The Shadow of Darkness

Magic of the Realm
Book Four

Kimberly Marraffino

The Shadow of Darkness
Magic of the Realm ~ Book Four

Copyright © 2025 by Kimberly Marraffino
All rights reserved

No part of this book may be used or reproduced in any manner whatsoever without written permission by the publisher, except for brief quotations embodied in articles or reviews. Map and symbol are owned by Kimberly Marraffino. Rights and ownership reserved and cannot be used or reproduced without written permission by the publisher

This book is a work of fiction. Names, characters, places, events, and incidents either are the product of the author's imagination or are used fictitiously. Any resemblance to actual persons, living or dead, events, locations, etc. are entirely coincidental or used only for fictional purposes

Cover by Stefanie Saw (www.seventhstarart.com)
Copyediting by Enchanted Ink Publishing
Proofreading by Dennis Doty
Map made by Kimberly Marraffino
Symbol designed by Kimberly Marraffino and made by DRIVEN Digital Services
Character Art by Beth Gilbert

First Edition February 2025
Printed in the United States of America
Published in Texas, USA
ISBN: 979-8-9861792-4-7 (Paperback)
Library of Congress Control Number: 2024922938

www.KimberlyMarraffino.com

To Isabelle,
Thank you for having more strength than I do sometimes
and for pushing me to finish this dream of mine.
Remember this kind of strength, resilience, and
determination as you navigate your way through life.

To the writers,
Never believe the voices in your head telling you no one
wants to read your story. Every story has an audience.
So, get up and write. You got this!

And finally…

To those who never feel good enough,
You are! No matter what you believe, you are enough,
and you matter. Find the people who accept you for you,
broken pieces and all, and live a life you can be proud of.
And remember, each day is a new chapter, so turn the
page and try again.

KILUEMAR
North Shores
Lunar Cave
Werewolf Highlands
Forbidden Coast
Dragon Cove
Demetrius Desert
Arista Bay
Full Moon Forest
Midnight Ridge
Dwarf Ridge
Dead Man's Bay
Elf Beach
Centaur Forest
Lucien Valley
Cursed Cave
Siren Sea
Forsaken Bluffs
Raven Lagoon
Enchanted Hills
Casteya Castle
Stoweward
Shadow Forest
Macein Mountains
Sunset Cliffs
Valley of the Giants
Mystic Woods
Drolnogard Peak
Nymph Grove
Guardian Lake
West Shores
Muse Meadow
Kitra Forest
Emrys Cave
Caerwyn Village
Cassil Cabin
Sunrise Mesa
East Shores
Cavern Beach
Half Moon Harbor
Dryad Forest
Grotto Bridge
South Shores
Ember Cliffs
0 1 2 3
Miles
N
W E
S

Note from the Author

I want my readers to be well-informed of any possible triggers or content that might not be appropriate for them. This book contains darker elements and quite a few subject matters that might be triggering or more mature for some readers. If you would like to know if this book contains any elements that might be of concern to you, please check the back of the book or my website for more details.

I would also like to point out that even though this series is classified as young adult, it is also considered coming-of-age and contains mature content.

Read at your own discretion.

Pronunciation and Translation Guide:
Both provided in the back of the book.

Table of Contents

Chapter 1

Message in the Night

Faint crackling filled the silent room, the slowly dimming embers within the stone fireplace fading and casting the space in darkness. Streaks of silvery white streamed in from the window, the break in the thick, dark clouds building outside, allowing the practically full moon to shine through.

Leaning awkwardly against the armrest of the couch, James slept, his chin tucked in against his chest and his arms crossed over his body with a blanket haphazardly draped over one leg, while the other hung off the side of the plush sofa. Resting a few feet away, Raina sat in an oversized chair, her legs flung over one of the armrests and crossed at her ankles. She held her growing stomach as her open eyes remained fixed on the ceiling.

Raina had not been able to sleep due to the fear and anxiety surrounding Kavana's disappearance. Not to mention the fact that Pavian had not returned the night before like he had planned. However, Raina strongly believed he had, in fact, returned, but once he had found Zarrius, he immediately went out to help with searching for his sister. At least, that was what Raina kept telling herself.

Glancing over at the clock on the wall, Raina sighed before angling her head to face James, who was still sound asleep. "James," she called quietly as she rose to her feet, cradling her stomach. Walking over to him, she gently nudged him. "James, wake up."

Eyes shooting open, James bolted upright, panic in his voice and on his face. "What's wrong?" He met Raina's composed expression. "Is everything okay?"

"Yes," Raina reassured him. "Sorry, I didn't mean to startle you. It's just, you were sleeping in a weird position, and you still have your shoes on."

James lifted the leg hanging over the side of the couch, taking in his black combat boots. "Oh." Sitting up, he dusted the top of the furniture where his other foot was, removing any potential dirt. "Sorry." Soreness pinched at his neck, and he groaned, rubbing the dull ache. "What time is it?"

"Just after midnight," Raina said, sitting down beside him.

Concerned, he asked, "Have you gotten any sleep yet?"

"Some."

"Have you eaten?" James observed the hesitancy in her response and the regret drawing her lips into a thin line. "You need to eat something." He stood up and started toward the kitchen. "When was the last time you ate?"

Raina followed behind him, trying to remember. "Uh . . . the last thing I ate were the eggs and toast you made me."

He halted and turned on the balls of his feet. "That was this morning." Disbelief and annoyance lined the statement.

"Yeah," she said matter-of-factly with a shrug.

"Raina Richards Ward!" he snapped with a mix of playfulness and irritation.

"Hey!" Matching his tone, she placed her hands on her hips, taking in his smug smirk. "Don't full name me, James Drolnogard Ward Cassil. I do not appreciate being spoken to like I'm a child."

"Well, stop acting like one, and I won't treat you like one." James closed the distance between them, the slight grin on his face fading into a serious expression. "I'm just worried about you." He gently gripped her shoulders. "Both of you." His eyes dropped to her stomach. "I know you're worried about Aunt K and Uncle Pavian, but you have to take care of yourself. And my little cousin is counting on you to take care of her too."

"Her?" Raina asked, smiling. "You think it's a girl?"

He nodded. "Yeah. I mean, Liam needs a little sister."

Tears threatened to break from her now watery eyes. "James . . ." His name was strained behind the tightness in her throat. Clearing the emotions, she continued, composed and assured, "They'll find her."

James pulled her into a hug. "I know they will."

With it being after midnight, Kavana had been missing now for over forty-eight hours. When Aidan had returned home a couple of nights ago, he had noticed Kavana had not—which was unusual for her since she was normally home, reading and ready for bed, by the time Aidan got back from patrolling. Even though Aidan had never officially joined the guard, he had opted to help monitor any and all activity from the skies to help maintain not only the continued protection needed around the island but to provide an extra set of eyes and ears for any potential threats or disturbances. Having some of the portals constantly moving and being completely unpredictable since the twins' return, Zarrius had grown uneasy with things and had asked for some additional help, hence why Kavana had finally stepped up in her Guardian duties and decided to take on more proactive responsibilities in helping to maintain the safety and stability around the island. But she never returned home after working late with her father, and since then, Zarrius, Aidan, and the whole guard had been out searching for her.

James had wanted to help look for his aunt, but his parents had insisted he and Rhiannon both stay within the protective barriers of the village—where Rhiannon currently was—and Stoweward after Kavana went missing. And with their grandfather agreeing to this idea, James had decided to stay with Raina and Liam to ensure they were safe. Although James valued his role in protecting and caring for his aunt and cousin— something Pavian had asked of him every time he had to leave to the non-magical world. And with things being chaotic over there, Pavian had not been back in Kiluemar for more than a short time since the attack at MUSE—the magical school that had been discovered by Merrick, leaving almost everyone either dead or still missing. But Pavian was supposed to return during the last full moon, the night before Kavana went missing. So now that both were unaccounted for, everyone was on edge and worried something might be coming. Knowing Raina should not be under too much stress, James was hopeful there had been some truth to her idea that, maybe, Pavian had returned, and he was out looking for Kavana with Zarrius. But, in all reality, James was not so sure, and deep down, he believed Raina was feeling the same way.

"Come on," James said, releasing her from their embrace and heading into the kitchen. "Let's get you some food, and then it's off to bed for you."

She followed behind him, humor in her tone. "And who's the adult here?"

He chuckled and faced her as he continued to walk backward. "Look, I'm just taking my duties seriously."

Turning on the faucet, James filled a glass with water before handing it to Raina as he placed a small frying pan on the top of the cooker along the back wall of the kitchen. Stoweward had many modern upgrades compared to Caerwyn Village, and how the residents prepared meals was one of them. Most of the homes in the village had wood-burning stoves, whereas here, all the houses had cookers fueled by natural gas—a process James had learned was added to the island when Stoweward was built.

"So, you can really travel back in time?" James asked Raina nonchalantly as he pulled two eggs from a basket on the counter.

Raina not only needed to eat, she also needed a distraction. Something James was prepared to give her. And maybe he needed one as well. James had heard the story of how Raina first discovered her powers, but they had never really discussed her ability to actually travel back in time. Even though she had spent the last few months teaching him how to strengthen and control his astral abilities, they had never talked about the added powers of an Astral Traveler. But he had always been curious about it—intrigued and utterly fascinated by the idea.

"I only did it the one time, but yes," Raina said, carefree and accepting of the conversation, as she sat down in one of the wooden chairs at the small dining table near the window.

Dropping a slab of freshly churned butter into the pan, James swirled it around, the sound of sizzling filling the room. "That's so cool. Who needs a DeLorean when you have magical powers?"

"A what?"

Raina had lived in the non-magical world for seventeen years before she moved to Kiluemar, but her childhood had been sheltered, the access to modern technology something she never missed once she was here due to her upbringing.

"A DeLor—never mind. Keep going."

"Okay," she said with a raised brow, drawing out the word. "Well, what do you want to know?"

"Everything," James announced as he cracked two eggs and dropped them over the melted butter.

"All right. Well, Astral Travelers can travel to the past, but it's not something we can really control."

Raina had met only one other person who had the ability to do what she could. He had been an older man in his sixties, someone she had met thanks to the records that had been located at MUSE. She had gone there in the earlier years after coming to Kiluemar to see if she could learn more about the magic inside her. After meeting the man, she had discovered there had been over a dozen Astral Travelers reported in the last two centuries.

A wooden spoon moved through the eggs as James ventured, wanting to know more, "Really?"

"Yeah. And it's not something we do lightly either."

"How come?"

Raina straightened and arched her back, attempting to relieve some of the pressure building along her tailbone. "Because, contrary to what people think, the past is definitive. It's concrete. It can't really be changed. So, when someone who isn't supposed to be in the past shows up who could possibly alter the outcome, they tend to die there. Their existence there affects the cosmic balance. It's why I was almost killed. I wasn't supposed to be there."

"So, some people are supposed to travel back in time?"

"Yes. It's why the magic to do so exists. And it's all part of the balance and order of things. No one knows for sure who's in control of this, but many think it's a higher power outside our realm of time and space, while others believe it's Mother Nature. Either way, everything happens for a reason."

James turned the knob of the cooker and placed the scrambled eggs onto a glass plate. "Then you believe in divine fate? That everyone has an unbroken, predetermined destiny?"

"In a way, yes," she answered as James strolled over to her and lowered the plate onto the table before sitting down beside her. "I mean, I still believe in free will, but I also believe we are preprogrammed to know the choices we are supposed to make. We know when to go right or left, or when to say yes or no. When we alter from the course we are meant to be on, something or some event intervenes to put us back on the path we are supposed to be on."

"So, do you think—"

James cut himself off and tilted his head as his brows pinched together.

Observing his abrupt cutoff and baffled expression, Raina asked, worried, "What's wrong?"

His index finger gently tapped against his lips as he continued to stare at nothing, his attention wholly set on something else.

Raina shifted uncomfortably as her bare feet pressed into the cold, wooden floorboards, ready to spring into action if needed. Holding one hand against her stomach and the other flat against the table, she waited, the few moments seeming as if time had slowed down.

Eyes wide, James stared over at her, his expression a blend of confusion and dread. "It's my mom."

James shoved back from the table, the chair scraping against the floor as he bolted for the front door.

"James," she called, hurrying behind him, "what's happening?"

The front door swung open, the momentum in James's eagerness to rush outside sending it slamming into the wall. A bitter wind and harsh chill swept across his skin, his short-sleeve shirt and worn-out jeans doing nothing against the rapidly decreasing temperatures. Dark clouds thickened overhead as he searched the sky, the screeching cries of his Messenger, a bald eagle named Zeus, filling the desolate area.

The houses around the center of Stoweward were seemingly empty—most of the residents opting for the village now and the added protection of the guard, or more leaving the realm altogether due to the dangers still evident around the island.

James let out a strained and disjointed whistle as he mentally called out, *"Terramina! Oakley!"* He hurried down the steps of the porch. *"Raeth!"*

Over the last few months, James's Drolnogard powers had gotten stronger, more defined and precise. But distance was still an issue. He was not able to communicate as far away as Rhiannon could. But he still tried.

"Harkin!"

Raina exited the house, hurrying after him, her bare feet pressing into the chilled gravel just off the porch steps. "James?"

Turning, he faced her, panic laced in his every move and word. "Merrick is at the cabin. He's going to take my mom."

Stopping in front of him, she asked sharply, perplexed, "What? Why?"

"I—I don't know." James spotted Zeus flying overhead, the eagle soaring in tight circles, the fear emanating from the bird matching James's. "He's at the cabin now, I don't know—" Realization bloomed, the sensation like a knife to the gut. Shaking his head, he ran his hand through his hair, disheveling it. "No." The word came out breathy, the disbelief growing. His dark brown eyes blinked over at Raina, the glow from the porch light the only illumination around, the moon now disappeared behind the clouds. Chest heaving, he continued, "My mom made a deal with Merrick."

"What kind of deal?" she asked apprehensively.

"She never told us. But I'm guessing this is it. I think . . . I think she is giving herself over to him."

Her voice was tight. "But why?"

"Merrick promised to give us more time to prepare ourselves."

"Why would he do that, though?"

"Because, I think, my mom offered up herself in exchange."

Raina stared at him, dumbfounded.

Searching the sky again, James let out another whistle, this one loud and ear-piercing.

"What are you doing?" Raina asked, wincing at the sudden noise.

"Mommy?" Liam's soft voice said from the porch.

Raina and James observed the young boy rubbing the sleep from his eyes.

"Liam, sweetie," Raina said, walking up the stairs, "get back inside."

"I'm sorry, buddy." Calm settled in James, both his tone and demeanor shifting as he took the steps two at a time and crouched in front of Liam. "I didn't mean to wake you."

"Is everything okay?" Liam asked, the innocence and worry in his question pulling at James's heartstrings.

"Yeah," James lied. "Everything's okay. Go back inside. You'll freeze out here." Standing to his full height, he towered over Raina, the seriousness and protectiveness evident as he said, "Both of you."

"James," Raina started, pulling her shoulders back, the clear indication of maternal instincts kicking in as she ushered Liam inside. "Think about this first."

"I can't let him take her, Raina."

Her shoulders relaxed, sympathy taking over as she closed the distance between them. "I know. But maybe you can try something else."

His eyebrows narrowed. "Like what?"

Hope flashed across her face. "Try astral projecting. Maybe—"

Callie landed a few feet away from the porch, her sudden arrival sending a whoosh of wind sweeping across the ground.

Without hesitating, James headed for her, but Raina grasped his arm.

"Maybe check on them instead," she continued, her voice pleading. "Don't put yourself in danger."

"I can't, there's not enough time."

"But you've been doing so well. It shouldn't take you any more time than it would to get there." She paused, allowing him a moment to think. "You can do this—I know you can."

Glancing up at the sky, James eyed Zeus before returning his gaze to her. Dread filled his every nerve. "Rhiannon's going."

"What?" Raina said, just as terrified. "How do you know?"

"Zeus said Athena went to her, so I reached for her—mentally. I can sense her. She's scared. But she's going to try to stop him."

"Then go," Raina said. "She needs you." Hugging him, she added, her cheek pressed against his racing heart, "Please be careful."

He hesitated. "But what about you?"

"What about me?"

"Will you be okay?"

"Yes. I've been by myself many times before, remember?" She paused, taking him in. Seeing the uncertainty mixing with his need to help his family, she added, "I can take care of myself. I promise. Now, go."

James gave her a quick nod and headed down the stairs.

"Wait!" Liam called from behind the small crack of the door as he pulled it open. Running toward James, he held out something for him. "Here."

Raina and James watched the young boy as he held a thin jacket in his little hand.

"So you don't get cold," Liam added.

Taking the jacket, one James knew was actually his uncle's, he hugged his cousin. "Thanks, buddy."

"You're welcome."

"Be careful," Raina said again as James hurried away.

Callie lowered herself down, and he jumped onto her back and gave Raina and Liam one last look before the winged horse leapt into the sky.

~

"Grandpa!" Rhiannon yelled, racing down the cobblestone path and bursting through the front door of the two-story stone and wood-slated home with Ryan trailing behind her. "Grandpa!"

Darkness filled most of the house as Rhiannon ran toward a dim glow at the back of the house with her dagger gripped tightly in her hand.

"What's wrong?" Randolyn said in a panic as she exited the lit-up room with a robe tied around her, her face sunken from lack of sleep.

Rhiannon leaned over and panted. "Where's Grandpa?"

"He still hasn't come home. He's out looking for Kavana with the others. Why? What happened?"

"It's my—"

Her words were interrupted as James's voice shouted in her head, calling her name.

"What's wrong?" Ryan asked, his nervous gaze shifting between her and Randolyn.

"Rhiannon! Where are you?" James exclaimed telepathically again, his words loud and frantic.

Sensing him nearby, she twisted around and bolted outside. "James!"

The shadows of the night were dark even with the practically full moon producing slow, steady streams of light in between the moving clouds.

Wings flapped overhead, the heavy beating the only sounds echoing in between the quiet buildings as the cold air remained still and snow began to fall in light flurries.

Ryan and Randolyn retreated outside and scanned the sky.

"Over there!" Ryan shouted as a figure came into view to the north.

Rhiannon ran toward Callie, her long-sleeve sweater doing nothing to cut the cold chill slicing through her, as the winged horse landed down the path and trotted to a stop.

"Get on!" James demanded as he reached out a hand.

Ryan ran up behind Rhiannon and helped lift her onto the back of Callie, mindful of the outstretched wing.

"What are you doing?" Randolyn asked, her voice tight with worry. "What happened?"

"Merrick is coming for Karramis," Ryan answered solemnly.

Randolyn's dark eyes widened. "What?"

Backing away, Ryan peered up at the twins. "Stay safe."

Before they could respond, Callie took off in a gallop, driving her wings down in one swoop and lifting into the sky.

Randolyn glanced over at Ryan. "What are they going to do?"

Monitoring the winged horse disappearing into the night sky, Ryan said matter-of-factly, "They're going to try to stop him."

A moment passed before Randolyn asked, "How?"

"I have no idea."

Chapter 2

Waiting Game

Karramis glanced at the moon, a tiny sliver missing from the celestial body peeking out as it crested over the tree line and met the dark clouds, thick and heavy with moisture. Shades of navy, indigo, and rich charcoal painted the area around the cabin, the streaks of silvery-white beams illuminating small patches of the dry grass just outside the glow of the porch lights and the swaying trees in the background. The crisp air was filled with a harshness she had never experienced before, the bitter bite against her face and hands unnatural for Kiluemar—which always had the almost perfect temperatures year-round. A change becoming more evident as winter arrived on the island, the mid-December night filling with a chilly breeze scented with frosty, salty air and an unrecognizable yet unique aroma reminding her of cold rain and fresh earthy tones.

Going over the plan in her head again, she closed her eyes, imagining any and all possible outcomes, good and bad. She had prepared for everything—trained, practiced, formulated different scenarios, gone over every moment from the night at the manor eight years ago and all her mistakes at Château Rouge. She even primed her body for any possible injuries she might have to endure tonight to escape. And knowing James and Rhiannon were safe in the confines of the borders, she did not have to worry about them.

The deal was simple—Merrick would guarantee her children's safety until the full moon after their next birthday, but she had to offer up herself in exchange, and she had to go willingly. But in promising he would stick to his word, Merrick would leave her children alone. They could prepare and train for what might occur when it came to their destiny and what the prophecy foretold. And they would be able to live without fear of capture or death. At least, for a bit longer.

However, the agreement never stated she had to stay. A fact she reminded not only herself of but her husband as well, and she had done it daily since the deal was made five months ago. Being the only other person Karramis told, Will had helped her prepare for tonight with any possible mishaps and with training her mind and body to fight.

She was ready.

But even though she knew she could handle this, and she was prepared for anything they threw at her, something was still bothering her. Something was off about the whole thing.

"You're not dying tonight, darling," Will said adamantly behind her as she rested her forearms against the porch railing, a seriousness behind the teasing tone. "Do you understand me?"

Smiling, she angled her body toward him, pressing her back against the wooden banister, admiring him as he leaned against the doorframe with his arms casually folded over his broad chest. Every fiber of her being—her heart, mind, body, and her soul—loved this man.

"I know," she said, confident yet lighthearted.

Lowering his arms, he strolled over to her. "Then what's bothering you?"

Will could always tell when something was wrong with Karramis, the energy and demeanor of his wife shifting around her when she got lost in her head or started to overthink and overanalyze the intrusive thoughts and wandering ideas filling her mind. Karramis was a worrier, a worst-case scenario and what-if kind of person—always fearing the possibilities, preparing for the unexpected, and cautious of the unknowns.

"I don't know," she said with a heavy sigh, her eyes never leaving his as condensation blew from her mouth. "Something just doesn't feel right. And I hate this waiting around crap. It's like he enjoys these mind games or something." Stepping in closer, she placed her hands on his forearms, trailing her delicate touch up along his jacket before gliding them over his chest, her fingers gently gripping the thick, dark material. A calmness filled her nerves, a softness returning to her face. "Look, I've thought about this—many times. And dying is not part of my plan."

Will leaned his body into her as he slid his arms around her waist, pulling her into him. "That's wonderful to hear because if you did, I'd be very upset."

"Just very upset?" she asked at the teasing declaration, playfully clenching the material along his stomach, the warmth of him welcoming and his scent intoxicating.

His hands trailed down her lower back. "All right, I would be *extremely* upset—downright mad and utterly heartbroken. And in a fit of rage, I would slaughter everyone who stole you from me, making sure their deaths were slow, torturous, and excruciatingly painful."

Karramis slid her hands under his jacket and shirt, the feel of his skin against her palms releasing the tension in her shoulders. Running her fingers along his stomach, she said with a grin, "Much better."

Taking hold of the band of his pants, she pulled him into her body, the gesture an invitation.

Will ran his hand along her neck, lacing his fingers through her hair and kissing her. The embrace was gentle and passionate, each swipe sensual and meaningful as he trailed one hand down her backside, pressing her harder into him.

Drawing back, Will stared into her dark brown eyes and ran his thumb along her puffy, pink lips. "But seriously . . ." he started, his tone stern and nervous, "tonight is not the night. Do you understand me?"

She smiled, trying to lighten the severity in his gaze. "So bossy."

"Karramis—"

She kissed him again, quick but equally as passionate.

Taking a moment to enjoy the feel of her, the taste of her, he surrendered to her, the passion and lust-filled encounter awakening every part of him.

Chest heaving, Karramis stepped back, the gleam of desire in her eyes matching his. "Listen," she said, the yearning now fighting with a determined urgency, the cadence in her voice stern and her posture tense. "I think, maybe, you shouldn't be here tonight."

Will's eyes opened wide in disbelief. "Pardon?"

Calm yet hurried, she continued, "I know it's kind of late to suggest this, but maybe the dragons can take you—"

"Absolutely not," he interrupted pointedly, no room for argument.

"Will, something doesn't feel right about this and—"

"Even more reason for me to stay." Nothing but purpose and love shone in his eyes, his stance stoic and his energy pragmatic. "Do not ask me to stand back and watch them take you away from me again."

The truth of tonight was evident, something she had known would happen for months now. "But that's exactly what he is going to do. Merrick is coming for me, and I have to go. I can't fight this, and you can't stop it either."

"I know what needs to happen, but still, I need to know you are all right. I refuse to wait idly by while you put yourself in danger. Please don't ask me to do that."

"I'm not," Karramis admitted wholeheartedly, an unease against her worried expression. "I'm asking you to trust me."

Placing a palm against her cheek, he kissed her forehead. "I do."

"Then please," she pleaded, her anxiety grating against her nerves, "let me do this alone."

"No." There was a finality with the single word, an unquestionable no-backing-down fortitude behind the soft but firm declaration. "Don't think you're the only one allowed to protect the ones you love. I told you when you returned to me that I would never again leave your side, so don't even think about asking me to break my promise." Kissing her forehead again, he added, "We're a team, remember?"

She nodded, gently lifting the corner of her lips. "Partners."

"That's my girl," he said with a grin, lifting her into his arms and carrying her inside.

"What are you doing?" she said with a shocked chuckle.

"Making him wait just a bit longer," he admitted, deep and husky as he closed the front door behind him.

~

Karramis sensed it, the tension in her chest and the gut-twisting awareness of something, or rather someone, nearby—the all-too-familiar sensation of magic swirling to life as a steady rumbling rattled somewhere nearby, the cloud-filled night currently hiding the moon and blanketing the area in darkness. The energizing vibrations intensified, a tiny shock wave of power resonating closer before everything stilled.

Silence surrounded the cabin as the crisp air of the cold night remained calm. Nothing could be heard outside of the steady breathing coming from Karramis as she searched through the dark hues, eager for the soft, luminescent rays of moonlight to peek through the slow-moving clouds.

"What kind of magic was that?" Will asked from the opposite side of the porch, his attention set on the area where the sound originated.

Karramis strolled over to him, squinting to inspect the vicinity where the once still trees slightly swayed. "Portal magic."

Eyeing the sky, Will searched for the moon, only to find its soft glow emanating from behind the clouds. "But the full moon was last night."

"I know," Karramis declared, her thoughts filled with uncertainty and unease.

A quietness settled around them, even their breathing slowing as time passed, each moment filling the air with a keen sense of dread—a realization that Merrick was out there somewhere. Waiting.

Will placed his hand on the curve of her hip, drawing her into his side. "What is he waiting for?"

"I don't know," she said with a shrug, her voice uneven as the warmth from her mouth billowed in a misty cloud in front of her face. Swallowing, she pulled her shoulders back and called out with a smug undertone, "Come out, come out, wherever you are."

A figure moved through the shadows off to the side of the cabin, the slow, steady advancement like a predator. A break in the clouds opened up, casting some of the field just beyond the porch in a soft moonlit glow, the subtle illumination directed along the dry grass. The dark shadow moved closer, each step calculating. More light shone overhead, the moon gracing them all with its presence, the giant celestial wonder itching for a front-row seat.

"Darling," Will said quietly as his fingers pressed into her hip, the gesture both a tense warning and playful tease, "let's not provoke the man."

"I'm not," she said, squeezing his hand at her side. "I'm just not in the mood for these mind games." Taking a deep breath, the freezing air filling her lungs, she headed over to the landing of the porch steps. "Let's get this over with."

Coming into view, Merrick continued closer. There was so much control in his movements, so much casual confidence to his stride. A smoothness to his arrogant swagger and stoic posture. Pale blue eyes met hers as he stepped into the illuminating glow from the porch lights, his stare burning with dominance, a gleam radiating an undeniable truth—he held all the power, all the control.

"Over with?" he said charismatically with a devious smirk. "But we're just gettin' started."

- 24 -

Chapter 3

Life for Life

Karramis stared at Merrick for a moment, taking in the fitted, long-sleeve black shirt, black jeans buckled with a black belt against his lean waist, and the black boots tucked inside the hem of the pants. His light brown hair was combed back, and the beard along his sharp jawline was perfectly trimmed. Eyes a stunning shade of light blueish gray remained fixed on hers, the sight of them captivating.

Merrick was definitely a beautiful man. Deadly, but beautiful nonetheless. He appeared so normal, so natural and relaxed, so picturesque. There was an allure to him, an almost hypnotic appeal—a wonderful mix of mystery, darkness, danger, charm, and raw power. And yet Karramis wanted no part of it. No amount of charisma and beauty could take away from the fact that a monster stood before her.

A heaviness dipped in Karramis's stomach, the trepidation roiling deep in the pit of her soul as Merrick lifted one corner of his mouth, the wicked smirk displaying a hidden secret before disappearing as quickly as it came.

The heat of Will standing next to her warmed her as a chill crept up her back. Sensing her body tense, Will slid his hand into hers, interlocking their fingers and gently squeezing, calming her emotions and reminding her he was there.

Squaring her shoulders and lifting her chin, Karramis acknowledged, her voice steady, "Hello, Merrick. It would seem you're still dedicated to adding dramatic flair with your arrivals. The stalking through the darkness wasn't really necessary, since I knew you were coming."

"Hello, sweetheart." He grinned again, the gesture both devilish and enchanting. "It's lovely to see ya again." Strolling closer, Merrick ascended the steps, lifting a hand as he made his way up, stopping before his fingers reached the ward along the porch. "Come here."

No games, no small talk, just a soft, sensual command—an alluring request given by a man who knew his power and always got what he wanted. But Karramis remained still, her vigilant gaze never wavering.

There was something malicious to his presence, an energy rolling off him Karramis could sense, her gut feeling and overcautious instinctual nature sending her into fight or flight mode.

"Come here, love," he requested again, adding a patronizing yet charming lilt to the final word. A nickname he knew she hated being called. "Unless you've decided against our original agreement." Something dark flashed in his eyes as tension pulled at his features. "Which, of course, would negate my contractual obligations, and that will definitely not do. You see, it's quite imperative ya refrain from any impetuous or disingenuous ulterior motives tonight. Or I just might have to take matters into my own hands."

Something was definitely wrong. What Karramis was experiencing earlier, and her current high-alert mindset was not just nerves—this, in fact, did not feel right. A sense of dread filled her entire being as every alarm of warning blared in her gut, her intuition and innate instincts informing her of an impending danger.

Fighting her need to react, to organize a last-minute escape plan, she steadied her racing thoughts and regained focus, her attention wholly on Merrick once more as a stern composure settled back into her. "The theatrics are unnecessary. I said I would go willingly with you, but only if you continue to keep your word and not allow any harm to come to my children in any way until the agreed upon time."

Lowering his hand, Merrick slid his arms behind his back, seeming to interlock his fingers as his softened gaze remained fixed on Karramis. "What is a man's word worth these days?" An arbitrary question delivered with a reverent yet dominant connotation, a soothing smoothness laced with steady arrogance. "Fer me, my word is worth my weight in gold and the very immortal life grantin' me the ability to stand before you."

Pausing, he ascended the last step, the spell around the cabin non-existent to him, and stopped in front of Karramis.

Remaining unfazed physically, she lifted her chin, his six-foot frame causing her to have to glance up. Eyes stayed plastered to his without a flicker of emotion on her face, but everything in her mind and body and soul was telling her to run. But she would not. So instead, she would stand her ground and show no fear.

Merrick leaned into her, the short whiskers of his trimmed beard grazing her cheek. He inhaled, long and deep, before he pulled back and continued, "Now, sweetheart, let me ask you. What is *your* word worth?"

"Is there a reason for this rather tedious show?" A bold question, her need to fight coming out through her outspoken and unfiltered mouth. "Again, your theatrics are unnecessary. And to be honest, a little beneath you." Karramis could almost hear the silent warning emanating from Will as his hand pressed into the small of her back, her brazenness coming front and center. "There's really no need for the not-so-subtle mind fuckery."

A spark of intrigue brightened Merrick's features. A challenge. Something he was hoping would come out of tonight as thirst for both blood and power coursed through him. Hunger and lust burned like acid along his nerves and in his veins—a rush of adrenaline filled with an undiluted, uncontrollable mix of wants and needs.

"Let's just go," she added shamelessly, brushing past him and heading down the stairs. "Stop with the intimidation tactics and taunting."

"Now, witch," a familiar voice said, closer than expected, the casual, cunning tone both terrifying and pleasing, "if anyone is going to taunt you, it would be me."

Karramis halted mid-step, both feet on two different stairs as she and Will turned and squinted through the darkness off to the side of the cabin, catching sight of Leif stepping into the glow of the porch lights and coming around to the front of the building.

Lingering at the base of the stairs, just a few feet from where Karramis remained frozen, Leif crossed his arms, the movement relaxed as he grinned up at her. "My, you sure are adamant about dying tonight. You still can't control that mouth of yours, I see. Well, I'm all for it. Let the games begin."

Dark brown eyes rolled, the involuntary action joining an exasperated chuckle as Karramis placed both feet on a single step and said, "Well, I never took you as one for playing games, Leif."

"Oh, now, you know that's not true. I do love a fun game of cat-and-mouse every now and again." A playful and sinful teasing lilt lined every word. "In fact, how about we play it now. You run, and I'll come chase you. I promise, I won't bite this time." A salacious smile rose on his lips with the next statement. "That is, unless you want me to."

Leif advanced slowly, each step up the stairs calculated.

"Can I play too?" Will challenged, both the humor and condescension tight in his question.

Karramis tilted her head back toward the porch and glared at her husband, slightly irritated but trying not to laugh as she lifted her index finger to her mouth, shushing him.

He gave her a knowing smirk as one of his brows lifted in time with a carefree shrug. "What?"

Matching his nearly inaudible tone, she said, heading back up the stairs to stand near him, "Could you please not entertain him?"

"Oh, why not?" Leif asked. "It makes this all the more fun." Leif inched closer to the barrier, his advancement slowing as he reached the protective wall, his attention on Karramis. "In fact, why don't you come back out here and play?" His eyes shifted to Will. "Both of you. I could really use a snack."

Merrick closed the distance between him and Karramis. "And we do love playin' with our food first." He lifted his arm and glided the back of his fingers down her cheek, soft and sensual.

Reflexively, Karramis slapped his hand away. "What the hell is this?" Annoyance rang in her tone, her expression fierce as her eyes narrowed and jaw clenched. She glanced over toward Leif and back at Merrick. "What kind of sick game are you playing at? I said I would go. What's he"—she lifted a chin at the vampire, a sneer scrunching her nose—"doing here?"

Raising a hand again, Merrick traced a finger along her neck, a warm, smooth pad gliding over her pulse.

Magic rushed from Karramis's palm, the power weak but controlled, the energy a gentle warning as Merrick staggered back, the few retreating steps shocking him.

"Don't touch me again," she warned, a hateful bite in her tone.

"Naughty, naughty girl," Leif said, condescension dripping from his words.

"Seriously, Leif . . ." Karramis chastised, her mouth running wild as an emotional charge shot through her, a mix of anger, disgust, and fear.

Trying to calm her brewing tirade, Will took hold of her hand and interrupted, "Karramis—"

"—go fuck yourself," she blurted, ignoring her husband's composed plea.

Lifting a brow suggestively, Leif smirked. "I'd much rather fuck—"

"In your fucking dreams, you sick bastard," she snapped, knowing what he was about to say. "I wouldn't touch you if my life depended on it. No sane woman would. Hence why you're a lonely, miserable man. What's the matter, Leif, no one ever loved you?"

Rage filled Leif's expression, his bright blue eyes disappearing behind a pool of blackness, his attention pulling inward as if remembering something. "You fucking bitch!" He slammed a fist against the barrier. "I'm going to kill you, just like—"

Merrick swooped over to Karramis, grasping her neck and shoving her backward toward the front door until she slammed into the cold wood, a loud thud reverberating through the freezing night air.

Surprised, Karramis gaped at him, her eyes wide as her hand clasped around the wrist at her neck. "Let me go." Her words were choked behind his tight hold, but the demand was still there, her fear hidden behind her need to fight.

Will reacted, hurrying after the man now holding his wife's life in his hands. But before he could reach him, magic erupted from Merrick, the powerful burst of undiluted force sending Will through the air. Karramis watched in horror as her husband sailed backward, his head barely missing the rafters as he flew over the railing and landed hard against the ground.

An inaudible gasp blew from Will's mouth, the breath-stealing collision with the frozen ground expelling all the oxygen from his lungs. Pain shot down his spine, the piercing sensation pulsating along his back. Rolling onto his side, he took in a deep breath, the act jagged and strained as he lifted to all fours and struggled to gasp in more air.

"Well, isn't this a turn of events," Leif said, strolling over and lifting Will to his feet. He twisted Will's arm behind his back, nearly snapping his wrist. "I think you should stay here with me." Letting out a sinister chuckle as he exhaled, Leif added mischievously, "Time to watch the show, pretty boy."

Will struggled against his tight grip, the movement sending a wave of agony through his arm. "Karr—"

"Nuh-uh-uh," Leif cautioned, tapping a finger against his lips. "No talking."

Merrick studied Karramis for a moment, her gaze watching him with a cautionary gleam as the seconds ticked by, his hand still pressed firmly against her neck.

Her pulse beat steadily as his thumb pressed into her artery, the gradual pounding resonating through his own veins, along his skin, deep down in the very core of his body. It was like a drug—an intoxicating elixir of desire, quenchable thirst, and satiable hunger. His eyes dipped shut and he leaned into her as he angled her head, exposing the soft, luscious skin along the rest of her neck. The tip of his nose grazed her nape just below his thumb.

Karramis continued to steel herself—her posture taut, her expression unflinching, and her breathing as steady as she could manage under his hold and uncomfortable caressing. She would not surrender to his intimidation tactics. She would not acknowledge his desire for her to show fear or to submit.

"You smell absolutely divine," Merrick uttered unabashedly as he loosened his grip on her.

"Last I checked," she stated matter-of-factly, pausing to take in a few short breaths before continuing, "groping me while you get some sick pleasure out of smelling me, completely disregarding my personal space, I might add, was not part of our deal. So, if you would so kindly release me, I would greatly appreciate it."

Noting her impassive nature, he went on reverently, her courage and boldness tantalizing. "I find it quite extraordinary how you've managed to survive all these years. I will say this, you're certainly a persistent and audacious woman. But it would also seem you are incredibly resilient as well. I would very much love to discover what exactly flows within those veins of yours."

Eyeing Leif over Merrick's shoulder, she glared at the vampire still holding her husband hostage, Leif's expression emotionless yet highly entertained. "Well, take a number, buddy. It would seem I'm on the desired menu for another."

"My, sweetheart, are you tryin' to provoke me?" Merrick asked with a tilt of his head, his grip around her neck slowly tightening again as a thrill coursed through him, a rush of a potential hunt.

Karramis stayed silent, the dread surrounding the position Will was currently in, not to mention her own, stifling her response.

Merrick tsked, taking in her reluctant silence. "It would appear your rather defiant mentality and impudent mouth is keen on huntin' fer the monsters." He paused, his apathetic countenance contradicting the mischief in his tone and the devious glare staring down at her. "But ya may want to be careful with the insolence and temerity you so loosely and foolishly exhibit, love." His demeanor shifted, the air around them seeming to darken, the energy seeping from him menacing and immoral as he leaned into her. "Because," he whispered, his breath hot against her ear, "once my beast comes out to play, ya won't be so eager to meet it. Understood?"

Karramis swallowed but nodded, submitting for now to get this entire thing back under control.

Merrick gave her a quick, smug smirk. "Good girl." Releasing her, he offered her his hand. "Shall we?"

Refusing to humor him, Karramis brushed past him and sauntered down the steps and over to Will and Leif. "Let him go," she demanded, a non-negotiable command.

Leif glared at her, his blue eyes fierce behind hooded lids. There was a challenge in the way he focused on her. A game he was eager to play. But Karramis wanted no part of it. Unflinching, she held her ground before Leif finally released Will and lifted his hands in mock surrender.

Observing Merrick as he rubbed his wrist, Will caught a noticeable change in his persona over Karramis's shoulder, the man communicating silently to Leif through simple expressions.

"Karramis," Will warned quietly as he took hold of her hand.

She squeezed, the unspoken confirmation delivered in her eyes—she knew something was not right. Holding her breath, Karramis clutched his hand one final time before letting go, slowly easing the burn from her chest as she exhaled.

"I'll be okay," she mouthed, and Will gave her a curt nod, the faith he had in his wife evident as he kissed her goodbye. Angling herself toward Merrick, she demanded, not wanting to draw this out any longer, "Let's go."

"After you," he said, gliding his upturned palm across the area in front of him, directing her away from the cabin.

Karramis started toward the trees as his hand rested against her lower back. His fingers were warm despite the temperature outside, but the feel of him against her skin, even through her jacket, sent an unease racing through her veins, a visceral distress signal making the hairs on her neck stand up and chills skitter along her spine.

"No, that's quite all right," she argued softly, coming to a stop. "I'd much rather you be in front."

"Of course," he said coolly, strolling by her without a second thought. "As you wish." Continuing forward, he paused after a few steps and faced Karramis. "Oh, I almost forgot . . ." He eyed Leif, his pale blue eyes gleaming with satisfaction as he shifted his attention to Will. "He's comin' as well."

"What?" Karramis blurted, horrified, her attention shifting between Merrick, Leif, and Will as she shook her head. "No. No he's not."

"Aye, sweetheart," Merrick said arrogantly, the presence of pure enjoyment lining his tone and forming along his features. "He most certainly is."

Gut-twisting panic shot through her nerves. "No, that wasn't part of the deal."

"Oh, but it was." Merrick interlocked his fingers behind his back and slowly started to circle around her. "You see, I was promised life fer life. Well, what, pray tell, do ya reckon that implies?" A rhetorical question. "Clearly there are two of 'em, so why would you assume I would not require two in exchange?"

Confusion and fear struck Karramis as Merrick slowed to a stop. He stood there, assessing her with delight sparking in his eyes.

The words of their deal rattled around in her head as she remembered each section agreed upon in specific detail. Along with his exact words, she recalled how Merrick would use careful wording and wittiness to manipulate things to work in his favor.

Life for life.

Shit.

A life for a life. Two lives for two lives.

Shit!

An electric charge filled the space as a powerful energy thickened around them, the air coming to life. The sensation built in Karramis's core—the distinguishable momentum of power, a familiar thrum coursing through her nerves and tingling in her stomach.

Magic.

But not just any magic. This was a power she recognized all too well, a magic branded into her very existence—a proverbial ability she had long since developed and grew to master. Portal magic.

However, she was not the one creating this power, nor was this sensation linked to her Guardian abilities since the full moon was long gone. And this was not just any pulsating surge linked to the portals.

Or was it?

This powerful energy was similar, yet it felt very different to the magic she was used to, something familiar yet foreign, a strange yet comforting awareness. It was as if the energy around her was being altered or manipulated, just like she did when she created and controlled her portal, but there was something wrong about it.

Merrick angled his head, his eyes kind and inviting but his features predatory. "Oh, I nearly forgot," he announced, his tone unnervingly relaxed yet eager, as he pointed off to the side of the cabin, a section blanketed in darkness.

Karramis's eyes snagged on a watery vortex swirling, something she had missed earlier when he had first arrived. Night still consumed the area, but there was no doubt a portal rested a few yards away, the magic gently flowing in a slow circle and sending fallen leaves and dead grass rustling nearby. Darkness danced with the circular, swirling water, the whirlwind transparent and mystifying.

Will pushed past Leif, the vampire untroubled and seemingly thrilled by the scene unfolding, most likely from the pure confusion plastered on his and his wife's faces and from whatever was about to come through. Taking hold of Karramis's arm, Will gently pulled her behind him, shielding her from whoever was about to arrive.

Two figures stepped out of the portal and strolled into the illumination of the glow from the porch.

Haydrin and Lucas.

Karramis could not believe what she just witnessed. Merrick had somehow created a portal. Not only that, he had kept it flowing for all this time—only using his mind, not even having to pay attention to it, and he did it without any real effort. Plus, he somehow mastered allowing not one but two people through it without any noticeable struggle.

"Hello, love," Lucas said with a saccharine grin, his gaze narrowing as he shifted his attention over to Will, the cockiness still in his tone. "This'll be fun."

Chapter 4

Change of Plans

"How?" Karramis questioned Merrick evenly, ignoring Lucas's comment, her cadence persistent and accompanied by an analyzing glare as she stepped around her husband, taking in the full view of the four men now standing in front of the cabin. "How are you able to create a portal?"

Merrick remained quiet for a moment, allowing the anticipation to thicken between them. "Well, unfortunately, I am inept at creatin' an entry point—my magic limited and unable to counter the strong, natural power of the entrances."

"So, you're not able to create your own portal, then?"

"Precisely. However, I am capable of manipulatin' one once inside and shiftin' the location fer my exit by guidin' the closest portal to a new area and then departin' as usual."

"Then you're the reason the portals have been moving."

"Not entirely. It is not I who is solely manipulatin' 'em. Nevertheless, I am responsible fer a few relocations, but only with the ones inside the realm. I have yet to master the portal magic outside Kiluemar. That particular magic is a tad more complex and quite enigmatic."

Mulling over this information, Karramis regarded the men, but her next words were still directed at Merrick. "What exactly do you want?"

He tilted his head down ever so slightly and gave her a wide, mischievous grin. "Final payment."

"Clearly," Karramis shot back wryly. "But what the hell is all of this? Why the audience?"

"Why, sweetheart, are you questionin' me?" Merrick ventured, delighted by her impervious and petulant nature. "Well, if ya must know, I would deem this right here a contingency plan. Among other things. Like I mentioned already, I'm here to collect what is owed to me—life fer life. Or have you forgotten our deal?"

"No, I haven't forgotten," she stated matter-of-factly. "It was my deal, remember? Not to mention, we've already had this discussion, or have *you* forgotten?"

Excitement flashed across his smug face, matching his brazen and flirtatious tone. "My, ya sure do have a mouth on you." A deep rumble rattled in his throat, a near-feral growl. "And I do fancy a sharp tongue."

Nothing but pure stubbornness and confidence settled in her body language and voice as she reiterated her statement from before, avoiding the retort she desperately wanted to utter. "Like I said before—no. Will was not part of our deal."

"Now, I beg to differ," Merrick said. "It's not my fault you were unable to grasp the full extent of our agreement."

Karramis let out an exasperated exhale.

Will stepped into her, and Karramis instantly leaned into him, welcoming his touch against her back and his hands on her waist, the hard squeeze a clear warning to be careful as she kept her eyes on all the men—observing each posture, each set of eyes, and every demeanor.

"Darling," Will said softly, turning her to face him, his hands cupping her face. Imploring eyes bored into hers, the silent resignation on his face palpable. "Listen to me—"

"Will, no," she announced, sharp and pleadingly, shaking her head. "You aren't part of this."

"Clearly I am."

"No." Her voice dipped low with the single word. "This isn't how it's supposed to go." The somberness faded from her, a new resolve, one of determination taking over. "No, you're not going." She faced the others, pulling away from Will. "He's not going." Turning back to her husband, she repeated with an unwavering declaration, her voice softer, quieter, "You're not going. Do you hear me?"

Will placed a hand on her cheek, and Karramis eased into the caress. "I watched you walk away once before, not knowing when or if I'd ever see you again. And I will not do it now. So, please don't ask me to. Just the thought of you walking away from me yet again was eating me alive, and this way, you won't have to."

Pleading eyes blinked up at him as tears formed. He could not go. They would surely kill him.

"I thought I lost you once," he continued, wiping away the emotion glistening on her lower eyelashes. "I love you, and I will not stand by and watch you being forced to leave me behind again. Either you allow me to fight *with* you, or I shall bloody well fight *for* you." He stared at her for a moment as he caressed her cheek with his thumb, a glare of stubbornness equal to hers shining through. "I'm going, my love. Full stop. This is not up for debate. Do you understand me?"

She gave him a gentle, resigned nod. "Yes."

He brushed the tip of his nose across hers before dipping down and kissing her, quick but sensual. "That's my girl," he whispered against her lips as he pulled away. "So, what's Plan B?"

Taking a moment to compose herself, she said under her breath, "Working on it."

"Now, you're not plannin' anythin' insanely reckless, are ya, love?" Lucas asked coolly, surprisingly composed.

Facing him, Karramis surveyed his easygoing disposition, the public display of affection she and Will just showcased seeming to have zero effect on him. In fact, his behavior was a mix of dismissive and completely uninterested. Yet there was something else, something analytical and highly calculative about the way he observed her, his blue eyes never faltering from monitoring her in a predatory way, his attention solely on her and her alone.

Lucas advanced closer, the motion unnerving. "That would not be a wise choice."

Ushering Karramis behind him, Will announced, savage and unapologetic, "Stay the fuck away from my wife."

"Oh, come now," Lucas said with a chuckle, carefree and composed, a persona Will had rarely experienced—an unfamiliar personality not usually present when Will was around. "Ya don't need to protect her, Will. I'll keep her safe from the likes of these men." He gestured to Merrick, Leif, and Haydrin. "They know you're not to be touched."

Karramis scoffed. "And who's going to keep me safe from you?"

"Just behave yourself and nothin' bad will happen to ya."

"If you so much as touch her," Will started, "I'll—"

"What?" Lucas challenged arrogantly. "What exactly do ya think you'll do to me?"

"I'll fucking kill you."

Lucas let out a sneering chuckle. "I'm fairly certain you've already mentioned somethin' along those lines before, mate. And yet here I am. But I do admire your gallant effort."

"I promise you, Lucas," Will warned, harsh and direct, "if I don't . . ." He nodded toward Karramis. "She certainly will."

Glaring at Karramis, Lucas declared with conviction, "She's not capable of harmin' me. It goes against everythin' she is and knows."

"Pardon the interruption," Merrick interjected with deliberate politeness, remaining next to Leif and Haydrin, all three still by the stairs, "but if we may continue. This incessant and rather vapid verbal diatribe is not at all entertainin'. We have other matters to—"

"Heads up," Lucas called, grinning at Karramis, his focus wholly on her. "We have company."

Flapping filled the air just as light flurries coasted down from the darken clouds, the moon now completely hidden.

Taking sight of the source of the noise, Merrick said, pleased with the unexpected arrival, "Well, this is a lovely surprise."

Callie landed behind Karramis and Will, both twisting as the winged horse lowered her outstretched wings and revealed James and Rhiannon.

Karramis's gaze swept the area, moving from her children back over to Lucas. He had sensed them coming, the grin on his face proving what she just now figured out—he had known the twins were headed this way. Karramis had always known Lucas's power to sense magic was strong, especially with extremely powerful abilities. It was one of the reasons he was always able to find her when they were younger.

Once Lucas was introduced to strong magic, particularly unique magic, that power would be imprinted into his psyche, like a magical beacon linking him to it. He could track other magic, even without having been around it first, but his abilities were stronger if he had. And when that magic was being used while he was searching for it, or when it was close enough to him, he would be able to sense and track it. That is more than likely how he was able to sense the twins' magic when they were at the manor. Because not only did James and Rhiannon possess very powerful magic, abilities most likely unique to them, but they were also an extension of Karramis and Will, both of whom wielded unique powers. Not to mention, Rhiannon possessed the same fire magic as her mother, something else adding to the connective link Lucas had on their bloodline. And with the twins' magic getting stronger by the day, Lucas most likely could tap into their magic much quicker and easier now, sensing when they were near. But Karramis was uncertain about one thing. Was he still unable to pinpoint them exactly? When they were at the manor, Lucas was unable to narrow down their exact location, stating he could still sense them, but there was a disconnect, like some kind of cosmic interruption. He knew they were nearby, like that magical beacon was going off in his head, but the sound could never be located fully.

Disregarding the curiosity brewing in her thoughts, she strolled over toward Callie and her children, the disbelief and nervousness seeping from her pores. "What are you two doing here?" she asked in a low, biting tone.

James held out a hand, hurrying to help Rhiannon off the winged horse. Ignoring his mother's question, he blurted frantically, "Mom, this is insane."

"Yeah," Rhiannon agreed, running her hands over her skirt, adjusting it over her skin-tight black pants, "you can't do this."

"I can," Karramis noted uncompromisingly, "and I did. And you two need to leave. Now."

"No." The word shocked even Rhiannon, the defiant nature unlike her. Continuing with a meeker tone, she added, "You know how you said there's a fine line between bravery and fear?"

Karramis gave her a slow nod and arched a brow, wondering where her daughter was going with this. "Yes."

"Yeah, well, there's also a fine line between doing something heroic and doing something stupid. And this, this right here, is stupid. It's downright reckless."

"It's suicide," James noted, assertive yet soft.

Rhiannon lowered her voice. "They're going to kill you." Worry creased her features. "Mom, you can't go with them. You have to fight. Even if it means we have to fight with you."

"That's rather magnanimous of you, sweetheart," Merrick said with a smirk, his posture relaxed. "But unless your mother would like me to reevaluate the terms of our agreement, then I would deem your courageous nature unnecessary."

"Just give us a minute," Karramis requested, the desperation thick in the air. Her chilled hands took one of theirs as she closed the space between them. "Listen to me. As your mother, it is my duty, and destiny, to protect you. You're not ready, and right now, this is the only option to keep you safe until you are. And when that day comes, you will take this"—she mouthed the next words—"son of a bitch down." She smiled. "But right now," she continued in her normal but quieted tone, "it's my turn to fight. To fight for the both of you. I would give a thousand of my lives if it meant you two would live a long, full, wonderful life." She kissed both of them, cupping their faces and giving them both a single peck to their foreheads.

"Can we hurry this up?" Leif asked, slightly annoyed. "This sappy shit is getting on my nerves."

Karramis pinned him with a hard stare. "You know, Leif, I'm going to kill you one day, right? Bet on it."

Leif scoffed, the arrogance poised in his expression. "I'm sorry to say this, witch, but that little promise there is one you will never keep."

A smile tugged on her lips. "I always keep my word."

"We'll see."

Giving him her back, refusing to acknowledge him anymore, Karramis said to the twins, "Listen, you two need to get out of here."

"Actually," Merrick drawled, "I have another idea."

Everyone faced him, confusion and anticipation flowing between them.

Karramis's eyes snapped to his, her defensive behavior shifting to one of caution and strategy. "I said I'd go with you without any trouble. There is no reason for them to be here."

"Well, as much as I appreciate your continued obedience when it comes to our agreement, I am quite keen on 'em stayin' here just a tad longer."

"Why?" Karramis asked, unnerved by the eagerness in his tone, steering James and Rhiannon behind her back as Will came up beside her, both aiding in protecting their children.

"Patience, sweetheart. All in due time."

Karramis wanted to shield them, defend her children at all costs. The urge to summon her fire magic to the surface burned in her veins, the heat bubbling and coming to life. A fierceness rattled in her core, this innate, instinctual nature driving her to protect her children. It was the raging beast of a mother hell-bent on destroying anything daring to threaten her offspring.

"What exactly do you want, Merrick?" Karramis asked him again instead.

"I'm not quite certain I know what you mean," he said, feigning innocence, his casualness unsettling.

"It's obvious there's some ulterior motive here, so let's hear it. You agreed to take me *after* the full moon, so it's pretty damn clear it's not my magic"—she gestured to Will—"*our* magic you want. So, what is it?"

Merrick cocked his head and took a step closer. "It would appear you have figured it all out. You're very astute, if ya ask me. A no-nonsense kind of woman. I have to admire that about ya. And aye, you are correct—your antiquated magic is not a beneficial piece to my plans." His hands clasped behind his back, his emotionless and authoritative stance domineering. "And, to my delight, I no longer require"—his gaze angled toward Will—"your magic either, Drolnogard. Not since one, or maybe both, of your children confirmed my suspicions and also possess your magical bloodline." Pale blue eyes shifted over to the twins, a wink aiming at Rhiannon. "So, with that wonderful bit of information, I was able to provide a slight amendment to both Lucas and Leif, thus allowin' me to still keep my word to 'em."

"What do you mean?" Karramis asked.

"It would appear Leif here has had a personal vendetta against ya fer quite some time. However, Lucas is still rather fond of ya and would very much fancy you fer himself. And when we originally came to an agreement about you, I never gave my word you would be alive once he acquired you."

Will glared at Lucas, his feet acting on their own accord as he started forward. "You bloody bastard."

Clutching his arm, Karramis stopped him, shaking her head in a pleading protest.

Eyes narrowed in irritation, Merrick cocked his head in warning and continued, "If you could all kindly refrain from any more outbursts, I would greatly appreciate it. I am attemptin' to explain the events leadin' to this moment, and I do not welcome interruptions." His features slackened. "Now then, where was I? Ah, yes. Well, in my need to rectify my side of the deal with Mr. Fraye, I devised another plan. So, rewind time a tad to a few months ago when you"—he smiled at Karramis—"so generously offered yourself up in exchange fer your children, I made certain to word my end of the bargain very carefully, so in the end, I would be able to take both of you. Nevertheless, I did initially want Will fer his magic, but when I arrived here after I returned, my plan was not to act in the manner which was played out, but rather to assess all of you. To see what I would be up against. So, I discovered some of your children's abilities, even the ones you all tried desperately to hide." A sly grin landed on Rhiannon. "And so, I formulated a new plan. One which would allow both Leif and Lucas an opportunity to get everythin' they want and therefore provide a resolution to my end of the deal."

"And what deal is that exactly?" Will asked, voice steady despite his heart pounded hard against his ribs.

"Well, that all depends on Mr. Fraye here."

"Again, what do you mean?" Karramis asked sternly but carefully, tired of his vague answers.

"Before we get to that," Merrick said, strolling back over toward Lucas, Leif, and Haydrin, all completely stoic and way too calm, "I would very much fancy if tonight's festivities were a wee bit more interestin'. I mean, we did come all this way."

With that, Haydrin marched over toward the portal, his stride wide and unhurried.

The sight of Haydrin again sent Karramis into a tailspin of emotions. Fear and anger from the last time she saw him as a human at the manor, the things he contributed to. He was just as intimidating and brawny as the first time she saw him all those years ago, yet now he was more put together, cleaner. In a way, handsome even. His black hair was shorter, resting at his shoulder blades, and his once bushy beard was trimmed. But now, burns marred his face, injuries Karramis could only assume were from when Rhiannon set him on fire when they were all attacked at the cabin at the beginning of the year. His eyes were hidden behind thick, black-framed glasses, which Karramis found odd since he was a werewolf.

Everyone watched as Haydrin disappeared into the watery vortex, the silence surrounding the area deafening.

"What is he doing?" Karramis finally asked, taking hold of Will's hand.

"He, too, is owed somethin' from me," Merrick said, "so I'm deliverin'." With a grin, he added, "Seems only fittin'—kill as many birds with one stone as I can." He paused, taking in the sight around him, pure joy flashing on his face. "Now, since your notoriety to circumvent certain situations eliminates any element of surprise on your part," Merrick chastised Karramis, a lilt to his tone as if a parent was scolding a child, "I reckon you halt any ludicrous notions ya may be concoctin' in that mind of yours. Because . . ." He strolled closer, his arms tucked behind his back. "How some of this ends tonight is solely up to you, sweetheart."

"Cut the crap, Merrick," Aidan's voice boomed from behind her, easing the tension in her shoulders.

Karramis, Will, and the twins twisted toward him, the dark green hoodie and light denim jeans barely noticeable outside the beam of light from the porch as light fluffy snow slowly fell from the night sky and obstructed their view of Aidan as he strolled closer.

Aidan must have seen the events unfolding while out patrolling, something he had been doing tirelessly since Kavana went missing. Having parted from Will and Karramis early in the evening, Aidan knew something was not quite right with them—their need to halt their own searching and return to the cabin tonight, something both Karramis and Will had not done since Kavana disappeared.

Bright emerald-green eyes took in the light, the unnatural and magnificent color nearly glowing as Aidan took in Rhiannon and James first, their parents now standing behind them. "Are you two all right?" After the twins nodded, he glanced up at Karramis and Will. "You two?"

Both nodded as Karramis said, "Yeah, we're fine."

"Well, well, well," Merrick drawled, condescension dripping from him, "it would appear the noble son has decided to grace us with his presence." A thrill sparked in his gaze, his expression filled with ease and eagerness. "I was hopin' you would show up. Stick around, you're goin' to want to see this."

Chapter 5

Not Over Yet

Everything about this was wrong. James was fully aware of it all the way to the very marrow in his bones. There was an ache in his stomach and a twinge of something strange tingling along the surface of his skin, this instinctive warning blaring throughout his whole body. Some of it was coming from him—the angst and uncertainty of what was going to happen to his mother and the concern of what Merrick might do again—but the absolute terror and unease exuding from his sister was what was flooding his system. It was palpable. Her thoughts ran wild, a silent plea screaming for help as she remembered the last time she saw Merrick and Haydrin, both attacks by the werewolf equally as fresh in her mind as the one with Merrick. Each event had left her traumatized, yet the strength and resilience she exhibited the night Haydrin and Ryan attacked them at the beach was the turning point for her. An awakening of sorts. But now, the timid, meek girl was back, trying desperately to hold it together.

Fingers wrapping around hers, he said to her, mind to mind, *"Just breathe."*

His words faded into the voids of her thoughts, her own inner voice taking over her consciousness.

"While we wait," Merrick said, his eyes focused on Aidan as James's attention shifted, the need to help Rhiannon fading behind his need to watch Merrick intently as the man slowly started toward all of them. "I must ask . . ." He stopped in front of Aidan. "How is our darlin' Nina?"

Tension built in Aidan's shoulders, and he squared them, attempting to appear taller, though he and Merrick stood eye to eye. "You leave my sister alone. Ye're never to go near her."

"How is her magic comin' along?" Merrick asked nonchalantly, disregarding the threat in Aidan's tone. "Has she mastered both shifts yet?"

Panic flashed in Aidan's eyes as Merrick's words settled between them, filling the space with an anxiousness James felt in his gut.

Rhiannon quietly gasped. "Oh no."

Ambivalent to what any of that meant, James's thoughts raced, the feeling of something bad about to happen building inside him.

A pang of magic surged deep in his core, the familiar sensation building and building, a sense of ease taking over. The power grew as a rush of recognizable comfort settled his nerves, the tingling of a well-known presence, of protection and companionship, erased some of the overwhelming emotions swirling through his body.

Wind whooshed overhead, causing Callie to shuffle behind James and the others, the winged horse huffing and ruffling her feathers as she took flight just before five dragons landed with a thud where she was once standing. The three Earth dragons—Terramina, Oakley, and Raeth—hurried to either side of the group, their eyes locked in on Merrick, Leif, and Lucas. Harkin and Ignara, the two Fire Dragons, chuffed thick plumes of steam from their nostrils, the vapors mixing with the cold air and creating an even larger cloud of condensation. Harkin strutted forward, the clawed knuckles of his wings pressing into the ground as his back feet marched across the lightly snow-dusted grass, stopping a few yards behind the others. His enormous frame, the mix of dark gray and black along most of his body, blended with the darkness, but his dark green eyes shimmered, the color nearly glowing as the dragon monitored the ones standing on the other side of the group he stood behind. Ignara remained where she had landed, her head cocked as she eyed the whole area, watching for any other potential threats. The bright red and scarlet scales along her underbelly radiated a glow from beneath, the soft illuminating contrast against the subtle gray of the other parts of her body like embers among ashes and soot. Black wings pressed into the ground, her haunches bent, ready to take flight at any moment.

Rhiannon had again called the dragons in her panic-induced whirlwind of memories and uncertainty currently unfolding before her. Despite not being able to fully hear her thoughts, James had no doubt they were here because of her.

"I'm sorry," Rhiannon admitted softly, the words barely audible. "I didn't mean to."

Terramina kept her head facing forward, but the dragon's voice filled the minds of all the Drolnogards. *It was not just you who summoned us.*

"It wasn't?" Rhiannon asked, eyes narrowed.

"We heard all of you," Harkin replied, the deep voice old but strong.

"All of us," James said, the inner monologue reaching the minds of Rhiannon and the dragons. The statement was not a question but rather a realization.

That meant not only had Rhiannon subconsciously called them, but he had too. And so had his father. Which also meant Will must be nervous about what was taking place, the situation more dire and far more dangerous.

Again, the feeling of something not quite right about everything bubbled in James's stomach. Something bad was about to happen.

Glancing over at Will, James noticed his father held his mother's hand firmly with her body slightly angled behind his. His body language was protective and on the defensive.

James had to do something. He had to protect his family. Mirroring his father, James took hold of Rhiannon's wrist and gently guided her back away from his side, stepping partially in front of her but still allowing her to see around him.

"What are you doing?" Rhiannon asked, her inner voice matching the bewilderment on her face.

Ignoring her question, James vowed to remain silent, remembering how his mouth had put his sister in danger before. He would not make that mistake again. This time he would be vigilant, observing everything with a keen sense of awareness, taking in everything with an alert mind and a cognizant intuition—allowing his instincts and rational side to take control of his actions. He would not be careless tonight.

"There they are." Delightful satisfaction beamed in Merrick's intense gaze, regarding the dragons for a beat, his lingering attention admiring the winged beasts.

James's gaze snapped to Merrick, pulling him from his thoughts.

"Absolutely magnificent," the man continued. "What a pleasure it will be to have you all on my side." Eyes shifting toward James and Rhiannon, he noted, confident and amused, "Soon."

The urge to retort sliced through James, the need to challenge him, to wipe that arrogant look off his face. There was something innately etched into him making him want to show this man he was not afraid, that fear was not something he would admit to. It was an unnatural sensation, one burning with the need to prove himself. Maybe that was why he always felt the need to speak whatever words came to mind. Or maybe he was just like his mother and never knew when to shut up.

But in this moment, everyone remained still. Quiet.

Snow flurries continued to cascade from the dark sky above, the thick, fluffy flakes creating a picturesque ambiance despite the tense and potentially grave situation unfolding. Silence loomed between the two groups, each set of eyes taking in every movement, every flicker of emotion, every breath, every blink—assessing each other with such intensity.

Karramis shuffled, a wandering, worried gleam flashing in her gaze as apprehension built in her posture, an agitation and anxious feeling building as that familiar sensation grew again. It thickened deep in her gut, the atmosphere around them shifting, creating a pulsing vibration combining with something recognizable yet unique. Glancing over at her children, she knew they could sense it too.

"James," Rhiannon said into her brother's mind, the concern sending chills up his spine just as a sound he was all too acquainted with drew his attention.

Rhiannon swallowed, the tingling in her lower abdomen growing. She could sense it, the portal. Its magic was churning, the same way it always did the night of the full moon. But it was not possible, the magic to open the portals from the non-magical world had long since passed. And yet the sensation was undeniable.

Her eyes found his, the paleness of Merrick's irises such a contrast to her vivid sky blue, the shade matching her father's perfectly. Something flickered in his gaze, something wild and malevolent, something malicious.

"Someone's coming," James replied, his response coming out audibly as a familiar sound filled his mind and body. He grabbed hold of his sister's hand again, his next words meant only for her. *"I'm right here. You hear me? I won't let anything happen to you."*

Exhaling, Rhiannon squeezed, her cold fingers clutching to him as a sense of control washed over her, the full awareness of all the emotions rattling around inside her coming together and forming a shield instead of crippling her.

The sound intensified, the portal a few feet away vibrating with an unusual frequency, a disturbance of some kind. One James recognized as the same one from the night Merrick returned all those months ago. But this one was not as powerful. It was weaker and unsteady—the reverberations more languid and unrhythmic, almost as if the portal's magical battery needed charging.

Since James and Rhiannon had received their Guardian powers, the magic linked to the portals had been inconsistent. Sometimes the twins could sense the portals nearby, and other times it was as if all the doorways inside the realm had disappeared completely. And the last time anyone came into Kiluemar, James and Rhiannon had not been able to sense them at all, not even the magic from the outside portals. And with Pavian not showing up like he was supposed to, James was unsure if he did arrive back home and something happened, or if he actually never made it through at all.

But this portal was definitely producing a magical link to the twins, one sending both of them into a state of unease as the power vibrating from it suddenly halted.

Eyes wide and trepidation blooming to life in James's stomach, he peered at a large figure stepping out of the portal, the oversized silhouette definitely not human. He swallowed, his mouth becoming dry as his once steady heartbeat thumped erratically as the strange creature he had long since forgotten moved closer toward the light.

Rhiannon gasped, quickly stifling it behind a hand, not wanting to draw attention to herself.

"Holy fucking nightmares," James muttered, unable to restrain himself. "What the hell is that thing?" He never could quite determine its identity when it had been at the manor.

Leif and Merrick grinned as Lucas crossed his arms over his chest, the movement relaxed as he let out a low chuckle.

"It's an ogre," Karramis said, monitoring the tall, monstrous, and ugly humanoid creature shuffling closer through the shadows, his enormous and plump frame dragging a much shorter person along, each step sluggish, unsteady, and forced.

Gastell tugged on the arm of the figure clasped in his grip, a small grunt falling from the very familiar feminine voice.

The world around Karramis froze as her heart dropped into her stomach, trepidation and shock taking root in her gut.

"K?" Karramis whispered, panic lacing her tone as she stepped around Will, her body angled toward her sister but her gaze landing on Aidan.

Will hooked an arm around her waist, pulling her into him as Terramina mirrored Karramis's advancement, his wife acting on instinct to help her sister. "Stop." The declaration was soft, not a demand but rather a plea.

The pliant and languid Kavana stumbled as Gastell held tight to her arm, her hands appearing to be bound behind her back.

Bruises colored the left side of her unnaturally pale face, and her eye was swollen shut. Different shades of red covered her forehead and hairline, signs of old and new injuries. Her hair was matted, and stray strands stuck to the blood coating her face and neck. Two deep cuts sliced through her right temple and along her cheekbone, blood trailing down and dripping off her chin onto her ripped, light gray sweater. Smaller and slightly lighter bruises mottled the bridge of her nose, a possible indication of it being broken. She was conscious but barely as her uneven breaths blew from her split lips, the condensation thick as it blended with the light snowfall.

Aidan pushed past them, the movement swift and fearless, his need to get to her superseding any politeness as he ignored all traces of danger from the men surrounding his severely injured girlfriend. Karramis tried to follow, but Will refused to let her go, his unwillingness to allow her anywhere near those men overriding whatever thoughts or irrational actions his wife was most likely rattling around in her head.

Gastell shoved Kavana, her weight nearly nonexistent behind the powerful thrust. She crumbled to her knees against the cold, slightly snow-covered ground, a grunt coming out in a guttural moan as the cold air mixed with the warm breath billowing from her blood-filled mouth. She slumped forward, all control of her own body completely gone as she started to topple over.

Aidan advanced forward, his mission clear as he remained in a trance, his movements fleeting yet inaudible.

Leif gripped Kavana's hair from behind, halting her descent. Tugging and lifting her head to face him, he towered over her and glided a finger down her exposed neck. "No sleeping." He squatted behind her, his nose brushing her jaw before he tipped down and licked the dried blood caked along the two puncture marks on her neck. "I'm not quite finished with you yet."

Eyes lifting, Leif released Kavana and stood just as Aidan charged at him, the shapeshifter's fist colliding with the vampire's jaw without any hesitation or concern for retaliation.

The blow was powerful but ineffective at causing any real damage to Leif, the vampire now raging with anger at the brazen attack on him.

"I guess it's your turn," Leif warned, cold and callous.

Aidan scooped a limp Kavana into his arms, the motion effortless as he ignored Leif and the others, his refusal to leave her anywhere near them erasing any concern he might be fighting against.

Annoyance grew as the enraged vampire swooped in front of Aidan, halting him in place. "Your little girlfriend here proved to be no match for me. Let's see how you measure up."

Pulling a small dagger from under his shirt, Leif ran the blade along one of Aidan's hands holding Kavana, the pressure behind the slice making the shapeshifter wince as blood began to well along the gash.

Deep sapphire eyes turned solid black, pooling outward until two dark orbs peered back. Mouth opened, fangs appeared among the top row of perfectly straight teeth as Leif inhaled, taking in the sweet, rich scent of Aidan's blood. Veins protruded around the eyes, the deep red among them turning black against the pale skin. A hiss erupted from the vampire as he launched at Aidan, his sharp fangs aimed to kill.

"Stop!" Merrick demanded, a tautness coating the usually calm and collected tone—a strained cadence that almost resembled fear. Advancing over to them, he announced, the dominance in his demeanor not allowing any room for debate, "Stand down. Now."

Shifting back to normal, Leif grinned, the gesture unapologetic as he sheathed his dagger and uttered, "Apologies."

Aidan glared at the vampire before stepping around him.

Karramis urged herself out of Will's hold and raced toward Aidan and her sister as she hurried to remove her jacket.

Will's instinct to follow her was evident as he turned to his children. "If something happens, both of you are to get out of here. Just take the dragons and go. Do not stick around. Understood?"

Before they could answer, Will bolted after Karramis, his attention wholly on Lucas and the others.

Aidan's steps quickened as the terror and agony finally appeared across his features while taking in the semi-unconscious Kavana who was freezing and severely injured in his arms. Blood coated Aidan's hoodie, the reddish-brown fluid soaking in and making the dark green appear black. Tears threatened to break free as he reached Karramis halfway, both examining Kavana from head to toe.

One eye was open, the other fighting against the swelling against it, but there was a distance in her stare, the blue empty and all awareness lost.

"K?" Karramis whispered as she draped her jacket over her sister. "K, can you hear me?"

A moan grumbled from Kavana, the pained groan seeming difficult to manage, the only sign of life she could provide.

"I have you, my love," Aidan said softly, kissing her forehead. "Ye're safe."

Karramis and Aidan headed over to the others. Rhiannon and James remained frozen in place, the cold mist flowing from their mouths heavy and irregular as both continued to hold hands. Will monitored the area behind his wife and best friend, his gaze staying on the men across the way, the uncertainty of what was happening building in his chest. The mercurial nature of the men, as well as the morose energy, made the air around them thick with tension, the consternation of the situation causing everyone to become fully cognizant of their surroundings.

Fury slowly developed inside Karramis, the panic and fear lessening. Red-hot fire burned in her veins, the strange yet soothing sensation awakening something primal inside her. Something ancient and destructive. And yet it was dormant— hidden deep beneath the surface.

Heat radiated from her hands, the fire inside her rising. They had hurt her sister. They had taken her captive and tortured her. But why? Why her? The torrid fury burned hotter, growing and strengthening, wanting to show itself.

Feet halting, Karramis demanded, struggling to combat the indignation and contemptuous hatred she felt in that moment, "Aidan, get her out of here." She faced her husband. "Will, tell the dragons to get the kids out of here."

James released his sister's hand. "Mom, what are—"

"You two are not supposed to be here," Karramis said adamantly, closing the distance between her and her children. "This is my deal, my fight."

"Mom, you can't—"

"Yes, I can," she countered, tight and steady as she interrupted James's plea. "And I will." Blowing out a heavy breath, she added firmly but with a reassuring gentleness, her eyes pleading, "Listen to me, I stood back long enough, allowing you two to figure out all of this on your own, but not anymore. I wasn't going to let you both be taken or challenged when you aren't ready. Not yet. I know this is your destiny, but if I can delay it even just a little bit, then I'm damn well going to. I am your mother. It's my job to protect you. No matter the cost. So, for once in your life, listen to me and don't fight me on this. It's your turn to stand back and allow me to do something dangerous."

"You've done enough, Mom," James said, his voice soft. "You nearly died for us once before."

Determination and unwavering conviction gleamed in her expression. "And I would gladly do it again without hesitation."

Rhiannon's breath shuddered as she spoke. "But Mom . . ."

"End of discussion," she said with finality.

Clearing his throat, Merrick announced eagerly, "But the show is just beginnin', sweetheart. I'd seriously hate fer you all to miss the best part."

"Haven't you done enough?" Karramis asked, venom in her tone. She moved closer to him, each step slow as her brown eyes monitored all three men and the ogre now standing off to the side. "What is all this? Huh?"

She paused her movement as Will came up beside her, placing a hand at the base of her back, the presence of him giving her comfort and strength—the strength she needed being far more mental and emotional rather than physical, the former being exceptionally unruly and arduous to control.

Merrick locked his cunning gaze on her, his attention unnerving as he remained silent with a gleam of amusement in his eyes.

No one spoke as an ominous tension filled the air.

Karramis waited, refusing to back down. She despised this insufferable tactic, this method of intimidation and ploy for dominance. It was something she learned from her father and became even more familiar with when it came to her relationship with Lucas. Her father often did it to prove a point—he was the boss, the authoritative figure, and what he did and said was for her own good and to protect her. Whereas Lucas had often done it to control her, dominate her. It was all about power to him, and when the power balance was not in his favor, he would often become something else completely.

The cold, brittle air sent goose bumps rising along her body, Karramis feeling every snowflake melt against her bare skin, the lack of jacket reminding her the thin shirt she wore was not sufficient in this weather. "Could we hurry this along, please, before I freeze out here?"

Lucas chuckled. "My, my, love, ya sure are feisty tonight."

Karramis fought the urge to roll her eyes. She was seriously tired of the games. "What is all this?" she repeated, her questioned aimed at Merrick again as she crossed her arms, the movement seeming defensive or defiant but, in all reality, she was attempting to erase some of the chill taking over her body. "Huh? First, you tricked me. Then you kidnap my sister for some sick, fucked-up game. What the hell are you playing at, Merrick?"

"Tricked you?" Merrick questioned with a low, mocking snicker. "Sweetheart, there was no trick. It was merely a play on words. It was not my fault ya failed to read between the lines. And I hardly see what was done to your sister as kidnappin'." He glanced sideways, his gaze landing on Leif as they both smirked. "Nah, I simply perceive it as commandeerin' her in the hopes of obtainin' a far more lucrative item to help fulfill my end of yet another agreement."

Merrick stood next to Lucas and Leif, who were all waiting where the light mingled with the night, their features almost unnoticeable in the uneven shadows. All three remained utterly still with their hands behind their backs, a picture-perfect stance of soldiers waiting for their orders. Leif and Merrick steeled their faces, zero emotion showing across their impassive features. Gastell, however, shifted from foot to foot, his enormous body hard to ignore even as he stood a good distance from the others just outside the light, more of his frame cloaked in darkness.

Scanning the open area for any more potential threats and a way to get Kavana out of danger, Karramis spotted Lucas glaring at her, a different set of emotions filling his eyes and tightening his expression. Even through the darkness, she could sense the shift in his behavior, the clear-cut jealousy boiling off of him as she held on to Will's arm. A different person glared back at her, one unlike the dismissive and arrogant man who had not even flinched at her and Will's embrace only moments ago. A shift she had grown to anticipate over the years. One man stood before her, but two different personalities rested beneath the surface— one of possessiveness, anger, jealousy, and hatred, and the other being one of love, protectiveness, compassion, and kindness. But both contained two things in common, the absolute foundation of who Lucas was—obsession and pride.

Observing the hostility coming from Lucas as he and Karramis stared off at one another, Merrick grinned, pure satisfaction on his face as he addressed Karramis. "What is it about you that drives people to covet you so fiercely? First, you have Leif over here, who desperately yearns to drain the life from your body. Then there's my faithful companion who is rather insistent on me procurin' your magic. And, of course, you have me, and the absolute fascination I have with ya, and the longin' to taste your intoxicatin' blood. All of us wantin' you dead more than anythin'. And yet, ya have another who wants you fer an entirely different motive." He gave Lucas a little smirk, the gesture warm yet mischievous. "Ya know, I find the story of you two to be quite poetic. The anticipation of how this all will conclude is rivetin'. I absolutely cannot wait. But until then . . ."

Magic pulsed, the portal's power vibrating to life again just as Haydrin stepped back through, yanking a bloody figure behind him.

Shocked, Karramis breathed, "Dad?"

Chapter 6

A Debt Owed

The urge to vomit churned, the nausea roiling deep in her stomach as every emotion rattled her nerves. Fear swelled in Karramis's gut, the combination of horrified disbelief and panicked helplessness causing every alarm throughout her body to kick into overdrive. Every nerve prickled, an overwhelming sense of apprehension, uncertainty, and dread coasting over her chilled skin. Anxiety plagued her every thought, the strategy she had planned out now slowly crumbling to the ground in a fiery heap at her feet. Every scenario, every what-if completely shattered in a matter of minutes as she continued to stare at her father, all feeling of control and readiness vanquishing as Haydrin forced Zarrius to his knees.

Still cradling Kavana against his chest, Aidan slowly began to step backward, his gaze shifting to the twins. He gave them a curt nod and a quick flick sideways with his eyes, gesturing them both to follow him. All three moved at a steady pace, the retreat barely noticeable, moving only a few feet behind Karramis and Will. With his eyes still focused on the group across the way, Aidan lowered Kavana to the ground, the action noted by both Merrick and Leif.

Haydrin remained towered over a kneeling Zarrius, the brooding man now gripping the Guardian's salt-and-pepper hair, more grayish than white, in his hand as Lucas moved ever so slightly forward, the act purposeful. As if on cue, Merrick and Leif sauntered closer, all three men stopping right next to Haydrin, the line of them creating a looming wall behind Zarrius as Gastell remained close to the steps near the cabin, his filthy clothes stretch tight against is plump frame.

The unswollen eye of Kavana cracked open as she took in an unsteady breath. Pain laced her expression, her body recoiling in on itself as she hissed, the sound disjointed and strained.

"Don't move, Aunt K," James whispered, kneeling down to help Aidan put his mother's jacket on Kavana. Her skin was so pale and splotchy, all warmth in her battered frame sucked away by the cold.

Words formed in her throat as she forced down a swallow, whatever she was going to say lost behind the heavy lassitude taking over her body. The mottled bruises on her cheek and eye were a mix of deep black and rich blue. Dry blood stuck to her face and along her neck, the numerous puncture marks lining her throat clotted but still new. There was no sign of healing, a clear indication the Guardian magic inside her was not only weaker but possibly nonexistent.

"Shh," Rhiannon said as Aidan tucked a strand of blood-coated hair behind Kavana's ear, "don't speak, Aunt K."

Shuffling sounded, Raeth and Oakley coming to stand on either side of the group sitting on the ground, the snow coating the deadened grass with each passing moment. Harkin and Ignara closed the distance, taking just a few more steps closer. The energy between the groups thickened, a nerve-racking tension building even the dragons could sense.

Lifting Kavana back into his arms, Aidan handed her to James. "Like yer father said, if somethin' happens, you two"—his bright emerald green eyes landed on Rhiannon—"get out of here."

James and Rhiannon shook their heads, the need to protest evident in their postures.

"Yes," Aidan insisted, no room for arguing. "Take your aunt and get somewhere safe."

The urge to have them leave now was eating Karramis alive, her eyes glued to the others across the way but her focus solely on the ones she loved behind her. They were not safe here. No one was. But if she could only get Kavana and her children out of here, maybe she could focus on not only getting herself and Will out of this mess, but her father too. Knowing Aidan could shift and fly away, she was not worried about him. However, with things not happening how she thought they would, she was not so sure her assessment of that theory was entirely accurate.

Hand gripping Will's, Karramis waited, the chill in the air washing away some of the warmth coming from him. She hated the silence. There was too much power in silence, something Merrick seemed to know all too well. He was controlling the entire narrative, something she hated as well. There was this desire to take back control, to switch this around to be in her favor. But how? This was not something she had prepared for. There were too many variables to consider. Too many possible outcomes. And she was not going to jeopardize anyone tonight. This was not how this was supposed to go at all. So now, all they could do was wait.

"I don't know about anyone else, but I'm freezing," Karramis declared. "So, if we can move this along, I would appreciate it."

The tone accompanying the statement was not at all frightened despite how Karramis was actually feeling. In fact, there was a playfulness to it. A cadence laced with a nonchalance and a surprisingly relaxed smoothness. But in reality, she was terrified about what might happen next.

Zarrius kneeled on the ground, the snow seeping into his dark brown khakis and leaving a wet stain along his knees. The light behind him shone from the porch, casting a bright shadow along the frosted-white grass as flakes continued to fall. His eyes lifted and landed on Karramis, the icy blue almost glowing silver through the darkness and flurries. Blood trailed down his chin from a split along his lip, the mark the only noticeable injury. Hands unbound, Zarrius appeared calm and unfazed by the events—something Karramis could only assume was from the years of having to be level-headed and dignified in his position, even when faced with obstacles or danger. But she knew her father better than anyone else here.

Karramis analyzed his posture, the perfect etiquette of a leader—head held high, even with a hand gripping his hair, shoulders back, arms relaxed yet flexed, jaw tight, and eyes razor sharp and focused. But it was the look beyond his fixed gaze that gave him away, the look of defeat. It was hidden deep inside, but Karramis could see it in the slight twitch of his eyelids and misty haze he was desperately trying to fight back.

Erasing the silence, she finally said softly, the question directed at Merrick, "What do you want? With me?" She lifted a chin to her father. "With him? With all of us?"

Merrick waited a few beats before he answered, "It's not what I want. At least, not in this particular moment. Nah, what I want shall come in due time."

"Then what exactly is goin' on here?" Aidan asked, moving up next to Karramis.

"Now, that is a splendid question there, son." Merrick squatted beside Zarrius, both men eyeing one another. "It would seem the exterior portals caused a wee bit of an issue with my initial plan to tie up loose ends. And I am quite curious as to why such an incident occurred."

"Care to elaborate?" Will asked, the need to pull Karramis behind him crawling up his spine.

Merrick stood and focused on Will, sensing the shift in the man's posture and demeanor, the need to protect his wife unmistakable. Grinning, he glanced over at Lucas, trying to gauge if Will's actions were caught by the one intently staring at Karramis. Intrigue gleamed in Merrick's expression, the not-so-subtle way he flashed his devious smirk making the hostility and unease around them thicker.

"Come here." The demand was aimed at Will.

"No," Karramis countered, firm and unyielding. There was no room for debate, nor did any sign of regret show on her face.

"Protectin' him, are we, love?" Lucas chuckled, low and callous as he glared at Will. "Should ya not be the one protectin' her, mate?"

"She can handle herself." Confidence filled the statement, the sheer pride in how far his wife had come in the last few months with her training radiating in the cocky smile Will flashed.

Lucas scoffed, the sound a breathy exhale and low laugh. "From past experience, I would haveta disagree." Advancing closer, he added, "So c'mon, mate, protect her. I dare ya."

Karramis bit her tongue, the metaphorical pain clamping down on the words wanting to escape. Clearing her throat, she focused back on Merrick as she squeezed Will's hand, the need to remind both her and her husband they were in this together. "What did you mean about the portals?"

Merrick hesitated, the urge to continue stirring the proverbial pot between Lucas and Will itching just below the surface. It was a game he definitely wanted to play. A strange form of entertainment he had collected over the last few months with Lucas's hatred toward Will being a constant topic of discussion again. And Leif did not help the matter. The vampire's desire to encourage Lucas to act on his unpredictable and more malevolent urges was like adding fuel to the fire. Leif was, without a doubt, quite insistent on Lucas finally putting an end to his obsession once and for all after Merrick's return to the realm.

Karramis swallowed, the intense way Merrick examined her making her want to break eye contact as her heartbeat quickened. The energy around her sent her senses into high alert, this strange feeling of dread building in the pit of her stomach.

A perusal of predatory intensity remained on her. "Are you not aware one of the portals malfunctioned when your children returned?"

She blinked at her father, his expression neutral as she shook her head. "No, I wasn't aware."

Merrick eased his arms behind his back and widened his stance, the action seeming unintentional yet somehow purposefully executed. "Oh. Well, that is actually quite fascinatin." A light brown brow arched as an inquisitive gleam filled the depths of the blue gaze peering down at the head of the Guardians. "I reckon daddy here kept some very important details to himself."

"What do you mean malfunctioned?" Rhiannon asked, her voice strong as she stood next to her brother, who was still holding a now sleeping Kavana in his arms.

Merrick beamed at her, the memories of how her blood tasted coating his tongue. "Hello, sweetheart."

Blocking some of his sister's body with his, James repeated her question, the sternness in his voice and the power behind his stance clear—he would protect Rhiannon this time. No matter what.

"Still the weakest link, I see," Merrick muttered to Rhiannon, taking in how she was guarded by her brother and four of the five dragons, each monitoring the events unfolding with an intense, watchful gaze.

"When the twins came through," Zarrius stated, trying to take the focus off Rhiannon, "there was a rift in the powers around the island." He grunted as Haydrin's hand gripped tighter to his hair and jerked his head back.

"Who said you could speak?" Pure ire thundered in the werewolf's deep voice.

"Now, now, Mr. Tevlak," Merrick scolded playfully, "let the man speak. I fer one would very much welcome an explanation as to why the outside portals have caused such a nuisance lately."

"What are you talking about?" Karramis asked Merrick before she eyed her father. "What's he talking about?"

Zarrius let out a heavy sigh, the cold mixing with his heated breath. "For a while now, there's been a . . . an issue with the barrier around the island, and over time I guess it seeped into the portals on the outside. There was no real notice inside the realm because the portals were sealed. But occasionally Meadow and I would sense the portal magic in the non-magical world flicker slightly, similar to when they opened, but only for a few seconds at a time—and it only happened maybe half a dozen times over the last year or so before you all returned. We just assumed more power was being siphoned away from the island. The power we felt was almost as if the magic left here wanted out, like it was trying to run or hide."

"Or tryin' to find somethin'," Aidan added under his breath but still heard by those close to him.

Rhiannon stepped up next to her brother, both eyeing each other.

Zarrius continued, not hearing Aidan, "But when James and Rhiannon came through and their magic presumably returned, I believe there was a major rift in the magic around the island, especially with the portals. Despite the Guardian magic fading, I could still feel it—the strength behind it was so powerful. But then it was gone. I felt this small zap before the power started to faulter and fade, it was like the charge behind the magic was flickering in and out. It was the strangest feeling. That's how I knew you all returned, because I could feel the portals from the outside again, but not the same way. It was weaker. Broken almost. But there was another issue we soon discovered."

"And that would be?" Karramis asked, drawing out the last word, the confusion as to why her father chose to stop talking making her uneasy.

"Yes, please," Leif said, bored, "indulge us without the pausing for dramatic effect."

"It would be a whole lot easier to discuss this if I wasn't being manhandled and sitting on the freezing ground," Zarrius declared sharply, the smooth cadence of his authoritative tone replaced with a condescending quip.

Black boots strode toward him, stopping a few inches from his bent knees. Hands still behind his back, Merrick towered over Zarrius. "Try anythin' foolish, old man . . ." Nothing but pure dominance filled the space between them, the threat clear in every facet of Merrick's being. "And I will surely deliver Haydrin's end of our deal in the manner in which it was originally agreed upon."

Zarrius swallowed and nodded. "Understood."

"Release him," Merrick demanded.

Without arguing, Haydrin loosened his hold and stepped back, placing his hands behind his back and presenting himself as a dutiful and obedient soldier.

"Now then," Merrick announced, "continue."

Zarrius thought for a second, trying to remember where he had left off, a glimpse of something sad in his eyes. Remembering, he continued, the confident and respected tone firmly in place, "When you all returned"—he regarded James and Rhiannon—"the portal you all came through, well, something went wrong." Ignoring the confusion riddled on Karramis's, Will's, and the twins' faces, he noted, "As head Guardian, I felt the crack in the magic, the separation of sorts."

"Separation of what?" James asked, shifting behind his parents and Aidan, the weight of his aunt's relaxed body in his arms causing fatigue to his muscles.

The dragons waited, unmoving and vigilant. Terramina remained close to Will with her wings tucked into her body, her head lowered slightly as her narrowed eyes focused in on Lucas, who inched closer every few minutes. Raeth and Oakley stood on either side of the twins, their stance ready to react at any moment, their observant instincts and defensive nature honed to attack if necessary. Harkin, the oldest of the group, and the most territorial and protective of all the dragons, monitored each movement carefully—every billowing exhale, every shift of a body, every blink, and every tilt of a head, even the way the trees swayed, the snow fell, and the gentle way the darkness changed as the clouds moved overhead and the faint moonlight peeked through and cast a silvery sheen across the wintery backdrop. As Harkin watched intently, Ignara focused all her attention on the sounds surrounding the cabin and deep within the forest, as well as the emotions looming within the three Drolnogards standing before her. She concentrated on the wind dancing through the trees, the gentle breeze like waves brushing along a shore. The Fire Dragon took note of the way each person breathed and the distant footfalls of a four-legged creature stalking a few yards away, the large animal creeping steadily closer, the unnatural stealth poised and determined as if watching and listening for its potential prey. Ignara remained engrossed in the scene playing out in front of her, all the while being mindful of everything around them, taking in every sound and scent not obvious to the humans she was bound to protect.

Strutting over to the twins, Aidan said, "Do you remember when we first arrived, how I went and retrieved yer belongin's?"

The words floated around in Rhiannon's head. A question she never seemed to formulate on her own burning a hole deep in the pit of her stomach as she pulled up the memory, the conversations and research playing back in her mind.

Realization hit her like a ton of bricks, slamming into the side of her head. How could she have missed that tiny bit of information? Why had she not put two and two together and questioned how Aidan had gotten their belongings in the non-magical realm, handled the vehicle rentals, and returned without the full moon opening the portals? Something she definitely would have caught if she had been paying more attention. But she clearly had not been. Months and months of never catching this inconsistency on how the magic of the island worked.

Understanding seeped from his sister and pulled his thoughts inward, fast and alert, as James uttered, "How is that possible?" He glanced over at his parents. "How's any of this possible?"

Aidan noticed the same confused expression on Karramis's and Will's faces that was plastered on their children's, the similarity of the parents and the twins uncanny in this moment. "Do you remember how Pavian and I went into the village to get supplies after you returned?" The question was directed at Karramis. When she nodded, he continued, "Well, that wasn't all that happened."

Karramis flashed a look at Will before giving her full attention over to Aidan, trusting her husband to not only watch her back but to keep an eye on her father for her. "Meaning what exactly?"

Merrick advanced over toward Karramis, a knowing grin angled at Will's attentive gaze. "Leif, would you care to fill 'em in on what we discovered?" He turned slightly before reaching her, the movement relaxed as he strolled in a wide circle around the others, his pace steady. He weaved around Terramina, the space between him and the Earth Dragon only a few feet wide. He made his way closer to the other dragons and the twins, his features emotionless.

There was a silent plea in Karramis's eyes as she shot Aidan a quick glance, an earnest declaration to protect her children and sister as every fiber in her body filled with trepidation. A sense of an ulterior motive being played out continuing to take shape.

Leif cleared his throat, the sound loud and showy.

Karramis twisted toward the vampire, the jerking motion quick and frantic. Settling her nerves, Will slid his hand into hers and ushered her in between himself and Terramina, shielding her from Merrick and his calculating saunter around all of them. As Merrick made his way closer to the twins, Raeth and Oakley hurried in between him and the young Drolnogards. Ignara snarled, lowering her head and glaring at Merrick as her chest began to glow a fiery orange under the red scales along her neck. Harkin lifted his wings and flapped as a low growl rumbled from the back of his throat, the threat clear.

But Merrick remained calm, no reaction, not even a hint of anything flashing across his face or even in his eyes. "Leif, please proceed," he said, disregarding the dragons completely.

Leif crossed his arms over his chest, the thin, gray, long-sleeve shirt pressing against his biceps and across his chest, the three buttons unfastened and exposing a silver chain around his neck and a scattering of hair just beneath the collar. His laid-back appearance and relaxed body language made him seem more human than monster, his handsome features and arrogant twitch of his lips almost charming and flirtatious.

"Well, as you all are probably well aware, the lovely Kavana is a rather vicious little kitten when backed into a corner, a splendid trait she surely learned from years of training as a Guardian. And though her attempts to fight and escape were admirable and downright stimulating to experience, they were futile."

The need to punch Leif in the face again burned deep in Aidan's core, the impulse like a moth to a flame.

Perplexed by where the vampire was going with his bizarre monologue, Karramis studied the others carefully, surveying each one of them as she plotted an exit plan for her children. Something was surely going to happen any moment now, and she had to get them out of here.

Lucas had finally stopped his advancements just a few feet away when the Fire Dragons reacted to Merrick being too close for comfort. But Lucas's stance was wide, and his attention was focused as if ready to jump into whatever scheme Merrick had formulated. Haydrin remained stationary, his hands still clasped behind his back and his gaze zeroed in on one particular thing. Following his line of sight, Karramis took in what he was staring at with such intensity. Rhiannon. The predatory glare he gave her was uncomfortably attentive. There was an animalistic nature in the way he observed her, a wild and brutal penetrating assessment of not just a predator wanting its prey but of a killer wanting blood. Glancing behind the others, Karramis eyed the ogre, his presence known but inconsequential. It was as if he was only here to be an additional piece in this unpredictable game Merrick was playing—a potential pawn to maneuver only when needed. Despite being the one to bring Kavana here, his true role was unknown. But Karramis knew why the others were here.

Merrick was here for obvious reasons—the payment of their deal. And with the vampire, that too was evident, Leif always being by either Merrick's or Lucas's sides when things got dangerous, any chance to draw blood being one of his favorite pastimes. And it was also clear why Lucas was here, something she was sure she would find out soon enough. But it was Haydrin who baffled her, because since they had all returned, Karramis had not seen him in his human form since the night at the manor. However, tonight, it would seem, Merrick was adamant about having him part of all this. Maybe he was the reason Merrick waited until after the full moon to move forward with their deal.

"—with some very effective tactics on my part," Leif said, pulling Karramis from her thoughts, "she provided Lucas here with some very interesting facts." Crouching down next to Zarrius, he smiled. "Wanna fill them in on the rest?"

Zarrius heaved a heavy sigh. "The portal you all came through never closed that night."

"What?" Rhiannon and James blurted, both sets of eyes wide.

"When Pavian and I went to get medical supplies," Aidan chimed in, "Zarrius saw me. He didn't know who all came back with us, but he knew somethin' was wrong with the portals' magic. He and the rest of the guard were frantic tryin' to protect the open portal in the non-magical realm, but they needed help. So, he asked me to go out and see if I could find anythin'. And when I did, I took care of all traces of us, as well as collected all the items we left behind. Luckily, with it bein' winter, that area had very little activity, but we still had to be certain, so I continued to monitor it for a few days."

"What happened afterward?" Karramis asked. "With the portal?"

Aidan's eyes landed on Zarrius, allowing him to answer her question.

"That particular portal eventually disappeared completely."

James let out a small huff as recognition hit him. "So that's why we only felt four when our Guardian powers arrived over the summer."

Zarrius nodded. "Yes."

"But why?" Rhiannon questioned, confused. "Why did that happen?"

"We aren't sure, honestly. But the pulse of magic that was felt by not only me and Meadow but by many people around the island, it was like a surplus of power. It was as if too much magic was in one place at one time, and it disconnected the power anchoring it to the island. Then over time, it burned out completely."

"Power overload," James uttered.

"Now," Merrick stated, "to advance this discussion ahead a tad here, since I am becomin' quite complacent with all this tedious nonsense. This brings us to just a few days ago when we discovered the younger Mr. Ward had yet to return from his lawful duties." He tsked. "Such a shame what happened to those innocent bystanders." Faux remorse lined his words. "All those unfortunate souls taken too soon."

Karramis closed her eyes, remembering the horror in Pavian's eyes and the sadness and anger in his voice when he told everyone of what was discovered at MUSE—the massacre that had taken place, the incident never having a motive nor a person to blame. And yet Karramis was certain Merrick knew the truth behind the attack on the school and all the lives taken that night.

"Nevertheless," Merrick continued, his entire mannerism shifting back to one of casual charm and cunning leadership, his presence all charismatic yet dominating, "Pavian's absence caused a slight setback with the events scheduled to take place tonight. Therefore, a new plan was formulated, one Leif here seized as a perfect opportunity to relish in—the pleasure and enjoyment of breakin' someone, one of his favorite forms of entertainment."

Amusement sparked in Leif's bright blue eyes as he winked at Karramis. "You're next, witch. Your sister was fun, but I'm itching to get you behind closed doors."

"Be careful, Leif, I bite back."

"Oh, I'm counting on it."

Merrick clapped his hands together, the single slap loud and attention pulling. "Now then, shall we move on with tonight's revelries?"

Brows creased, Karramis was afraid to ask but did anyway. "And what might those be?"

"Well, ya see, sweetheart, your sister was not our initial target. She was simply the bait. With Pavian not present fer a pivotal moment in my plans, I needed an alternative." He gestured to Zarrius. "Case in point."

Her heart pounded in her chest. There was nothing in her deal about her father or anyone else. Life for life. Her agreement with him was life for life, a fact she overlooked before, but now, it was clear. Her and Will's life for the safety of their children. Two lives for two lives. This was something she could still work with, creating a new plan from the moment she discovered her mistake, her lack of reading between the lines. But what plan did Merrick have with her father? And why was Pavian also involved?

"I don't understand," Karramis said, trying to remain calm.

"Oh, it's rather straightforward, sweetheart." Merrick prowled closer as he slid his hands into his pants. "Your father is goin' to die tonight."

Chapter 7

A Debt Paid

Merrick's words seemed to be the catalyst everyone was waiting for, the scene unfolding fast and chaotic, each person reacting at once.

Leif swooped across the open area, his figure blurring, the sudden rush sending a swirl of flurries dancing through the air as he zoomed behind Will and seized him, drawing his dagger and placing the tip of the blade under his chin, taking the Drolnogard by surprise. Terramina reacted, baring her sharp teeth with a snarl, eyes narrowed, and body positioned to attack.

Karramis twisted and gasped, the swift movement of the vampire surprising her just as Lucas wrapped himself around her, pinning her arms to her sides. The strength he possessed matched that of Will's, the training with her husband likely aiding in her potential escape from his hold, but she was unable to focus on freeing herself as her attention pulled in all directions.

Pain shot through the back of one of Zarrius's legs, the blunt force of a steel-toed boot driving him to his knees again. A guttural grunt fell from the Guardian as Haydrin kicked him again, this time along his back and making him topple over, his hands pressing into the cold, snow-covered ground.

James grabbed for his sister's arm as he held tight to Kavana, the presence of Aidan swiftly in front of them apparent, the shifter now guiding them smoothly and quietly closer toward the Fire Dragons. Raeth and Oakley hurried forward, creating a barrier of protection in front of them. But Harkin had his wings outstretched, the narrowed gaze of his glowing green eyes aimed toward the cabin.

Taking Kavana from James, Aidan carried her closer toward Ignara, his eyes pleading as he hesitated, the fear of what the dragon might do to him filling his mind, but he trusted the twins would never allow her to harm him, or their aunt.

Harkin took to the sky in a flash, the force of his wings beating, mighty and relentless, causing Aidan to curl his upper body over Kavana, protecting her from the icy shards of snow blasting around them.

Aidan lowered Kavana to the ground a few feet from Ignara's enormous frame, steering James and Rhiannon in front of their aunt's prone body.

Afraid of what Merrick might do if the twins took to the sky—the malicious and scheming man's laser focus zeroing in on every person and every action with intense observation—Aidan instructed, "Protect her and each other." He peered over his shoulders at Oakley and Raeth, the two dragons with their attention zoned in on the action playing out. "Have them protect you. And when Merrick is distracted, take her, and all of you get the hell outta here."

Harkin rose a few yards in the air before aiming his hurried descent toward the ogre racing his shuffling stride over to Lucas, who was trying to tame the now wild and flaring Karramis in his arms, his struggle to control her hands proving to be his main focus. A roar exploded from the Fire Dragon as his chest glowed, the fiery light maturing deep within his body and becoming brighter beneath his smoke-colored scales, the smoldering radiance traveling up his long neck. Fire erupted from the dragon's mouth, the bright blaze blinding in the darkness, the flames narrowly missing Terramina as she drew up her wings to shield Will from the heat soaring across the open field, all traces of snow melting and turning to steam. The fire rocketed across the grass, a trail catching the ground ablaze. Waves of flames slammed into Gastell just as Harkin closed the distance, the giant mouth snapping shut, the sound of sinew squishing and bones cracking echoing through the chaos.

Haydrin dropped and rolled sideways just as Zarrius flattened himself against the ground, both barely missing being taken out by one of Harkin's wings. The stench of burning flesh filled the air as the dragon landed with a thud on the roof of the porch, the weight of the creature too much for the structure as it caved in beneath the dragon's massive body, one corner of the covered deck opened to the elements, the snow now coating the splintered pieces of wood. Wings flapping, he hovered over the cabin, his chest lustrous again, the glow rising. Intent clear, Harkin's green eyes brightened and focused on Merrick, who was still standing in his original location, taking in everything but remaining unfazed and highly entertained.

"Harkin, no!" Rhiannon yelled pleadingly, the challenge coming from Merrick's expression aimed at the dragon sending every bit of her body and mind into a state of panic.

But it was too late.

The dragon drew in a breath, the exhalation coming out with a forceful roar, flames blasting outward, the bright orangish-red glow beneath the scales on his neck and chest like magma bubbling and raging to life.

Rhiannon raced forward, the attempt James had made to stop her falling short as she dodged his outstretched hand and ran past Aidan, but Raeth and Oakley blocked her, the slick soles of her boots sliding along the thickening snow.

The world around them slowed as the raging blast shooting out of Harkin charged toward Merrick. Silence fell, only the sounds of the fire roared as it traveled across the night sky, all remnants of snow and the bitter chill in its path evaporating. Heat seared, the extreme temperature unbearable as all the darkness vanished behind the bright illumination of the flames, the deep hues of red and orange shadows dancing along every surface.

Impervious, Merrick remained in place, the blaze reflecting in his eyes as it soared closer. The corner of one side of his mouth lifted. Hands rising, the movement so carefree and unhurried, he tilted his head and glared at the dragon, defiance and dominance conveyed in his expression. Victory radiated in his gaze as the fire halted a few feet in front of him, the wall of heat vanishing, the chill of the night returning and covering him once again as the blaze slammed against something solid yet not really there.

Zarrius rolled as the flames bounced off the invisible shield protecting Merrick and roared directly toward him, the wave of fire and heat curving back against the hidden wall of power.

Karramis knew her father would not make it out of the way in time as the fire grew closer. Bending her knees, she widened her stance and ducked down, twisting slightly and sliding her leg behind Lucas's, the movement quick and effective as his hold on her loosened. Power surged as she flattened her palm and rammed her open hand into his stomach, the force of the blow and the magic erupting from her sending him stumbling backward. Without a second thought, she faced her father, praying she could still use her telekinetic powers to remove him from the danger headed straight for him. But as her eyes lifted, she spotted Zarrius being yanked out of danger by Haydrin, the werewolf saving him from the fire but clearly not for any benevolent or honorable reasons since he proceeded to grip her father's throat. Haydrin's dark eyes burrowed into him, the fixed glare delivering not a warning but a promise.

Karramis stood there, her attention pulling to the still-raging flames in front of her. Magic hummed around as Merrick's steady hands flexed and his fingers twitched, the power coming from him curling around the fire. But there was control to it, a strong and solid maneuvering. The flames pulled together and slowed, the fire moving with purpose. It was no longer untamed and wild, but rather, it was stable and calm.

Merrick was manipulating the element.

Eyes wide in surprise and confusion, Karramis could sense the magic ebbing and flowing from the element she had become all too familiar with over the last few months. One of the hardest powers to control, fire was highly unpredictable. Not to mention complicated. By far the most difficult element to manage, fire was wild, fierce, powerful, and destructive. Dangerous.

Harkin balked, his mouth twisting into a snarl as the fire he had created became stationary, the flames still flickering wildly, the sound still raging, but all flowing pausing in midair.

"I am becomin' rather efficient," Merrick said, brash and self-assuring. "Would you not agree?" The question was aimed at Karramis. Satisfaction beamed in his expression, the significance to his current actions clear to her—he no longer needed her magic. And maybe he never really did.

Pale blue eyes focused on the dragon airborne over the cabin, Harkin's wings flapping rhythmically and keeping him in place. Drawing his open palms back, Merrick forced his arms forward with an even thrust, pushing the controlled flames skyward, the fire aimed for the dragon. The blaze raged back to life, the intense heat and magical flames soaring toward its creator.

Flames sliced along the roof of the cabin, the powerful element setting a section of the structure ablaze. Banking, Harkin dodged the forceful impact but faced it as it zoomed by, drawing in a deep breath. The fire slowed and began to flow backward, retreating inside the dragon's open mouth.

Karramis hurried and lifted her hands, drawing her own fire magic to the surface, taking control of the residual flames remaining on her home.

Sensing Lucas closing in on her, she angled her head toward him, rage burning in her eyes as she gradually extinguished the flames. "Touch me, and I will not hesitate to reignite these and send them straight into you. Don't fucking test me, Lucas." With the flames out, she lowered her arms and aimed her anger at Leif and stalked over to him, the vampire still pressing his dagger to Will's throat. "Unhand my husband. Now."

"Ooh, I like when they're feisty," Leif teased, releasing Will without arguing, his amused expression set on Lucas behind Karramis. "She's going to be fun later."

Will twisted, his hands fisted, a clear threat in his stance and posture, but Leif lifted his dagger again, the movement fast and barely noticeable, the tip of the blade breaking through Will's skin under his chin. A piercing pain sliced through Will, and he winced at the sudden penetrating contact. Blood trickled down the silvery blade, the trailing droplets bright red. Leif flicked his wrist, the dagger jerking forward and slicing a small gash on the underside of his chin, the mark just deep enough for blood to well along the surface of the cut.

Terramina growled, low and deep, her weight shifting.

"Don't," Will told the dragon, halting her attempted attack. Two sets of blue eyes remained unblinking as Will added to the vampire firmly, "If you so much as touch my wife—"

"You'll what?" Leif challenged. "Kill me?"

Will shook his head with a grin. "Oh, no," he said without doubt, the declaration smooth as he glanced over at Karramis, pride filling his expression, "it won't be me."

"Her?" Leif scoffed. "You think she can take me down—a vampire?"

"Ashes to ashes," Will mocked.

Licking the blood of his blade, Leif said, derision and arrogance in his tone, "We'll see."

"Enough," Karramis ordered with conviction, the authoritative finality in the demand like a mother scolding her children, surprising not only herself but the others. With her shoulders squared and features even, she said, "This has gotten way out of control, and it ends right now."

Merrick's eyes darkened with intrigue, a captivated gleam of mischievous interest as he regarded her, his full attention on her every word.

Catching sight of the quirking of Merrick's mouth in her direction, Karramis disregarded him completely, making her way over to her children, her stern gaze flicking to Lucas as he started to move behind her, attempting to follow her retreat.

"I'm not going anywhere, Lucas, so back off."

Lucas halted, well aware she was right. She had nowhere to go.

"I will stick to my end of the deal," she continued, her eyes lifting to Merrick, "but whatever is about to happen, will *not* be taking place in front of my children." Tears threatened to break free as she faced her father, Haydrin's grip around his neck still firmly in place. She inhaled, the cold air burning her lungs before she released it, holding herself together and remaining level-headed. Weakness and fear would not surface. Not tonight. She had to focus if they were going to survive whatever was in store for them.

Snow fell, the flurries gone as thick flakes fluttered from above, the gusts growing colder. Rustling joined the gentle breeze and swaying trees, some of the dragons shuffling as their heavy bodies pressed into the ground and their feet moved across the frozen sleet. Five sets of beastly eyes monitored, their intense scrutinizing of the four remaining enemies across the way not at all inconspicuous.

Terramina had stayed near Will, refusing to take her eyes off Leif, who remained far too close to the Drolnogard. Raeth and Oakley had never left their positions next to the twins, the Earth Dragons ready to take flight with them in tow as soon as word was given. Ignara had shuffled closer from where she once stood. With one of her wings lifted, she shielded James and Rhiannon from the increasing snowfall. Her chest glowed, the flames deep within her body burning along her red-scaled chest and neck, the warmth melting the snow under the exhausted

Kavana, the heat radiating from the dragon washing away some of the paleness along her cold skin as she flooded in and out of consciousness. Harkin had never landed, his patrolling now taking place from the sky, his black-and-charcoal figure dipping out of sight occasionally within the darkened and white-speckled backdrop.

Pondering her next move, Karramis closed the distance between her and the twins, giving a quick glance to Will, an unspoken reassurance flashing his way.

Eyes fixed on Aidan, she declared firmly, "Get them out of here."

James protested, "I'm not leaving."

"Yes, you are," she countered.

Rhiannon peered over her mother's shoulder, taking in her grandfather. "Are they going to kill him?"

"Aidan," Karramis said, unsure how to answer her daughter's question. Uncertainty bloomed in her stomach, the unknown of what Merrick had planned churning with a nauseating fierceness. Why was her father now a target? "Take care of my sister and children. I'm counting on you to keep them safe."

"Mom, no," Rhiannon pleaded.

"Yes," she retorted sharply, a tightness growing in her throat. "This right here is not your fight. Not yet. Now, get on those damn dragons and get the hell out of here. Go. Help Aidan with Kavana. Make sure she's okay."

Voice cracking, Rhiannon whispered, "Mom . . ."

"Please." The word fell from Karramis in a matching tone, the distress in the single word causing tears to form in her eyes. "For once, just listen to me." Her declaration from earlier rang through her, needing to brand it deeper into her children. "I need to do this. It's my job to protect you . . . And I will do anything to see you two live through this. So, if that means I have to go blindly into the lion's den, then so be it."

Warmth caressed her back, the familiar touch sending goose bumps throughout her body. Will remained silent, hanging on every word he understood his wife needed to speak. He trusted her. He knew she was already planning something to get them out of this mess—he was certain tonight was not his last night with her. No matter what, she was not dying tonight. And he had no doubt she would do everything in her power to save him. To save them both. And he would fight like hell to do the same for her. Something they both provided for one another, protecting each other. Equally.

"Mom," James said imploringly, "but they're clearly going to kill you." Brown eyes moved between his parents and over to Zarrius. "All of you."

Karramis shook her head. "No one is dying tonight." Although, she feared her words were a lie. There was a foreboding presence lingering around them as if death was lurking in the shadows.

"I wouldn't make promises you can't keep, witch," Leif chimed in loudly, the vampire now standing next to Merrick—

Lucas and Haydrin also back by their sides as Zarrius knelt in front of the werewolf.

Karramis seriously despised the vampire, his unrepentant persona and callous nature making her skin crawl with fuming annoyance. Closing her eyes for a second to stop them from rolling back, she went on, "This is not up for discussion. Now, go." A pleading expression locked in on Aidan. "Get them out of here."

"Mom," James argued.

"Go." Her voice was tight beneath the demand as she pulled her children into her, hugging them and kissing their foreheads before stepping back. "I'll be right behind you."

Memories flooded Rhiannon's mind, the thoughts flowing freely within James's head as well, both unsure who was pulling forth the recollection. Sadness and terror filled the twins, those exact words reminding them of the last time their mother spoke to them, the events from the night at the manor coming to the forefront of their minds.

Mouths open, they both went to protest, but Karramis interrupted them, "Go. Please."

Sorrow and defeat seared threw Karramis's chest, the numbing pain burning a hole in her heart. She had no clue what was going to happen, even though she continued to strategize. But the unpredictability of what Merrick had planned with whatever deal he had made with Lucas and the others, and the uncertainty as to why her father was here, were causing her nerves to charge with anxiety.

"Aidan," she went on, "get them out of here."

"Come on," Aidan urged solemnly, a subtle resignation masked behind the firm command, turning and heading over to Kavana, who was still nestled under Ignara.

Eyes filled with tears, Rhiannon took in her grandfather, their gazes locking.

Zarrius gave her a gentle but forced smile, his blueish-gray eyes soft and sad as he flicked them between the twins. "Take care of each other."

The words rushed through Rhiannon, the comprehension of his statement taking her breath away. This was not just a request to protect each other, it was a goodbye to them. Their grandfather would not make it through the night. And he had known all along. He had accepted his final fate. And he had chosen not to fight it.

James marched toward his mother, his body tense and his features pinched with worry and despair, every part of him wanting to fight her on this as Rhiannon's thoughts raced through his head and her emotions swelled inside his own body. "You better come back to us." His eyes landed on his father. "Both of you."

Karramis's mouth quirked in a half smile, her eyes expressing a silent vow as she said quietly, her words meant only for him, "We will."

His voice lowered, matching hers, but there was determination present. "Do not surrender."

"Never." An unspoken vow rested between them, a tenacious declaration she could live by. She would never give in.

"And you're going to fight, right?"

"Of course."

"Promise?"

"Yes."

"Say it."

Placing her hand over his heart, she said, soft and confident, "I promise, I will fight like hell."

Releasing a relieved sigh, he nodded. "Good. I'm going to hold you to that." Pivoting, he strolled over to where Aidan stood, who was holding Kavana close to his body, and took Rhiannon's hand, ushering her to follow. "Let's go," he whispered to her.

Without a word, Rhiannon climbed onto Raeth's back as James mounted Oakley, getting situated before reaching down and taking Kavana from Aidan and cradling her in his lap.

Opening her eyes, Kavana groaned as she blinked up at her nephew. "James?" Her voice was gravelly, her throat sounding dry as her effort to say something else faltered, her weakened state showing in both her body and tone.

James gently shushed her. "It's okay, Aunt K, I've got you. We're going to get you some help."

Apprehension lined his features, the intoned delivery of his statement sounding distant and hollow. Anxiety and fear coursed through him, the defeat he felt by leaving his parents at the mercy of Merrick and the others—along with the haunting heartbreak of never seeing his grandfather again—engulfed him, his nerves vibrating with a burning uneasiness and his blood raging with an unsettling anger. The sensation was overwhelming, pulling him down into a strange new place, a place of darkness. A void of some kind. A place where guilt, shame, and regret dwelled and flourished.

But James refused to allow himself to fall into this foreign place. He would fight it, completely rejecting this mysterious and hollow emptiness. It would never take him. Not if he had any say in it. Like his mother, he would not surrender. Never.

As the twins took flight on the dragons, Aidan gave Will and Karramis one final glance.

"Thank you," Karramis mouthed.

Aidan nodded, the hope he would see them both again and the silent promise to protect their children displayed in his warm expression.

Shifting into a golden eagle, Aidan soared upward, following closely behind the twins and Kavana, both dragons camouflaged within the snowy night.

Will searched the sky as he angled back toward Ignara, a silent conversation taking place. The Fire Dragon huffed as if protesting before spreading her wings and rising upward, her body aimed in the direction of the other dragons. Terramina shuffled and chuffed before following Ignara over the western tree line of Kitra Forest. It was clear Will was sending them off to protect the twins as Karramis continued to watch her children fade away, her emotions raging—the roller coaster of contradicting feelings swelling in her core.

Clapping filled the area. "Fair play," Merrick praised as Will and Karramis faced him. "That was a spectacular show ya just bestowed upon us." No condescension in his declaration, the statement directed at Karramis, the awe in his reverent tone mirroring his charismatic energy. "Your persistent and dominant temperament has always enraptured me. That assertive disposition is so . . ." He pulled in a deep inhale as if smelling the air. "Intoxicating. Somethin' emanates from you when ya allow yourself to take control, to fully acknowledge whatever powerful force is dormant deep within that vessel of yours." An intense set of eyes remained fixed on her, an animalistic hunger and preternatural thrill analyzing her every move. He was hypnotized by her. "You exude this absolutely luscious, mind-altering aroma, a unique blend of somethin' sweet and spicy, a magical and delicious fusion of sin and danger." He licked his bottom lip and sauntered closer to her. "Of fiery passion and succulent pleasure. You are the forbidden fruit . . ." Black seeped into the whites of his eyes, a ravenous yearning radiating from his penetrating glare. "And I, fer one, am desperate to taste you."

Merrick's skin along his cheeks began to slice open, the small gashes forming as if tiny razors glided over his pale flesh, creating paper-cut-like marks, half a dozen or so on both sides of his face. Longing filled his blackening eyes as he craved whatever he smelled coming from Karramis, the pheromones mixing with her already tempting blood making him feral for her, a hunger and thirst he no longer could fight.

Cutting in front of Karramis, Will blocked his wife from the view of the advancing man, his posture taut. "Stay the bloody hell away from her."

Harkin landed with a thud not far behind Karramis and Will, the last remaining dragon taking his place as their only line of defense, refusing to leave them unguarded.

Merrick slowed, the desire to take what he craved fading behind a wide grin as his eyes returned to normal and the cuts sealed. Tossing a glance back at Lucas, he said, "Apologies." There was no truth in the statement, the word flat. "It would appear I am far more ravenous than expected." Blue eyes settled on Karramis, a predatory gleam behind his dilated pupils. "And the current scent comin' from her is so . . ."

"Intoxicating," Karramis uttered with a slight bite to her tone, uninterested and a bit annoyed by the idea of being a target of his interest because of the way she smelled. "Yes, we heard you."

The confidence and brazen honesty were at an all-time high, and Karramis recoiled at her own actions. Pressing her lips together, she regretted this newfound defiance and boldness, the trepidation she fought to control clearly hidden behind a wall of snarky insolence, the audacity to test the waters of the situation not part of the new plan she was trying to devise. The bottled-up fear and anger and sadness were taking control, the hatred toward the men in front of her for forcing her to run and hide, for taking years away from her, for robbing her of a different life, were finally surfacing completely.

Leif chuckled, placing a hand on Lucas's shoulder. "Well, it would seem the witch's mouth is determined to get her into trouble tonight." He analyzed her, something like hunger, or maybe it was malice, flashing in his deep observation. "You really don't know when to shut up, do you?"

Eyes narrowed, she glared at him, words rising to the surface.

Whatever she was about to say was cut off by her father. "Karramis." His tone was deep and imposing, the authority behind it causing her to snap her mouth shut.

"Oh, I almost forgot about you," Leif added with a snicker, making his way over to the man again kneeling on the ground with Haydrin standing behind him.

The snow had coated everyone, the steady storm showing no signs of letting up. But Karramis ignored the chill, trying desperately to remain warm under her thin shirt. It had never been this cold here, and this was the first time she had experienced snow up close. There had been a few times when she was younger when the weather on the island was colder than normal, usually because an Arctic freeze had coasted over the northeastern Atlantic, the bitter chill blasting into the barrier and causing some snow to fall on the higher elevations along the mountains, but even that was rare. Kiluemar had always been a perfect temperature, even the sandy oasis of Demetrius Desert giving off the best kind of warmth, the heat like a hug and not at all suffocating.

"If we could get on with this," Haydrin said, his deep voice jarring since he rarely spoke, the brooding man of very few words. And yet, he was the most intimidating with his tense energy, menacing nature, and dark scowl beneath his thick-framed lenses. Not to mention his height, his six-foot-six frame towering over everyone else.

A question burned in Karramis, the need to find out something about the werewolf still plaguing her. "Why do you wear glasses?"

Haydrin stared at her, his stance going taut more than usual as his brows drew together, something like anger or frustration irritating him. But he did not answer her. Instead, he asked Merrick plainly, dark and demanding, "Are we going to do this or not?"

Zarrius shifted, his knees pressing into the sodden, slush-covered ground, the heat of him melting the snow. Fear flashed in his gaze, something Karramis caught immediately, the terror emanating from her father something she had never witnessed before, along with the resignation she could sense also coming from him.

"Dad," Karramis said in a strained whisper, realization of what was most likely about to happen taking root in her stomach, the roiling anxiety in her gut making her nauseous as she took a step toward him. She had to stop this.

"No," Zarrius warned, shaking his head.

This was all wrong. Why was this happening? How had all of this manifested into her sister being taken, her father being the target of an execution, and Will also being forced into her deal? Things were happening here that were not at all things she had prepared for. Everything was so convoluted and overwhelming.

"Why?" Karramis asked, her question pointed at Merrick.

"Why what, sweetheart? I cannot read minds, so you are goin' to have to be a little more specific as to what you are inquirin'."

His blasé demeanor not only made Karramis nervous, it infuriated her. That and the silent and watchful gaze of Lucas—him quietly and eagerly sizing her up like she was some prized possession he wanted. It was unnerving and downright disgusting. The need to fight the toxic energy, narcissistic tendencies, and possessiveness coming from him itched beneath her skin. She so badly wanted to wipe the arrogant grin off his face.

"Why," Karramis continued, her jaw clenching as she paused and swallowed, "are you doing this?"

"Which part?" Merrick answered.

"All of it? Insisting on Will being part of our deal. My sister." Her eyes locked with her father's. "Taking my dad."

"Well, as I stated before, ya vowed to deliver me life fer life. Thus, two lives given and two lives taken. The results of our deal will depend on the events of which still await you both later. In addition, I simply suspected you would find some way to undermine our arrangement, since I, too, worded my end of the deal carefully. Therefore, takin' your Drolnogard here would also provide an additional safeguard, since ya have this keen ability to escape the confines you often find yourself in. Now, your sister was never my target, but she was a great alternative. And the outcome of her capture was simply the results of her insubordinate nature and inability to refrain from tryin' to fight her way out. A family trait, I suspect. However, she discovered rather quickly she was in no way trained nor prepared fer challengin' a vampire, especially with her lack of magic or enhanced skills." Merrick circled around Zarrius as Haydrin remained planted behind the Guardian. "Now, your father here is compensation—penance, if you must. He is payin' fer his sins. Or rather, he is payin' fer the sins of another. Life fer life." He smiled, wide and full, pure satisfaction in the gesture. "Quite poetic, if ya ask me."

Terror squeezed in Karramis's chest as shallow breaths fell from her mouth.

Acceptance and remorse entered her father's features, drops gliding down Zarrius's face, the tears cold against his cheek. "It's okay." A soft, reluctant smile tugged at the corner of his lips, his gentle, knowing eyes beaming at her as he wiped away the tears.

She had never seen her father cry before. He had always been detached, stoic, and commanding, never showing any true emotion other than casual boredom or a domineering politeness. There was a laziness to his enthusiasm, only seeming to express happiness in the form of gentle smiles, constructive criticism, or subtle acts of service. He was a man of rules and structure, one who valued routine. Karramis had never truly known the man behind the mask of being a leader or beyond the veil of the protector. But in this moment, she saw it, the love he had for her—everything he had ever done was to protect his children, to protect her.

"Dad." Her voice was strained.

"It's okay," he repeated, taut and quiet. "Let me do this. I'm ready."

"Please." She started toward him. "Let me try—"

"No," he argued, holding up his hands for her to stop. "It'll be okay." Another tear slid down his face as he gave her a reassuring wink, forcing another smile. "We'll see each other again."

Karramis wiped her face, the steady stream warm against her cold skin as Haydrin moved closer to Zarrius, his frame monstrous behind him.

"Don't," she pleaded to the werewolf. "Please."

He dismissed her, not even glancing up, his dark gaze fixed on her father.

"Dad." The imploring tone behind the word accompanied a breathy exhale, thick condensation flowing from her mouth.

Haydrin leaned over, and Zarrius stiffened, his pained and watery gaze staying on his daughter as the man's massive hands grasped the sides of his face from behind.

Zarrius let out a shuddering breath. "I'll tell your mother you said hi."

Karramis launched forward, determined to stop what was about to happen next, but Will slid an arm around her waist, her backside instantly warmer from the heat of his body pressing into her. A trembling sob broke free, the single, shaky cry rattling her body.

"This," Haydrin said through gritted teeth into Zarrius's ear, loud enough for everyone to hear, "is for *my* mother."

Zarrius let out a low exhale, his attention never faltering from Karramis. "I lov—"

A snap echoed as Zarrius's head was jerked sideways, the force behind the werewolf's muscular arms and enhanced strength making the movement effortless as the lifeless body slumped in his grip. Releasing his hold, Haydrin watched with pure enjoyment and satisfaction as Zarrius toppled to the ground.

Gasping, Karramis covered her mouth, her knees buckling as she turned and sagged in Will's arms, the heavy sobs muffled behind her hand.

Harkin roared, the dragon's anger explosive as he bolted upward, the gusting blast of the cold air sending a wave of snow and ice swirling around him.

Will held Karramis tight, the lack of warmth from her cold body seeping through his jacket as his own figure grew tense, the dragon's unpredictable actions unknown to him. Removing his jacket, Will quickly slid his wife's arms into the sleeves and tugged it up over her shoulders, taking no time to zip it up before pulling her back into him, his eyes focused on Harkin.

The Fire Dragon soared upward, his large, dark figure disappearing. Wings flapped, the powerful force behind the fast-beating descent downward echoing across the snow-packed meadow.

Will's body went rigid. "Don't do it," he whispered. The plea was flat as if he had repeated the words over and over, this last set of lines seeming to escape him.

Karramis jerked her head upward, catching sight of the dragon headed straight for Haydrin and the others, the glow emanating from the creature bright against the dark sky and within the falling snow.

Opening his monstrous maw, Harkin let out another powerful roar, this one exploding outward with a steady flow of fire. Flames jetted through the sky, aimed directly at its targets.

Leif sauntered without a care in the world behind Merrick as Lucas and Haydrin stood there debating if they should stay put or attempt to get out of the way.

The fire halted for a second as Merrick raised his hands, the flames shooting sideways and straight into the cabin. The building exploded as the fire crashed through the front of the structure, the blaze erupting into an inferno.

"No!" Karramis screamed as she lifted her hands, her magic building inside her.

But before she could summon her powers, Merrick threw out both arms. His telekinetic abilities zoomed outward and slammed into her and Harkin. Karramis flew backward and landed on the ground, a heavy grunt bursting from her. The flames burned brighter in a thunderous blast as the Fire Dragon was thrown into the fiery blaze, his large body swallowed by the flames. An agonizing bellow echoed from the fire as Harkin sprung from the destruction, his membranous wings singed and a splintered wooden board protruding from his side.

Will watched as the dragon fell to the ground, the sizzling sound filling the air as Harkin collapsed in the snow.

"I guess Fire Dragons' wings aren't fireproof," Leif said with a chuckle. "Shame."

"You fucking bastard," Will snapped, attempting to go aid the dragon, but Leif swooped over and stopped him.

Little cuts began to slice through Merrick's exposed skin along his neck and face, spreading and splitting open.

"Come now," Merrick said, joyful and exuberantly, "shall we proceed to the castle fer the remainder of tonight's events?" He strolled over to Zarrius's body. "But first, I am rather famished."

Dark red oozed beneath cuts as strips of flesh peeled apart, creating deep fissures along Merrick's skin. Pain erupted across his face as he let out a controlled yet guttural groan, the sound muffled in his chest.

Karramis and Will backed away, the scene unfolding sending fear racing through their bodies.

Black sinew appeared beneath the peeling flesh as dark, leathery muscle thickened, the remaining pale skin melting into the new body forming. The whites of Merrick's eyes disappeared behind deep pools of darkness, cold and empty as his gaze shifted to Zarrius's dead body, the hunger in his intense stare building. His body swelled as he grew taller, his shoulders stretching wider as his clothes ripped from his humanoid figure.

A muscular frame tore from the old body. Sharp, hooked claws sprouted along his fingertips. Shards of something black broke through the new skin along his arms, sharp points connecting to thin, transparent tissue. Wings. Large, gnarly wings had erupted from his shoulder blades, connected to his arms. The flesh of his face shredded away as if his skin rubbed aggressively against fragments of glass over and over. Blood rose from the continuous slices roaming along his face until black bone and thick, taut membranous flesh stretched across a monstrous skull forming from the once human head. Giant, round ears sprang out where his hair once was—bat ears. Screams escaped him, the sound booming across the meadow. His jaw cracked as cuts sliced through the corners of his mouth. Thin lips curled up in a snarl as the monster unhinged his jaw. Jagged, uneven teeth and fangs lined the inside of his unnaturally wide mouth, the yellowish points dripping with saliva.

The deep obsidian figure was a creature of the night, a monster of epic proportions. Merrick had become a nightmare on two legs.

Karramis stood terrified and awestruck, never having seen a creature like this before. Despite no longer fully fearing the man, she definitely feared the monster before her.

Solid black eyes peered at Karramis, the creature seeming to reach into her soul and take what it wanted, but he hesitated as his two slitted nostrils flared. Head cocking, Merrick sniffed, his attention pulling to the dead body a few feet away. His mouth opened, exposing his sharp teeth and vicious snarl, a thick stream of saliva trailing off his thin lower lip. Wings shot out and, in a flash, Merrick was airborne, his sharp-taloned hands reaching out and swooping down to snatch Zarrius's body.

Karramis reached up and stepped after him, the attempt to try to retrieve her father's body and save it from being mutilated pointless as both disappeared into the night.

"My, that was quite entertaining," Leif said mockingly with a boyish smirk. "Now then." He gestured toward the portal, just a few feet from the dragon lying motionless on the ground. "After you."

Haydrin stalked over and grabbed Will's arm, forcing him along.

Jerking back, Will said pointedly, "We can follow without the need of an escort."

Haydrin pointed at the portal. "Walk."

Will obeyed as Karramis made her way over to him, but Lucas strolled up behind her and wrapped his hand around her wrist, pulling her to a stop. When Will stopped and faced them, Haydrin stepped in front of him, crossing his arms and glaring down at him.

"Behave, love," Lucas said evenly. "Or Will's dead before we even reach the castle."

Karramis pinned him with a heated glare, her gaze burning straight into him. "If you don't let go of me, you'll be dead before we reach the portal."

Releasing her, Lucas smiled. "Ya might wanna be careful there, love."

Karramis returned the gesture, hers a bit more menacing. "And why is that?"

"Because . . . how tonight ends is now up to me."

Chapter 8

The Infirmary

The icy wind sliced through the air as each snowflake crashed into James's exposed skin, the tiny shards painful behind the force of the swift movement through the darkened sky. Branches swayed below, the mix of deciduous and coniferous trees creating a soft melodious tune in sync with the flapping of wings.

Reaching the western edge of Kitra Forest, Oakley banked right, the change in direction causing James to squeeze his thighs tighter against the dragon's back and hold Kavana closer to his chest. His aunt's face was cradled against his body as a hand shielded her from the onslaught of snow crashing into them. James could feel the chill seeping from her body, his every attempt to keep her warm failing as his own limbs grew numb.

"Ignara," James called, his inner voice somehow showcasing just how cold he was as the shivering he was struggling to control flooded his entire being.

The Fire Dragon soared downward and coasted alongside Oakley, mindful of the distance between her large, outstretched wings and the Earth Dragon. *"Is everything all right?"* she asked James, the dragon's pleasant, raspy voice gentle but a trace of bitterness hidden behind it.

James understood the indignation racing through the dragon's nerves, the instinctual nature to turn around and protect the ones left behind. To help fight a battle they would surely lose alone. An unfair fight that was equivalent to one against a hundred.

With no active magic, James feared his father would never stand a chance against Merrick, Haydrin, or Leif—possibly Lucas, depending on the fighting skills the man had compared to Will. But even so, even if his father had the advantage, going up against a werewolf and a vampire was not in his favor, let alone a cursed creature with a plethora of stolen magic. And despite the powers his mother possessed, she was still no match for all of them. Yes, she had outsmarted them before—twice actually—but could she do it a third time? James was reluctant to believe she would be so lucky yet again because she would have to not only outwit and outmaneuver the same three men as before, but now she had to do it with a fourth—Merrick.

His parents were seriously outnumbered and nowhere near powerful enough. And it took James everything he had to stay the course, to get Kavana the help she needed, and to make sure both his aunt and sister were safe from whatever nefarious deeds were planned tonight.

"She's getting too cold," James said to Ignara, refusing to acknowledge is own body's inability to fight the freezing temperatures as he glanced down at Kavana, her face unnaturally pale. *"Can you help her somehow?"* He pulled the collar of his mother's jacket up over his aunt's neck for the second time since taking to the sky. *"I'm afraid she's going to freeze to death."*

"We are nearly there," Raeth offered reassuringly as he flew a few feet in front of Oakley, both dragons navigating through the snow-filled darkness.

Ignara flapped her wings and went skyward. *"I may be able to reduce some of the snowfall and heat the air in front of you and your sister."* All traces of the adverse cadence were gone, replaced by the rough yet sweet, familiar tone he had associated with the Fire Dragon.

"Yes, please," Rhiannon interjected, paying close attention to the ongoing internal conversation as she and Raeth led the way. *"I'm so cold I can barely hold on anymore."*

"I would never allow you to fall," Raeth promised.

Rhiannon laid her chest against the Earth Dragon's back and outstretched her arms around his neck. *"I know."*

A bright red glow exploded a few yards in front of James and Rhiannon as the location of Ignara became unmistakable. Fire tore through the darkness in the direction away from them as the radiant blaze lit up the entire sky around them.

A snow-coated meadow lay below, untouched and desolate. The trees lining Caerwyn Village illuminated, their once hidden silhouettes blanketed by a wall of light along one side. Mist and steam floated through the air as the flames and heat collided with the falling snow.

A warm embrace slammed into James as the bitter cold fought to remain, the storm above still going strong. Tiny droplets of water trickled down his face, the warmth melting the snow and turning it into rain.

Ignara continued to push the flames through the air, the controlled fiery breath lighting the way toward the easternmost part of the village. Sucking all the fire back into her, the dragon veered sideways before flying upward and disappearing behind the wall of falling snow, her presence remaining close by but on high alert.

Raeth landed first, his four large, clawed feet slightly disappearing beneath the white-covered ground near a two-story stone building resting in the middle of a wide-open field. The structure was the only thing around besides the outlines of a wall of trees circling the old building. An eerie silence coated the area, the air thick with a foreboding sensation of trouble on the horizon, a gut-wrenching caress of something sinister waiting to jump out and strike.

Rhiannon slid off the dragon, her movements hurried as her booted feet slammed into the slick ground. Crunching combined with the subtle breeze of the wind, the need to alert those inside of their arrival and the dangerous condition her aunt was in the only thing driving Rhiannon up the stone steps. Adrenaline pumped in her blood, erasing all the numbness and warming her from the inside out.

"Hello?" Rhiannon shouted as she shoved open the door, the hinges releasing a bone-chilling squeak with the rapid movement.

Someone had to be here, because a single window upstairs flickered with light and the smell of burning wood filled the air outside—all signs of a fireplace roaring to life.

But instead, inside was nowhere near warm. The only remnants of heat still present rested in what Rhiannon could only assume was a fireplace on the side wall, the soft embers barely visible due to the entryway being pitch black.

"Hello?" she called again, softer but equally as loud, through the darkened foyer, her eyes scanning the area and adjusting to the lack of light.

"Rhiannon," James said eagerly behind her as he carefully carried Kavana up the steps. As his sister faced him, he pulled something from his jacket pocket, careful not to loosen his grip on his aunt. "Here."

Taking the lighter, the metal case cold against her palm, she struck the top of it against her leg and jerked forward, the movement swift and effortless as a flame sparked and ignited. An extra-long table lit up a few feet in front of her along a wall directly across from the doorway. Candles perched in multiple iron tabletop sconces on the wooden piece of furniture, and just to the left of it was a single rounded, wooden door.

Racing toward the other entrance, Rhiannon snatched a candelabra from the table and lit the candle. She flicked her wrist and stifled the flame behind the metal lid before pulling down the collar of her sweater and sliding the lighter into her bra, the lack of pockets not a problem for her at the moment.

Rhiannon pushed open the closed door to the rest of the infirmary, this entryway exposing a long hallway illuminated by a hidden light source at the far end. The glow from her candle and the light at the other end cast the entire corridor in an ominous glow, the flickering of the flames she carried dancing on the walls and adding an even spookier ambiance to the space. Half a dozen closed doors sat on one side of the limestone corridor while only one door rested on the other. Dark gray colored the entire hallway, the rectangular stones covering all sides on the other side of the door. At the end of the hall, an open space and another door waited, this one much wider than all the others.

"Hello?" she called forcefully, her voice shaky but still powerful as she stepped under the threshold and jogged down the hall, the fire dimming against the wick from her hurried steps. Feet pounded down the stony corridor. "Is anyone here?" Reaching the end of the hall, she took in the other foyer as she glanced back down the corridor, realizing they must have entered through a back door instead. "Hello?" she yelled up the stairs, the stone steps lining one side of the hallway. "Is anyone here?" Turning, she observed her brother at the threshold of the second door, waiting—his focus on Aidan racing toward the building outside—before she made her way up the stairs. "We need help!" Her voice echoed off the walls, her loud tone amplified.

Creaking came from upstairs, the sound sending a chill shooting up her spine. Rhiannon froze for a moment, intrusive thoughts warning her of haunted places and scary ghosts. A concept not too unbelievable now that she lived in a world of vampires, werewolves, dragons, witches, and shapeshifters. By this point, she would not be surprised if ghosts were real.

"Nina!" Aidan yelled from down the hall, pulling Rhiannon from her thoughts, the baritone of his voice frantic and strong, though slightly strained. "Nina! Alfina!"

James twisted and handed Kavana to Aidan as he entered the infirmary, the movements between the two of them perfectly in sync. Almost like a silent conversation was happening between them.

Rhiannon had witnessed her brother becoming more and more at one with his powers for nearly a year now, but she had also witnessed, since the last attack at the cabin, the way he took charge of things. Rose to the occasion in a way that radiated leadership. He never allowed his emotions to fully take control, unlike Rhiannon. Even now, he remained calm and focused, never giving in fully to the feelings rolling around inside him or the need to stand up to the threat. She could feel the charge inside him, the powerful mix of want and need building with each passing moment. The deep yearning to return to the cabin and fight.

But he fought it. He remained fully in control of himself.

Ever since his actions contributed to her getting hurt, James had changed the way he handled things. And with Pavian gone,

Rhiannon was certain her uncle's absence had added to the responsible and more mature nature taking over her brother.

Shuffling reverberated along the ceiling, the hurried footfalls moving around upstairs.

"Aidan," a familiar voice called from upstairs, the soft, Scottish accent of Nina sounding groggy and confused. "Aidan, is that you?"

"Nina! Get down here!"

"What's wrong?" Her bare feet slapped against the stone stairs, her steps somehow matching her panicked tone. "What's happened?"

Aidan raced farther into the hallway. "I need you! Now!" Stopping, he kicked open one of the six doors on one side of the wide corridor, the powerful force sending the hinges ripping from the threshold and the thunderous boom of the unrelenting single blow racing throughout the whole building. Entering the room, Aidan carried Kavana over to an elevated bed and gently lowered her down, his hands never leaving her cold body. "It's goin' to be all right, my love. Ye're safe now." He carefully brushed the strands of blood-coated hair from her face and kissed her forehead. "I got you. You hear me? I got you, mo ghràdh. Nina's goin' to help make you all better."

Nina pushed past Rhiannon and James and switched on the overhead light. The twins stood just inside the overly bright and immaculately clean room lined with off-white walls, stainless steel utensils, and an oversized hospital bed. One side of the space was lined with metal cabinets and various medical supplies and monitors. The room was a top-notch medical space, equipped with everything one would need to perform surgery, as well as fully stocked and designed for an emergency. The only thing different from this space and an actual hospital was the smell—the unique blend of cloves, lemons, and tea tree mixing with the slight hint of a strong alcohol. It was almost therapeutic. Most likely a special blend of ingredients to provide the most sterile environment without requiring any material from the non-magical world. A feat a majority of the residents valued most about Kiluemar—the ability to be self-sufficient in as many aspects as possible.

"Oh my—what happened?" Nina said, her demeanor shifting from worried to composed in a matter of seconds, the professionalism taking root as she twisted her long, coppery hair into a bun and fastened it atop her head.

The light in the room was bright, revealing the severity of Kavana's injuries along her face. The sight of her made Rhiannon's stomach drop, the sensation adding to the shock racing through her. The night had masked just how bad her injuries were—the brutality she suffered.

"Is she alive?" Rhiannon choked out, afraid of the answer.

Kavana's skin was unnaturally ashen, and her lips had lost all color, appearing slightly tinged with blue. A cut sliced through the bottom of her lip, the gash deep and split open. Shades of blue and purple colored the left side of her face along with black undertones, the multiple bruises all delivered at various times throughout her capture. Her left eye remained swollen, but tiny cuts lined her eye sockets, the thin skin sliced open and covered in dry blood. Two other lacerations were visible on her right temple, these gashes deep and almost parallel to each other. Black and blue also covered the top part of her nose, the slight misaligned arch and outward bruising confirming she had a broken nose. More dry blood crusted along the creases of her nostrils as well as the inside of both, and red smears coated the top of her lip and across her cheek. Reddish-brown fluid lined her hairline and matted in her black tresses. A small trail of blood smeared along her chin, but it had faded as if someone had tried to wipe it away.

Dressed in a set of pale pink wrinkly scrubs, Nina rested her sleepy but fully alert gaze on Kavana and placed two fingers on the inside of her wrist.

Seconds ticked by as the room fell silent. Every breath held, the fear filling the room suffocating.

"Yes," Nina confirmed, her own exhale coming out relieved. "Her pulse is faint, but she's alive." Emerald eyes lifted, the same bright green matching her brother's water-filled gaze. "Go get Alfina. She's in—"

"No," Aidan protested, his tone leaving no room for argument.

Nina faced James and Rhiannon. "One of you to the cellar and get Alfina. I'm goin' to need help."

"Where's the cellar?" James asked without hesitation, backing toward the door, his entire behavior giving an air of confidence and undeniable calm.

"There's a door under the stairs—"

Without allowing her to finish, he raced out of the room.

"She's too cold," Nina said, rushing over to one of the metal cabinets and pulling out a stack of blankets. "If we don't get her body temperature up, she's goin' to get hypothermia—if she doesn't already." Unfolding one of the blankets, she draped it over Kavana's lower half. "I need to remove her clothes. Here." She peered over at her brother as she reached for a pair of large scissors. "Help me."

Snipping and rustling sounds bounced off the walls as Nina unzipped the jacket before cutting into the blood-covered sweater. She tossed the scissors on the table nearby, the echo of it hitting the metal causing Rhiannon to jump.

"Something is wrong," Ignara said, her voice distant and panicked.

"What do you mean?" Rhiannon asked, lifting a hand to her throat, her fingers pressing against her pulse as she stared at the shiny, white tiled floor, trying to calm her worry and focus on the Fire Dragon. When Ignara did not respond, she prodded insistently, *"What's happening?"*

"I need to go back," was all Ignara said.

Tears filled Rhiannon's eyes, the burn building in her throat.

He was gone. She knew it. She knew his final words to her had been his way of saying goodbye. And it was. Her grandfather was dead. They had killed him.

Rhiannon could feel Oakley, Raeth, and Terramina itching to get to her, to comfort her. *"I'm okay."* The lie tasted like acid on her tongue. Swallowing, she pleaded, the need to take control of herself and not feel lost or alone by masking her emotions again, to admit to herself what she was feeling was valid, *"Don't leave me."*

"We are not going anywhere, child," Terramina said, soft and comforting.

"We are right here," Raeth admitted soothingly.

Oakley, wanting to confirm his presence, added, *"I will go monitor the area. Nothing will happen to any of you. You have my word."*

"Pardon me, dear," a voice said just as a set of hands cradled Rhiannon's upper arms and gently moved her aside as a woman rushed past her.

The authoritative tone was firm but melodic, a beautiful fusion of feminine silkiness and raspy smoothness. It was commanding but still welcoming, and it was highlighted with a faint accent, an intonation sounding exotic.

Alfina had her long black hair pulled back into a tight French braid, not a single strand out of place. With the most silky, smooth bronze skin Rhiannon had ever seen, she wondered if it was simply because she was an elf or if she had some magical skincare secret allowing her to have such a flawless complexion, especially since Rhiannon knew the woman was likely hundreds of years old but didn't look a day over fifty.

"Rhiannon." James quietly entered the room, her name laced with a masked pain.

Twisting around, Rhiannon was surprised by the sudden force of being pulled into a hug, the warmth of her brother beneath the chilled material against his body a welcomed surprise. Muscled arms wrapped around her and squeezed, forcing her deeper into his hold as his chin rested on the top of her head.

He knew.

James had heard every word spoken between Rhiannon and the dragons. He felt every emotion, the realization like a stab to the gut. And so, he held her. No words needed to be exchanged. The only thing they needed were each other as tears started to shed from both sets of eyes.

It was too much. Everything they had dealt with tonight, the last few months, all of it was too much. James could not contain the ravaging emotions battling inside him. How much more could he handle and continue to suppress before it all broke free and took control of him. It was all too much, too debilitating—the anger, the guilt, the regret. This was his family, the ones he loved more than anything, and they were getting hurt because of him. And now . . . now they were dying for him.

His mother's words echoed in his head. *No one is dying tonight.*

She had promised him to fight, to not surrender. But she never promised no one would die. And he understood why now. Because his mother knew some of them might not survive the night. And so far, she had been right.

His grandfather was dead.

Glancing over at Kavana, he muttered internally, *"Please be okay, Aunt K."*

The words filled Rhiannon's mind, and she pulled away, wiping her tears and facing her aunt. Everything played in slow motion, the entire scene muted except for the rapid heartbeat pounding in her ears.

Kavana was still unconscious, the blood loss, freezing temperatures, and state of her injuries lulling her into a deep sleep. Thick blankets covered her lower half, but everything above her waist was fully exposed. The only thing remaining on her sallow frame was her red-stained, nude-colored bra. Blood had trailed down her collarbone from bite marks along her neck and smeared along the front of her chest, the material of her sweater having soaked up most of the crimson fluid, but still some of it had rubbed across her skin and seeped into her undergarment.

Without warning, Kavana startled awake, only one eye trying to remain open as her arms flailed wildly. She screamed, the sound piercing and animalistic, the fear and fight in her both rising to the surface as she attempted to fight off Aidan, Nina, and Alfina.

Rhiannon gasped and covered her mouth, the helplessness aching in her chest as she watched all of them struggling to calm her aunt from the frantic state she was in. It ripped at her heart, the pain in her chest tight and burning. A sob rattled from her, the inability to do anything to comfort her aunt making her knees shake.

"Can I do anything?" Rhiannon asked weakly, a shuddering breath following as James came up beside her and wrapped an arm around her shoulder and tugged her into him.

Kavana's thrashing slowed as Aidan whispered into her ear, the recognition of who was with her and where she was diminishing her pained expression and morphing into relief as tears sprang from her eyes.

"Rhiannon?" Nina said softly as the adrenaline eased from Kavana, and Aidan held her pliant body to his chest, hugging her and rubbing her back.

"It's all right, my love," Aidan whispered, fighting back his own tears as Kavana cried into his shoulder.

"Rhiannon?" Nina said again, this time a little more firmly, trying to pull her attention.

"What do you need?" James asked for his sister, his protectiveness and sympathetic nature securely in place next to her, his tone not at all threatening but rather kindhearted and supportive.

It was Alfina who answered, "Will you please go relight the fire in the parlor in the back?"

"Of course." James ushered Rhiannon out the door and down the hallway as he took her hand, stopping just short of the entryway to the parlor. Stepping in front of his sister, he hugged her again, tight and filled with as much silent comfort as he could convey, allowing his simple presence to wash away some of her emotional overload. "Just breathe, Sis." He rubbed her back. "Breathe." Pulling away, he met her eye to eye. "In." He took a deep breath, watching her as she pulled in a matching inhale. "Out," he said as he exhaled.

Closing her eyes as she blew out her breath, she steadied herself. Blues opened to a set with a kind, deep brown gaze. "Thank you," she whispered.

Lifting his hand, palm up, he offered her a soft smile. "Of course."

Rhiannon returned the gesture and retook his hand into hers as they both aimed toward the parlor room, a sense of serenity and unfettered resilience, a deep, unknown strength, flowing through them.

Knowing there was nothing else they could do, they leaned on each other for support. To remind one another they were not alone. To fight in the only way they knew how to right now—by not allowing each other to surrender to the emotions flooding their veins. Offsetting the fear into bravery and pride into rational humility, morphing everything into an evenly balanced mindset.

Apart, there was chaos, but together there was stability, control.

Making their way through the threshold, they both glanced outside through the main door leading out of the infirmary—left open in the rush of things—just in time to see the snowfall slow to a gradual descent and the moonlight stretch out across the white-covered field.

The storm overhead had passed.

Yet the one their parents faced was far from over.

Chapter 9

Decision Made

Rustling came, the wind and creaking of the deadened trees no longer the only sounds as footsteps resonated inside the dark and ominous forest. Snow descended in gradual blustering flurries as the clouds began to part, casting the woods of Shadow Forest in streaks of moonlight, the reflection off the white-coated backdrop of the night luminescent. Silhouettes stalked within the darkness, each step steady, the snow crunching beneath the various footfalls. The barren canopies overhead groaned as the dead trees swayed, the branches brushing against each other, the sound like hollow wind chimes clanking together. The figures moved without a word, their steps becoming one with nature.

The journey through the portal was different, Kiluemar's swirling vortex not containing the same familiarity and comforts Karramis had known so well from her own doorway. This magic was foreign. It was constant and dense, a concentrated phantom of power that felt heavy and suffocating, like trying to move through water, but the thick air within was hot and sticky. It was nothing like her portal, her magical doorway wispy and cool, almost cloudlike. The air was clean and fresh inside, the misty presence lingering within welcoming and peaceful.

Karramis snuck a glance back at Will, who was being monitored closely by Haydrin as the werewolf exited the portal just a few steps behind her husband. Lucas remained next to her, his presence looming. He had insisted he needed to help guide her through the portal, reminding her she had never traveled to this side of the island before, let alone through one of the portals unaccompanied. But he was incorrect on that assumption, having no clue she had used one of Kiluemar's portals to leave soon after the birth of her children. However, Karramis did not care to divulge any of those facts. Nor had she allowed his assistance with traveling through the portal, her own knowledge of the island enough to bring her to the only portal on this side.

Leif strolled at the front of the group, his focus on navigating through the trees and over the snow-covered underbrush profound, but Karramis was certain his hearing was zeroed in on every step behind him, every heartbeat, just waiting for one to waver.

Controlling her breathing and calming her nerves, she pulled her mind inward, the conscious awareness of her thoughts coming in visions rather than words. She had to formulate a plan, and fast. Karramis would not allow Merrick, or any of them, to hurt Will. Her children would not lose their parents tonight. And even though she had every intention of getting out of this alive herself, she still needed to make sure he was safe. And she would. Karramis would do whatever was necessary to get Will out of the danger they were walking into.

The trek to the castle was ominous, the air thick with warning. The snowfall slowly dissipated as the clouds continued to part, the brunt of the storm seeming to dissolve as it traveled farther away from the island, the strange occurrence a fluke among the various malfunctions happening around Kiluemar. Karramis was well aware of how cold it became in the northern parts of the world this time of year, but despite having knowledge of the Arctic weather, it had never broken through the barriers like this before. Nor had she ever experienced the air element quite like that—the system centered on a focal point, the clouds stationary yet still moving somehow, as if dancing, continuously swirling around one another. But as the storm disappeared completely, she wondered if, maybe, magic had played a part in its development. Or maybe she was just being paranoid by the uncertainty of what abilities Merrick might now possess and how powerful he really was.

Karramis had never seen Casteya Castle in person, her only expertise of the massive structure provided by the facts presented in her schooling, as well as the records she had discovered over the years, her love of reading having to bleed over to the archives and documents of Kiluemar when she had consumed all the other books on the island. Well, all the ones she could find at least.

Even her father rarely spoke of the affairs of the forbidden side, his contentment widely known among the guard and his family. Zarrius was a firm believer in allowing them to live freely, as long as they did not disrupt the safety of the others on the island, and they did not jeopardize the protection put in place to shield Kiluemar from the outside world. Even the rule of never killing another being on the island fell to the wayside through the centuries, each new Guardian losing more and more control over the malevolent creatures, their actions most likely heavily influenced by Merrick and his animalistic and vicious nature.

However, there was an unspoken truce to the dangers of the island, a silent agreement so to speak. Anything and anyone who entered within the boundaries of the forbidden side—including all areas on the eastern side of Maevis Mountain and Midnight Ridge, from Forbidden Coast down to Mystic Woods, plus Siren Sea and all the waterways from just north of East Shores to the bend just before Dragon Cove—belong to the creatures of the night, the bloodthirsty monsters, the beasts who craved death, and all those who were deemed a danger to Kiluemar. As long as they stayed on their side of the island, peace would remain.

But when Karramis returned, she learned so many people and creatures had gone missing, causing others to flee in fear. The residents less likely to be discovered in the non-magical world left Kiluemar, deciding the dangers on the outside outweighed the threats living within the boundaries. This had caused the guard to be even more proactive with protecting the realm. Her father had always been a man of information, having more knowledge than any normal Guardian had contained in the past, but she had always assumed it was simply his need for control, for his obsessive nature to know everything that was going on— something he had been consumed with since before she was born, something he most likely fell victim to due to the loss of her mother and the unanswered questions he had to live with day after day.

Stepping out of the desolate forest, Karramis took in a wide, open area stretched out in front of her, the snow covering what she realized was rocks beneath, the pebbled stones slick. The path extended out in both directions, the trail to the right heading toward a vast, flat mesa. Pale blue light shone across the wide openness beyond the blackened trees, nothing but white blanketing the open plains. Shades of navy and indigo covered the sky above as a rainbow of lights haloed the moon, the celestial giant making its descent toward the horizon. Silence loomed in the darkness, the crunching snow the only sound. Even the wind had slowed. Bare and blackened trees were now still, their thick, twisted branches menacing, like bony fingers reaching toward the sky.

Casteya Castle rested along the base of Maevis Mountain, the stone fortress consisting of two separate structures and various towers and parapets. Dark boulders lined the outer walls, the perfectly shaped rectangular stone lying slightly uneven, giving the building a natural and archaic aesthetic. Rose bushes lined the ground along the foot of the castle, and ivy vines crept along the walls, the plants long since dead. Two large gates came into view, the entrance to the grounds blocked as the two sets of iron bars remained closed.

Without a word, Leif strolled over to the first arched threshold, the gate opening with a loud rattling, the sound echoing around them before a loud thud resonated as the door locked into place within the crevice of the stone portcullis. Leif continued forward, the same action happening as he neared the second gate.

A heavy odor slammed into Karramis as she made her way under the gated entrance, the stench of death and blood erasing all traces of the unique blend of snow, sea salt, and nature filling the air. Trying hard to ignore the smell, she observed the lack of footprints among the new fallen snow, the beauty of her surroundings not at all matching the nerves sending unease coursing through her body or the vile aroma making her stomach churn.

The area inside the castle walls was enormous, the first structure long and narrow but stretching out in a large rectangle. Overgrown grass peeked out from beneath the snow, the thick blades showing no signs of life. Circular parapets lined the top of the castle, their tops open to the elements and attached by a narrow walkway. Stone walls jutted out along the first castle, the various irregularly placed, connected buildings most likely assorted accommodations and chambers.

Another building lay just beyond the gate off to the side, not far from where they continued forward across the grounds.

Stone-slabbed steps ascended along the dark and discolored structure. The moonlight lit up the exterior walls, which were a mix of concrete bricks—the large blocks in shades of gray and a deep red—oak columns along two of the corners visible on this side of the building, and warped and faded wooden pine slats. As the stairs curved upward, they disappeared within the night, Karramis assuming they angled upward and stopped at a door on the other side. Windows lined the walls, their half-circle stone openings high off the ground and reinforced with iron bars, the small framing lacking any glass panes. No lights shone from the windows, nothing but an eerie darkness lingering within the walls.

An open area rested in between the two castles, the inner ward blanketed with a layer of fresh snow. The grounds lacked many of the traditional makings of a castle during the time of its construction. With no real threat to the residents of the citadel, Casteya Castle was simply a home—a place of familiar architecture and standard ways of living. The fortress was meant to be a luxury, a lavish dwelling filled with accommodations fit for royalty. This was something many of the original inhabitants of the island deemed a necessity to continue the comradery and harmony within the realm. Many never wanted those forced to isolate themselves to feel less than or as if they were banished. It was always meant to be a way to protect all those who lived on the island. Kiluemar was meant to be a place who welcomed all magical beings, even those who were unable to control their malevolent nature and more animalistic urges. The inner ward had been one of those luxuries, providing a massive open field, filled with room to run and animals of all kinds to hunt. However, with the need for more room, the grounds diminished into nothing more than a large yard between the two castles.

A chill swept over Karramis, the bitter cold making her body shake uncontrollably. The adrenaline from earlier was starting to fade at a rapid pace, reminding her just how unacclimated she was to this type of weather. Goose bumps forming and teeth chattering, she fisted her hands, sliding them into the pockets of Will's jacket, thankful for his sweet gesture but guilty for how much her husband must be suffering right now, his shirt not nearly enough to maintain some semblance of warmth for his body. The bite of the freezing temperatures made her skin hurt, the numbness and icy burn a contradiction to her senses. How could she feel so much pain, yet feel nothing at all? The only part of her that remained somewhat warm were her feet, the thick wool, calf-high boots a true blessing. A gift from Fayemeara, something she had surprised Karramis with two weeks prior, the shoes were the only thing keeping her moving—that and her need to get inside, the hope there was a fire pushing her to walk faster. Something Lucas noticed as he matched her pace, both now closer to Leif, the three walking with the same stride.

Karramis fought the urge to peer over her shoulder, the need to reassure herself Will was not only back there but also all right. But she remained focused on keeping her gaze forward, her thoughts still devising a plan. She did not want to draw attention to herself, let alone to Will. Not until she could gauge the scene they were stepping into and definitely not without a plan in place.

The second building was newer than the first by a century, but as Karramis strolled closer, she could not help but notice the derelict nature of the once beautiful structure—the paintings and photographs she had seen proving the castle would never be the exquisite masterpiece it once was. Sections of some of the towers attached to this castle along the front had collapsed over time. Most of the towers along the back wall appeared to still be intact, but many seemed to be leaning, or possibly part of the design. Parts of the exterior walls had crumbled. The windows along the front of the castle were broken, the dirt-coated panes either shattered or missing large chunks of glass. Dead bushes and ivy lined the stone walls, similar to the outside of the castle grounds, but these were trimmed and neatly spaced, as if someone once took pride in managing the foliage. Brown moss, mud, and grime covered most of the thick limestone boulders, the structure appearing almost black within the night, the area lit up in a dark blue as the moonlight bounced off the snow.

Only one tower appeared to be in near-perfect condition. This one rested off to the side along the eastern wing of the castle, the stone structure reaching hundreds of feet into the air. Not much could be made out about it through the dark hues of the night, other than a large window rested along the upper section of the circular building, a slight glow coming from within.

Nearing the castle, Leif stopped at a large wooden door. The entrance was massive, the arched threshold nestled within an equally sizeable alcove. The hinges creaked as Leif pushed effortlessly, the vampire showing no signs of distress, the weight of the door clearly on the heavier side, something Karramis took note of as she entered.

The hallway stretched out in both directions, one leading to the east wing and one heading toward the west side of the castle. There was nothing noticeably different about the long corridor, except one side was lined with iron sconces with red pillar candles, the flames flickering as wax dripped down the sides. Nothing could be seen down the other side of the hallway, the walls cast in shadows beyond what light shone from the candles.

A chill filled the air, the dreary hall again reminding Karramis how cold she was. There was no warmth inside the castle despite the flames along the dark gray stone walls. Following Leif, they all made their way down the damp and musky corridor, the sounds of whistling wind seeping in from somewhere nearby echoing with the disjointed and thunderous footfalls, the stone walls amplifying the various steps.

Karramis's blood hummed with unease, her anxious and restless thoughts fighting to reveal themselves as they raced to the surface. She was running out of time. A decision needed to be made. Now. However, her ambivalent thoughts waged war against her pragmatic nature. The uncertainty of what was coming twisted in her gut, but her optimistic side whispered to her, the silent voice in her head telling her to fight back, reminding her she was no longer going to cower and run away in fear. There was no fight or flight. It was simply fight.

A smile fought to escape as the image of Will flashed in her mind, her own strength magnified by his auspicious mindset. He had never allowed her to feel anything less than capable, providing her with so much love and support. Karramis had always been strong-willed, but his faith in her amplified her determination. He knew she could achieve anything if she truly wanted it, if she really believed in herself. And in this moment, she wanted nothing more than to save him from whatever lay beyond the door at the end of the hallway they just turned down.

A narrow pathway extended in front of them, one side lined with floor-to-ceiling windows, the Gothic-style frames dirty but still clear enough to allow in some of the moonlight still present outside the glass panes. Two wooden doors filled the hallway, the enormous entrances similar to that of the exterior one, but these were slightly smaller and rested within a carved archway lined with large boulder-sized, rectangular dark gray stones. There was something eerie about the closed doors, like a decision to choose which evil one wanted to face awaited on the other sides.

The moment to decide was now.

Karramis knew what needed to be done. She was certain she could do it, she just needed to find the strength to accomplish what she had to do. But there was little room for mistake. That was also something she understood. Without the right amount of control, she would fail. And if she failed, neither of them would make it out of here alive.

"Don't even think about it," Lucas said plainly, his voice deep and quiet from beside her, his stride coming to a stop as Leif halted next to the first door across from the windows.

Karramis glanced over at Lucas as she stood next to him, her gaze taking in how much he was concentrating and unsure how long he had been watching her. Had her thoughts voiced themselves? Pondering the last few minutes, she found the urge to avert her eyes. There was no way he knew what she had decided, the reassurance her inner monologue had remained silent adamant.

Refusing to acknowledge Lucas, Karramis pressed her lips together. The need to see Will finally took over, and she glanced his way, her eyes going wide as she spotted Haydrin behind him, his large, veiny hand gripping his throat.

A grin flashed across Lucas's face as he pulled his gaze from Will back over to Karramis. "Now then . . ." He gestured toward the door as Leif opened it, the hinges letting out an echoing squeak. "Afta' you, love."

The room was dark, completely pitch black, and reeked of mildew and something earthy, a foul mix of dirt and rotting vegetation.

Shaking her head, Karramis argued, confusion bringing her brows together. "I'm not going in there."

"I was hoping you'd say that." The corner of Leif's mouth lifted, giving her a devious smirk. Lifting his chin toward Haydrin, he demanded, nodding his head toward the darkened room, "Throw him inside." His blue eyes landed on Karramis, the gleam of pure exhilaration and control radiating in them. "Only him. We'll deal with him later."

"What?" Karramis blurted, the argument still front and center as she twisted toward Will. "No, he's—"

Her objection was cut off as Lucas seized her wrist.

Will struggled against the werewolf's hold, his neck straining under the constricting grip. "Get your fucking hands off her!" There was vigor behind the choked demand, a savage command.

"Or what, mate?" Lucas patronized, his grip tightening as he stepped closer to Karramis.

"Now, now," Leif taunted, interrupting any response Will had lingering on his lips as the vampire strolled over to him. "He just needs to have a little chat with her."

Eyes lifted, Will declared, voice deep even behind the restrictive hold, "Like hell I'm going to leave him alone with *my* wife." There was an edge to the statement, a sharpness to the protective possessiveness.

Leif pulled the dagger from under his shirt and ran the blade along the clotted scar under his chin. "Well, you don't really have any other choice now, do you? Unless, of course, you'd rather wait in the Keep." There was a pause, a break given for dramatic effect but to also allow recognition to settle in, the vagueness of what exactly the *Keep* was proving to be a slight advantage in the situation. "Although . . . I don't really recommend that particular option."

Will gritted his teeth. "If you so much as touch her—"

"No one is gonna touch her," Lucas interjected, the certainty in the biting declaration leaving a hint of matching possessiveness. "Except for me," he added with a grin, yanking Karramis behind him. "*No one*." The last part was directly aimed at Will, the words a promise to take what was his.

Karramis's stomach dropped with unease, the sensation tight and tingling low in her abdomen. Heart racing, her pulse thrummed in her ears, pounding like a death toll, sending a warning with each hurried thump. But giving in to fear meant she was surrendering. And she refused to give Lucas, or any of them, that satisfaction. Not again.

A nonverbal communication flickered in her eyes as they settled on Will, her need to have control over the situation a silent plea.

Giving him a barely noticeable nod, she conveyed, soft and calm, "I'll be okay."

Wanting to protest, Will allowed his trust in her to settle the nerves vibrating with the need to protect. He returned the gesture as he accepted whatever plan she was playing out, but the resignation left a sour taste in his mouth.

Karramis pulled in a breath, the tension in her chest tightening as Will suddenly stiffened, locking eyes with Leif.

Danger and tension grew thick as Leif glided the blade upward, the pressure behind the movement leaving a faint white line along Will's jaw.

Turning to face Karramis, Leif watched her for a moment before stating with a clear threat in his tone, "Try anything stupid, witch, and I will rip his heart out from his chest and hand it to you." He angled his head, his watchful gaze taking in Karramis's shallow breathing. "This is just a little insurance." Flicking his wrist, Leif drove the sharp blade over Will's skin, slicing a clean gash diagonally across his cheekbone. "A reminder, so to speak."

Karramis swallowed a gasp, desperately trying not to react. Will winced in pain as his body was pushed forward, his movements being controlled from behind. A hand around Karramis's wrist tightened, the fingers squeezing, the crushing force sending a piercing wave of agony deep in her bone as she was yanked in the opposite direction. Body tensing from the sudden onset of pain and hurried movement, Karramis steadied herself as the sounds of voices echoed behind her. A new kind of agony coursed through her body as she rounded the corner, the terror of what waited for her husband . . . and for herself.

They had separated them.

Lucas had to have known she would try to plan some kind of escape, even if she had blocked him out of her mind. He knew her too well by this point. Karramis had only ever once been able to find Will on command, her very being somehow linking to him when he had followed her through the portal when they discovered his Drolnogard magic. But she had never figured out why, or how, it had happened. It was as if there had been some cosmic bond between them in that moment that allowed a deep connection. However, she had never mastered it. It was not an ability she had ever been able to replicate again. So, how would she be able to find him? How was she going to be able to get him, and herself, out of here. And certain Leif would jump at the opportunity to follow through with his threat, she could not take the chance in getting caught using her magic. It was just too dangerous.

Fuck!

The silent word escaped, the disbelief and fear taking control of her mind, body, and soul.

"My, such foul language," Lucas said, a patronizing lilt to his tone. "And if ya so much as think about tryin' anythin'—"

"Yes, I fucking get it, Lucas," she snapped with a venomous snark as she reluctantly followed behind him.

There was no need for him to finish the threat—Karramis knew exactly what would happen, the repeated threat seeming to strike a chord. Yet, despite knowing the possible ramifications, she could not help herself.

Lucas paused and curled his mouth into an amused, wicked grin. "Ooh, I think I quite enjoy this fiery side of ya, love. The fearlessness, it's fittin' for ya. I was neva' convinced ya were so meek. Ya always had a fight in ya. But the girl I found had become a pathetic version of you. But this version . . ." He blew out a breath. "I could get used to this version of ya. It makes me wanna tame ya."

"Maybe you should go get a dog, then. You'd have a lot more luck with one of those."

Lucas let out a laugh, a real, authentic laugh. "I definitely love this version of you."

The sound of footsteps traveled down the hall as Haydrin came into view.

Lifting his chin in Karramis's direction, he asked, his expression even but his deep voice curious, "What is it about her that makes you want her so badly?"

Karramis arched a brow, genuinely interested in his answer—the response a potentially crucial part to her newly developing strategy—just as the door down the hall slammed shut.

"Because," Lucas said, tilting his head, a gleam of absolute conviction in his gaze as it zeroed in on her, "she is *mine*. And I don't fuckin' share."

The urge to roll her eyes surfaced, but she clamped it down as she pursed her lips.

Haydrin glanced between the two as Leif came up beside him, his next question pulling Lucas's attention back to the werewolf. "And what makes you certain she is yours?"

Leif crossed his arms over his chest and smirked, the fact of knowing the exact response Lucas was about to declare equally amusing and irritating.

"Because I fuckin' said so."

"And if she disagrees?"

"You do know I'm standing right here, right?" Karramis asked with a comical undertone.

"Shh," Leif teased. "Now, now, witch, let the grown-ups talk."

This time Karramis did roll her eyes, adding an exasperated scoff.

Ignoring her insolent and juvenile response, Leif straightened, his demeanor serious as he pulled Lucas aside, his expression solemn but his words firm. "You harbor so much admiration for her, yet you also hold so much animosity—this enigmatic love-hate constantly waging war inside you." There was something candid in his words, something like understanding. "But I think it's time for one side to finally win. It's time to take back control of your life completely." Leif's eyes shifted to Karramis, his voice anything but quiet, the need to guarantee she heard the warning in the rest of his declaration clear. "Which one will it be, Lucas? Can you live the rest of your life without her? Yes, of course you can. But the real question is this . . ." He placed a hand on Lucas's shoulder. "Can you live a life knowing she will never be yours? Or would you rather have to live a life where neither of you have her?" Sympathy filled his expression, a side of Leif Karramis had never witnessed before. "You've already lost her, brother. Now, the decision as to how you want to move on and mourn her is solely up to you. Remember this moving forward, okay?"

Lucas nodded, the action conveying not only consideration but also a dismissal. Like he was not ready to ponder his words fully.

Haydrin twisted and headed back down the hall as Leif and Lucas stared at each other for another moment, a silent conversation happening between them before Leif followed the werewolf.

Lucas closed the distance, his proximity again too close for comfort. "I'm gonna take great pleasure in makin' ya submit." All pretenses of the last few minutes gone as he stepped right back into their previous conversation.

"What do you want from me, Lucas?"

"Oh, love, there is plenty I want from ya."

"Are you going to kill me?" There was no sign of fear, but Karramis was every bit worried by his response.

Running the back of his fingers across her chilled cheek before tracing the scar on her face, he said coolly, "Well, that depends."

Swallowing, she denied him a reaction to his touch. "On what?"

He pivoted and headed down the hallway toward the front of the castle, seemingly to ignore her question. But he paused and angled himself back toward her, offering her a roguish, haughty smirk. "On you."

Chapter 10

Contingency Plan

"Now, now, he just needs to have a little chat with her."

Despite the teasing tone of the vampire's words, the cadence was pointed and laced with menace, and they slammed into Will, pulling him completely into the present, his focus no longer on the conversations he was having in his head.

Through the whole ordeal at the cabin and the few feet he had until he reached the portal, Will had remained attentive to the whereabouts of the dragons, his intended mindset determined to convey as much as possible before he lost connection with them.

Distance had always been a downfall of the Drolnogard magic, the space separating a dragon from the human a flaw in the ability. Many Drolnogards could enhance their powers over time, the strength and connectedness growing through the years. When Margaret Dagley, the first Drolnogard, received her powers, her ability was powerful, having the capability of reaching out for hundreds of miles. But as time went on, the magical bloodline started to diminish due to the Drolnogards dying off, as well as the dragons—their very existence nearly wiped out when the non-magical world vowed to annihilate the creature. Therefore, with centuries of the magic linked between the dragons and Drolnogards limited, the ability weakened. And with Will having only arrived in Kiluemar when he was in his early twenties, he was not born into a world where he had an immediate connection with them, nor was the magic itself very powerful. And the last known Drolnogard who had lived with the dragons, allowing for a constant bond, was well over a century ago.

As Will exited the portal, he allowed his mind to focus on each dragon. Knowing there was no point in trying to evade being escorted to the castle, he held onto the connection. Fear continued to twist in his gut and strain in his chest, the dread of not being able to protect his wife a nightmare he truly did not want to face. Nevertheless, Will understood, in the moment, cooperating was his best option in not only surviving the night but being able to save Karramis from what lay beyond the stone walls of Casteya Castle. And he could recognize the wheels churning in his wife's head—Karramis was currently concocting a plan to get them out of there with her thoughts being shielded from the intrusiveness of the man walking a little too close to her.

All he had to do was remain fixated on the dragons, staying within their minds until the link was severed.

Lucas's ability to invade Will's thoughts had always been a problem. Will had never mastered the ability to block his inner monologue from the intrusive violation. But somehow, Karramis had conquered this skill long before she had ever met him, a talent he eventually learned she was taught to do by one of her best friends.

Avery Leibovich, now Kittleman, was a telepath and had helped Karramis understand the dynamics of telepathy, as well as train her to control her inner voice, shifting it into visual representations instead of actual words. But something Will had learned from Avery was that telepathic powers were not a constant ability. One had to literally access their power by clearing their own mind and opening it up to outside sources. She also taught him both telepaths and Telematras could not be within the mind of the same person, nor could they eavesdrop when other magical beings were using telepathy with each other, thus allowing Will some protection, since Lucas could not invade and hear the conversations between him and the dragons. This being one of the main reasons he remained in constant contact with them throughout the evening, thus blocking any thoughts he had from being heard by Lucas. The other reason being to monitor what was happening throughout the rest of the island.

Will had already lost contact with the Earth Dragons as he exited the portal—the three of them now in Caerwyn Village with the twins. Raeth and Oakley had taken James, Rhiannon, and Kavana to the infirmary, both dragons taking to the sky as

Terramina followed to monitor the area for any potential dangers. Phosmeratae had remained hidden at the request of Will, the Drolnogard asking for the Air Dragon's help in safeguarding the residents still living within the boundaries of the village and Stoweward after Zarrius's death.

When Will had felt the dragons coming, he knew having all of them there would cause some higher tensions, possibly putting himself and his family in even more danger, and even the dragons, since Will had no idea all the power Merrick possessed. So, he had insisted Phosmeratae remain concealed, staying above the clouds of the storm but in constant contact with him and the twins. But once Will saw the state of Kavana and witnessed the death of Zarrius, he sent the Air Dragon to patrol both locations, knowing the wards had most likely been weakened, especially since Pavian was also not currently within the boundaries of the realm.

Harkin had been Will's biggest concern due to him not knowing the state of the Fire Dragon when he left through the portal. But Ignara had returned to the cabin and informed Will just in time before their connection was lost, throwing it out to him in one final push as he stepped out of Shadow Forest. Will had been relieved. Harkin was badly injured, but alive. And with the help of Phosmeratae—his ability to control the air and work together with the Water Dragons—the fire had been extinguished from their home, but the damage was extensive. After the fire was put out, Will insisted the Air Dragon remain on guard, the fear of what else Merrick might have planned the sole focus of Will's command.

But with Leif's blade now at his cheek, Will could not help but be pulled back into the situation entirely as the sharp point pressed deeper into his skin, the pinprick pain pulling his full attention to the cold and dreary hallway. His focus was no longer on trying to reach the dragons for any updates but rather his wife and the dire state he was currently in.

Going stiff as Karramis sucked in a small gasp, Will shifted his gaze upward, his eyes connecting with Leif's.

The blade remained on Will's face as the vampire turned toward Karramis. "This is just a little insurance."

Will winced as pain sliced across his cheekbone, the sting burrowing deep beneath the layers of skin.

"A reminder," Leif added. "So to speak."

A hand slapped into his back as Will was shoved forward, the sound of Karramis's gasp echoing down the long corridor lit up with candles and soft moonlight.

Lucas's voice sounded over the footsteps as Will was forced toward the open door. "My, such foul language. And if ya so much as think about tryin' anythin'." There was an edge to the statement, a hidden promise. One Will knew all too well Lucas would love to follow through with.

"Yes, I get it, Lucas."

His wife's statement was calm yet clipped, the brazen tone ringing true to everything he knew about her. She would not go down without causing some chaos first. She would fight, and fight like hell. It took everything in him not to grin as he was directed under the threshold.

Darkness surrounded Will as Haydrin thrusted his hand one final time against his back, the force causing him to stumble before catching himself. The room appeared empty by the hollowness of the sounds reverberating off the stone walls. It smelled of dirt, smoke, and something familiar, something Will could not place. There was a comfort to it, though, not at all unwelcoming.

Haydrin entered the room just as Will attempted to hear more of the conversation beyond the door, but the voices were fading.

Every alarm bell sounded in his head, the need to protect and not back down taking over every nerve of Will's body. He could not allow Lucas to take her to a separate location. But as he charged forward, the ornery man stared him down, his arms folded over his broad chest, stopping him in his tracks.

Will had always cherished his magic, but he had often wished he had physical powers as well. And this was one of those moments. The chance to literally see what a magic he possessed could do. To be able to defend, protect, and rescue beyond just brute force and cunning fighting skills. And even those abilities were limited, considering the man in front of him probably outweighed him in pure muscle alone.

Entering the room, Leif tapped on Haydrin's shoulder as if giving him a silent dismissal.

There was nothing but silence beyond the threshold as Haydrin left the room, a clear indication Lucas and Karramis were gone. Dread coiled in Will's gut at what his wife was walking into and what Lucas had planned for her. Will was certain she would fight, but without her knowing the state he himself was in, he could not be sure she would protect herself to the full extent she had been training for. He was now a pawn in this game, one he was certain she would not sacrifice. Even if it meant sacrificing herself instead.

Will observed Leif standing under the stone doorway, his stance relaxed as he crossed his arms and leaned against the doorframe.

"Where is he taking her?" Will asked, frustrated by the vampire's cocky expression and his current situation.

Leif pushed off the wall and closed the heavy door with an echoing boom, the question remaining unanswered.

~

Time seemed to slow. Unsure if only minutes or hours had passed, Will sat on the freezing floor with his head resting against the wall. Desperation clung to him as the need to escape this room and search for Karramis remained his top priority. But all he could do was wait, so his thoughts continued to drift to the dragons, their voices no longer within range from where he was being held. But he still tried. Over and over again.

Pain throbbed against his cheek as the blood dried along his skin. The rough stones were hard, and the chill had taken root in the material of his shirt, making him even more uncomfortable.

But there was a familiar presence to the room—the darkness, bitter chill, and stony interior reminding him of Emrys Cave, the place he had called home for years. With his current surroundings and the icy temperature, Will had been able to withstand the discomforts. Having grown acclimated to his isolated life with the dragons inside the cave, Will was not entirely too bothered by his predicament. Well, not the actual room itself, that is. Even with the cold currently blanketing him, he was able to ignore the chill, despite no longer having his jacket or any source of heat. But it was not knowing what was happening to Karramis leaving him on edge and feeling the worst kind of discomfort—guilt and defeat.

Unable to see, he had navigated through the room blindly as soon as the door closed, feeling for anything to possibly provide him with some light or even a shred of warmth, but he had come up empty. The room was completely barren. It even lacked windows. There was no fireplace, no furniture. Only a large rectangular chamber, leaving Will to believe this was some sort of storage room. After inspecting the entrance, he had discovered the icy metal handle was the only piece attached, no signs of a lock on this side of the wooden door. It had taken everything in him to not open it, knowing his actions would most likely end up hurting Karramis in the process, or even lead him into an extremely dangerous situation.

But there were no sounds outside the door, at least none he could hear through the thick wood. However, Will was well aware of just how silent vampires could be, and there was no telling where Haydrin was, and with there only being one exit Will was aware of, he did not want to take any chances.

So, he waited.

And waited.

The minutes grated on his nerves—the unbearable, slow-moving seconds ticking by like a timer counting down to a bomb just waiting to explode. Even though the device on his wrist remained masked behind the darkness, he could almost feel the rhythmic, mechanical pulsation of the second hand rotating around the watch dial.

A slight illumination finally came from under the tiny crack of the door, most likely the first light of dawn, meaning Will's assumption was correct, Karramis had been with Lucas for a while now.

Footsteps echoed down the hallway outside the door, the sound magnified in the empty room. The pace was even and unhurried, but the stride was heavy and loud. There was no hesitation, no desire to be stealthy. And by the reverberations of the powerful thuds moving swiftly, Will could only guess the footfalls belonged to the werewolf. Haydrin was somehow the quietest of the bunch as a man of so few words, and yet he was the loudest due to his extremely muscular and lofty frame, his stride alone when walking by himself undoubtably outmatching Will's by a step or two. Now, add the power behind his advancement, and there was no hiding the werewolf's arrival.

Will pushed to his feet and brushed the dirt and grime off his backside, the chill soaked into his pants matching that of his entire body. He would give anything for some form of heat, if nothing else than to warm his extremities—his need to feel his hands dire if he was going to have to attempt to defend himself.

Light creeped in as the door swung open, the force behind the act effortless. Creaking filled the area, and the old, rusty hinges protested. Standing in the doorframe was, as Will suspected, Haydrin, the brooding, petulant expression having never left his face. Will wondered if this man had ever smiled, let alone been happy.

"Let's go," Haydrin demanded.

Battling the need to ask where he was being taken, Will stepped back into the hallway. A soft blue hue rested just outside the large, arched windows along the wall, the early dawn morning casting the snow and surroundings in a dim light. The candles lining the cobweb-filled corridor were no longer lit, creating an ominous presence, a mix of danger and vile, volatile deeds. It was as if death itself hid within the dimly lit hallway, awaiting the chance to take what lingered for too long.

Turning the corner, Will spotted Leif waiting by the main door to the castle, his usual laid-back demeanor firmly in place.

"Let me ask you something, Drolnogard," Leif said as Haydrin and Will slowed to a stop next to him. "What are you willing to do for her?"

Will realized the answer before he even had time to register the question, knowing the vampire's words were a hidden threat, a promise that was most likely aimed in Karramis's direction. "Anything."

Narrowing his eyes in consideration, Leif asked calmly, his tone lined with intrigue and a relevance only known to him, "Anything? Are you sure about that?"

"Yes." The word exited his mouth with the strength of a vow.

A sly grin creeped into the vampire's features. "Good."

Chapter 11

Losing Control

The large ornate wood-and-iron door at the end of the candlelit hallway swung open, the arched threshold revealing the west side of the castle. Soft blue filled the new corridor as the moonlight coasted in from the enormous vaulted, wood-framed windows lining the outside wall.

Awe entered Karramis's expression, the beauty making her mouth drop open as the chill along her skin met the subtle heat sweeping through the hall.

This wing was nothing like the location she had just left as she stepped farther into the new section of the castle. This area was warm and welcoming, both physically and psychologically, her body and mind relaxing in the seemingly cozy space. But it was not just the fact it was completely different from the east wing in a comforting way, and it exuded an energy more light than dark, it was because it appeared as if it was constructed from entirely separate material and by the hands of people who took pride in their work. Not to mention the actual heat filling the hall, the smell of smoke and burning wood causing Karramis to assume multiple fireplaces were lit somewhere.

Polished white and black square tiles lined the floor, the slick slabs perfectly placed in an alternating pattern. Rounded gray stone pillars rested evenly along smooth white stone walls, their counterpart on the opposite side of the corridor stretching upward and arching at the top, the two forms meeting at a point. Chandeliers lined the flat ceiling in between the stone archways, their black iron and glass frames housing cobwebs and dust, the untouched light sources all lacking candles and the only imperfect feature within the spacious hallway.

No candles rested among sconces on this side. Only the moonlight cast the area in light, the illumination enhanced by the reflective snow outside the frosted glass and the glow bouncing off the numerous mirrors placed along the walls, their placement perfectly spaced in between old but masterful artwork.

There was something peaceful about the area. Something giving her hope as to what Lucas had planned and where he was taking her. But the silence falling between them and the way she caught him side-eyeing her a few times made her question this feeling—reminding herself she had no idea what Lucas and the others were planning, their actions far from admirable. In fact, everything about this evening, and all the events leading up to right now, were far from impetuous. No, this was strategic. Something was clearly happening. And it was not just calculated in a simplistic manner. This was deliberate. All pretenses stored away, all dominant civility firmly in place, each step carefully thought out, and all the mercurial behaviors hidden deep within.

A game was occurring, and unfortunately, Karramis was unsure how to play.

Yet.

"Where are you taking me?" she asked, her voice pleasant as if the question was being delivered to a friend.

Rounding the corner, Lucas answered coyly, the charismatic persona she knew all too well in place, "My room."

She did not react to his answer, but her inquisitive mind still questioned it. "Why?"

Lucas lifted a hand and ran it through his dark brown hair as he continued his steady pace down the new hallway, this one lacking windows but housing a number of large oak doors, medieval armor, more artwork, and multiple statues. "I needed to talk to ya privately, and this is the only place I felt comfortable doin' so."

Karramis recalled when they were younger and how Lucas always preferred being alone with her when he had something to discuss, his feelings always remaining internal until he felt safe to express them. Lucas had been a very private person, especially after losing his mother when he was thirteen. She had always been the one person he could go to with his problems or when he just needed someone to talk to—this need shifting completely to Karramis soon after his father left him because he could no longer live in the realm without Lucas's mother, the daily reminders too much for him, and he was unfit to take Lucas with him.

The memories of their friendship had never left her, but she could no longer trust the man before her, his previous actions proving to be far too unpredictable and manic. She just could not do it, a fact she came to terms with a long time ago. But a part of her still cared for him—the part of her that still saw the boy who found her that day and held her, the boy who had vowed to always protect her. The boy who she shared her first kiss with, and the first person she ever loved aside from her family. Karramis still struggled with letting go of that boy. But Lucas was not that boy anymore. He was a man. A man who had a hidden agenda and a personal vendetta. A man who had taken it upon himself to make her life a living hell simply because she had not chosen him.

Erasing the happy childhood memories and bringing forth all the abusive, emotionally traumatic, and volatile moments she had suffered because of him throughout the years, she refocused her attention on Lucas as he came to a stop at a giant oak door, the carved designs and bronze studs and handle adding to the beauty of the etched-stone archway.

Lucas reached for the curved handle, his blue gaze landing on Karramis as he pushed on the door and held it open. Giving her a sideways nod, he motioned for her to enter.

A hand cradled her lower back, soft and gentle as the door closed behind her, leaving her in total darkness except for a slight, partially hidden orange glow coming from one side of the room. His touch was gentle, almost comforting, the heat from his palm and outstretched fingers penetrating the two layers of clothing she had on. But it was wrong. Unfamiliar. It was strange and made every inch of skin beneath the touch crawl with unease, like tiny bugs were skittering along her back just waiting to bite.

She shivered, the movement causing her to slink forward a few inches and just out of his reach.

"Are ya cold?" Lucas asked, genuinely sounding concerned and caring. "Ya must be, that jumper is not adequate for this sort of weather." There was a slight emotion masked in his voice, an almost patronizing undertone of irritation. "Maybe ya should remove it," he added as his voice moved away from her, his invisible frame only providing his location when it blocked out the glow emanating from a section off to the side.

The darkness filled her with a sense of dread, the inability to see her surroundings creating a slow-moving panic trailing up her spine. There was something overwhelming and anxiety-inducing about experiencing a prolonged moment of blindness. It was debilitating and restrictive, almost like being trapped in a tight space or stuck underwater with no way to breathe.

Shuffling sounded just as a heavy thud filled the room, followed by the strike of a match a few seconds later, the noise almost grating as it glided across a rough surface. Karramis folded her arms over her chest, the feel of the material giving her strength. She pulled in a deep breath and closed her eyes, lifting the collar of the jacket to her face. A whiff of wild nettles, cedar and suede, and soft blooming flowers filled her nose, the scent bringing her solace.

Light flickered behind her eyelids, the dancing orange glow getting brighter. Her eyes opened and landed on Lucas as he stood in front of a roaring fire, the heat reaching her as she remained near the door.

If Karramis thought the hallway leading to his room was beautiful, then this space was absolutely breathtaking. No, it was magical. And not at all how she would picture a bedroom of this magnitude and extravagance in a place built on an isolated and forbidden part of the island. Everything about this room screamed royalty—old royalty maybe, but royalty nonetheless.

The walls were painted the deepest shade of blue, so blue it was almost black. Elaborate designs consisting of straight lines and wide swirls rested atop the navy color, the silvery strokes adding a feminine touch to the room. Dark hardwood floors lined the whole area, the shade a lighter contrast to the black rug resting in front of the black marble fireplace. A slate-colored upholstered wingback with black iron legs sat off to the side of the moderate hearth, one of the few less than extravagant features in the expansive space.

Karramis monitored Lucas as he silently made his way to the other side of the room, the light from the fireplace barely illuminating a raised dais that appeared to be housing a king-size bed. Striking another match, Lucas lit two candles, the thick white pillars sitting atop a silver platter. The wicks flickered to life and created just enough glow to reveal a large, half-circle alcove with three floor-to-ceiling bookshelves, a dark, round area rug covering most of the floor—the color changing from black to navy under the flickering light—and an oversized chaise longue with the end table that was containing this side of the room's light source.

Lucas continued to walk around the room, his focus on casting the area with more light as he lit a few more candles. The ambiance was no longer eerie but rather romantic, intimate even.

Karramis had never realized this side of the island was never provided with electricity like Caerwyn Village, Stoweward, and even the cabin. It did not occur to her that the few people who learned all the ins and outs of electrical work and who built the various solar panels, wind turbines, and water wheels to create the energy needed to supply them with electricity never provided the same service to the forbidden side. But she could understand why no one wanted to take on that task, especially since all of the electricians who had lived here had been non-magical and only learned the trade to be useful and help create a more modern and convenient lifestyle.

Brown eyes moved across the room, taking in a large grand piano, two violins, and a desk in the opposite corner near the fireplace.

Lucas had always been an extremely talented musician, mastering both instruments placed in his room, as well as composing his own music and singing. His talent for not just hearing the music but feeling it had always been something Karramis admired.

"I haven't played since France," Lucas said, his gaze set on her as she stared at one of the violins.

"Why?" A softness settled in her tone, the confusion as to why he would stop doing one of the few things he loved coming to the surface and the slight fear of what happened at Château Rouge triggering her anxiety.

Closing the distance, Lucas stepped up behind her, not touching her but making his presence known as his breath blew against her hair, the wavy locks resting along her upper back. "I played every single day I was stuck there"—he circled around and stopped in front of her, his expression thoughtful—"just for you. And when ya left me, I just couldn't play anymore."

Karramis wanted to argue, saying she did not leave him, but rather she went home. But she knew that would not go over well, so instead she remained silent.

Blue eyes held hers, the kindness in them familiar yet foreign. It was strange, this side of him. There was a sweetness, one she had not witnessed in a long time. Yet there was also something else, something concealed behind the mask of gentle innocence he was trying to keep firmly in place.

The back of his fingers softly stroked the side of her cheek. "You're beautiful." Sincerity rang in the declaration as he leaned closer to her, his palm cupping her jaw. "I've missed ya so much, love."

Blinking up at him, Karramis was not sure what to say, nor did she want to react to his touch. Even the slightest rejection might set him off, and she needed to keep him calm. She grinned up at him, subtle but noticeable as she eased away from his touch and twisted away, appearing to take in more of his room.

"Oh," Lucas announced loudly behind her, excitement in his voice, "I haveta show ya somethin'."

Along the raised dais where Lucas strolled over to was a king-size bed with a thick comforter, the slick black material perfectly placed and unwrinkled on top of the mattress. The enormous bedframe consisted of a decorative footboard with intricate Celtic designs etched into the dark wood—no, not wood, stone. The bed appeared to be made of granite. The headboard's pillar-like corners were smooth but arched at the top, but the main section had similar designs on the footboard but with a large bird arching its wings in the center, the feathered creature reminiscent of a raven. Everything about the massive bed reminded Karramis of a gothic cathedral, with the dark colors, stony structure, and the sharp, arched points throughout the entire framework. Even the black comforter with its paisley designs woven into the soft material and black velvet pillows added to the gothic vibe.

Reaching what Karramis could only assume were the windows behind the bed, Lucas wrapped his hand around the thick black tassel-like rope hanging down and tugged. The dark blue curtains parted, the two sides gliding effortlessly and revealing a set of floor-to-ceiling cathedral-style windows.

Mouth parting, Karramis gazed out at the expansive sky just beyond the crystal-clear panes, the colors of night matching that of Lucas's bedroom. Stars sparkled within the deep blue sky, each constellation visibly bright and luminescent. Feet moved closer to the window as Karramis's eyes refused to look away.

Stargazing had always been a favorite pastime for her, the sight of the giant balls of gas flickering lightyears away calming her somehow. Lying out at night and just staring up at the night sky had always relaxed her, sent a sense of peace throughout her body. It was like a warm bubble bath on a cold night, the sounds of a gentle thunderstorm at bedtime, or the beauty of a sunset over the ocean's horizon. Mother Nature had always been a friend to Karramis, providing comfort in the simple things like a rainy day, starry night, or the sounds of the waves crashing against the shore.

"Do ya like it?" Lucas asked, pulling her from her thoughts.

She faced him, but her answer vanished as his hands clutched her hips and she was forced against him. Palms pressed firmly against his chest, trying to shove him away, but he held her in place.

"Where do ya think your goin'?" he crooned, giving her a lascivious grin.

"Lucas," she drawled in a sweet yet forceful tone, her expression tight with warning, "let me go."

"Why?" The question was genuine. "But I designed this for ya." He peered upward. "Do ya not like it?"

A pinch of confusion forced her eyes to narrow almost imperceptibly, not from his words, but by him. She could not trust the softness in his expression. But she also could not jeopardize the fact he was not actively a threat to her at the moment. And so, she answered truthfully, "It's beautiful, but I would really appreciate you letting me go." The word *now* lingered on her lips, but it was quickly erased with a steady, "Please."

He tucked her hair behind her ear, the gesture intimate as the tip of his finger trailed down along her earlobe. "Do ya know what you do to me?"

The question caught her off guard, even the way he watched her lips and the unusual tenderness he was exhibiting being a version of him she had long since forgotten. "Please, let me go, Lucas."

"I've loved ya for so long." His eyes stayed fixed on hers, nothing but raw honesty filling the space between them. "Every day, ya were the first person I thought about when I woke up, and the last person on my mind as I closed my eyes. It was always supposed to be me and you against the world . . . But ya shattered all of that for me." For a moment, he allowed her to see his hurt and heartbreak, his regret. There was a vulnerability there. A glimpse of the friend he once was—a boy who loved her and the man she always knew he could be. "Why?" He drew out the question, the pain clear in the tightness in his throat as he leaned into her, his face lowering so they were eye to eye. "You were always supposed to be mine."

Guilt ate at her, the remorse of how everything between them happened. Words failed her as she stared up at him. She never wanted things to transpire the way they did. It was a constant thing she thought about. This nagging what-if playing on a loop in her head, the what-if being, what if she had just done things differently? Lucas had been her best friend, her everything, for so long. But it did not matter. Not anymore. Because Karramis knew, deep down, the story would have always ended up the same. Will had always been part of her future, her destiny. It had been and would always be him. There was no life she wanted without him in it. Will was hers, and she was his. Always and now. And forever.

The hands clutching her hips tightened, the grip unrelenting.

A mix of pain and adrenaline shot through her. Had she voiced her thoughts? No, not possible. Karramis knew she was still actively shielding his powers. However, she could not guarantee her wandering gaze and expression did not give her away—that her mind had shifted to Will.

He loosened his hands and exhaled. Pulling back, Lucas drew in a deep breath and flared his nose, disgust evident behind the subtle twitch of his lips.

Loosely taking hold of her wrist, the gesture gentle, he said, "C'mere."

Moving away from the bed, they both made their way over to the fireplace. The flames crackled and the heat was filling the space, the warmth welcomed and appreciated as Karramis continued to fight off the chill coating her body.

Lucas ushered her closer to the fire, stopping her a few feet away and stepping in front of her. His hands trailed up her arms and began rubbing along her biceps. There was something romantic about his actions.

"Better?" he asked benevolently.

The heat wrapped around her, the warmth instantly relieving some of the chilling ache in her bones.

Lucas had noticed she was still cold. Something she did not even realize she had been making known, her actions never once seeming to reveal any obvious physical signs of being bothered by the temperature in the room.

Karramis nodded, appreciating his attentiveness. "Yes, thank you."

"Good." His hand dropped and something shifted in his stance as his gaze narrowed. "Now, take it off."

She did not miss the undercurrent of violence in the command. "What?" The question was innocent, but it had a heavy dose of childlike perplexity lacing the word as she gave him a nervous sideways grin.

"The jumper," Lucas said calmly, regaining his composure, a man fighting to remain in control.

But Karramis saw it, that shift she had witnessed at Château Rouge. It was always in his eyes—his beautiful blues hiding something dark and eerie. There was this evil inside him fighting to take over. It was daunting, this unrecognizable darkness. His demeanor was impassive and apathetic, like there was no longer a soul inside him. Like something else was controlling his actions. He was someone completely different—a man yet a monster. A beast begging to come out and play.

Locking her metaphorical armor firmly in place, she lifted her chin. She would not show fear. She would not falter, and she sure as hell would not yield. This version of him thrived on her weakened emotional state, and she would never allow him to steal that part of her again.

"Take. It. Off." The demand held a warning.

Karramis held her ground, refusing to respond or obey.

A hand closed around her throat, the constricting force restricting some of her airflow. "Fine, I'll do it for ya." Lucas's jaw ticked, and his nostrils flared. "And if ya so much as think of usin' any of your powers on me, I will make sure his last moments are very, *very* painful." The threat was delivered through gritted teeth as his hot breath brushed across her ear.

Karramis wanted to fight, the voice of Will floating through her mind, but the promise of danger to his life was the only thing holding her back. Slowing her breathing, she instead fought to remain in control of the situation, her need to not pass out under the constraints of his grip her main focus.

The sound of a zipper hit her ears as tugging made her body jerk side to side. Air pulled into her lungs just as she drew in an inhale. Lucas had released her and began twisting her around, yanking the jacket down her arms. But before Karramis could turn around, the material of the jacket zipped behind her and a whooshing filled the room in time with the sounds of the logs in the fireplace shifting. Facing the hearth, Karramis watched in shocked silence as the flames consumed Will's jacket.

"Seriously?" The word burst from her, annoyance pinching her features together. She pivoted toward Lucas, her hand gesturing wildly as she pointed toward the fire. "Was that really necessary? It's just a damn jacket, Lucas. A jacket. It's not like it was Will standing here, keeping—"

A sting sliced across her face, the pain forcing her head to the side. Heat filled her cheek as her hand flew to cradle it.

Lucas had slapped her, something he seemed to enjoy doing lately. And something Karramis was growing extremely tired of.

He gripped her chin, hard, and forced her gaze upward, their eyes locking. Karramis refused to balk at the intimidating harshness, the need for her to submit. But without knowing, a tear slid down her cheek, the force behind the strike making her eyes water.

His thumb glided over her smooth skin, wiping away the pain he caused. He eyed her for a moment, a flash of something sparking in his gaze, something like regret. "Fuck," he breathed through gritted teeth. He jerked away from her and ran his hands through his hair. "Fuck!" The word exploded from him, guttural and harsh. "Goddammit, Karramis!"

Karramis backed away, unsure what he might do next.

Sensing her cautious disposition, he closed the distance, his expression remorseful. His hands lifted, aiming for her face, but Karramis took another step back, the defiance and refusal to have him touch her clear in the action, not a single word needing to be spoken.

Lucas's gaze was almost physical, like an actual burn searing into her, as he glared in her direction. Anguish and bitterness burned in his expression at the rejection, all sense of control fading as eyes assessed her with quiet rage.

Squaring his shoulders, he stepped into her, but halted as the words he was about to say disappeared from his mouth. Instead, he twisted and stormed over toward the door.

Stopping under the open threshold, he pointed at the ground. "Stay put," he demanded. "And don't ya dare test me. Or you will fuckin' regret it."

With that final threat, he exited the room, slamming the door behind him and the booming echo rattling the walls.

Chapter 12

Right Behind You

Pacing the large open room, James glanced around, finally taking in the space and fully understanding the name Alfina used for this area.

The back entrance to the infirmary appeared exactly like the chambers of a medieval parlor room rather than a place where medical procedures took place. Complete with a massive stone fireplace—almost similar in size to the one in the Grand Hall— the room was anything but bright and sterile. The walls were a dark gray plaster with various cracks along the framing around the two large, arched windows with even darker stones lining the windowsills. Dark red curtains covered the glass panes, the heavy and thick material pulled open to showcase the fading darkness as dawn approached. Rich, worn-out floorboards lay beneath a crimson rug covering most of the area in the center of the room, the dark wood slats uneven in some spots. Two sofas sat parallel from one another, directly in front of the edges of the fireplace. An enormous clock, measuring a few feet, hung over the pewter-colored fireplace, the rounded pebble stones lining it similar to that of river rocks. Candles of all shapes and sizes lined two wooden tables each behind one of the sofas. Passing the banquet-style table, lined with candelabras and various-sized pillar candles, beside the door leading into the hallway, he strolled mindlessly throughout the room, taking in the comforting scent of lavender, sandalwood, and the smoky aroma of cedar and pine coming from the roaring fireplace.

It had been hours since they arrived, the hectic and heart-pounding events morphing into a stagnant stalemate. The air was thick with trepidation and uncertainty, the nervousness and tension like a house of cards just waiting for a swift breeze to blow past.

The time waiting was like a mind game, a psychological battle between his own thoughts—the rational and hopeful side of him fighting to win against his intrusive thoughts. But it was harder than he wanted to admit. The struggle to fight his mental warfare was like trying to breathe underwater—no matter how hard one tried, the attempt would be futile. Impossible. There was no winning against the voices waging war inside his head, the ones only heard by him—blocked behind a wall to shield Rhiannon from them.

Everything that had unfolded over the last few hours had started to take a toll on him. And all he could do was wait around. Something which did not sit well with him.

This was his destiny. *His* fight. And it was his family who were paying the price for it.

The Earth Dragons had lost connection at some point with his father soon after Will entered through the portal, the relaying of information delivered to James and Rhiannon vague. It was as if they were told to remain silent, keeping the twins in the dark about what had happened at the cabin. But both he and Rhiannon were certain something had happened to Harkin, the magic between the dragon and the twins thrown into overdrive, like a spike of adrenaline searing through them. But it had faded as soon as it filled their veins, the sensation going from hot to cold in a matter of seconds.

After Ignara left, she had gone quiet, even ignoring Rhiannon when she tried to contact her. Or maybe the Fire Dragon had retreated out of range of his sister's powers, but even now, there was no communication. And the three Earth Dragons, who still remained monitoring the area from the sky, had also remained silent, keeping their inner voices muted as their attention became hyper-focused on something, or someone, else.

Kavana still had not woken up, the combination of blood loss, mild hypothermia, exhaustion, and now medication keeping her in an almost comatose state. Alfina and Nina were able to return her core temperature to normal, but a blood transfusion was needed. Not only had she lost a lot through her injuries, but she had also been a victim of one of the blood-sucking men who had taken her. James had no doubt it had been Leif, the vampire clearly taking some sort of pride in the state of his aunt earlier.

But Kavana had put up a fight, the bruises and cuts on her knuckles proving she did not play victim while she was being held captive. However, she could not win against them, and now she was fighting for her life. Not only had his aunt been outmatched, but she most definitely had been outnumbered.

Just like his parents were right now.

If they were still alive.

Strutting by one of the couches with his arms crossed, the tension and worry like acid in his chest, James peered down at Rhiannon. She had fallen asleep a few moments ago, the weight of the last few hours, the roller coaster of emotions she was trying desperately to protect him from, the death of their grandfather—an unknown not yet verified but somehow certain on a deep, instinctual level—the strain of not knowing what was happening with their parents, and the tears she finally allowed to fully surface forcing her eyes to close as she surrendered to the exhaustion evident on her face and throughout her lethargic demeanor.

James was just as tired, just as emotionally distraught and physically and mentally drained, but the idea of sleeping did not sit well with him. How could he sleep when his parents were in danger? The thought of what was going on at Casteya Castle erupted an anger inside of him, a fury of not being able to protect his family. He understood why his parents did what they had done, but it was not something he had to agree with—and he sure as hell did not. These people wanted to take them from him, after only finding them again less than a year ago. It was not fair. Why was his life, and the life of his sister, destined to be riddled with so much heartache and obstacles? And so much loss.

"Hey," a deep, quieted voice said behind him, the familiar comfort of Aidan's presence easing the tension in James's shoulders as he turned around.

This was the second time Aidan had come to check on him and Rhiannon, the worry in his expression never faltering.

James examined Aidan's clothes again as he strolled closer, his stride sluggish and posture slouched. In Kavana's startled state earlier, some of her blood had gotten on his hoodie as he held her against him. And after soothing her to sleep as he stroked her hair, he had wiped the remnants from his hands due to her blood-soaked wet hair—the snow having melted along her black tresses—along his jeans. The contrast against the light denim and dark green made it appear as if new and old blood soaked his clothes.

Emerald-green eyes filled with worry landed on Rhiannon. "How long has she been asleep?" His question was whispered and laced with relief, sounding concerned and caring at the same time, almost parental.

"Not long."

Aidan studied James, taking in his droopy and distant gaze, his languid stance. Even his simple reply had sounded tired and hollow. "You should rest," Aidan muttered insistently.

"No, I'm fine." His eyes dipped to his sister. "I need to be awake."

"Ye're no good to anyone like this, lad. So, rest." Placing a hand on James's shoulder, Aidan offered a gentle and reassuring squeeze. "We have to believe they're all right." One side of his mouth quirked up, a hopeful gleam flashing in his eyes. "Their magic can't be taken today."

James swallowed the doubt rising in his throat and lowered his gaze to the floor before lifting it, his brown eyes settling on Aidan as he detached himself from the contrition he was feeling, the shame and irritation of not fighting harder. "How's Aunt K?"

"She's still sleepin', but Nina is with her now, and Alfina says she's goin' to be all right."

Nina and Alfina had not only administered a blood transfusion, but they had also stitched up some of her injuries before cleaning her up and moving her into the general ward across the hall. Due to the mild hypothermia, most of the previous hours had been dedicated to monitoring Kavana's breathing and pulse, while warming her up slowly and safely. But thanks to the large fireplace in the parlor, the area downstairs had warmed with a steady increase to a more comfortable temperature, allowing Kavana's body to adjust gradually with the added help of blankets and the removal of her cold, wet clothes.

"Are you hungry?" Aidan asked. "Alfina said there's a pantry and kitchen downstairs in the cellar."

"No."

"All right. If you change yer mind . . ."

"Thank you, Aidan."

Aidan gave him a curt nod, sympathy pressing his lips together. "I'll come back and check on you both in a bit." Heading toward the door leading into the rest of the infirmary, he paused just over the threshold, concern in his gentle expression. "James?" he called tenderly.

James glanced up from staring down at his sister, the mask hiding his emotions firmly in place. "Yeah?"

"Try to get some rest. Please."

James nodded, the action convincing as Aidan strolled down the hall, leaving the door open.

A tear slid down James's cheek as the words his mother spoke hours prior echoed in his head.

I'll be right behind you.

Panic and desolation and shame clawed deeper, reaching even further inside his body, his core being overrun by poisonous roots—branches of malicious intent digging their way into his soul. The darkness was slowly taking over again, this shadowy, inky wall of power and control. A darkness shifting everything he was feeling into something different, something raw and immoral. Something dangerous. It was a drive to fight, to win. To face the path he was forced upon with an iron fist, with an unrelenting determination to rise to the challenge. To not only win the battle but win the whole damn war. He wanted to face the enemy, to show he was not afraid. He wanted to shield those he loved from the dangers, to protect them from an unknown fate.

But James pushed against it, refusing again to allow it to fully take control.

Sitting down on the floor in front of the sofa, he leaned against the couch, the company of his sister behind him comforting.

"James?" Rhiannon whispered, her voice thick with sleep.

Shushing her, he twisted sideways and lifted a hand, offering it to her. "Everything's okay. Go back to sleep."

She slid her hand into his and closed her eyes, drifting off again.

Taking a cue from her, he placed his free arm along the top of the plush cushion next to her and lowered his head against it.

I'll be right behind you.

With his mother's voice in his head, James closed his eyes, giving his body permission to rest, even if for a short while.

As darkness fluttered behind his eyelids and sleep took hold of him, James hoped, wherever his parents were, they were safe. And no matter what happened, he prayed his mother would keep her promise to him and fight back.

Because this time, he wanted to believe, more than anything, that she would be, in fact, right behind him, and that she would be there when he woke up.

Chapter 13

The Love of an Enemy

The logs in the fireplace had turned to ash as dawn filled the area outside the large window, the deep shades of blues and violets adding to the beauty of the fading stars. A chill had returned to the room as the smooth, plastered walls fought to hold any remaining heat.

Karramis held herself, her folded arms tight across her body as she rubbed her arms and paced the room. Everything about the last few hours did not sit right with her. From the cryptic deal being altered, to all of them arriving at the cabin, to Merrick not being worried about the dragons showing up, to her sister, to the murder of her father. The memories poisoned her thoughts—the words he uttered, the raw emotions on his face, the tears he shed, the sound of his neck breaking and his body slumping to the ground.

Swallowing down the tightness rising in her throat, she shook the replay from her mind and wiped the escaped tear from her cheek. Karramis knew there would be a time to mourn, but right now was not it. If being a Guardian taught her anything, it was to compartmentalize her emotions in times of distress. As her father once told her, "If you allow yourself to be broken in a time of weakness, you will never be able to put yourself back together. Fight now, fall later. Only then will they never see you fail."

So that is what she would do, she would use any weakness and form a shield around herself.

"Fight now, fall later," she whispered to herself.

Her pacing slowed as she neared the fireplace, allowing the small bit of heat to warm her. Karramis was well aware there was some sort of hidden agenda happening, but she had no clue what it was. And this made her anxious and even scared. The whole uncertainty of it all made her uneasy, and it was making it hard to fully commit to one plan. Nothing was going how she imagined. Even Lucas was not acting entirely normal—well, normal for him. In all honesty, she was not fully confident what exactly Lucas wanted anymore. Whether it was her or something else, she did not know. But there was something. And until she figured it out, Karramis had to be careful not to expose herself in any way. The element of surprise was her best line of defense right now.

And it might be the only way to save Will, and herself.

Footsteps pounded down the hall, and the door swung open. Lucas entered the room, all signs of the anger gone. He gave her half a smile, the confidence in his posture and the charm in his gaze fully in place again.

Karramis paused her chaotic stride and eyed him, the silence between them uncomfortable.

"I'm sorry," he declared, the regret in his blue eyes seeming genuine, a look of sympathy forming along his brows.

The apology caught her by surprise, it being completely out of place hours later. And it was almost forced as always. Lucas's apologies had never been given without an excuse to his actions. A justification rendering the other person to blame.

"I regret the mistakes that were made." His tone was now flat. "But this wasn't my fault."

And there it was.

"Ya know I'd neva' intentionally hurt you," he continued. "I didn't mean to do it." His proximity to her was close as he reached up and cupped her face, Karramis allowing the unwelcomed touch, if only to gauge his intent. "I neva' wanna hurt ya, love." Sincerity flashed in his eyes.

But she knew better by now than to trust him.

"*Never.*" Lucas noticed the slight haze lingering in her eyes, the emotion placed in the back of her mind for now having nothing to do with him. "It's just ya neva' know when to shut your mouth. It's like ya enjoy pissin' me off. Like ya want me to hurt ya. Why do ya always haveta be so defiant?"

Silence lingered between them as several heartbeats pounded in her chest. A crease formed along her forehead and her head cocked slightly. She was uncertain how to respond. Was he actually wanting her to answer, or was this rhetorical?

Lucas released her and headed over to the chair next to the fireplace. Sitting down, he let out a heavy sigh and leaned into his thighs.

The room hummed as the space became too quiet.

"When we were in France, I took care of ya."

Karramis's brows creased even harder as she folded her arms over her chest, not sure whether it was from the cold filling the room or because she was shielding herself from whatever uncomfortable conversation was about to take place. The segue was random, but again, her curiosity won as she made her way over to the opposite side of the fireplace, her watchful gaze staying on him and keeping the distance between them. Taking in the full sight of him, she knew from this position, she had a better chance of not being taken by surprise again. The throb along her cheek was still present and pulsated in warning, reminding her to stay vigilant.

Blue eyes lifted, and his lips twisted in a grin. "Did ya know that?"

"How could I?" she asked warmly. "I wasn't even aware I was alive or where I was, let alone who had my body."

"Well, I did," he muttered, soft yet proud.

Memories of waking up at Château Rouge flashed in her mind. The pristine room. The dread of not knowing where she was or whether or not her children were safe. The red-stained and filthy nightgown. Camille and Leif. The confusion as the events continued to unfold, especially since she had appeared just as she had the night at the manor, covered in blood and mud, and with an injury that had never stopped bleeding. And yet years had passed.

She rubbed along the now healed wound that had been cauterized just below her ribs, the night still fresh in her mind.

"I cleaned your face," he continued, pulling her from her thoughts. "Ya looked so peaceful, like you were sleepin'. And I sat there for hours each day, just hopin' you'd open your eyes." He took a deep breath. "Leif begged me to change ya and throw away that disgustin' garment, to wash away the blood and remnants of that night—saying the smell of ya was both enticin' and unappealin'." Lucas caught the grimace on Karramis's face and chuckled. "Ya didn't smell bad, love. I mean, ya kinda did, but not in the way ya think. Like I mentioned before, all aspects of ya just stopped, so it's not like ya laid there for eight years just rottin' away or sittin' in your own filth. But ya did smell like blood, and the mud on ya had a very earthy musk to it afta' some time passed."

"Oh," Karramis said faintly, relieved by the statement before another emotion filtered in. "Then why didn't you? Do what Leif asked."

"Because I needed the reminder." Guilt lingered in his admission, but it did not seem genuine. "I wanted to rememba' every detail of that night. I needed ya to remain as ya were to remind myself as to why it had to happen the way it did."

Unable to combat the accusation in his tone, Karramis said, "So, I was a token to justify your actions." It was not a question.

Lucas rose to his feet as a light chuckle left him. His stride was slow and held so much purposeful advancement, his domineering and eager gaze sizing her up. He stroked her face with the back of his fingers, the touch sensual. "I coulda been the hero in your story," he stated, his charm laced with a hollowness. "But instead, ya made me the villain." The room fell quiet, and he dropped his hand, the space between them still minimal. "Why?"

"I didn't," Karramis admitted sincerely.

"Yes, ya did," he insisted. "Because it wasn't me who did it. No, everythin' I did, I did for you. For *us*."

She let out a delicate snort. "I don't think hunting me down and trying to kill me was really in my best interest."

His shoulders lifted dismissively as his head shook and a cocky smirk pulled at the corners of his lips. "I neva' tried to kill ya, love. You're bein' a tad overdramatic."

Mouth open, she scoffed before saying, "You stabbed me."

"You were the one who ran."

Karramis unfolded her arms and dropped them to her sides. "And what about France?"

"What about it?" he asked with a shrug, moving back a few steps and sliding his hands into his button-down coat pockets.

She arched a brow. "You almost killed me."

"Ya clearly wanted to get under my skin. And ya succeeded. So, I reacted accordingly."

Well, he had a point there.

It was true, she did act rashly with how she handled things when she woke up after thinking she had been dead. And it was a mistake she had to live with—the scar on her face her own daily reminder of the things she caused to come into fruition and the danger she put herself in.

"You've been able to block my powers for years," Lucas continued, "and yet ya were tryin' to piss me off with your incessant need to run your mouth all the damn time. It's not my fault ya weren't prepared for the consequences of your actions." The space between them was nonexistent as he glanced down at her, his hands no longer in his pockets but on her forearms. "And ya wanna know what I think?"

Karramis pressed her lips together, biting back the words *not particularly* as every part of her wanted to back away from him.

Lucas zeroed in on her mouth, his eyes slowly trailing upward to take in the rich brown of her gaze. "I think ya quite enjoyed it. I think ya like when I'm rough with ya."

Her brow arched, the movement happening on its own accord. Was he serious? Did he really think she enjoyed having the shit beat out of her?

One of his hands slid across her cheek, his caress so sensual. "Why else—"

She leaned her head away from the touch.

His fingers rushed into her hair, gripping and yanking down, making her head snap back and their gazes locking as his jaw ticked. "Why else would ya constantly want to make me so angry?"

"It's a gift," she retorted boldly, unflinching despite the pain searing along the base of her head.

He released a light chuckle. "No, I think ya like bein' dominated. I think ya like bein' controlled. Am I right?" He tugged harder on her hair. "Do ya secretly like it rough, love?"

"No," she said through a slight wince, "I think I just don't know when to keep my mouth shut, like you all keep mentioning."

"Now, that I can attest to."

"And I think you're the one who likes to be in control," she countered.

"I do love a good submissive." His voice was deep and husky, his face coming closer to hers.

"No, I think it's more than that. It's not just about submitting, it's about the control. You thrive on the power behind it. I think it's the fact you get some sick pleasure out of the fight."

"Well, I don't wanna fight with ya anymore," he announced honestly, releasing her and strolling toward the fireplace.

Karramis rubbed the dull ache on the back of her head. "You don't?"

He faced her and gave her a soft smirk, his eyes imploring. "No, love, I don't." He swallowed, vulnerability and hope displayed in his expression. "I neva' wanted to fight with ya. That was not my intention." He made his way back over to her, this time leaving a notable and intentional distance between them. "And I promise, if ya allow me, I can love ya like I was always meant to."

Her eyes went wide, and lips parted, the declaration not at all where she thought this was going. Nerves rattled to life deep inside her body as her stomach twisted, the unease of what might be coming making goose bumps sprout along her cool skin.

If he noticed her shift, he did not show it as he continued, "No one knows ya like I do." He took a single step closer. "And I've missed ya so much—missed us." Another step. "I just want us to go back to how we were. Just you and me." Step. "I can do better—I *will* be better. If ya let me." He stopped a few inches from her, causing her to have to glance up at him. "Please, love. Forgive me."

There was something so raw and real in the words he spoke, and it sent a tightness racing through her chest. He seemed so genuine. So vulnerable. So exposed with laying himself out for her to see.

"Lucas, I don't know what—"

"*Please*," he said, more a demand than a plea. "Give us anotha' chance. Ya hurt me first, remember?" The question was clearly rhetorical because he continued. "And I forgave you." He took hold of her hand. "I'm sorry. I'm sorry your actions got ya hurt. You know I didn't mean it. I neva' wanted to hurt ya . . . But ya just kept fightin'. But I don't wanna fight anymore. I said sorry, so please let's just move on." He freed her hand and traced a finger along her scar, the scar he gave her, a mix of regret and admiration in his eyes. "I love you, Karramis."

Still and calm, she did not balk at this touch, nor did she stray from his watchful gaze as she spoke, a softness in her tone. "I'm not sure you really know what love is."

"But I do." Cupping her jaw, he gently glided his thumb just below her lower lip.

Karramis wanted nothing more than to remove herself from the situation, the close proximity, the touching, all of it setting off every alarm in her body.

"I've always loved you," he stated matter-of-factly. "I can feel it deep in my soul."

"It's so much more than a feeling or even a declaration." The sensation of him touching her was foreign and nerve-racking, but she steeled herself, the steadiness of her expression and voice neutral and friendly. "It's about surrendering yourself to something you have no control over. It's about the willingness to give something without expecting anything in return. It's about faith and honesty. It's about trust and providing protection without hesitation. It's about giving something over and knowing you may never get it back but still allowing the universe to take control. It's a bet but without the urge to cheat." Pausing, she considered her next words carefully, the memory of the best friend she once had fresh in her mind. "I loved you. Once. And I might've loved you more than what I did if things had been different, but we'll never know. I'm sorry. I truly am. But if you really believe what you say, if you really love me, you wouldn't put yourself before me. Because love is about sacrifice.

That's what true love is, putting the other first. And if you really had loved me—"

"*Love*," he interjected firmly. Love, as in present tense.

"If you really love me," she corrected, allowing his truth to be known, "you would be willing to go to the ends of the world to protect me, not hunt me. And you never would've sided with those who want me dead. Or those who want my children dead. If you truly love me, you would want me to be happy. You would move on and just let me go."

"But I can't because I know we're meant to be togetha'. You're mine. Ya always have been. You belong to me."

"No, Lucas," she said with a gentle shake of her head, his hold on her never faltering. "I belong to *me*. You have no claim over me. No one does."

Dropping his hand, Lucas leaned back away from her, his eyes narrowing with irritation. "What about *him*?"

Karramis recognized the venom in that final word. "Yes, I am his, but only because *I* gave a part of myself to him. I did it— me. Not him. He didn't take it. He didn't demand it, or steal it, or claim it. He earned what I gave him."

Lucas scoffed and rolled his eyes. "Let me guess, it was your heart?"

"No." She shook her head again and shifted uncomfortably. "I gave him my trust. The heart is weak and ruled by inferior emotions, but trust is something only your soul can give. We can love anyone, but to truly trust someone is the purest and strongest form of love."

"So, ya really want me to let ya go, then?" It was a sincere question, a curious and yet calm inquiry.

Karramis stared at him for a moment, the gentleness and almost surrendering cadence and expression unfamiliar. "I do."

"But what if I can't?"

"If you truly love someone, you want them happy. Even if it means that happiness isn't with you. Let me go, Lucas." This time she closed the distance between them and clasped her fingers loosely around his forearm. "Please."

"I won't," he admitted, lowering his gaze to the floor, defeat etched in his slouching posture. "I can't."

"Yes, you can."

He exhaled and lifted his eyes to hers, raw determination gleaming within them. "But I don't want to. I don't wanna lose ya. Can't ya see that? I'm tryna fight for ya."

"There's nothing to fight for," she said, delivering it in the most delicate way. "You're trying to steal something that can't be taken. You're not fighting *for* me, you're fighting a*gainst* me. You're trying to force something that isn't there."

Lucas twisted his arm around, the movement making her lose her grip as he grasped her wrist. "I refuse to believe that."

Standing her ground as his fingers squeezed, she announced truthfully, "I will always choose him."

Lurching forward, he gripped her face, his fingers lacing through her hair and clutching the back of her jaw and the base of her head. "You're *mine*," he argued, low and gravelly through gritted teeth. Anger raged in his eyes, his tone shifting to one of control and power. "And if I have to beat it into ya, I will."

Karramis did not flinch, the sharpness in her expression unyielding. "See, you do get some sick pleasure out of it, don't you?"

Lucas yanked her into him, his lips ramming into hers in a not-so-graceful, hard motion. Hands slid farther into her hair, urging her harder into his chest. Karramis gasped as her body leaned uncontrollably. Taking advantage of her open lips, he glided his tongue into her mouth and lowered one of his hands, gripping her waist and pressing her even harder into his body. He pushed forward as if directing her backward somewhere. The motion sent another gasp escaping her. Taking her surprised inhale as another invitation to continue, Lucas slithered his tongue deeper into her mouth, invading and claiming.

Heat coursed through her body, the anger and disgust raging beneath her skin, her entire core igniting in a violent protest. Her veins filled with a fiery, lethal cocktail of defiance, outrage, and hostility at the invasion. A repeating offense she no longer would allow him to get away with, nor had she ever wanted a part of. Karramis was going to put a stop this blatant disregard for boundaries and respect in a barbaric and rather disgusting way, consequences be damned.

Without allowing this for another second, Karramis bit down on his tongue. Hard.

Lucas jerked back.

The momentum of his jolting retreat caused her to become unsteady on her feet and sent her downward, her backside hitting the floor.

"Fuckin' bitch!" Wiping his mouth, he peered down at the blood on his fingers. "Ya fuckin' bit me."

Karramis spit, the blood-tinged saliva splattering on the rug as she glanced up at him, satisfaction present on her face but disgust in her tone. "I'm getting really fucking tired of you doing that." Hurrying to pull her legs underneath her, she rushed to her feet and readied her stance for a potential fight.

A deep, sadistic laugh filled the room. "Ya really think ya can take me? How'd that work out for ya the last time?"

"I wasn't ready then," she challenged, "but now I am."

He gave her a bored smirk and chuckled, the sound dismissive but still arrogant. "I'm a trained fighter—you'd surely lose."

"Well then, you have nothing to worry about, right?"

Silence settled between them as he began circling around her, his stride coming slightly closer with each step. Keeping her eyes on him, Karramis matched each movement perfectly, retreating away with an equally steady pace.

Lucas halted, noticing her awareness of his actions. "I'm not fighting ya, love." His attention stayed fixed on her, observing her perfect stance and her hands lifted at the ready.

"What's the matter, Lucas? Is it less exciting when I fight back?"

"No, I just don't wanna hurt ya." There was truth to the statement, but an underlying thrill flickered in his voice and lifted the corner of his mouth.

Karramis glared at him. "I highly doubt that."

His eyes took in every inch of her features, the urge to touch her, to caress the newly formed bruise on her face, to trace the scar, his handiwork burning in his gaze. Remorse lingered in his deep blues, but there was also a glimmer of satisfaction there, a gleam of reason and justification.

"I love you, Karramis," he admitted amiably, truthful and forthcoming, nothing but raw honesty in his loving tone. He lifted a hand to touch her but quickly dropped it. "It's always been *you* for me. There's been no one else who has ever made me feel the way I feel when I think of ya, or when I'm with ya." Lucas could not help himself—he gently pushed a strand of hair from her forehead, carefully gliding his hand down her wavy locks.

Karramis pulled in a ragged breath, the sound barely audible as she steadied herself. His touch was unnerving, and his proximity made her tense, but it was the way his piercing blue eyes examined her, his gaze fixed on hers. There was a look of hunger in them.

"I love you," he repeated. "I neva' wanted to hurt ya. I neva' meant to hurt ya. I was just . . . upset. You broke my heart—ya ran from me. You abandoned me. I loved ya, and ya left me without a single care about how that would've hurt *me*."

"Lucas, I never left you," she said calmly, the softness in her gaze and tone real and sympathetic, a friend talking to a friend. "I was here. I never went anywhere."

"No, ya left." His voice was firm, insistent. "When ya disappeared—when the whole story of how ya died in childbirth came about . . ." He shook his head as if trying to erase the memory, pausing to collect himself. "But I knew, I fuckin' *knew* that son of a bitch was lyin'." The air grew eerily silent for a moment as he fought the anger flashing across his face. "You *left* me when ya decided to run. I loved you, and you left. Why?"

It was as if he wanted to see into her soul, to dig deeper and explore parts of her she refused to show him. Parts of her mind, her heart.

"I ran because I was afraid," Karramis admitted honestly. "Afraid of the prophecy, afraid of Merrick." She paused. "Afraid of you."

"Bullshit." The word flowed from him evenly and without hesitation. "All I eva' wanted to do was protect ya. I fuckin' loved ya, I still fuckin' love ya, and ya were makin' a mistake. All I eva' wanted from ya was to make ya happy and for you to love me back. But you chose wrong." It was more than love he wanted from her. It was possession. Something shifted in his eyes, his energy taking on a dark persona. Lucas stepped back and ran his hands through his dark hair. "He had no right." The words exploded from him, powerful but controlled, the sharpness not at all loud but still forceful as he stepped into her, his voice low. "He had no right to take what didn't belong to him." Agitation filled the room, the irritation building as he lurched forward and grabbed hold of her wrists, the grip making his knuckles white. "You are fuckin' mine. Ya hear me? *Mine*."

Karramis fought against the pain crushing her wrists, trying to not only ignore the discomfort and tingling along her fingers by the lack of circulation but attempting to maintain control of the situation. Keep him calm. Do not provoke him. "Lucas," she said smoothly, the sharpness in her expression unyielding, "let go of me. Please."

Lucas did not release her but instead pulled her into him, their chests pressing together. Peering down at her, he grinned, a look of intent in the boyish gesture.

A ball of anxiety lodged in her chest.

Don't you dare fucking do it.

Karramis allowed the words to flow freely, her thoughts clearly hitting their mark as Lucas's grin deepened.

"You've changed." His eyes remained on her, fully taking her in as he thrust her back and released her. "Ya know that? It's a shame, too. Because I'm not sure I like who you've become. Maybe everyone was right. Maybe all this is just a lost cause."

His words conveyed an elusive insult, a cryptic meaning behind the almost manipulative statement.

"No, I didn't change," Karramis stated plainly, conviction in her stance, her expression. "I simply found who I was always meant to be, and you didn't like who I became. But this is me. All of me. And I refuse to allow you to make me regret who stands before you." Her dark brown eyes blazed with determination and certainty. "This *is* a lost cause because I will never submit to you. Ever. And I sure as hell no longer feel guilty for the choices I've made. I'm not afraid of you anymore, Lucas, or those who deem to try to control me. I am the flame which can no longer be tamed."

He laughed, the sound deep and grating and lacking any humor. "How fuckin' poetic. But far from accurate. Because . . ." His voice became low and rough. "In the end, you *will* submit. One way or anotha', I promise ya. And if ya don't, you will surely regret it. How you play the rest of this game and how ya come out of it all depends on your next move. So, choose carefully, love."

"What does that mean?" she asked, dread curling in her gut.

"Oh, you'll see."

Strolling over to the front of the room, Lucas opened the door. "C'mon, let's go."

Karramis remained firmly in place. "Where?"

Grinning, Lucas announced, "To settle this."

Chapter 14

Unfair Fight

Head held high, Karramis moved leisurely through the doorframe, graceful and poised in her every step. Fine, she would play along with all of this. If he wanted a worthy opponent, she would give him exactly that. Because that was exactly what this was to Lucas, a game. A way to show who had the upper hand. A power play. A twisted attempt at the age-old cat-and-mouse game, prey versus predator. And she would entertain him. Let him think he had won.

But she had to be smart. Everything moving forward had to be calculating, strategic. There was too much happening and not enough to go off of. Too many people were playing with their own set of rules and own personal end game in mind. At least, that was what seemed to be happening. No clear agenda had been presented in regard to her and Will. The deal with Merrick had a whole new agenda, one she had not yet figured out. But she was going to. Eventually. Whether by putting the pieces together herself or discovering it as they unfolded. So, she had to be ready. And the only way she could do any of that, to fully plan to be a step ahead of the others, or come up with a defensive attack, was to keep herself focused and to maintain control for as long as possible. Therefore, she had to remain vigilant and organized, composed and docile—compliant yet not fully submissive—as well as continuing to hold her emotional and mental armor firmly in place. But more importantly, to keep her magic just below the surface, ready and waiting. Even now, she could feel it vibrating along the surface of her skin, thrumming in her veins. Lingering. Preparing. Waiting.

She had relied on her powers before to save her, their arrival in the past being either slow to finally appear or faulty once present. But Karramis was the one to blame for this, having resented her magic, being fearful of it, and thus never fully embracing what she was capable of. But that had stopped after Château Rouge. She had trained almost every day to prepare for this moment, to gain the physical strength to rise to the challenge, to fight back. However, she had not only been determined to strengthen her skills physically by training to defend herself through the means of brute force, cunning maneuvers, and evasive tactics, but she had also been strengthening her mental abilities, honing her mind's innate capabilities to control her body and soul. Mind over matter.

And no matter what happened tonight, she knew, without a hint of uncertainty, her magic would present itself. Because she would not allow Will to be a victim in this stupid game she was being forced to play—a game that had nothing to do with her children and any of their powers. At least, she assumed as much by the strange interaction and seemingly pointless conversation she just had with Lucas. The only way to protect Will was to remain in control of herself, in all facets of her entire being. And for her, that meant standing her ground and never allowing Lucas to gain the upper hand.

A door opened at the end of the long hallway just before the bend, the slight creaking of the hinges loud within the quiet space.

A man with blond hair, combed and slicked back, stepped into the hall and glared at them, his narrowed brows conveying either confusion or disapproval. His eyes, the deepest shade of green, the vibrance of them reminding Karramis of the leaves surrounding the cabin in the spring, moved between her and Lucas before settling on her.

His tall, lean frame and hair color mirrored Leif's, but this man was muscular and just a few inches shorter. And surely, a decade separated them in appearance—age having no significance here—possibly even more. They could almost be brothers, or maybe even cousins. And based on the pale skin and darkness lingering in his gaze, a lost soul searching for a home it will never find again, Karramis could only assume this was also a vampire like Leif. But there was a softness to him, a kindness. Not at all like the brazen, arrogant vampire she had grown to despise over the years.

"The Fire Witch," the young man announced flatly with a Russian accent, the brogue recognizable but not at all thick. "What is she doing here?" The question was clearly meant for Lucas, but the vampire's gaze never left Karramis.

"Unfinished business," was all Lucas said as he lifted his chin down the hall, urging Karramis forward with the jerking motion. "Move."

Rounding the corner of the immaculate hallway, the corridor a well-kept visual of history frozen in time, Karramis observed the doorway leading back toward the main part of the castle. Her heavy boots pounded against the tiled floor almost in sync with Lucas, his frame remaining in her peripheral vision. The distance between them was purposeful, just within an arm's reach of each other. Most likely a ploy to keep her compliant. An act that did not go unnoticed by Karramis the entire time they had been within close proximity of each other. He had kept himself entirely too close to her throughout her time at the castle, along with pushing his limits with the constant embraces, which he had been closely analyzing as if taking in her reactions. Again, something Karramis also took note of.

He had been testing her. For what? She did not know.

They both remained silent as Lucas pushed open the door leading outside. Cold air crashed into Karramis, the icy blast reminding her of Will's jacket and how it was now a pile of ash back in Lucas's bedroom. Fighting back the urge to huff in annoyance as she rubbed her sleeved arms, Karramis followed behind Lucas as they headed east along the front of the castle, trudging through the freshly fallen snow lying undisturbed along the grounds.

The early morning hour was peaceful, welcoming, even on this side of the island. There was something serene about that moment right before the sun crested the horizon, slowly washing away the darkness. It was not just the visual representation of a new day, a fresh start, but it was also a reminder that even within the dark, light was never too far away. One just had to be willing to persevere through the darkness long enough to see it again.

Through the soft shades of black and gray, rich blues and dark purples colored the area, the snow not white but rather a deep royal hue. The horizon line was painted with pinks and yellows, fading upward into an ombre of more blues before disappearing into the last remaining obsidian of the night, the stars twinkling their final goodbyes.

Something unique filled the air, something distinct and familiar but still foreign, almost ominous. A metallic twinge and something reminiscent of old, rotting flesh yet somehow sweet coated the bitter breeze, but it was faint and masked behind the clean, fresh earthiness of the powdery flakes covering the ground. It was somehow an eerie blend of life and death.

As they turned the corner, Karramis's stomach dropped, the fear she so adamantly refused to allow to take over slowly starting to seep back in. Not only was Leif waiting for them, leaning casually with his arms crossed over his chest and a smirk grazing his smug face, but they were headed straight for the tower—a tower she knew belonged to Merrick. A tower not only designed by him, commissioned by him, but had also been built as his own personal torture chamber and feasting grounds. This structure was a thing of nightmares and horror stories. It had never been proven if all the tales told were real, but bodies had been found over the centuries, mutilated and violently dismembered throughout the castle grounds and outside the exterior walls. And to the young girl who eavesdropped on the stories and witnessed the panic throughout the guard when more and more bodies had been discovered throughout the years, this was not a place she ever wanted to visit—the forbidden side, let alone the tower of death. And even as an adult, the feeling was still there. There was something so sinister about the structure, even the way it sat there, isolated and menacingly towering high above the rest of the castle grounds. It screamed danger, as if the ghosts of those who roamed the land around it were yelling for her to run.

Suspicious brown eyes focused on the deep blue irises of the vampire before her as she neared the structure reaching hundreds of feet into the sky. Their gazes were locked, both carefully examining the other. Karramis had never trusted Leif, his preternatural abilities, lustful urges, unmistakable desire to dominate, malicious personality, and his unpredictable nature causing an emotional response she was unable to control at times. He always had this way of simultaneously infuriating her yet absolutely terrifying her. It was a constant internal battle she struggled with, this need to fight and flee at the same time. To challenge yet cower. To run but with the hope of being chased.

To hide yet be found. It was a strange conundrum, a dichotomy of contradicting responses she still, to this day, could not explain. There was a hate there yet an intrigue. A fire that wanted to burn—both physically and metaphorically—from the inside out.

"Hello, witch," Leif said, his tone deep and almost flirtatious. A gleam of anticipation and delight flittered across his features, the upward twist of his mouth and slight arching of his brow suggesting he had been waiting for her to arrive. "Are you ready?"

Her face wrinkled in confusion, the unease in her stomach churning but a subtle thrill accompanying the nervousness. "For what?"

"To see how this ends."

Karramis let out a slow scoff, glaring up at him and offering him a bold, confident grin. "If it means I finally get to end you, then yes. Let's do this."

Leaning into her, Leif hooked a finger under her chin and angled her head upward. She did not recoil at his touch or flinch at his closeness. He smelled of earthy musk, spicy citrus, and something soft and floral, like lavender, a perfect mix of woodsy and earthy. The scent of danger and pure dominance.

"This will be fun." The delivery was husky with a hint of mockery, the arrogance fully in place. He stared at her for longer than he had ever watched her before, the scrutinizing turning into something like admiration. The cockiness faded from his expression and turned into one of lust and possessiveness. "You look just like her."

The statement sent Karramis aback, the words hitting her like a punch to the gut. "What?"

Leif ran his hand down her dark wavy hair, the touch gentle and barely noticeable as his fingers caressed her locks. "But she had the most beautiful hair—straight, silky, and the deepest reddish-brown color." He would not avert his newly pained and distant gaze as he soaked in her watchful, bewildered expression. "But you have her eyes." He peered down at her mouth and glided his thumb over it. "Her lips. She had the most delicious mouth." The back of his hand caressed her cheek sensually. "Her skin—so soft and warm."

He was talking about her mother. A mother she never knew. A mother she had never even seen a picture of.

"You even have her personality," he continued, his eyes back on hers as his hand trailed down her arm. "Stubborn. Vivacious. Passionate. Fiery. A total fucking brat. Annoying as hell. Smart mouth, even when she knew she should keep it closed. Lovesick." The last word came out rough, the delivery edged with bitterness. He retreated away from her, the gentleness in his expression and the affection in his tone fading, the memories he was remembering vanishing. His eyes darkened, the longing and peacefulness morphing into animosity and anger and resentment. "She, too, made the wrong decision."

An uncomfortable twisting sensation filled her chest, the rawness of it wringing a slew of emotions sinking into the pit of her stomach like heavy rocks. Had Leif loved her mother? Had he killed her because of it? Disbelief and shock sliced through her. The pain of not only losing her mother but the terror of nearly dying along with her coursed through her veins.

"You fucking bastard," she gritted out through clenched teeth, rage bleeding from her tone, the anger consuming her and swallowing up the grief threatening to escape. "You killed her." It was not a question but rather a fact, the truth of his words slapping her in the face. "Didn't you?" She needed to know, needed the confirmation, needed to hear it from his own mouth. This man had loved her mother, but he had still killed her. "Why?" she breathed.

"Like I said," he declared nonchalantly with a shrug as he made his way through the stone archway leading into the tower, "Keya made the wrong decision, and she paid the price for it."

Her head jerked toward Lucas, the pressure in her chest intensifying. Heart pounding, her entire body went rigid, paralyzed by the admission. Sweat formed along her hairline, the chill doing nothing to erase the rising of her core temperature. Incredulity and fury vibrated through her bones.

"Now, none of that, love," Lucas said casually as his hands stretched out on either side of her from behind and snatched her wrists, driving her arms backward at an uncomfortable angle.

Leif stepped behind them, the sound of metal rattling filling the entryway.

Pain and an icy tightness clamped around her wrists. The harshness of a bone-chilling touch and the unbearably constricting grip digging into her skin sent a surge of agony racing up her arms and trepidation filling her chest.

Shackles.

They had bound her wrists behind her back with metal cuffs.

Leif appeared in front of her, grinning as he quietly tsked her. "Naughty, naughty, little witch. Don't forget, we still have your precious Drolnogard. And I won't hesitate to kill him right in front of you."

Karramis's breath hitched.

"That's right." Leif stood tall, satisfaction in his tone. "Don't test me. Actually . . ." He paused and cocked his head. "Please do."

"Enough," Lucas said calmly, humor filling his tone. Hitching a head toward the castle at Leif, he added, "Go."

Silence lingered, but a plan was definitely being played out as Leif strolled away, determination in his stride and a joyous gleam in his eyes.

"Move," Lucas said, gesturing his head toward the stairs.

Karramis blinked at Lucas, unsure what to do or even say. He had the advantage—Lucas knew whatever was coming, he knew whatever plan lay at the top of the tower.

"Go on, love. Now." It was a demand, but one laced with pacifying conviction.

With her hands bound behind her back and worry creeping up her spine, Karramis ascended the stairs.

~

The wooden slabs creaked beneath Will's weight as he made his way up the unstable steps, littered with protruding splinters and rusty nails, along one side of the circular tower, Leif trailing closely behind. Haydrin had chosen to forgo whatever was about to take place, the werewolf deeming his part in this particular plot completed and to call him if another task was presented.

In spite of the well-worn stairs and the bite of the freezing air filling the open interior, the stone structure seemed to be fairly maintained. No stones were damaged, and all of the walls appeared to be firmly intact, not at all like certain sections of the castle just outside the door. A landing appeared as they made their way up the stairs, displaying an arched wooden door leading into a room partially lit up by the rising sun. A single bookshelf was in view and what looked like the edge of a dark wooden desk. Making their way higher into the tower, Will caught the whiff of an unrecognizable foul stench hidden behind the smell of smoke. Warmth filled the stairwell as they climbed, a welcome reprieve from the cold air seeping into his bones. At the top of the steps rested a stone landing and a wooden door opened just a few inches. Fire roared inside, the smell and warmth blanketing the entire upper floor.

Stopping just before the door, Will turned, hesitant to walk through, the fear of what rested beyond the threshold forming in his gut. It was quiet, too quiet. Not a whisper of anything could be heard beyond the crackling flames, and the vile smell was far more potent, an odor Will now understood was the scent of death. But a calm settled over him, a serene and familiar sense of peace. It hummed through him, a soothing connectiveness he not only knew well but also craved.

"Move," Leif demanded as he stepped up onto the landing.

Will obliged, knowing Karramis waited inside. He was desperate to be near her and ensure she was all right, safe. The last few hours had been absolute torture for him, not understanding what exactly was happening or whether or not his wife was in danger. The urge to protect was hard to control, but Karramis had made him promise to play along with her decisions. To trust her. And he did. But when the deal was altered, he wanted nothing more than to shield her from it. From the dangerous situations and manipulation being played out. But he knew she was formulating a different plan, and he had to allow her the time to figure it all out. But the simple act was difficult to combat because there was nothing harder for a man to fight against than being asked to step back and allow someone else to take control of a situation. Especially when it came to not being able to protect the woman he loved. To protect his family. That was their duty, to provide and protect. To be the foundation and the safeguard. And right now, it took everything in him to follow through with his promise.

The door hinges squeaked as Will pushed it open. Heat blasted into him and smoke floated upward from a fire pit, the flames dancing inside a stone circular recess in the center of the massive and open space. Unlit candles lay ensconced along the limestone walls, and a single arched window opened up to the outside along the far side of the room. The smooth, rectangular stones beneath his feet were discolored, and the grooves were tainted an odd shade, the coloring Will could only hope was from years of dirt and grime, but in reality, he knew it was not.

Scanning the room, Will's eyes widened in shock before narrowing in anger. "I'm going to fucking kill you." His tone was deep and venomous, the gravelly undertone sounding wild.

Karramis knelt on the floor with her arms bound behind her while Lucas leaned against the wall just a few feet away from her, grinning like a lunatic with his legs crossed at the ankles and his hands in his pockets.

Will charged at Lucas, intent on striking him, but a hand wrapped around the back of his neck and yanked him, the sudden jolt forcing his entire body off-balance as Leif pushed him downward. His knees slammed into the stone floor, the pain shooting through his legs at the impact.

"Again with this shit?" Lucas huffed a mocking laugh and pushed off the wall, the stride forward relaxed and unhurried. Crouching in front of Will, Lucas stared at him, a callous and evil smirk slowly forming. "You could neva' best me, mate." He tapped his temple, his voice composed but threatening. "I can hear every single thought bouncin' 'round in your head. Includin' your little idea that Karramis here"—he turned his head toward her—"will use her magic and get ya both outta here." His gaze returned to Will. "Well, unfortunately for ya, we've already taken that into consideration." Rising to his feet, he made his way over to Karramis and took hold of her chin with his thumb and index finger, forcing her to look up at him. "She's not gettin' away this time."

"Don't fucking touch her," Will warned, struggling under Leif's grip.

"Oh," Lucas said with a snicker as he faced him, "I already have."

Glaring, Will announced, coolly and confidently, "I will kill you one of these days."

"Highly unlikely, mate." Pivoting, he turned, returning his attention to Karramis. "Now then, where were we? Oh, yes." He snapped his fingers. "Leif, if ya will. I believe it's time to begin. Merrick will wanna answer once he arrives."

Leif released Will with a shove to the back of his neck, strolling over to Karramis and grasping the metal chains of her cuffs and yanking her to her feet. The motion made her wince, a muffled groan coming in unison at the harsh tug against her wrists and abrupt movement forcing her to her feet. Pain shot through her knees, the combination of the pressure of her weight releasing against the joints and the awkward angle of her ascent making the bones pop and muscles strain.

"No burning through these," Leif said as he yanked on the chains again, hauling her toward the corner of the room and attaching her iron shackles to a set of chains hanging on the wall, the metal links attached securely to the stone interior.

Reaching behind, Leif pulled a torn piece of black cloth from his back pocket and lifted it to her mouth, but she jerked her head sideways. He clasped a hand around her neck and drove her into the wall, her body smacking against the stones.

Will moved, trying to stand, but Lucas reared back and slammed a fist into Will's face. His head jerked to the side as the impact sounded through the room. His body toppled over, and his palms slapped into the warm stones.

Karramis yanked on her chains. "Will!" The metal rattled again as she landed a challenging gaze on the vampire, his hand still tight around her neck. "Let me go."

Hot breath coasted across her face, his lips stopping at her ear. "No." The self-assured smirk returned to his face. Dangling the cloth in front of her face, he added, "Now, open that pretty little mouth of yours before you regret it."

Another grunt came from Will, but Leif was blocking her view, the added sound of a thwack coming in unison.

"Lucas!" Karramis stared Leif down, disregarding his threat as she continued to address Lucas with ire in the tone. "What the hell are you doing?"

"Taking back what's mine." Lucas's voice was throaty and raw.

Not this again, this incessant need to take back something that was never his. But before she could respond, the fingers wrapped around her neck closed, restricting her airflow.

Her gargled gasp and choking expelled from her throat.

"She's not yours," Will objected, emboldened by a wave of adrenaline. "She's fucking mine."

Will was on his feet ready to throw a blow, but Lucas twisted just in time to evade the punch, dodging and pivoting at the right moment. Fisting his hand, he rammed it into Will's abdomen. Lucas's eyes blazed with possessive anger at Will's words just as the air whooshed from Will's lungs.

"Open, witch," Leif demanded.

Her breaths came quick and shallow as she cracked her lips apart, tears welling in her eyes. Air sucked in as Leif dropped his hand to take hold of the other side of the cloth.

Sliding the material between her lips, his eyes alight with something carnal and dominant, the vampire added smoothly, "Good girl."

Another punch landed, this one splitting open skin and blood rising to the surface as the momentum of the blow twisted Will sideways. Will licked the warmth from his mouth as a steel-toed boot struck the side of his leg, hard, driving him down to his knees with a heavy thud.

Anger and defeat surged through Karramis as she fought against the gag being placed into her mouth. Leif jerked her around and pressed her front into the wall, fastening the cloth behind her head. Karramis grunted in protest under the binding preventing her from speaking. Heat swelled in her hands and radiated against the rough metal.

"What's the matter?" Leif ventured, turning her to face the others and inclining his body closer to her, condescension dripping from his tone. "Does that pretty little mouth of yours have something to say?" He traced a finger over her bottom lip, and she quickly jerked away from his touch. "Well, too bad. You're not ruining anything this time. If you can't keep your mouth shut, I'll gladly do it for you."

A deep, sadistic laugh filled the room, pulling Karramis's attention back to Lucas and Will.

"Time to watch the show," Leif added as he gripped her hair along the back of her head, making sure she was in the direct line of sight of the others.

"Ya shoulda died a long time ago," Lucas announced bitterly. Heavy footfalls circled around Will as he panted for breath, the bruises deepening along his face. "That arrow was meant for you, not her. But no, she had to go and fuck it all up—get in the goddamn way."

Karramis recoiled, and her eyes went wide at the admission.

Lucas had been the one who shot the arrow that day, the one that nearly killed her. He was the reason she had a hole in her heart and relied on the blood of the dragons to keep her alive. Will had been the target. Lucas had tried to kill him. And if she had not stepped in the way at that exact moment, Will would not be here today.

Lucas landed another blow to the face, his quick reflexes and powerful strikes never allowing Will to counter the attack. "You were neva' supposed to live—ya were supposed to die. Ya weren't allowed to steal her away from me." A hard kick to the stomach. "Did ya really think ya could take what belongs to me and get away with it?"

Lucas struck him again and again, fists colliding with Will's face a few more times before another kick landed against his ribs.

Karramis screamed, her muffled pleas going unnoticed as Lucas circled around Will again, who was now hunched over on all fours.

Taking in a ragged inhale, Will managed, "She's not some chattel or toy, you bloody prat."

Lucas!

His name rang out in her mind, but it never reached its mark, her thoughts not being focused on by Lucas. He was inside Will's head, anticipating his every move.

Lucas grabbed Will's hair and yanked his head back, forcing his eyes to him. He lowered his voice, the next words only for him. "No, she's not. But she *is* mine."

"You're fucking mad." Will spit in Lucas's face, the saliva and blood slapping against his cheek and dripping from his chin. "And she will never be yours."

Eyes emitting hatred and fury widened with intent as he yanked harder on Will's hair. Lucas turned menacingly toward Karramis, gradual and determined. Focused. His unnerving gaze searched her face, analyzing her, deciphering her. Decoding her in the only way he could—through her mannerisms, her expressions. Through her thoughts.

She shook her head, her own gaze stark with warning. *"Don't. Don't do it. If you touch him—"*

"What?" He prowled toward her a few steps, his sneer cold and dark. He removed a pocketknife from his pants and sliced through the cloth. "What're ya gonna do, love?"

Dread and hostility warred inside her, fighting for dominance. This unbridled battle between her frightened and anxious side was now plagued with reluctance—the basic animalistic nature to never taunt a hungry beast—and the relentless, determined side of her that wanted to fight, the side that wanted to be ruthless and vengeful, if it meant saving the one she loved. The latter rose to the surface, the restraint she held on to falling to the wayside as her mind and heart joined forces, all logic leaving her body, the rational side of her disappearing completely.

"You're dead," she said, her jaw tight and her eyes blazing with a heated threat, sounding nothing short of a woman in love, sure and absolute. "Touch him again, and I will fucking kill you. Past be damned. Duties be damned."

A chuckle rumbled up his chest, his darkness flicking back to the cool, collected side as a flash of arrogance filtered into his features. "Is that a fact?"

"No." Brown eyes stared into his, the glare burrowing deep and taking root. "A fact is something that has already occurred. No, that was a threat—a promise."

Lucas clicked his tongue against his teeth. "I thought ya neva' make a promise ya can't keep."

"I don't."

"Well, challenge accepted, love." His gaze flicked to Will, who was clutching his stomach, and over to Leif. "Bind him." The corner of his mouth lifted and aimed at Karramis. "And release her."

"No," Will countered with a strain in his voice followed by a guttural cough as he fought to stand.

Leif closed the distance and lifted Will by the arm, moving him toward the opposite side of the room to another set of chains and iron cuffs hanging off the wall. He shackled Will, taking in the Drolnogard's weakened state and battered face before strutting over to Karramis and unbinding her with amusement and excitement clear in his expression.

A dull ache throbbed along Karramis's wrists as the bindings lay at her feet. Skepticism and apprehension pinched her features as she eyed everyone in the room.

"What is all of this?" she asked curiously, bewildered by this ongoing game, rubbing her wrists and zeroing in on the knife still in Lucas's hand.

Lucas followed her gaze, closing the pocketknife and tossing it across the room, the sound of it hitting the floor almost like an alarm blaring, a warning of sorts. "Ya wanted to fight, so let's fight."

"No," Will protested, the pain in his voice matching his hunched-over body.

"You"—Lucas pointed at him—"shut the hell up."

Eyes watery from the constant blows to the face, Will pleaded, "Karramis, don't do—"

"I said shut the fuck up!"

Leif laughed quietly to himself, taking up a spot against the wall and enjoying the show entirely.

"C'mon, love," Lucas said more calmly. "Ya wanted a fight, so here's your chance." He circled around her.

Karramis countered his steps, never allowing him to get behind her or too close. "I'm not fighting you, Lucas. I'm far more powerful than you."

He monitored her, the way she carefully scoured the room and observed every square inch of the space, every exit. Every person and their demeanor. Her thoughts may be silent now, but Lucas knew her well enough to know she was not going down without causing a lot of trouble along the way.

"No, no," he countered. "No magic. No weapons. No tricks. Just you and me, fair and square. Equally matched."

Karramis continued to mirror his movements perfectly. "That seems to be balanced more in your favor. I highly doubt this would be fair. As you mentioned before, you're a trained fighter."

"So be it, then." He pointed to the pocketknife across the room. "To make things more evenly matched, I will allow ya one weapon. But no magic."

Strategy was in play, her mind scrounging to find some sort of escape route. "And what makes you think I will fight fair and stick to these rules?" Her question was a distraction, a way to give herself more time.

"You're forgettin' I know ya all too well, love. Your word is your honor."

"Not to mention," Leif added, his stance relaxed against the wall, "you wouldn't jeopardize him." His chin lifted toward Will. "You would never violate the agreement or even dare to try to escape with him acting as collateral."

They both had her there, but it was more of what Leif said that settled like a rock in her stomach. She would never actively put Will in danger or risk them taking him away. They could not be separated again.

But she also doubted her ability to fight Lucas. Even with the months of training, she still only believed her skills could be enough to counter an attack, a defensive tactic rather than an offensive one. Lucas was fast and cunning, and he had impressive reflexes and an innate way of reading an opponent, even without his magic.

"And what's the point of all of this?" Karramis queried, genuinely curious at the reasoning for this dramatic turn of events and this never-ending, and seriously unnecessary and immature, mind game.

"The point is," Lucas answered, "that if ya win, ya can walk out of here freely. You will be released from your obligations to Merrick."

Ignoring the fact that she had already held up her end of the deal, a fact she kept to herself, she declared, "I'm not leaving without my husband."

His expression creased with annoyance. "Well, that's not up to ya now, is it?"

"I'm not leaving here without Will," she announced adamantly, each word precise, the edges landing hard against their target.

She did not necessarily want to piss him off, but her patience was thinning and the anxiousness bubbling up inside her was starting to morph into stubbornness, the need to challenge him. Test him just as he had with her. It was a toxic trait of hers—giving in to the bratty side of her personality, the one who tested her limits. This was the side who controlled her mouth. The side that often got her into trouble.

Her eyes widened as Lucas crowded her with his body as he pushed her backward, the movement seeming to take forever as they crossed the room. Her back slammed into the stone wall as his hand wrapped around her neck, his fingers not constricting but secure. His grip forced her head upward, and they peered at one another.

Lucas scowled down at her. "Those lips belong to me, so ya will not speak anotha' man's name—" He cut himself off as Karramis rolled her eyes. He cocked his head slightly, the action purposeful and predatory. His gripped tightened. "You're tryin' to get under my skin again." He tsked, the sound grating against her nerves.

"No, I'm not," Karramis admitted truthfully. "I'm just tired of this game. It's tedious, and frankly a bit foolish. You're wasting your time here."

Leif snickered. "You're one crazy bitch, you know that?"

Struggling against Lucas's grip, she shifted her eyes sideways. "Say it again, but this time put a little more emotion into it. I don't think it had the effect you were hoping for."

Will grunted as his feet shuffled. "Let her—"

"Shut up," Lucas barked.

Leif sauntered over toward them, disregarding Will, his blue eyes on Karramis. "I'm going to take great pleasure in murdering you, witch, when the time comes." His fingers tapped against Lucas's shoulder, the silent communication conveying a shift in control.

Lucas retreated away as Leif slipped in between them, both sets of eyes never leaving Karramis.

Trailing a finger along her collarbone not covered by her sweater, he continued, hunger and malice in his tone, "The pure satisfaction and glorious euphoria of draining the life from your body while you writhe beneath me has been a fantasy of mine for a *very* long time."

That was both highly amusing and yet equally repulsive, the imagery of his words floating into her head. "Wow, I'm not sure what to do with that, but I'm flattered you fantasize about me. Just make sure you draw it out a bit. Savor it. I mean, you don't want to jump right into it too quickly and ruin it prematurely."

His warm breath blew across her face. "Oh, I'm definitely going to enjoy every second of it."

Not sure why, but she decided to poke the beast. "Seconds, huh? Can't even last a full minute, Leif?" She curled her bottom lip, giving him a faux pout. "Too bad."

Air slammed into her as he zoomed to the other side of the room, striking Will across the jaw, another split slicing into his lip.

"I swear, I'm going to slaughter you," she declared, her voice calm and controlled, even if she appeared crazed. "And I'm going to make sure it hurts. I'm going to make you beg for me to stop. And I'm sure as hell going to make you scream the entire time."

He was back in front of her, the strands of hair around her face blowing wildly as she blinked, the sudden onset of wind drying out her eyes.

"My, such a naughty, delicious mouth." He lifted a hand, but she jerked away from his touch. But he grabbed at her, tightly cupping her jaw and holding her head in place while his thumb traced her bottom lip. "I bet you're mighty talented with it." He tossed a mocking gaze over at Lucas. "Is she? Oh, that's right, you wouldn't know." Eyes settled back on her. "Well, I'd love to try out this beautiful, wicked thing . . . just once. Watch you choke before I drain the life from your body very, *very* slowly."

"Fuck you," she scoffed.

"Now, that can be arranged as well—I mean, if you're offering. I'd love to get a taste, a feel, of that fire inside you."

She spit in his face. "In your fucking dreams."

He wiped his face, amused by her antics. "Well, I've never been particularly interested in the whole spitting thing. No, but I would definitely consider doing *your* kink . . ." He choked her and she gagged. "If you do *mine*." He glanced back at Lucas, who appeared oddly entertained by their interaction. "Care to watch?"

"Ya know I don't share, mate."

Leif stepped back, feigning disappointment. "Fair enough."

Karramis was getting whiplash from these two. It was like two sets of men with two completely different sides to them. It was not only confusing, but it was extremely unnerving. She never knew which pair was going to show up. One minute it was two evil villains, dark and malicious. Then she was dealing with one good and one bad, the devil and angel, the contradicting personalities a constant back and forth between them. And now, it was two morally decent guys, yet slightly demented, having a jolly good time with their salacious behaviors, joking displays, and carefree, rakish comments. It was absolutely tiring trying to gauge the constant shift of her surroundings.

The only thing she was certain of was that she had to get Will out of here. He was badly injured, and he was definitely in no shape to fight to protect her, let alone defend himself. The only plan she had solidified was getting him out of here. Come hell or high water, he was a priority.

It could not be that hard, right? She had escaped them before.

And despite the unpredictable nature of her portal, she had been practicing, taking her time to master her ability to transport someone else without the use of a spell. Will had gone through without any consequences once, maybe there would not be an issue having him go through again. Maybe she should have practiced it with him before today, but she did not know Merrick would require him to go too. That thought still ate at her. The fact that she missed the careful verbiage he spewed to trap both her and Will into protecting their children for as long as possible. And now look at them—Will was hanging on by a thread, something she blamed herself for, while she struggled to figure out why she was here. What was in store for her by the end of all this? Lucas had said he wanted to take back what was his, but what did he mean by that? Why was she the focal point of what happened to them?

The answers to these were neither here nor there at this point, though. She had to get Will out of here, first and foremost, and get him the medical attention he needed. She would worry about herself later, once he was safe.

But as the plan she had been contemplating formed in her mind, the pieces coming together, fear forced her eyes to widen. All optimism drained from her body along with the blood in her face as she spotted Merrick at the door, his hair freshly washed and wearing an entirely new black outfit, smiling over at her . . .

And holding her father's severed head in his hand.

Chapter 15

Brazen Beauty

"Have the festivities commenced?" Merrick teased, pale blue eyes trailing over the room. "Or am I too late?"

Pain-fueled, heartbreaking anger flooded Karramis, the agony at the sight of her father's head hanging loosely at Merrick's side like a stab to her chest.

The dark discoloration along the ripped skin at the base of her father's neck held the last remaining remnants of blood. His skin was ashen, the gray coloring almost matching the silvery strands gripped in Merrick's hand. Silver-blue eyes rested open behind a film of glossy white haze.

Karramis swallowed down the bile threatening to flow from her mouth as a sob lodged in her chest. Desperation clung to her as she tried to hold herself together.

"You fucking sick bastard," she delivered around the burn in her throat and sting in her eyes, allowing the anger to show through rather than the dejection taking root.

Leif held back a laugh at her boldness, reveling in the way Merrick turned a sharp-eyed and merciless gaze toward her.

"Well, that was rather rude," Merrick chastised mockingly, his demeanor relaxed in spite of the slight bite to his tone. "But I will choose to disregard that insolent, uncouth mouth of yours, considerin' your current predicament, and simply presume an apology is forthcomin'."

Enraged shock tore through her. The nerve of this man, so shameless and bold. "You have my dad's head in your hand," she shot back impetuously, it taking everything in her to not look down at her father or show anything other than the wrath she felt. "You burned down my fucking home, you tricked me, you kidnapped my sister, you are part of the reason why my husband is bleeding over in the corner, you want to kill my children . . . and you have the audacity to *presume* I owe *you* an apology." Condescension dripped from the final part of her recap of the events having played out recently. All civility drained away as she tossed him a heated glare. Standing her ground, she continued, the venom in her tone coming out clear and drawn out, "I don't owe you shit."

This time Leif coughed out a laugh, his fist lifting to stifle it as Lucas came up behind her and gently pulled her behind him. There was something gallant about his actions. Protective and noble.

Merrick inclined his head ever so slightly and lifted an imperious brow as he regarded Lucas for a beat. "Your proclivity to love this woman is astonishin', Mr. Fraye." Fixing Karramis with a cold, vacant glare, he went on, "I find it both romantic and repulsive. Such a complicated thing—love. There's a hinderance to it. A fault in any way you perceive it. You either love to hate it or hate to love it. And yet, either way, someone always winds up heartbroken in the end." He strolled over to the fire pit in the center of the room. "Case in point . . ."

Merrick lifted his arm, exaggerated and deliberate, as Zarrius's head dangled from his fingers over the flames. Observing with rapt curiosity, he monitored Karramis as all the color drained from her face.

Her shoulders sagged, defeat and a silent plea washing over her. Steady heartbeats began to pound harder, the blood rushing through her veins.

Merrick's hunger burned in his stomach, the thirst building with a rapid and mouthwatering current as her blood raced just below her skin. He could almost taste her, the saccharine, fieriness raging inside her—this perfect mixture of caramelized sugar, toasted vanilla, and campfire smoke with a hint of something exotic and rare like saffron and aged spiced rum. Her blood was definitely unique and the most succulent he had ever encountered—most humans tasting like a glass of fresh, cold ice water on a hot day, and all magical creatures either consisting of the ideal blend of something sweet and salty or sugared spiciness. But not hers. Hers was almost like a drug he just could not wait to taste. And as the anguish, disdain, wrath, and heartbreak grew inside her, it became an almost palpable, mercurial essence filling the room. The fervor, the delicious passion behind it called to him like a siren in the sea.

And he wanted it. He wanted all of it.

Amusement tilted the corner of Merrick's lips upward as he studied her, the ravenous gleam narrowed with resolve and desire. Releasing his hold, Merrick dropped the head into the fire, the sound of flesh singeing and embers crackling following the soft thud of it landing against the burning logs as the last of Zarrius was swallowed by flames.

A sob rose in her chest, but she shoved it down and covered her mouth as her knees buckled, her entire body sagging in grief.

He was gone. Her father was really dead.

It was a realization she knew would hit her eventually, but she hoped it would be with her family around her. She wanted a chance to say goodbye to some part of him—no matter how morbid or strange that sounded. But now there was nothing left of him on this plane of existence. She would never see him again.

Sensing her sullen and forlorn disposition, Lucas surveyed her, the barest hint of emotion flickering in his blue eyes, and for an instant, he seemed human again to her, all traces of evil gone. Nothing but the boy she knew, the one who her father loved like a son, standing before her, the urge to hug, to console her, present in his apologetic expression.

Shaking off the emotions threatening to escape, Karramis wiped away a tear escaping and gliding down her face. Rage and revenge quickly erased the sadness trying to win, and she allowed it. Panic-fueled anger flooded her, the agony of everything happening around her burning like a fire in her veins.

Sensing the shift, Lucas reached out for her, attempting to calm her and prevent whatever she was planning to do.

"Love," he drawled in warning.

The nickname for his wife grated on Will's nerves, giving him a tiny boost of adrenaline. But the languidness sweeping through his body was overwhelming. His shoulders sagged, the energy it took to stay upright becoming more difficult with each passing moment. Everything hurt. His face throbbed and head pounded, and the taste of blood made him want to vomit. But it was his midsection causing the worst of his pain. Not only was it difficult to breathe, but the slightest movement tore through him, the multiple assaults to his abdomen, back, and sides most definitely forming deep bruising along the gnawing tissue and pulsating muscles. And he was convinced one of his ribs was fractured. The worst of it all was not his injuries, but the reality that he could not protect her. The one he swore to himself he would do anything to defend. His wife.

However, Lucas and the others had prepared for her this time, knowing she would have some distraction and escape plan ready to go. Even without Will's too-loud thoughts giving away any predetermined or on-the-fly decisions, it was clear that Lucas knew Karramis almost as well as Will did. And why would he not? He had known her far longer than Will ever would, and her tenacious ways had followed her into adulthood. In fact, it was worse now—the years of all the trauma she faced providing a newfound courage and an indomitable drive to face any challenge head on. It was downright inspiring, but it was also extremely imprudent. And in this case, deadly.

Chest heaving, Will wanted nothing more than to voice his warning to Karramis, to remind her that the prey within the darkness can only remain hidden when silent, but once you draw attention to it, the predator will strike.

But it was too late.

Karramis had crossed the room, her magic vibrating off her, ready to attack. "Enjoy the power now," she seethed, her glare deadly, "because when the prophecy finally comes to slap you in the face, you will be nothing more than dust when it's all over. You *will* die. And I hope—I pray—that I will be here to watch you fucking fall."

There was nothing Will could do. Too many people were between him and his wife. And even if he could reach her, what could he do? His magic was useless here, and despite his years of training to fight, he was just too weak to do anything now. And like Lucas had pointed out and made abundantly clear with the attack Will just suffered through, his inner monologue was just too vocal—the reminder apparent as his and Lucas's eyes met for a split second. In all the years preparing to stand beside his family, to protect and fight until his final breath, Will had never considered he should train his mind, like Karramis did, to become undetectable by Lucas and any other telepath.

Lucas gripped Karramis's wrist and pulled her back a few steps, but this time he did not stand between her and Merrick, allowing Merrick to address the formidable energy coming from him as he clenched his jaw and his glare became lethal.

"So audacious," Merrick said, a tone seeming to stop everyone in their tracks, his entire being radiating with virility as the room became tense. He moved with indolent grace toward Karramis, stopping half an arm's length away from her. "Such candor. So much exuberance and courage." He studied her a moment. "The reverence I have fer you is quite titillatin'." Gentle admiration and sensual energy flowed off him, his tone now relaxed. It made Karramis nervous. "In fact, I find ya absolutely mesmerizin' fer some bizarre reason. And yet . . ." He flashed her a crooked, roguish grin, a hint of pure wickedness present. "Equally as foolish." He gave Lucas a side eye, his silent understanding clear in his expression—*I see it now, she is a wildfire begging to be tamed*—before his attention returned to rest on her again, his closeness causing her to have to glance upward. "And it's the latter you should be cautious with, sweetheart. Or ya might just find me in a rather foul mood. And I can assure you, ya do not want that . . ." He leaned in and whispered, "'cause then I will surely put that mouth of yours to use fer somethin' other than the vitriol you so boldly spew."

Karramis wanted to scoff, wanted to roll her eyes, something she was becoming all too familiar with lately, but she pushed those urges aside and instead delivered a retort to his lascivious comment. "Well, that seems to be a rather redundant and perverse theme today."

Merrick inclined his head and arched a suggestive brow at her as he took in her pink, plump, and perfectly pouty lips, a flash of interest shining in his eyes. "It is a very lovely mouth, if ya ask me." He wanted to trace a finger over it but resisted the urge. "Would you not agree, Lucas?"

"Yeah, it is," he admitted with a slight bite to his tone. "When she keeps it shut."

"Well, that kind of defeats the purpose," Leif added teasingly just as multiple footsteps pounded up the stairs. "Fuck," he drawled, his lust-filled amusement turning to annoyance in an instant. "Killjoy's here."

Tressa strolled into the room, poised and graceful, with Theseus, the minotaur, and Niko behind her. "What is going on here?" The simple question was delivered with a luscious, silky tone. Dressed in a deep purple gown, flowy and simple, and a black corset, she focused all her attention on Karramis. "What is she doing here?"

Blinking, making sure her eyes were working properly, Karramis stared at the beast behind the beautiful woman with her ample chest falling with an exasperated yet hesitant exhale, something Karramis would ponder in a moment because there was a minotaur standing a few feet away from her. An actual minotaur.

She had heard about Theseus before, of course, but seeing him up close and personal was a whole different reality. She did not know whether to chuckle in disbelief—the fantastical beast proving she, again, was existing in a live-action fairytale like the novels she read, a world many, to this day, still did not know about, let alone believe existed—or pinch herself to make sure she was actually awake, considering most of the last few hours seemed outlandishly perplexing and nothing short of a living nightmare. But this, this was unreal. She had seen many magical beings over the years, but it still surprised her when she came face-to-face with a rare creature. And this one was definitely rare. His stature was monstrous—the irony of that fact not going unnoticed, nor the irony of his name, something Rhiannon often found highly amusing.

Having to stoop to prevent his head from hitting the top of the doorframe, Theseus also had to turn slightly to cross the threshold, his broad shoulders and muscular torso perfectly proportioned with his towering height but just a bit too wide for the narrow opening. Making a mental note to simmer the emotions boiling over inside her, as to not poke the beast again right now—the multitude of them now in the same room as her and Will pulling her back into the more rational side of her thought process—Karramis studied the room, gauging her surroundings in an observant and strategic manner.

The man she had run into earlier in the hallway with Lucas was far less intimidating standing next to the giant half-man, half-beast, but both towered ridiculously taller behind the curvy and absolutely gorgeous woman with smooth, tanned skin waiting utterly dignified and statuesque a few feet inside the door. Karramis could not be certain, but based on her posture, she could only assume the woman was wearing heels, but the hem of her dress rested just above the stone floor.

"Tressa, dear," Merrick stated sweetly, facing her, "what a pleasant surprise."

Trying to decipher the sincerity in his words, Karramis snuck a peek over at Will. Black and blue colored the left side of his face, and two cuts sliced across the bottom of one side of his mouth. More bruises covered his upper arms, the injuries most likely due to evasive maneuvers causing the blows to strike elsewhere. He was slumped over and leaning against the wall, the fight to remain upright evident on his face. He was in a lot of pain. And based on the way his arms drooped at his sides, no longer cradling his injured midsection, he was also weak—his poor battered and lacerated body struggling to function against the various bruises, soreness, and possibly broken bones.

With the additional threats now in the room, and with Will being on the opposite side, Karramis worried her tactics to get him out of here might not work. But it was still there, just below the surface—her magic. She had kept it calm and steady, taking every emotion she was feeling and controlling it, keeping it in check, until it was time. And based on the realization all the delays over the last few hours were due to Merrick and his desire to be present for some reason, she could conclude, whatever was supposed to happen would be presenting itself shortly.

"To what do I owe the pleasure?" Merrick asked Tressa, drawing Karramis back into the conversation.

Clasping her hands together in front of her, Tressa offered, her even-keeled disposition and feminine energy presenting an air of credence about her, "I was simply curious as to why she is here? You can't possibly think you can keep her contained for an entire month." Her dark brown eyes flicked to Karramis, fast yet purposeful. "And pardon my transgression, but she has proven to have the fortitude for . . ." She paused, ruminating a way to end her sentence. "Removing herself from a difficult situation."

Merrick considered, the careful scrutinizing of the woman blanketing the room in silence, thick and taut. It was obvious their affiliation with one another was not so evenly matched as Karramis originally thought. There was a hierarchy here, an order of authority that was palpable.

"Apologies," Tressa presented, lowering her gaze for half a second, submitting to Merrick's silent show of dominance. "I may have spoken out of turn. However, I do recall you mentioning a change in plans. And . . ." Hesitating, she blinked before asking. "If I may speak freely?"

Merrick inclined his head indiscernibly. "Proceed."

"I still have not been privy to those details. So, I am simply requesting an update, especially since it would appear a crucial part of *our* agreement is currently standing before me utterly stupefied and completely out of her element. It's as though she's a lamb waiting to be slaughtered." Two sets of dark brown eyes stared back at one another. "No offense, dear."

Dear? The way she said that, with such a matriarchal and superior intonation, was strange. This woman could not be much older than her. Maybe mid to late forties. Definitely no older than fifty. Karramis knew she was technically in her early forties, but not aging the last eight years made her appear younger, but still, being called *dear* in such a condescending way by a peer was irritating and equally confusing.

And what did this woman mean by all of that? Why was Karramis again part of another agreement with Merrick? And who was this woman exactly? Karramis knew the name, but other than being a witch, she did not know much about Tressa.

Swallowing down every retort, every question burning a hole in her mind and threatening to escape, Karramis concentrated on her surroundings. On every person—how far apart they were from each other, their mannerisms, their energy, how far away they were from the open area on the opposite side of the room, who they were watching. On Will and how he was also analyzing the room, taking in every factor standing between him and her. On how the flames continued to burn in the sunken fire pit, the vibration of energy coming from the element comforting. The huge, arched window with no glass—the only exit other than the door. But they were hundreds of feet off the ground. That kind of fall would be deadly.

Tressa's movement drew Karramis's attention back toward the group, the woman's body language becoming tense and hostile. Bewilderment and annoyance flashed in the woman's gaze as her stance widened and her arms crossed.

Shit! What had Karramis missed?

Everyone else seemed completely rapt in the conversation between Merrick and Tressa. Everyone except Lucas, who was watching Karramis with a keen eye and knowing smirk.

He shook his head, the warning expression fixed on her before it turned toward Will then back to her, the implication clear.

A sickening twist churned in her stomach.

Lucas had his sights set on Will—a target firmly planted on her husband's back if she tried anything.

"I don't understand," Tressa announced dryly, clearly trying to understand whatever she had been informed of.

"Oh, my dear Tressa, it's quite simple," Merrick declared unapologetically as he stood with his hands clasped behind his back, his posture completely relaxed. "Our agreement is null and void. Ya see, it would appear a more advantageous opportunity arrived after the discovery of the children's additional abilities. And so, I decided to offer up an alternative arrangement with both Leif and Lucas here."

"And that would be?"

"Well, I'm not exactly at liberty to answer at the moment."

"And why's that?"

Merrick scowled at her tone, the ploy to get the upper hand of the conversation, to pull every detail from him, irritating him. "Are you questionin' me?"

"No," Tressa said timidly, realizing her mistake. "Of course not." Her shoulders slouched ever so softly before pulling them back, the confidence returning. "I just feel if you're going to alter our deal—"

"The deal I made with you was that I would not take her life until the ritual. But if Lucas here accepts the revised agreement in regards to the Fire Witch, then *I* most definitely will not be the person at fault fer takin' her life."

Nausea rumbled in Will's gut, and he had to fight back the bitter taste of bile creeping up his throat.

They were going to kill Karramis.

Will had realized the probability of it happening was high due to the nature of tonight's events, but hearing it firsthand was gut-wrenching. He had continued to hold on to the hope that they would have to wait for the next full moon, or that Lucas would never allow them to hurt her. Even though Lucas had made a habit out of doing that himself, and he even came close to killing her twice now in his fits of rage. But the idea of Lucas being part of a well-thought-out plan to actually murder the woman he claimed to love seemed highly unlikely. Because despite Will loathing the man and thinking he was certifiably insane, Lucas did seem to love his wife—even if it was in his own eccentric, extreme, unhealthy, and delusional way.

Will shifted against the wall and forced himself to stand upright. His gaze flicked to Karramis, and almost as if she could sense his eyes watching her, she glanced over at him smoothly, being careful not to draw attention to herself.

"Run," Will mouthed, a desperate plea creased into his features.

She shook her head, the movement subtle but the certainty was there. She was not going to leave him here to defend himself.

The stubborn woman.

"You need her magic," Tressa whispered as she stepped into Merrick. "She's a lot more powerful than—"

The flames in the fire pit exploded upward, the sudden onslaught of heat, smoke, and harsh cracking startling everyone in the room.

Merrick had finally showcased his fire abilities in front of Tressa, his control of the flames effortless. He was not even facing them, but his palms were up at his sides, the manipulation of the element flowing from his hands.

"When did you get fire magic?" Tressa asked coolly.

"That's all you have to say?" Merrick asked, almost offended by her nonchalant disposition.

"Congratulations." There was very little emotion in her flat statement.

"Ya seem rather indignant, my dear. I was under the impression you would be elated by this discovery."

"Not at all," she said completely monotone as she fought the urge to grin.

There were days when she loved testing him, but today was even more satisfying. He had used his play on words against her. A mistake she would have to deal with. But still, she wanted it rectified. And so, she would see just how far she could push him.

She knew Theseus and Niko would protect her, their loyalty bound to her and her alone.

Annoyed, he asked, "To bein' indignant or elated?"

Tressa pulled in a deep breath, the exhale sounding petulant. "May we talk in private?"

"Whatever for?" he accosted coyly.

"Don't play dumb, Merrick. There are matters we need to discuss here . . ." Dark brown skimmed over the room, landing for a moment on Karramis. "And the audience seems to be dealing with other matters."

The boldness of this woman was something Karramis admired. Even though she was certain Tressa feared Merrick, she still stood her ground. Something she had to believe Merrick valued about the woman, since she was still standing. Maybe that is why Merrick admired Karramis as well—because of this woman. Or maybe it was because Merrick loved a challenge. Either way, the respect was there as Karramis took notes. Even the slightest action could be beneficial moving forward and getting out of here alive.

However, based on the look on Merrick's face, the same look he gave Karramis just a short time ago—a look of pure evil and hunger—she concluded that he most likely enjoyed the thrill of the hunt rather than her previous assumptions.

"Niko. Theseus," Merrick said, the authoritative cadence firm as he glared at Tressa. "If you would so kindly remove my dear Tressa here from my premises and escort her to my chambers, I would greatly appreciate it." Addressing Tressa, he said, "This matter will be discussed at a future time. You are dismissed fer now."

Tressa did not move, the protest on the tip of her tongue.

"Tressa." Merrick casually strolled toward her. "Did ya have somethin' else to say?"

"That depends," she snarked.

"Pray tell."

"On whether or not I will be allowed to keep my tongue afterward or be able to walk out of here in one piece."

Gesturing with his hand, palm up toward the ceiling, he offered, "Speak."

Exhaling, she said matter-of-factly, "You're making a mistake."

"Pardon me?" He was so calm and relaxed it was unnerving.

"With her." She nodded to Karramis.

"I will take that into consideration. Anything else?"

Pivoting around, Tressa's heels clanked against the stone floor, somehow acting as the silent cursing she wanted to deliver, before twisting back around, a hand flying to her hip. "Yes. When can I expect you? I don't want to be waiting all morning."

His eyes narrowed in irritation, the anger coming off him undeniable, but he replied calmly, "You will wait until I deem to grace you with my presence."

"Very well, then," she said, turning on her heels and strutting through the door behind Niko and Theseus.

"Oh . . ." Merrick followed a few steps behind her. "And Tressa?" He stopped, waiting for her to face him. When she did, he added darkly, "Disrespect me like that again, and you won't live to see another full moon. Understood?"

"Yes."

"Yes, what?"

"Yes, Merrick. I understand."

"Good." He flicked his wrist. "Dismissed."

"Hey, Merrick," she uttered from the top of the landing.

His blue eyes focused on her, but Merrick remained quiet. He had a way of showing stoic patience. A hidden strength to wait, to manipulate a situation with silent intimidation.

When he did not speak, sensing his defiance, she continued, again poised and confident, "In a room of many, it's the quiet one you should always be cautious of. Be careful, Merrick. You're not the only one with teeth." Her gaze landed on Karramis. "Never underestimate the silent opponent, for they only speak when they are about to win the game. Good luck."

Karramis was unsure if that last part was for her or Merrick, but as Tressa descended the stairs, all eyes landed on her.

Chapter 16

Element of Surprise

Had Tressa known Karramis was planning to fight, to try to escape again? Or was it simply a ploy to remove all attention from herself as she bounded down the stairs, the annoyance and disgruntled energy rolling off her in waves.

And what deal had Tressa and Merrick made? And why? Why was she the focal point of yet another agreement despite Merrick clearly already having fire magic? Was it her portal magic he wanted? Or maybe her Guardian powers? She remembered how Merrick had tried to take Guardian magic before from Adalaide Stowe—her however many times great-grandmother—but it had somehow backfired on him, causing Merrick to never try it again with any other Guardian. But maybe because her magical link to the portals and the island were weaker, he wanted to try again with her. Or was it something else? Was it because her own fire magic was like her mother's? Being able to summon it at will without the aid of the element actually being nearby. Based on what Karramis had witnessed at the cabin, it was clear Merrick's fire magic was on the simpler and less advanced side of the ability, only able to control and manipulate it and not create it. But why was her magic so coveted in particular? Especially since Merrick already had fire powers and some control over the portals. And why did Tressa care?

But as the thoughts floated around inside her head, Karramis considered something—Merrick never really wanted her magic. It was obvious in not only his lack of interest when Tressa brought it to his attention, but it was also something Karramis slowly began to understand throughout the last few hours' events. There was something else happening here. Something that revolved heavily around Lucas and whatever decision he had to make. Something, Karramis realized, would end in Will's death, no matter what outcome came to pass regarding herself. Lucas wanted Will out of the picture. For good. And this was the only way he knew how to do it. And after Merrick's conversation with Tressa, the odds did not look good in Karramis's favor either—her life was on the line too. And by the look on Merrick's and Leif's faces at the moment, a gleam of anticipation and a desired thirst beaming over at her, they were awaiting the moment Lucas finally made his decision.

Welcoming the heat in the room, Karramis pushed aside the chill creeping into her body, the spine-tingling crawling sensation trailing up her back and the gut-twisting trepidation surging through her veins.

Just breathe. And think.

A small furrow appeared between her brows, faint and discreet. But the act did not escape Will's notice. He had been watching her carefully since he retreated against the wall, the other's paying him no mind—out of sight, out of mind. But he knew, in this moment, she was going for it. His wife was about to do something equally foolish and extraordinary. But more than anything, he knew she was about to cause some serious problems for them, something he had learned was her go-to for kicking things into gear and allowing herself the adrenaline rush she needed to rise to the occasion. And in doing so, would raise hell while doing it.

Lifting her arm, Karramis flicked open her hand, her fingers splaying outward—

Without hesitation, Lucas moved, fast and efficient, and lifted the hem of Leif's shirt, removing the vampire's dagger and flinging it at Will in one fell swoop as Lucas twisted toward the Drolnogard.

Karramis moved on reflex as her telekinetic powers reacted, her hand flying out and shoving the dagger sideways with an invisible swipe.

Will ducked, realizing his mistake just in time. But as the dagger clanked to the floor, he let out a relieved exhale.

That was too close.

Storming across the room, Lucas wrapped a hand around Will's throat, lifting him upright and slamming the back of his head against the wall. "Ya should really work on that, mate."

Fire soared through the room from the fire pit and sailed into her open palm. The flame grew hotter, stronger—the calm blaze building to an inferno, engulfing her hand and trailing up along her forearm.

"Let him go." The command was nonnegotiable but steady. Her determined gaze flicked between the three men staring emotionless and uninterested at her, as if she was not at all threatening and they were unaffected by her magic or antics. "Let. Him. Go."

"No," Lucas said with equal parts arrogant charm and sweet innocence. "Why don't ya make me."

"If you insist."

The fire grew, reaching upward as Merrick and Leif watched, immersed in the scene, enthralled by the heated display of dominance and tenacity spewing from Karramis. She saw it then, the lack of concern. They did not see her as a threat.

"Cheating now, are we, witch?" Leif taunted.

A cold, deadly stare landed on him. "Fine," she conceded, her arms dropping to her sides as the fire in her hands vanished and the flames in the pit slowed to a gentle roar again. Spacing her feet shoulder-width apart, she readied her stance. "Let's play fair."

"No," Will protested faintly under Lucas's choking grip.

Lucas squeezed and turned a hard glare toward him. "What's the matter? Afraid I'll beat her? Or are ya ashamed it's her doin' the fightin'?" His body leaned in, his face stopping inches from

Will as his voice lowered. "You're pathetic. How she ever chose you ova' me, I'll neva' understand."

"Lucas," Karramis warned firmly.

Merrick and Leif both moved toward the wall near the door, both leaning casually as if settling in for front row seats of what was about to take place.

Focus. Play this right.

This was her best option. With Merrick and Leif letting their guard down to enjoy the show, and Lucas rising to the challenge—thus removing Will from his literal death grip—this was the best logical plan. The only problem was, she had to again rely on her wits, brute strength, and cunningness. Magic would, most likely, cause the others to step in, and with their speed, that would be deadly.

Staring at her, Lucas lifted both hands in the air in faux surrender as Will coughed and rubbed his neck.

Rearing back, Lucas slammed a fist into Will's stomach, the sound of the impact just as loud as the grunt expelling from Will.

"Lucas!" Her anger permeated the space, sucking all the oxygen from the room as she charged forward, her feet acting on their own accord, her fight instincts taking over. "What the hell?"

"For good measure," he admitted with a grin.

Karramis did not slow as she closed the space between them, gripping his collar—just now noticing the material of a sweater clutched in her hands. When had he removed his coat? Probably before he started to attack her husband. Focusing, she pushed him back and slammed him hard against the wall, his back slapping against the stones.

"My, you've gotten a tad bit stronger," he said with a chuckle. "I like it."

She landed a punch to his jaw, the surprise on his face by her swift and imperceptible movements making his eyes go wide.

Pain shot through her knuckles and surged down her hand. She would never get over the agony of punching someone in the face. It really freaking hurt. Bad.

He laughed and opened his mouth, popping his jaw. "Ooh," he cooed. "Well, well, well, very nice, love. It would seem that strength came with some new skills. It seems someone's been trainin' ya." Blue eyes shifted to Will, catching his slow advancements toward them. "Nuh-uh-uh," he tsked. "You stay put." His gaze returned to rest on her again. "This is a lover's spat." He winked before shoving the palms of his hands against her midsection, the force behind it causing her to release his shirt and stumble backward and lose her footing.

She landed with a thud on her back as a grunt burst from her. His weight pressed into her and urged her hips hard against the floor.

Straddling her, he pinned her arms beside her head. "I see your still not up to par on your defenses, though. Clumsy as always. Looks like ya still need some more trainin', love. I can teach ya."

She bucked but the action was futile just as the weight of Lucas disappeared, followed by Will hurtling himself into

Lucas's side. They both landed hard against the stones, Lucas taking the brunt of the tumble.

Rushing to her feet, Karramis got to Will as movement flashed in her peripheral. Her palm flew up, the blur becoming visible as she stopped Leif in his tracks.

"No fucking cheating," she scolded mockingly.

"Nice reflexes," Will admired, the two of them standing upright as Merrick's laugh rang out, the amusement disconcerting.

The pain coursing through Will was excruciating, his body screaming in protest. But a sliver of adrenaline kept him upright as he moved Karramis behind him, shielding her and backing them both toward the wall.

"Bitch," Leif snapped, the insult deep and guttural in his chest as he remained stuck behind a solid, invisible partition of power.

"Stand down, Leif," Lucas said, the irritation and anger present in his furrowed brow and darkened gaze as he rose to his feet and dusted himself off.

Leif retreated but not before strutting over and picking up his dagger, eyeing Karramis the whole time as he returned to his place next to Merrick.

The muscles along Lucas's shoulders pulled against the fabric of his long-sleeve sweater. Tension strained against the thick material, taut and rigid, just like his expression, and his voice as he muttered to Will, "Move."

"Fuck off," Will argued. "I'm not moving. If you want her, you're going to have to go through me."

"That's the plan."

"He has nothing to do with this," Karramis pointed out behind her husband.

"But he does, love," Lucas said smoothly, the arrogance coming off him in heated waves. "He has everythin' to do with this. And ya know it."

The way he said that sent every part of her on alert.

"Leif," Lucas called, the tone relaying an unspoken command.

Facing the door slightly, Lucas lifted a hand just in time to catch the dagger Leif had tossed in the air, the motion of the two men flawless and perfectly in sync—the expert flick of Leif's wrist sending the blade rotating before the hilt landed just right in Lucas's open palm.

"Don't," Karramis rushed out, moving herself in front of Will the moment she realized Lucas's intent.

His predator gaze remained fixed on the desperation and fear in her beautiful, deep brown eyes. "The best way to fix a problem is to remove it."

Karramis shook her head in a mix of warning and plea, her posture matching her expression, unmoving and composed, completely ready to counter his attack.

"There's no stopping it, love." Lifting the dagger, he ran the point of the blade along her jaw, the act sensual. "It's inevitable. This will make things so much easier. On both of us."

"Go to hell," she said tartly.

"I'm already there." There was no anger, no condescension, just raw truth. The blade lowered to her neck, trailing down so deliberately and seductively slow. "But not for long." Lower and lower. "You'll see." It slid between her breasts—

A hand reached around Karramis and snatched Lucas's wrist. Will stepped around her and twisted his arm, driving Lucas to his knees under his hold. But there was no surprise on Lucas's face as he drove a fist into Will's back, connecting with a kidney. Will's body crumbled from the incapacitating strike.

Kicking out a leg, Karramis acted on instinct, putting as much space between Lucas and her husband as she could. And it worked. Lucas flew backward from the powerful thrust, her legs having more force behind an attack than her arms. Her attention jerked upward, mindful of the others, but Merrick and Leif had remained in place.

This time she straddled Lucas, the acrid taste of resentment and ire taking its place in the forefront of her actions. Fists flying, she aimed for his face, but he blocked just as his legs moved behind her, a strange sensation following as she jerked sideways. Her back landed against the floor, and weight crushed against her hips, driving them harder into the stones, pain lacing her sides as Lucas's thighs clamped around her.

Her magic thrummed as the blood in her ears roared. It wanted out. The months of training her powers resulted in an effortless reaction to fight back. But she fought against it. Not yet. She had to release it at the right moment.

So, she looped a foot around Lucas's leg, trying to counter and take the guard, but he slammed a fist against her upper thigh, the nerves going numb as her muscles weakened.

"Don't even try it," he uttered, delight lacing his tone. "Quick thinkin' though. There's hope for ya yet."

On his feet, Will charged forward, but a rush of air swooped around him just as a hand pressed into his chest and he was again against the wall.

"Let mommy and daddy play a bit," Leif said, smirking down at him.

"Fuck off," Will declared, all fear gone.

The flames in the fire pit rose higher, the crackling getting louder. Karramis could not contain it for much longer, the rage, the panic, the dread and the irritation taking over. She was so over this—this stupid, childish game. This constant ploy to control her with threats, fear tactics, and intimidation.

"Karramis, don't do it," Lucas warned gently as he glanced up toward the two men. "Do ya really want to test Leif's patience?"

A fist connected with his face, Karramis providing him with a silent answer, the landed blow surprising even her.

"You're gonna regret that," he seethed, jaw clenched.

She tried to strike him again, just wanting him off of her, but he was faster, taking hold of her wrists. She bucked, trying to hook her foot under him, but he lifted both feet and pinned her legs down, the muscles in his legs proving she was outmatched. Trying a different tactic, she jerked her arms down, driving him forward, but before she could thrust one of her hips to roll him off her, he released her wrists and drove a hand across her face. But she did not give up, she continued to thrash as she shook away the sting along her cheek.

Screw this, she was going to cheat. If it meant getting her out of this position, she would gladly do it. Splaying her hands, she called forth her magic.

"Don't!" Lucas snapped, gripping her wrists again and slamming her arms into the floor, a harsh sting shooting through the back of her hands as they connected with the hard stones. "Stop fuckin' fightin' me!"

"Do you really want me to stop?" she shot back, bitterness and anger burning in her veins.

"Yes!"

"Then you're going to have to fucking kill me!"

The pressure around one wrist loosened just as a deep, gut-wrenching pain smacked through her midsection, Lucas's fist making contact right in the middle of her stomach. The air whooshed out of her, her eyes closing just as Will's voice filtered through the thrumming in her ears, the desperation in the way he called her name forcing power to show itself.

Her power faltered as she gasped in air.

The weight above her shifted, and Lucas pushed to his feet. He seemed remorseful about his actions, the regret in his tone as he said, offering her a hand, "C'mon, love. Get up."

But the softness of his tone was anything but gentle. It was manipulative.

After a few moments, she pressed her hands into the floor and sat up, grasping her stomach.

Lucas squatted down in front of her and ran the back of his finger across her cheek, wiping away the tear that slipped out when he struck her, and brushed the stray strands of hair from her face.

"You'd really die . . ." There was something so kind about his eyes, so much gentle emotion behind his blue gaze, but just as fast as it appeared, he blinked, and the monster controlling him returned. "For him?"

Confused by the strange shift in his personality, she answered honestly. "Yes."

"Why?" Vulnerability and hurt came with the simple question. Again, there was something flickering behind his expression. Something Karramis could not quite understand.

But again, she answered truthfully, allowing her own weakness to shine through. Something she knew was a fine line to cross with Lucas. "Because I would rather die than live another day without him again. Or my kids."

"So, you'd gladly sacrifice yourself . . . for *him*?"

Not wanting to say anything, afraid the answer might set him off, she remained silent.

Spotting her reluctance, he added, "But what if that final breath of yours didn't save him? What if your life was simply a pawn in a game he would neva' win? What then?"

Still she refused to speak, her eyes never faltering from the heat of his gaze, the love and dominance behind it.

"Answer me," he demanded softly.

Exhaling, she said, "Then I'd fight like hell to take down as many of you as I could. If it meant giving him a chance, I'd fight to the death."

He stood, all emotions gone. "Well, I guess that's it, then."

"Meaning what exactly?" Karramis inquired, genuinely curious.

"Leif," Lucas said.

Again, the way he delivered the vampire's name communicated some hidden dialect between them, and by now it was starting to irritate her.

"No," Karramis snapped, refusing to allow them to follow through with whatever they were planning. This was not happening. With Will in a dangerous situation, and Lucas eyeing her husband with satisfaction and raw hatred, she would not take any chances.

It was now or never.

Flames sprouted from under her skin along one hand, the flickering growing as she faced Leif. "Release him and I won't kill you. Yet."

Leif actually had enough sense to appear scared. Or maybe it was just a distraction. Either way, she was going to run with it.

Lucas cleared his throat and stepped in front of her, blocking the vampire from her view. "Why don't ya put out that fire and we can discuss this like civilized people."

Karramis did not miss the patronizing tone as she stole a glance over at Will, bruised and battered, the need to criticize Lucas's use of the word *civilized* on the tip of her tongue.

But instead, she understood when to cut her losses, despite her need to prove she was anything but weak. However, the moment to surrender was now, at least in terms she had full control over. She needed to allow the enemies to think they had the upper hand, that they had won. For now.

Closing her hand, the fire sucking into her skin, Karramis conceded, "Fine."

"Good girl, love," Lucas teased.

"Tell me why we are here," Karramis demanded, paying close attention in her peripheral to how Leif forced Will to the ground, pointing a finger and gesturing him to stay put just before the vampire, too, faced her fully, his strides closing in, his steps barely noticeable as she kept her eyes glued to Lucas.

"I don't feel all the details are necessary," Lucas stated, "but I do feel an explanation of sorts is somethin' fair I could offer ya."

This is what she wanted, to hear whatever plan they had in place for them. To hear exactly why they were here and see what she had to do to prepare. She just hoped after learning the truth, she would have enough time to follow through with the plan she concocted—a plan that would surely get Will killed if she did not plan it just right. A plan that would definitely defeat the purpose as to why she was doing it as Merrick moved closer.

Taking a slight step back, she took in the space, her attention pulling three ways, reminding herself of all the threats in the room. Words clipped, Karramis said, "Stop with the games, Lucas."

"Now, witch," Leif said playfully, "I thought you enjoyed playing games."

They were trying to surround her, trap her.

Her magic hummed to life.

"Nuh-uh," Lucas chastised, followed by a tsking sound. "Don't even think about it, love."

Karramis shrugged dismissively. "I don't know what you're talking about."

"I know you're plannin' somethin'. I can see it all ova' your beautiful yet readable face."

Lucas lifted both hands, the action signaling the other two to stop their movements. Why was he suddenly in control right now? Merrick and Leif had never handed over command so easily. What the hell was going on here?

"Lucas . . . ?" She was not sure what she wanted to ask.

"Yes, love." There was so much conviction behind the way he said that, so much underlying passion.

"What do you want with me?"

"I want you, of course."

"And what about . . ." Karramis did not want to draw attention to Will, but she wanted to know—needed to know. But with her delayed wording and the way she shifted her eyes ever so slightly toward her husband, her actions had delivered the rest of her question.

"Oh, well, he's gonna die," Lucas said casually. "But ya already knew that."

Her eyes widened.

Hearing it out loud was like a punch to her gut and a stab to her heart.

"No matter what happens," Lucas continued, "he will not survive the day." He took a few steps closer. "Ya see, love, the deal is, if I decide I want you, he dies. But if I decide I don't want you, ya both die. Either way, he dies."

She stared into his cold, callous eyes before slapping him across the face, the strike coming as a surprise even to her, the action surely a reflex as she declared, her teeth clenched, "You will not touch my husband."

There was a moment of absolute silence, the stillness like a ticking bomb.

She felt Leif and Merrick move, their fast-moving abilities humming to life and coasting across her skin as goose bumps erupted. Hands flaying outward, palms facing the two vampires, Karramis stopped them mid-advancement.

"Do you understand me?" Karramis added, unrelenting in her hold on them. "I will kill you if you so much as lay a single finger on him again."

"Not if we kill him first," Leif said with a low, demented chuckle, shooting himself across the room and out of her magical hold.

Magic exploded from her, her telekinetic powers wrapping around all three of the men and tossing them into the side wall near the main door, mere feet from one another. Will rushed to his feet just as he was suddenly yanked forward, his body moving swiftly toward Karramis. The abrupt movement was painful as Will struggled to fight the numerous injuries complaining at the tight hold Karramis's magic had on him. Holding the others in place with one hand, she carefully released Will with the other, placing him against the wall near the window before rushing over to him.

Cradling the uninjured side of his face, she kissed him, the blood on his lip coating her mouth. "Are you okay?" She kissed him again, this time softer after seeing the wince he fought to hide at her touch. "Will, listen—"

"No." Will shook his head. "Don't you dare—"

"I'll be okay." She kissed him again, long and hard, savoring it for just a moment. "Just let me do this."

"Dammit, Karramis!" Lucas yelled just as Leif called out, "Stop her!"

She still had a hold on them, but she could feel Merrick's magic fighting against her.

Time was running out.

"Always and today," she muttered, nothing but love in her voice and on her face. The secret vow between them landed with the intention she was hoping for. "It's my turn to save you."

Will cupped her cheek, his blue eyes burrowing into her, the passion and reverence and love he had for her burning like fire.

"I'll come back for you," he accepted reluctantly, knowing there was no arguing with her. "You know that, right? I'm coming back for you."

Smiling, she admitted softly, "I expect nothing else."

"Karramis!" Lucas yelled across the room, pushing against her magic. Jealousy hit him at the sight of the two of them embracing, the emotion slamming into him like a blow to the face.

Karramis ignored him and the others, rushing to conjure her portal. But something pushed against her telekinesis, ripping through her powerful shield guarding them. Something hard and powerful.

Merrick.

He was countering her abilities, a pain accompanying the fight.

Without warning, Will was tossed to the other side of the room, crashing with a deafening slap against the wall before landing with a thwack against the stone floor.

"Will!" Karramis shouted, but Merrick's magic wrapped around her, snuffing out all her magic and holding her in place, the pain of his abilities constricting around her causing her to go mute.

Flames exploded from the fire pit, the blaze dancing wildly as Karramis's eyes remained focused on the inferno rising higher and higher. Smoke filled the area, the thick haze choking everyone in the room. Coughs sounded just as more magic soared around the room like a bird swooping down from the sky, circling around the fumes and driving them out the window. A trail of fire blasted across the floor, creating a straight line and dividing the room in half. The flames grew, reaching toward the vaulted ceiling, blocking the two sides from each other.

Karramis gasped as Merrick's magical hold on her faltered, the tightness making way for her to breathe in again.

She drew in steadying breaths.

In and out.

In and out.

Her mind focused on the wall of fire as she ran toward Will, using both hands to lift him to his feet. Shock filled his features at the sight before him, the power she was exhibiting and control she had over the element absolutely astonishing and mesmerizing. And how she was not even using her hands to focus on her magic.

Feeling Merrick push against her powers, she shoved back, the pain to hold on to the element slicing through her.

"Come on, let's go," Karramis pleaded as she wrapped an arm around Will, the agony of what she was doing in her voice, the pain intensifying as she struggled to maintain the power she was creating.

Will limped in her arms as she directed him toward the window. "What are you doing?"

"Saving you, remember?" she said through a pained chuckle.

Merrick shoved again, this time combining his fire magic with his air abilities, trying to morph the two forces together and drive them into Karramis and Will.

Will cupped her face, his eyes imploring. "Come with me."

She winced, the pain making her knees buckle.

"I'm not leaving without you."

"Yes . . ." She panted. "Yes, you are. Just trust—" A scream tore from her.

"Karramis!"

"I'm okay," she lied, panting.

He held her gaze, his hand shaking against her cheek as his eyes welled with tears. "Karramis—"

"Don't," she interrupted, shaking her head, knowing exactly what he wanted from her. "I'm not dying."

"Please . . ." The word was a broken plea, one filled with fear and sadness. "Let me—"

"No," she said, her voice unsteady, but confidence still radiated in her tone. "Not yet. Not today."

And with one final kiss, Karramis lifted Will into the air with her telekinetic powers as another wave of pain shot through her, searing into her bones, and Will stumbled as she lost hold of him.

Fury swelled and exploded inside her, clawing and ripping its way out from her core. Every emotion tumbled out of her— the fear, doubt, apprehension, every moment of regret, sadness, and torment. All of it pulled back like the waves of the ocean, the surge of what awaited building into something raw. Something powerful. And as it all exploded outward, so did her magic.

The entire room was engulfed in flames, the fire not only coming from the fire pit and the wall she created but from herself. Flames licked across her skin and danced in her hair as her mouth opened and released a deep, guttural scream. Will shot backward in one fell swoop, exiting the arched window as the inferno erupted inside the tower, the blaze discharging across the cold morning sky. Heat consumed the room as the stones soaked up the intense, blistering temperatures emanating from the powerful fire. From her. The flames flowed from her body, her skin glowing a soft blue underneath the bright colors of red and orange. It was hard to distinguish whether she was the element or if the element had consumed her—blanketing her or coming from her.

But Karramis was the fire and the fire was her.

As her mind focused on Will, she called her portal.

Trees.

That is all Karramis could think about as she summoned her portal just outside the window. But all senses linked to an exact destination to send him faded in unison with her magical doorway. She had hoped Will would end up in Kitra Forest, to their home and to Harkin, but as the magic faded and the pain took over, all she could think about was trees.

Karramis crashed to her knees and panted, leaning her palms against the floor for balance. The entire room went cold as if all the fire had been completely doused.

"Son of a bitch!"

Lucas's voice filtered through the haze in her head, the mix of pain, disorientation, and elation taking over her mind.

But she had done it.

Will had made it into her portal. She had felt it, felt him travel through it. She had gotten him out.

But where he actually ended up, she had no idea.

"How the fuckin' hell did she do that?" Lucas snapped, his words muffled and echoing disjointedly in her head.

Everything hurt. Her head, her body, her insides. All of it ached like nothing she had ever felt—no, scratch that. She *had* felt this before, it was like she had been beaten, that throbbing pain radiating from the inside out. Giving in to it, she collapsed on the floor.

"Well, Mr. Fraye, it would appear the witch is far more powerful than I originally gave her credit for."

Karramis had whetted his interest and curiosity, her powers exceeding previous expectations. Maybe there was more to the witch than just the uniqueness of her blood and her very existence. Her magic had clearly grown, the full extent of the power inside her no longer dormant. The mediocrity of her abilities had proven wrong, a fact Merrick understood would be a focal point to an argument surely on the horizon with Tressa, her intuition about the Fire Witch being accurate. But Merrick could handle Tressa.

"Fuck!" Lucas roared, followed by a loud booming sound as he kicked the door hard against the wall.

Hands gripped Karramis, pulling her from her fading slumber.

Lucas lifted her into his arms, the anger coming from him felt even with Karramis's eyes closed.

"Come now, Lucas," Leif said with a teasing tone, "you're going to kill the poor, defenseless witch when she's down? Where's your pride?"

"Fuck off, ya cunt," Lucas spat at his own words being thrown back in his face. "I'm takin' her back to my room."

"Have you made a decision, Mr. Fraye?" Merrick asked.

"Ask me again later."

"Very well."

Footfalls pounded down the stairs as they all exited the room now covered in charred remnants.

"What makes you think she won't escape now that the Drolnogard is gone?" Leif pointed out, following behind the others.

"Because," Lucas answered, annoyed, "afta' that display up there, she's too weak to try anythin' like that again."

"And how can you be so sure?"

"Trust me, I know her. That was nothin' like she's eva' done before. It was too much for her."

The bitter chill sliced into Lucas as he stepped out into the morning air, exiting the tower.

Merrick slowed, eyeing the windows of his chambers, the one now housing Tressa staring over at him. "And what exactly do you have planned fer the rest of the mornin', Mr. Fraye?"

"I don't know."

"Very well. Well, summon me once you have made your decision. Remember, no matter what decision ya make—"

"I know."

Merrick glared at Lucas.

Lucas cleared his throat. "I know, sir. I remember."

"Good," Merrick said, heading toward the castle, leaving the others behind. "Oh, and Mr. Fraye." Merrick turned back toward them.

"Yes."

"Make a decision already. Conclude this. Today. We will deal with the Drolnogard later. Oh, and one more thing . . . She better not escape this time. Finish this already. Understood?"

"Yes, sir."

"Good. Now, I will leave you be fer now. If I am needed, I will be in my chambers dealin' with a rather petulant witch."

"Good luck," Leif joked, catching sight of Tressa and giving her a devilish smirk and a quick wink.

"I do not need luck, Leif. I simply need to remind her who is in charge."

Chapter 17

Confessions and Consequences

Tressa braced herself for the discussion she was about to endure as she moved away from the Gothic-style arched window. Or rather the argument she was determined to have. She did not care at this point. She was angry. Annoyed. Pissed. Merrick did not just lie to her, he went behind her back to do it. He preached for years about loyalty and trust, but he never held himself to the same standard. He believed himself to be superior. Above everyone else and not required to walk the same ethical lines as others. There was no solid moral code for him. And it was bullshit, something she would definitely tell him once he arrived.

On second thought, maybe not.

Striding across the cold, dank stone room—housing the dais with Merrick's throne-like chair, a decorative partition with various silk, black robes draped over the top, and the wooden table with the chessboard she often enjoyed playing to pass the time—Tressa made her way through the open threshold, entering a space she was rarely welcomed, leaving Theseus and Niko to stand guard by the main door.

Merrick's bedchamber was his safe haven, his sanctuary from the various planning, scheming, and volatile acts that often took place next door. In fact, his room was the complete opposite. This space was equally open and spacious, but his room was warm—thanks to the black marble and slate-gray fireplace she had lit upon her arrival—and inviting. The deep reds and blacks and silvers created an atmosphere of sensual awakening and surprising comfort. Extravagant furniture rested throughout the room, immaculate and regal. It was nothing less for the self-appointed king of the castle.

Footsteps echoed down the hallway, Merrick's heavy boots the only sound aside from the crackling fire. Exiting his room, Tressa made her way over to the main door she had left wide open, giving Niko and Theseus a subtle nod in preparation for whatever side of Merrick decided to show up this time.

Merrick was fully composed as he moved down the hallway, his posture relaxed with his hands locked behind his back. Tressa took note of the unhurried pace of his steps as if he wanted to remind her she was at his mercy, his time and presence a gift. As he strolled closer, the pure dominance in his expression made her straighten and lift her chin.

It was then she decided to remain as equally collected.

Merrick thrived on showing his dominance and reveled in the thrill of the hunt, the submission of his prey his favorite activity. But she would not give him the satisfaction. There was a time and place to demonstrate her own authority over him, to prove she was not someone to underestimate. That without her, he would not have the power he had today. However, right now was not the right moment. Nor did she have the mental strength to deal with his constant shifts in behavior and aloofness.

All she wanted right now was answers. Tressa had to know what was happening. And why the plans had changed.

"Hello," she said evenly as he entered the room, sauntering past her and into his personal chambers.

He stopped, his shoulders going rigid as he canted his head, clearly taking in his room. "Were you given permission to enter my bedchamber?" He did not even bother facing her.

"It was cold," Tressa acknowledged faintly, her timid tone not matching the irritated roll of her eyes.

Merrick peered over his shoulder, his brows lowered and his blue gaze glaring at her.

Theseus let out a low growl of warning.

"Apologies," she offered genuinely, trying to settle the tension. She did not want to start this conversation off on his bad side, nor did she want to deal with the repercussions following a brawl with her trusted companion. Then she would surely never get answers, and she quite enjoyed the minotaur's company. "It won't happen again."

"Now then," he said almost dismissively, strolling onto the large circular scarlet rug in the center of the room and by his crimson-clad, dark mahogany bed, stopping in front of the fireplace. His hands reached out, soaking up the warmth, the flames dancing across the logs in a way that told Tressa he was admiring his new ability.

When he remained quiet, Tressa spoke as she made her way over to him. "If you so please, I would appreciate an update on whatever is happening here." She paused. "Is the Fire Witch going to die?"

Focusing on the fire, he answered simply, "That is up to Lucas."

Tressa was the epitome of class and refinement, of femininity and self-confidence. There was a softness to her, yet there was also an underlining firmness that rivaled most men. She had control, yet she never stole it. She was dominant and determined but knew when to submit. It was a balance she had mastered being around Merrick and Leif for so long. And she understood that despite their need for power, for authority over everyone in a room, they still valued her company—both seemingly for very different reasons. But Merrick appreciated her willingness to question everything. He respected her tenacity and bravery to challenge him. To never fully cower at his feet. It was a strength no other human, although magical, had ever shown him. But Tressa often found herself walking a very fine line lately with him, his sudden shift in reasoning and strategy falling to the wayside of an entirely different endgame. One she desperately wanted in on.

Hesitating as to not sound too eager, she waited a few seconds before asking, a picture-perfect display of elegance and grace filtering into her regal persona. "Care to elaborate." It was not a question but rather a humble request.

Blue eyes met brown, the emotion behind them solemn. It was as though the companion she had known over the years now faced her. "Are you positive ya want all the details? You might not be so copacetic on the matters at hand."

"I would like to know anyway. I have been in this with you, standing by your side as not only your confidant but also the witch who helped aid in your newfound abilities, so I feel I am, if nothing else, owed the truth. All of it."

Merrick studied her, absorbing the reality and honesty of her words. "Very well."

Tressa let out an imperceptible sigh of relief. *Finally.*

She had waited months for this—ever since he had returned from his six, well five, months away this past summer. She had waited six months. Six months of uncertainty and anticipation. Six months of not knowing where she stood in terms of being part of this team. Six months of fearing the worst yet being so annoyed by the omission of an answer to every question she asked. Six months of wondering why he had no longer needed her, let alone never spending more than a few hours in her presence each month. It was six long months of wondering, worrying, and wasting time. At least, she thought it was wasting time, but now she was not so sure, considering the plan to take Karramis's magic was no longer a focal point as she thought it to be.

"Why?" Tressa asked, plain and simple. "Why offer Lucas another deal? And what does Leif have to do with Karramis? And when did you decide you no longer wanted her magic?"

He strolled over to his bed, plopping down and leaning against the dark wooden headboard with bronze studs and a black embroidered cushion, crossing one ankle over the other and resting his hands in his lap.

Tressa had always thought Merrick was handsome. There was something so attractive about his casual confidence and ability to control an entire room with very few emotions and the composed way he spoke. Not to mention the dominance he exuded. He had an energy about him that was corporeal, majestic. Everything about him screamed power and authority. He was a mystery she often wanted to unravel. But over the years, his charm and eye-catching appearance grew mundane. Maybe it was the darkness hidden beneath his charisma or maybe it was because he had never shown any interest in her outside of the companionship he offered. Either way, being around his laid-back disposition and good looks barely registered to her. Except when he flashed her his signature cocky grin—something he was currently doing.

"My, so inquisitive, Tressa dear."

"Well, I've been out of the loop lately." A silent jab.

"The contrition you seek is justified. However, I shall not supply you with such a thing. I had my reasons fer the way things were handled."

"Again, care to elaborate?"

He stared at her as if analyzing his next move.

The tops of her thighs barely brushed against the edge of the bed. She crossed her arms over her plump chest, the action showing discomfort and annoyance. She hated waiting—and this was a tactic he often loved to use on people.

Slapping her arms at her side, she said, heading for the door. "Fine, I'm leaving. Summon me when—"

"You were not dismissed, Tressaya," he said, the tone deep and threatening.

The use of her entire first name made her halt, her dark gaze returning to his. "Then give me something, *Cillian*."

Tressa was treading in dangerous waters.

Footsteps moved toward her, the sound steady and unhurried. His very being was overwhelming. The energy coming off him was like the heat of a raging forest fire, and she was caught right in the middle of it.

But Tressa did not falter as she stood tall, her height just a few inches shorter with her stilettos adding a few inches to her average stature.

The corner of his mouth lifted, amusement twitching his lips. "I always loved the way you said my name." Fingers gently stroked her lips, gliding over the bottom with delicate precision before coasting across the top one. "However, say *that* name again, and I will remove your lips from your face. Do you understand me?"

"Yes." She nodded, her voice even.

"Yes, what?"

"Yes, Merrick."

"That's a good girl." He nearly growled the praise. Rotating on the balls of his feet, he began to pace the room, his usual habit when relaying information to her. Fingers interlocked behind his back, he moved with purpose. "In regards to your questions," he said, the stoicism and composed nature returning, "which one would you fancy an answer to first?"

Surprised by his willingness to give her a choice, she responded honestly, "What is going to happen to Karramis?"

"That was not one of your original questions."

"Okay then . . ." She exhaled, willing herself to focus and not scoff at his antics. "Let's start with this, when did you decide you no longer wanted her magic?"

"To be quite frank"—his gaze landed on her—"I was never the one who coveted her magic. You were the one who insinuated it was a power I needed."

"Yes, because she was the only one left after Keya died."

He tsked. "Such a tragedy."

Tressa caught the way his eyes flickered with delight, the pleasure hidden behind his expression barely there, but she had caught it then. "You killed her. Didn't you?"

"Nah, it was not I."

"But you know who did?"

"Aye."

"Who?" she questioned, the fury of their original plan being snuffed out rising to the surface.

"I am not at liberty to—"

"It was Leif." She scoffed. "Wasn't it?"

Merrick gave her a sly grin.

"That son of a bitch. He actually did it." She shook her head, disbelief replacing her anger momentarily.

Leif Nyland had been in love with Keya Llewellyn, having fallen for her when she was only nineteen years old after a friendship between them developed. She had reminded him so much of the wife he had when he was still human, not in terms of appearance but in her gentle and kind nature and the way she saw the good in everyone. But Leif was a vampire in his early forties, a taboo relationship even on the island of magical creatures, so he never acted on it. But that eventually changed because as Keya got older, his feelings for her magnified, the witch not only being a weakness of his but a desire he wanted to experience. And she was also at a point in her life where she wanted to live, to experience things all growing women craved. So, their friendship blossomed into something more. But it was never official between them, the casual relationship being more about lust than love. At least, that was the case for Keya.

However, shortly after Keya joined the guard, she had begun spending more and more of her time with Zarrius, something Leif did not approve of at all. And when he noticed she had started to fall for the Guardian, Leif professed his love for her, only to be rejected by Keya. Even in her mid-twenties, he was just too old for her, and being from a prestigious family—the first line of Fire Witches and the most powerful—she could not see herself getting romantically involved with a vampire, particularly one who was not only hundreds of years old biologically but also lived on the forbidden side of the island. Zarrius was a safer choice, and she had grown deeply in love with him. She had loved Leif, but not in the way she loved Zarrius, and that confession broke Leif's heart.

Over time, Leif began to resent Keya and her decisions, saying she had made a mistake and fallen for the wrong man. And when Keya and Zarrius wed, and Leif found out she was pregnant, Leif lost it. He had vowed to make her pay for breaking his heart. And so, he did.

"Why then, though?" Tressa asked, curious as to why he killed her when he did.

"Leif couldn't live in a world where Zarrius got everythin' he wanted. So, when he summoned Keya to the forest that mornin', he gave her one final chance to choose him. And when she refused him again, he killed her—breakin' her neck without a single ounce of remorse."

"And you allowed this? Knowing she was your only hope for gaining fire magic? And what about Karramis? How did she survive all of that—her mother dying and the fire? And who started the fire?" She paused, realization hitting her. "Wait, were you there?"

"Aye, I was. Leif had approached me with a proposition—if he found me another Fire Witch, he would be given the opportunity to take Keya's and her unborn child's life if he so chose to. And he did. Well, not exactly." Merrick kept a steady pace, back and forth, back and forth across the rug. "Leif had discovered from magic hunters that a Llewellyn descendant existed in the non-magical realm, but their powers had never fully developed due to a brain injury the woman had suffered from an accident many, many years ago. And due to her disability, her line never grew into their abilities. That is, until one of the members of the bloodline was trapped in a house fire, the fire being started by them after an attempted attack. But after the young woman was discovered, she was put into hidin'—most likely by another Fire Witch."

Tressa knew who the witch was. "Keya."

"Precisely. Leif had discovered Keya had known her own bloodline was sought-after, so when the witch declined her invitation to live in Kiluemar, Keya opted to conceal her instead. And the witch obliged. The only problem was, Leif could not find this witch. He had not been able to uncover where Keya had hidden her."

Tressa analyzed his words. "So, with the knowledge of another potential Fire Witch, you allowed Leif to kill the last two here."

"Correct again. That is, if he chose to do so."

"Of course," Tressa said with a shrug, the information seeming irrelevant. "So, back to my original question then, why didn't you just allow him to kill Keya and then take Karramis once her powers developed? Why kill her?"

"Well, those questions are slightly more complicated to answer."

A hint of irritation formed in her scowling expression. "Humor me."

Merrick loved the determination she exhibited, and the fiery sass. He always loved a woman with a stubborn side to them. They were always fun to play with. "Leif never wanted Karramis to survive. He believed the spawn would be a constant reminder of the woman who broke his heart. So, the plan was always to include her in his decision. Nevertheless, somethin' was off about the unborn child livin' inside the now dead witch. Her heartbeat remained, steady and strong. Never falterin' even after nearly an hour of Keya's body going cold."

Not possible. "What?"

"Aye. Leif and I were utterly dumbfounded by this turn of events. But I understood it to be somethin' more profound. She was an omen. Clearly the child was cursed in some way, bein' adept at livin' among the dead. So, Leif set the forest on fire. He desired nothin' more than to end the life of that child inside Keya. To kill the child she had with another man."

"But she still lived."

"Aye, she did. Somethin' even to this day not a single person can explain."

"Okay, see then," she pointed out, confident and resolute. "This is why you need her magic. She's a paradox of unexplained circumstances. She's rare. A mystery we can only know more about when you take her magic. Plus, the prophecy—"

"Is about her children, Tressa," he interjected, stopping and facing her wholly. "Not her."

"Right," she conceded, opting to get another question answered rather than starting a heated debate with him. "And what do Lucas and Leif have to do with all this? This new plan in place with her?"

He returned to his slow movements throughout the room, his hands sliding into the pockets of his black pants. "When Leif found out Karramis had again survived, I grew curious about her, so I had denied Leif's original request to kill her, stating our agreement was fer him to kill the unborn child. So, he was determined more than ever to find the last remainin' member of her bloodline. And bein' trapped outside the realm fer all those years proved quite beneficial. He had dedicated much of his time to huntin' 'em down. And he succeeded, havin' discovered 'em quite literally right under our noses."

He paused and took her in, the rapt attention she exhibited sending excitement through him. He fancied when things fell perfectly into place, chalking it up to his cunning abilities and strategic mindset. Always two steps ahead. The best way to overthrow your opponent.

"Here?" Tressa asked, sounding surprised but equally confused and annoyed by his dramatic pause, the anticipation to learn everything itching beneath her skin.

"Not quite." He strode toward her, his gaze wholly in her direction. "They were at the school."

"They?"

"Aye. Two of them. Brothers. Both Fire Witches. They were sent to MUSE when the oldest was nine after being abandoned by their mother—their father most likely from the Llewellyn line."

"Okay," Tressa drawled. "So, you then allowed him to kill Karramis?"

"Aye. The deal with Leif was he could kill Karramis, thus erasin' the last reminder of Keya from this world, if he found me another Fire Witch."

Tressa thought of Lucas and the love he had for the woman. "But Lucas made him believe that wasn't the case. Right?"

"Correct. See, Lucas had deemed the agreement between us superior to the ideologies of the previous deal set between Leif and I. Nevertheless, the deal I made with Lucas when he came to me was he could have her, a detail I was content to oblige him with. But what he failed to comprehend was my choice of wordin'. He never asked fer her to remain alive. The deal I made with Leif was simply that he could kill Karramis, and the deal I made with Lucas was that he could have her."

"And that deal has been altered?"

"So to speak."

"Meaning?"

"I have offered Lucas an alternative deal. Havin' taken the situation with Leif into consideration, and after discoverin' both of the children have abilities I long to possess, their parents are no longer pivotal in my overall plan. They are inconsequential. And frankly, they are simply in the way. And so, I decided to change some of the outcome. However, I had to be mindful of who I allowed the knowledge of this new plan. Thus, why you were not privy to such information until now. But the new agreement is this, Lucas has a decision to make. If Karramis allows Lucas to fully claim her and—"

Tressa rolled her eyes at the last part, something she was unable to control. No woman could ever be claimed by a man. And yet no man could be claimed either. Not fully. At least, not the way someone who professed their love truly deserved. Love was given, not stolen. And claiming someone was not love, it was possession. And despite her persistent nature that certain members of the magical community needed to die to further enhance the plan in place—a plan she hoped Merrick still strived to complete in spite of this detour—she believed no human deserved to be shackled. No chattel. No masters. No toys to be played with. No forced control over one's very livelihood. Tressa may have loose morals and questionable ethics, but slavery, of any kind, was a quality of life she never wanted anyone to endure. Being bound to something or someone was the worst kind of hell.

"Problem, my dear?" Merrick asked with a sharp tone, her disrespectful antics causing his posture to shift, the smoothness of his movements becoming rigid.

"No," she admitted, regretting her actions as she cleared her throat. "Continue. Please."

"As I was sayin', if Karramis allows Lucas to fully claim her, and love him in return, my deal with Leif will be voided. But," he said, drawing out the word, "Leif will be given the opportunity to do two things he has longed to do for many years. First, he will be allowed to drain just enough of her blood to keep her alive, thus allowin' her body to recover over time. And he will be permitted to end the life of Will—justice for not only Lucas but fer himself. He was never given the opportunity to kill Zarrius, that right given to another, but now he would in the form of poetic justice."

"And if Karramis denies Lucas?" This is the part Tressa equally wanted to know and yet worried about the answer. Karramis had always been part of the plan, her powers clearly, now more than ever, far more advanced than any other witch she had come across in life or documents. Why could Merrick not see that, see the potential power he could have with her magic? Karramis could very well be the one to break the curse completely. And with her magic, keep the prophecy's outcome on the side of evil. "What happens to her then?"

"If she refuses, then again multiple things happen. I, fer one, will be given the chance to finally taste her. Somethin' I will refrain from doin' if she does accept Lucas because her blood was promised to Leif in that scenario. Then, Lucas will be permitted to kill Will, endin' the life of the man who stole the love of his life. And Leif, well, he will finally be allowed to kill Karramis." He dusted off invisible dirt from his hands. "All problems solved."

"And in both situations, you still abide by our agreement? That she will not die by your hands unless it is during a ritual."

He tapped a finger against his nose. "Correct."

Tressa scoffed, dumbfounded and slightly impressed. "You sneaky little shit."

Merrick let out a laugh, completely amused by her boldness.

"So," Tressa continued, "you never really wanted her magic?"

"Nah. Her magic was far too complex and seemingly unpredictable. Even now, her abilities are progressive but in a more detrimental way. They are too capricious, just like her. And from the looks of it, even she had difficulty maintainin' control over 'em. Plus, I'm cursed enough. I don't need her wayward magic tryin' to alter the powers I have now. And like I said, she should have died that day, and she did not. I refuse to take in magic that may or may not be plagued in any way."

"Then why lie to me all these years?"

"I never lied, my dear. I simply refrained from agreein' in covetin' her magic. It was you who desired fer me to have it, and it was Lucas who followed along. And the rumors continued to spread over the years that her magic was what I desired when the prophecy was rediscovered. But I was never the one to admit such a thing. However, when I learned of the second verse hours before her children were born, those children became my priority. If it was not for Haydrin bein' at the right place at the right time when that seer had returned to the village to inform Zarrius, I never would have discovered what I did when I did. But by the time any plan was in place, Karramis and her children were dead and their bodies burned. At least, that was what we were led to believe."

Pausing to consider something, Tressa asked, her arms folding across her midsection, shielding herself from the potential shock and fear following her question. "How'd you do it? How did you steal the magic without my help?"

An evil and malicious smile lifted his lips, the satisfaction in his arrogant expression like a snake slithering at her feet. "You're not the only witch, ya know?"

Lucky for her, she loved snakes. "Yes, I'm aware," she said, the bitterness sharp and deadly. "But the ritual site."

"Not needed when you have all the right elements to duplicate it."

Trying to put the pieces together, all the things needed to help him steal the magic of others, she shot a wide-eyed gaze up at him, her dark brown eyes narrowed in understanding and anger. "You stole my spell."

He chuckled. "My dear Tressa, you have uttered those same words numerous times in my presence before. I strongly disagree that warrants an accusation of such magnitude. I simply needed to perform a ritual, and takin' your advice by leavin' the realm, I had to provide myself an alternative way of performin' it. So, I improvised."

"But the words in the spell states—"

"Easily corrected. I just needed a powerful and skilled enough witch to do so. Somethin' clearly accessible at a magical school."

"And they helped you? Willingly?"

"I would not say willingly. In fact, it took some serious coaxin' on my part, and the part of the others who deemed a visit to the school would be highly entertainin' and an advantageous escapade. And they were not wrong."

Her emotions boiled over inside her stomach, her anger and frustration and anxiousness driving her to ask, her voice steady and taut, "If you figured it out, then why keep me around? If you're so damn smart—Mister I Don't Need a Common Witch to Do My Biddings Anymore—Mister High and Fucking Mighty. If you've figured it all out, then why not just kill me?"

Merrick did not appreciate her tone, nor did he condone the way she glared at him, the fierceness he admired becoming nothing more than a hysterically irate woman challenging his authority. This was far different from the playful and stubborn Tressa. This version of her was walking on a fine line between curiosity and pure insanity. He loathed being questioned, but nothing infuriated him more than being talked down to in the manner in which she was currently doing. It was passive-aggressive and a very, very stupid move.

He stepped into her, the cold emptiness of his eyes intensifying as black began to bleed into blue. "I can surely arrange that."

Tressa backed away from him. She really did not want to die, and as Theseus and Niko stormed into the room, she did not want them to die for her. She needed them. "Apologies. I overstepped."

Merrick let out a breath, his face going stoic. "You have been a confidant for a long time, Tressa—providin' not only advice and encouragement but bein' the one constant in my darkest times. You have not only been valuable in those regards, you have been beneficial in helpin' to counter my curse. And fer that, I owe you my deepest gratitude. And, one day, I will aid you in the thing you seek most, as promised." He closed the distance between them again, anger now burning in his gaze. "But if you ever speak to me in that manner again, I will, in fact, kill you."

She nodded. "Understood."

"Good. Now, leave. I bore of you." Flicking his wrist, he added, "Dismissed."

Gliding around along the smooth soles of her heels, Tressa exited his room and chambers without another word, Theseus and Niko following closely behind her.

Merrick stood at the threshold of the main door as Tressa and her henchmen turned the corner at the end of the hall.

Striding through the stony room, his anger causing his boots to pound hard against the floor, he fought against the beast wanting to break through. The confrontation with Tressa made his mouth water and the fangs along his teeth to grow.

He was thirsty.

And hungry.

He needed to quench one of them. And soon.

His blood thrummed and heart pounded against his rib cage, the smell of every human within range growing stronger and becoming a beacon to the monster itching for a single taste.

This was the worst part of his curses, the heightened senses. Being a vampire was hard enough to fight against when the bloodlust and hunger seeped in, but the demon curse enhanced everything even more. And he could smell her.

Karramis.

Even from so far away, her unconscious body having been carried through the main door of the castle just a few hundred yards away, he could smell the lingering scent of her blood deep in her veins, its euphoric aroma trailing down the halls as if searching for him.

He wanted her. To taste her, to eat the flesh from her bones.

Lucas needed to decide her fate. Today.

And Merrick hoped Lucas's decision would end with the beast inside him finally being able to consume the blood of the one person it had craved since she was nothing but a baby in the womb of a dead woman.

Chapter 18

Punishment

The pain throbbed in her head, the slow beat of her heart pounding against her temples. Karramis groaned and forced her eyes open. They were so heavy as she fought the weight of them wanting to close. She could not see. Everything was so hazy. No, not hazy, dark.

The area around her was cast in a translucent orange glow moving in a wave-like motion along every dark surface. Resting on something soft, she slid her arms from her chest as she lay on her back, the position of her hands seeming out of place as if they were placed there on purpose. The act of moving was far more difficult than it should have been, her weakened state making every movement sluggish. Why were her arms so heavy? And why did it take so much effort to move them?

A dull ache pulsed in her veins, the discomfort coming from every muscle, the soreness seeming to bleed from her skin. Every inch of her body felt brutalized, like a stampede had trampled over her. She was positive bruises marred the various locations along her body more tender to the touch.

But just beneath the pain rested a numbness that was slowly fading with each conscious decision. However, the weakness was harder to fight.

Feeling the satin softness under her palms, Karramis gripped the material in her hands.

A bed. She was on a bed. A soft, warm bed. A bed that smelled very familiar.

"Lucas," she croaked, her mouth dry and her lips coated with a strange taste.

She wanted to move, to react and ready herself for whatever precarious situation she was now in, but everything hurt. However, it was more than simple pain. No, this pain was laced with something far worse. It was unfathomable, the ache burrowing deep into her bones, taking root in her marrow. It was incapacitating as it tunneled into the very core of her being. It was visceral, and powerful, and lethal.

Magic.

It was magic in its rawest, most primitive form. And she had just summoned it from the deepest parts of her very essence. Allowing it to join as one with the crux of her soul. The magic inside was no longer dormant. It was fully alive and breathing, never again afraid to come out and play. Now, all she had to do was acknowledge the power she possessed wholly, giving way for the magic to fuse together inside her, no longer a separate entity but rather joined completely. Only then would the pain subside, the agony being a driving force, a strength, rather than a weakness.

The thing was, she was weak. Undeniably so. Every sliver of strength was completely gone. This weakness was far worse than she had ever experienced before. It was almost unnatural. Far too potent. Had she really overexerted herself that much? Had her own magic been too much for her?

Slowing her breathing, she focused on the power humming through her, her own magic seeming foreign and incomplete. Like the fire inside her was not fully awakened. There was something still missing. Or rather, all the pieces before her were finally put together, but the picture was all wrong.

Exhaling the ridiculousness of her magic wanting to shift into something else, she forced herself to focus. Maybe it was the lethargy, this fatigue making her limbs feel weighted and her foggy brain making her think these things.

"Lucas?" she called again, her voice louder but still groggy.

Karramis was not even sure why she was calling him. He was the reason she was in this mess. But in this state, he was probably the lesser of the evils still lurking somewhere in the shadows.

Pushing herself up onto her elbows, she winced and sucked in a breath as she scanned the room, her entire body fighting the movement.

Sleep. All she wanted to do was sleep.

No. No sleeping.

Focus.

Okay, where are you?

Lucas's bedroom. That part she confirmed by taking in the familiar fireplace and furniture.

Okay, good. Now, are you alone?

The other half of the room was too dark, but based on the lack of any sounds other than the fireplace and the fact that Lucas did not respond to her, she could only assume she was, in fact, alone.

Karramis plopped back down on the bed, allowing a small reprieve against the exhaustion. She angled her head back, eyeing the glow of the flames flickering along the curtains behind her. She had no clue how long she had been asleep, and the drapes blocked out the view on the other side. For all she knew, she had been unconscious for days.

Did Will make it out?

Did the kids make it to the infirmary?

Is Kavana okay?

He's gone. I can't believe they killed him.

Fuck!

Focus, Karramis!

She had to get out of here. This was her one shot to escape, the idiots leaving her unbound and allowed to roam around this exceptionally large room, free to summon her portal without fear of anyone trying to stop her.

Rolling onto her side, she pushed herself up, the strain against her muscles from both the pain and the frail state of her body extremely difficult to counter. But she persisted. Karramis was not going to let some bruised body parts, weakened muscles, and silly fatigue stop her from getting the hell out of here.

Booted feet pressed into the wood as she forced herself upright, but her knees wobbled before buckling, and she caught herself against the bed. Shaking out her legs, trying to urge the blood through her veins, she tried again to stand. This time with more success, but she still had to combat the strange numbness flowing through her limbs. She blinked and pulled in as much of the light from the fire as she could, the darkness fading with each fluttering of her eyelids. Adjusted to the light just enough, she carefully stepped off the dais.

All she had to do was conjure her portal, then she was out of here.

But as she lifted her hands, she noticed the tremor in them. She had not even realized they were shaking so badly until now. Concentrating on the muscle spasms, she noted the slight trembling also present in her legs.

Nausea coiled in her stomach.

Extreme fatigue. Weakened limbs and muscles. The urge to just sleep. Uncontrollable shaking. Disorientation.

"Son of a bitch," she snapped under her breath through gritted teeth. "He fucking drugged me."

Outstretching her arms, she held her palms out, summoning her portal. The air in the room swirled to life, the gentle breeze blowing her messy strands. She struggled to hold on to it, but her magic flickered out, the air sucking back in on itself. It was just too difficult to hold tight to the magical doorway, her physical and mental strength having taken a toll with what had happened in the tower and whatever drug was still lingering in her system.

But still she tried again.

And again, the magic building but quickly fading.

She tried again.

And failed.

And again.

It was no use.

Defeated, she lowered her arms and sat on the dais, taking a moment to rest. "Dammit," she whispered with an exasperated exhale.

"Well, hello, love," Lucas said nonchalantly as he entered the room, Karramis not even noticing the door opening. "You're awake. Sleep well?"

Karramis wanted to stand, to not show him just how weak she was, but she could not find the strength to even care at the moment. "Why did you drug me?"

He closed the door and clicked on an annoyingly bright light. "Always so dramatic. I didn't drug ya—I simply sedated ya."

Karramis winced, shielding her eyes from the too-bright glow coming from a single bulb hanging over the sitting area by the fireplace.

Lights. There were lights in here. How had she not noticed the lightbulb set in a wired cage-like contraption hanging by a hook from the ceiling? Her assumption of not having electricity on this side had apparently been wrong. Quickly eyeing the light fixture, she noticed a thick black cord mounted against the ceiling and stretched out and attached to the wall, disappearing somewhere behind the furniture. Electricity had not actually been installed. It would appear Lucas had added the feature himself.

Karramis could only assume he had not used the light earlier because he wanted to create a more calming atmosphere, or possibly more intimate, with the candles. But now, he appeared all business and no pleasure, strolling toward her with purpose. Yet he was still composed. Calm even. Maybe Lucas was not as mad as she thought he would be at Will getting away.

Registering his words, she said through an incredulous snort as she stood, "It's the same thing. No matter which way you twist it, you still drugged me."

"No," he drawled, a hint of humor curving his lips. "No narcotics were used. I simply provided ya with a concoction of carefully measured medicinal plants to help aid in makin' sure ya remain asleep for a bit, as well as to provide some assistance to any pain ya might be endurin'." The space between them closed a few feet. "You should be thankin' me, not condemnin' me."

The back of Karramis's boot hit the edge of the dais as Lucas neared, causing her to fall with a thud against her backside.

"Ow," Karramis acknowledged, glaring up at him.

He chuckled, the sound playful rather than sardonic. "Hey, that was all you. I didn't even touch ya, love." Something flashed in his gaze, something Karramis could not place.

All the adrenaline had seeped from her body, every inch of her fully aware of the situation she was in as her instincts to protect shifted into survival.

"Are you going to hurt me?" she asked softly, curious and skeptical of the answer, remembering every other time he had laid a hand on her.

He crouched in front of her and inclined his head, a strange desire filling his expression. "Do ya want me to?"

"No," she said simply as she shook her head, her tone gentle.

"Then behave and I won't. Unless ya change your mind, of course."

"I won't."

Everything about him made her uneasy. He was just too composed, too unfazed by her honesty and everything that unfolded earlier.

Curiosity hit her. "How long was I unconscious?"

"You were *asleep* for only a few hours."

She stared at him, keeping her features neutral. "May I stand, please?" He was close, too close. And way too calm.

"Of course." But Lucas did not move away from her, his proximity blocking the needed space for her to lift to her feet.

"Can you back away, please?"

"No."

Her nerves vibrated with warning, but before she could ask why, he leaned his forearms against his thighs and said smoothly, his voice deep, "You know ya haveta be punished for your actions, right?"

She blinked—once, twice, bewilderment taking shape in her features. "Excuse me?"

Lucas pressed his palms into his thighs and stood.

A slap rang out as his hand collided with her face, the sting wiping away more of the grogginess from her head. It was nowhere near as hard as he had hit her before, but it still sent her head shifting sideways with a jolt.

All right then, maybe her earlier assumption was incorrect, and he was a little mad. And, if she was being honest, she did kind of deserve it—ruining their plans and all.

"Feel better?" she asked, unbothered as she rubbed her cheek.

"No," he admitted quietly, keeping his blue gaze on her. "But it needed to be done. Ya know why, don't ya?" he asked ruefully, his tone remorseful but justification written all over his face. His eyes focused on the red mark lining her cheek just for a second too long to go unnoticed by Karramis. "It's just . . ." He sighed. "What ya did back there—ya fucked everythin' up."

Yes, she had. And she would do it again in a heartbeat. "What did you want me to do? Just sit by and watch you kill him?"

"Ideally, yes."

Karramis caught the humor in his voice. "You can't be serious, right?"

His hand lifted, his index finger and thumb pinching together but not touching. "Only a little. I mean, with him outta the picture, ya would definitely be more cooperative, I'm sure."

She crossed her arms, realizing more and more of the lethargy in her muscles were lifting. He must not have given her too much of whatever he gave her. Just enough to subdue her until he returned. "You're insane. You know that, right?"

"So I've been told," he said with a shrug. "Now then, to settle a few—"

His bedroom door opened, and Leif came into view.

"Perfect," Lucas said lightheartedly. "We're just about to get started. Unfortunately, ya missed her punishment."

"Not a problem," Leif stated, his demeanor pleasant. "I'm sure there's plenty more to come."

Karramis was already uneasy about her current situation with Lucas, but now that Leif was here, fear and panic churned to life in her stomach. Her heart pounded so hard in her chest, she could feel it pulsing in her neck and hear it in her ears.

"Started on what?" Karramis did not like how meek her voice sounded as she rose to her feet, moving a few steps closer to the fireplace.

Lucas glanced over at Leif, grinning. "Care to share with her?"

Leif matched his expression as he observed Karramis with absolute delight, strolling over and stopping her advancement. "On whether or not you live or die today."

Well, his words were not at all surprising, considering everything she had already learned and the actions she took to save Will. "What else is new?" she asked, trying to convey a sense of boredom even though she was terrified. She could not show them any weakness. "This is becoming a rather common theme lately." She faked a yawn, regretting the act the moment she did it, and yet she ignored the twinge of stupidity. "And I'm growing tired of it."

Careful, Karramis. Now is not the time to be a smartass. Remember, they are much faster, and you don't even know if your magic will work right now.

"Yes," Lucas agreed, smiling with absolute satisfaction. "It's definitely a wise choice to remind yourself of your place."

Brown eyes shot over to him, wide with shock.

"That's right, love. I didn't just sedate ya so you wouldn't wake right away. I did it because it also weakens your cognitive abilities. No shieldin' my powers for the time bein'. So now . . ." He moved toward her, totally invading her space, the two men standing between her. "I can hear every single thing you are thinkin'."

Karramis took note of this and lifted her chin defiantly, wanting to show him she was still one step ahead of him. "Only *if* I'm verbally thinking it. You should know better than to believe I didn't have other means to stop your powers." And she had, using images rather than words to convey her internal plans. "It's not just a matter of shielding you. It's altering my thought process completely. You see, no inner monologue, no telepathic invasion." Now, all she had to do was push through the remaining remnants of the sedative in her system and she would be fine. "So, unless you also learned how to perceive my thoughts, I'd say I'm safe from your invasive powers for the most part." Patting his chest, she added coyly, "Better luck next time."

A hand wrapped around her fingers, squeezing and twisting. The sudden onslaught of pain pierced along her rotated wrist and drove Karramis to her knees. She winced at the slamming force of her body connecting with the floor. The twisting of her wrist made something pop, and she sucked in a hissing breath.

"Now, isn't this a sight to behold." Anger morphed into desire as Lucas took her in. "Such a good girl, kneelin' before me."

"Ugh." Disgust rose in her throat. "In your dreams," she said, fighting through the pain. Walking a fine line again, she added, "My skills are reserved for—"

Lucas twisted harder, the action making Karramis gasp at the sudden jolt of pain. "Don't ya fuckin' dare say it."

She could sense the small trace of her abilities below the surface, her telekinetic power the strongest one at the moment. She could not summon her other abilities fully yet, but maybe she had just enough strength and control for one of her powers. All she needed was a tiny amount to expel.

Releasing a small pulse of it, Karramis aimed her telekinesis at the back of his knee, the one closest to the open hand at her side. Lucas buckled as his knee bent forward, the action releasing his grip on her.

She rose to her feet, eyeing both the men as she rubbed her wrist. "Seriously," she declared completely annoyed by yet another questionable act done by him due to her almost mentioning Will by name again—although, she was baiting him, but that was beside the point. "You're a grown-ass man, Lucas, and you're still running around like some possessive, lust-drunk man-child who is a complete lunatic with this unrealistic ideology that you have some claim on me because of something that was said to you when I was ten. Ten." Her hand flew through her messy waves, her fingers catching on a few tangles before she tugged it free. "Jeez! Seriously, grow the hell up. Move on. It's over. It's done." She paused, taking in a few steadying breaths as her voice and features softened, and she offered him the truth. Some form of pleading closure. "Trust me . . . I'm not worth all of this, Lucas. Really, I'm not—I'm not worth all this pain I'm causing you."

On his feet, he shifted toward her, the need to close the distance itching along his skin. He wanted to feel her closeness. He needed to touch her. "But you are."

"No, I'm not," she confessed wholeheartedly.

"But . . . I love you, Karramis."

"No, you don't." She gave him a gentle shake of her head. "You only love the idea of me. This idea and dream you created in your head a long time ago. A dream you refuse to let go of. But it's not real." Taking a chance to console him while still offering him the cold, hard truth, she placed her hands on his forearms. "It's not real, Lucas. And it will never be real. But maybe, one day, you will find someone who can make it real for you."

"I don't want anyone else." There was a rawness to his truth, a vulnerability.

"And that's where I come in," Leif interrupted, excitement and anticipation dripping from him.

"Oh, you're still here?" Karramis offered in faux surprise, her sarcastic tone matching the derisive arching of her brow.

Leif snickered, low, deep, and dark. "I always knew that mouth of yours was going to be the death of you, witch." Wind blew across her body as he closed the distance, his face stopping inches from hers. "I guess I was right."

Karramis flinched ever so slightly as she attempted to control the way her chest heaved. His close proximity made the energy in the room thick and smothering, the change like a slap to the face, almost as if her body and mind were tapping into her instinctual nature. She could only fight the fear she was struggling to combat for so long. And the way he was sizing her up, the hunger in his eyes, was making every fiber in her body charge with warning. Whatever was about to happen, Karramis was not going to like it. And may not even survive it if Leif's wicked smirk and cold, soulless eyes had any indication.

The door to Lucas's bedroom opened, pulling Karramis's attention from the vampire.

"Afta' you." Lucas gestured toward the hallway.

Karramis shook her head, denying the request. "I'm not going anywhere with you until you tell me what is going on."

She did not like this at all. There was a strange feeling about whatever was happening, and an even weirder sense with whatever was coming. It honestly felt like her time here was limited. She could feel it in her soul.

She recognized it then—Lucas.

Lucas was still far too relaxed, but it was deeper than that. He was too nonchalant, too indifferent. There was a somberness to him, an emptiness. A dejected acceptance. He had detached himself from everything. From her. There was a hollowness to him. A sudden shift she had not even noticed until now. When Leif had arrived—as if the vampire had been some kind of harbinger. A reminder of sorts.

Lucas's posture was void of all confidence as his shoulders sagged in defeat. Blue eyes, once adoring and gentle and determined, lacked any emotion. "Now."

"If you don't move, witch," Leif announced, all humor replaced with seriousness, his frame moving closer, "then I will gladly make you."

Karramis did not move. "I'm not going anywhere."

A hand wrapped around her throat and squeezed, holding her in place. "Wanna bet?"

Panic filled her veins as he started to lift her onto her tip toes. He was going to kill her.

She clawed at the tight constraint gripping her neck as she forced out a plea through a strained inhale, "Lucas." Her eyes tried to find him, but Leif forced her gaze back to his.

"He's not going to save you. Not this time."

"I'm . . . not afraid . . . of you," she choked out through strangled breaths.

Leif smirked at the lie she was trying to convince herself of and declared darkly, his blue eyes fading to black. "You can act like you aren't scared of me all you want. But you're forgetting one thing." He loosened his grip on her throat and pulled her in closer. "I can smell the sweat seeping from your pores. I can see the uncertainty in your eyes. I can hear your heart pounding like a trapped, wild animal wanting to escape." His face morphed and his fangs lowered. "And I can taste the fear in your blood."

Leif's hand lowered as his mouth aimed for her neck.

Karramis lifted an open palm just as Leif's fangs drew closer, the magical force behind it blocking his advancement as he met an invisible wall.

Her powers were returning, more and more, slowly but surely. If only she could hold it in place long enough—

Leif let out a frustrated groan and disappeared, air suddenly whooshing past along one side of her, her skin registering the cool breeze at the same moment a boot collided with her lower back. Jutting forward, Karramis stumbled from the momentum, her knees crashing to the floor, followed by her hands. Karramis gasped on all fours, the force behind the kick driving the oxygen momentarily from her lungs.

A pang of frustration coursed through her. She had not generated enough magic to contain him fully, only focusing on stopping Leif instead of creating a full magical wall around him. She knew her powers were nowhere near strong enough right now to counter the vampire's speed, and she still had not taken that into consideration.

Sensing Leif moving closer, she pushed herself back on her heels, attempting to regain her footing. But Leif landed another blow, this one a fist to her face. As she lurched sideways at the impact, Leif caught her by the biceps, shoving her back just enough to cause her head to fly back, the motion following a swift punch to her stomach. Karramis expelled a grunt and bent at the waist, her body starting to sway just as a set of arms lifted her, her limp body hoisted over a shoulder.

"Like I said," Leif said as he began to walk, his features morphing back into his handsome, human face.

Her face stung. She had never been struck by a vampire before, and she was honestly surprised the strength behind it did not kill her on the spot. But she doubted Leif wanted her to die from blunt force trauma. However, despite the pain along her face, her stomach was the one part of her killing her. Metaphorically, of course. Well, she hoped it was anyway. Internal bleeding was a thing. But not only was a possible bruise forming along her abdomen, the bouncing pressure of her stomach against Leif's shoulder was pure agony. She was not sure if the urge to vomit was from the pain of the blow or the deep compressions against it.

"Put me down," she pleaded with a tap to the vampire's back. She did not like not knowing where she was headed or the lack of control she had. "Please, I'll go wherever you want, just let me down." There was only truth in her declaration.

And she would. There was no use fighting right now. If she even tried, there might not be any chance of her getting out of this alive. It was only a matter of time before her magic was fully restored and her body and mind were prepared, the physical and mental practice she had done over the last few months proving to be well worth it. It was a luxury she not only valued but had grown to love. Her magic was a part of her, and she would never take it for granted again. It had saved her life many times, and now it had saved Will. All she was hoping for was for it to save her once again.

It had to—it had to save her. Or else, she would never see her family again.

Leif slowed before dropping her to her feet, the descent down his six-foot-four frame making for a not-so-graceful landing as her knees wobbled, and she grabbed hold of Leif's shirt.

Surprised he actually obliged her request, she said sincerely, stepping back, "Thanks."

Leif's hand gripped her arm, holding her in place. He placed a finger under her chin and forced her eyes to him. "Don't read too much into it, witch. I just didn't feel like carrying your ass across the castle."

When she tried to step away, he tugged her back again and clasped his large hand along the underside of her jaw. Dark, sapphire-blue eyes studied her. He held her gaze, unblinking, before taking in every inch of her face, moving his hand and trailing a finger across each feature—her rounded chin, her angular jawline, the rim of her nose, her high cheekbones, the shape of her eyebrows. And she allowed it, unsure what to even do at this point. He was not hurting her, only invading her space in a weirdly intimate way. And his eyes held a story, one she knew housed memories he was likely reliving. He moved his finger along her temple and down the side of her cheek, tracing the scar on her face. Then he ran the pad of his thumb gently along her bottom lip.

Leaning in, he brushed his own lips against the shell of her ear. "Are you going to choose him?" He had asked it so quietly she was afraid she imagined it.

Pulling away, Karramis locked her brown eyes on him, confusion creasing her brows. But as the question settled in, the confusion faded. She understood exactly what he was asking— was she going to pick Lucas over Will.

She blinked, not wanting to answer the question. And what was the point? He knew the answer. Even Lucas knew the answer by now. She was never going to choose Lucas over Will. Never. She did not and could not love him in that way, nor could she ever trust him again.

"There ya have it," Leif declared, glancing over his shoulder with a malicious grin.

Angling herself to see behind him, Karramis spotted Lucas standing with his arms crossed a few feet behind Leif. Understanding hit her. This was all part of the plan, to get her to admit she and Lucas would never be together. And whether he had heard her thoughts or whether it was written on her face, her answer was clear. But she had told him this already, she had told him numerous times before, in fact. So why was now any different?

Without a word from anyone, the three of them made their way down the hall, turning the corner and heading to the east wing of the castle.

The tower. They were back at the tower, something Karramis took as a very bad sign.

Ascending the flight of steps along the inside of the circular structure, Karramis jumped straight into strategizing, feeling for not only the full capacity of her magic but also the full strength of her body. She was certain whatever lay at the top of the stairs was going to require not only her powers but her sheer will to survive.

And she was right.

Because as she moved from the landing into the room at the top of the tower, Karramis confirmed one thing as she spotted Merrick staring at her with hungry eyes.

They were going to kill her.

Chapter 19

Life Taken

Merrick stood so still. So statuesque and beautiful and majestic. Everything about him radiated allure and sophistication, passion and intrigue, hypnotizing charm and an undeniably captivating presence. Everything except his eyes. There was a flash of eagerness and desire in his analyzing and ravenous gaze, giving way to the monster prowling just below the surface.

Karramis hated the feeling of being backed into a corner. Every fiber of her body screamed at the idea of being a victim. She had promised herself she would never allow it to happen again. And she had also promised her son she would fight and never surrender to them. But it was the feeling of being defenseless and vulnerable causing her entire energy to sag in indisputable defeat.

They had won. They had outsmarted her.

Everything from using Will against her to not fight back, to the bindings and the drugs, and even now, it was three against one. And all of them were larger, stronger, faster, and far more advanced in fighting and with magic. Yes, Karramis had been powerful enough to save Will, but what were the chances she could do it again? The magic she called forth earlier was the strongest she had ever exhibited, and it had been driven by a deep, soul-crushing, heart-stopping need to save the love of her life. It was instinct. It was natural and so fluid it was almost as if the magic had been the one controlling her and not the other way around. It was not a matter of *if* she could save him, it was a deciding factor she had ingrained into her bones of *when* she was going to do it. But now, she was not certain of the fate she, herself, would be handed.

Hand wrapping around her arm, Leif ushered her toward the metal shackles on the wall, the same ones they had bound her in earlier. "Lucas wants you coherent and conscious for this next part, so these"—he chained her up, both arms bound behind her back—"will have to do." He threaded his fingers through her hair and pulled, making sure she took in the black pooling into his eyes and the veins darkening just above his cheekbones. "I'll be watching you . . ." His tone was rough and deep. "Very, very closely."

"I'm flattered," she said candidly, unable to help the sass she was feeling as she held his stare.

Karramis knew the dismissive retort would likely get her in trouble, but she still refused to showcase any sort of fear— knowing the brazen vampire would revel in the way he affected her.

Pain seared the back of her head as Leif tugged hard and forced her to her knees. "Still trying to play the hero, I see." He leaned over and yanked, making sure her eyes were on his. "Do I need to remind you," he warned with a mix of danger and seduction in his voice, "just how vulnerable you are, witch?"

"Leif," Merrick said with authority, his tone conveying a finality behind it.

"Keep it up, and I promise, I'm going to make it hurt." Releasing her with a final yank, Leif strolled away from her and leaned against the wall just a few feet away, carefully monitoring her every move.

Karramis swallowed, knowing his threat was imminent.

Appearing before her, Lucas lowered himself to her level, all serious and contemplative. "I'm gonna ask ya one final time, love, and afta' this, whateva' ya say will be final."

Karramis fought against the pressure of her knees pushing into the cold, hard stones beneath her, shifting uncomfortably as Lucas stared her down, waiting for her to reply.

Everything about this moment was riddled with doom. A fate she could not alter. From the dread coasting over her skin and trailing up her spine, to the damp, dank space, to the coppery and musky smell lingering in the air, to the sight of the fire snuffed out a few feet away. Even the room, which had been warm earlier, was now cold, both literally and figuratively, due to the window not containing any barrier from the elements and the three cold, calculating men standing before her. The tower had always had a darkness to it, but now it was even more so without the warmth or any light coming from the candles ensconced along the walls. And the sky outside was turning to dusk, the impending nightfall confirming she had been unconscious for a few hours—since the days were much shorter in Kiluemar this time of year, only getting roughly six to seven hours of sunlight at the peak of the season.

"She's never going to answer you, Lucas," Leif acknowledged. "Just accept it already and let's get on with this."

Karramis had the nerve to turn her head and glare at him. But she bit back a retort, not wanting to provoke the vampire any more than she already had. Silence was her ally right now.

"Is he right, love?" Lucas ventured, something akin to desperation clinging to his question. "Is there really no chance for us? Even afta' everythin' I did to make us happen? For us to be happy and together."

Still, she remained quiet.

"Answer him," Leif commanded with a deep, insistent, yet relaxed tone as he continued to lean with a casual arrogance a few feet away. He wanted her to admit what everyone already knew.

Leif wanted her to dig her own grave.

With pleading eyes, she whispered, "Lucas, please—"

"No," the vampire interjected as he pushed off the wall, snapping his fingers and pointing at her, "none of that." He towered over her and folded his arms over his chest. His presence was so overwhelming despite the relaxed nature of his stance and slight upward tilt of one corner of his mouth. He was enjoying this. "Answer the damn question."

Karramis regarded Lucas, still refusing to speak the truth—to hurt him again. This was never her intention. She never meant to break her best friend's heart by falling in love with someone else.

An imperceptible shake of her head conveyed another plea—not to make her do this to him. Not to do whatever they were about to do to her.

Leif squatted down beside her and caressed the scar along the left side of her face. "Your timing is slightly off, witch. Now is not the time to remain silent. So, if you don't answer him in the next five seconds, I'm going to start breaking some bones. Starting with your fingers."

Closing her eyes for a moment, desperate to remain calm, Karramis blinked up at Lucas, the softening in her gaze genuine. "I'm sorry for—"

A large hand slid along her bound arm in a flash and gripped her pinkie. "Try again," Leif demanded coolly as he twisted her finger at an awkward angle.

"Okay," Karramis conceded in a breathy panic, desperate for him to not hurt her. The idea of him breaking her fingers one by one was not a pain she wanted to endure. She needed her hands fully functioning if she was going to have any chance of protecting herself.

Releasing her finger, Leif grinned and stood. "Good girl."

Letting out a deep exasperated sigh, equally annoyed and terrified, she confessed with absolute certainty, her focus on Lucas, "I . . ." She hesitated, choosing her next words carefully. "I can never love you the way you deserve to be loved." Sympathy rose in her stomach at the sadness in his eyes. "I'm sorry."

"Say it," Leif insisted as he moved to the other side of her, his entire presence and closeness menacing.

Karramis knew what Leif wanted her to say, but she was too worried to speak, afraid she might set any one of them off with her admission.

But that was exactly what they wanted. Getting her to admit everything one final time out loud was the thing they needed to seal whatever deal was in place.

She could not give them that satisfaction.

No, she was not going to be a pawn in this game of theirs. She would do as she promised her son—she was going to fight back. Even if it meant she had to do so silently.

Silence was not surrendering. It was taking back control of a situation.

The back of Leif's hand drove hard across her face, the slap echoing off the stone walls as her body twisted and she landed slightly on her side, the bindings pulling against her wrists and the chain rattling. A sting of pain blasted across the side of her face as a metallic taste slid over her tongue. She swallowed, the warm and coppery tang making her gag. Rolling until she was more on her side, the pressure on her wrists and weight against her bound arms easing a bit, Karramis coughed, trying to drive the blood coating her throat from her mouth. She choked as a stream of crimson-tainted spit flew from her lips.

"Stop fucking hitting me," Karramis deadpanned, enunciating every syllable.

Leif lifted her to her feet in one swift motion, the ascent causing her entire body to tense with a piercing onslaught of pain.

"Fuck," she said with a breathy exhale as her back slammed against the wall, her arms aching due to the position they were in and how they were pinned between her and the wall.

"Then answer the fucking question," Leif nearly growled in her face, his eyes dipping to the blood coating her bottom lip and a small section of her chin.

Well, if she was going to die, she was going to do two things first. One, she was going to enjoy every minute of taunting all three of them. Why not have a little fun first, right? And the second thing was she was going to try to take as many of them down with her as possible.

Karramis slowly ran her tongue along her lip, licking up the blood.

Leif narrowed his eyes as her tongue swiped at the blood, the annoyance and anger tangible. "Do you think this is some kind of joke?"

"Am I laughing?" she asked defiantly, her expression stern.

"Do you have a death wish or something?" His hand clamped around her throat. "Because I will gladly grant it."

"Well, from what I gather, you already plan to, so how about this—you let me go, and you can go fuck yourself."

"Or . . ." The pressure built around her neck. "How about we just give you a little more of that sedative and give you a slight head start. Whichever one of us catches you gets to do whatever they want with you."

Dread coiled in her stomach, but still she said, "That sounds highly unfair."

He edged closer with a grin on his face, bending his head until he was eye level. "Who said anything about it having to be fair?"

Merrick's voice finally filled the room, so calm, soft, and controlled but full of raw command. "Untie her, Leif." Footsteps sauntered closer, the hand around her neck disappearing. "But she is not goin' to run, neither as our prey nor in general." He studied her so intently it made her skin prickle and a chill crawl along her spine. "Are you, sweetheart?" The rhetorical question not needing an answer, he continued, all charm under his alluring tone. "And do you want to know how I know this?"

Karramis did not respond, already anticipating a solid threat to her life—one she knew would arrive no matter what, so why should she care about his answer.

"Because . . . if you so much as *think* about usin' your magic again, I will not only remove your head from your body and devour you from the inside out, I will personally conduct the necessary means to guarantee your Drolnogard is beggin' fer death once we are all finished with him. Understood?"

There were no empty threats with him, just a promise.

Karramis nodded, not wanting to show his declaration was lodged in her chest, the pressure making it hard to breathe.

"Good." Merrick gave her a genuine smile before his expression went neutral and he glanced at Leif. "Proceed."

Uncuffing her, Leif lowered his voice and ordered again, "Say it."

She feigned ignorance. "I don't know what you want me to say."

His eyes burned with a fiery gleam. "Tell him the truth. Tell Lucas you don't choose him, so we can finally get this over with."

Running her hand over the red marks on her wrist, Karramis made her way over to Lucas, her entire disposition tight with worry and despair. She did not want to hurt him. Truly. But his actions had proven to be chaotic, unhealthy, and extremely toxic. So, if telling him one final time would be the thing she had to do to help him move on, then she would. But she also knew that no matter what she said, her honesty would be the catalyst to whatever was about to happen, and she knew what that was.

She was about to die.

Unless she could figure a way out of this *and* still keep Will safe from the wrath of Merrick, they were going to kill her.

Giving him a pleading look, she started, "Lucas . . . please just—"

"Nope!" Leif interrupted, shaking his head. "Try again."

She eyed Lucas and swallowed.

"It's all right, love." He was so sad and disappointed. "Say it." Everything about him radiated heartbreak and grief—the loss of losing her in the way he yearned finally settling in his expression.

Karramis never wanted this. "I'm sorry, Lucas. I know my decisions hurt you, and for that, I am so sorry. But I can't keep shielding you from what you already know. I choose him. I chose Will." She could feel the pain she inflicted by her words, his despair mixing with the fury raging in his eyes. "But, please, don't do anything stupid. You know you'll eventually regret it. I know you. I know who you are deep down. And this isn't you. So, please . . . if you ever loved me, just let—"

"If?" Lucas stood up straight and cocked his head, his emotions becoming darker. "It was neva' an *if*—I *do* love you. That's why I'm doin' this."

She let out a bewildered sigh, her brows narrowing. "Doing what?"

He was so calm and so somber as he monitored the rising and falling of her chest. "Finally sayin' goodbye."

"Why, though?" she whispered on an exhale, trepidation starting to take over her nerves, all her tenacity to stand her ground fading.

"Because . . ." He traced the scar on her face before pushing her hair behind her ear. "Sometimes destroyin' somethin' ya love is far easier than watchin' someone else get to enjoy it."

Fear flashed in her eyes.

"I finally realized the past is where ya belong, and it's where you're gonna haveta stay. There, the girl I love will stay. And that's where I will continue to love ya. But now, I haveta decide how I wanna go forward with my life. And I've finally made a decision." He stepped back. "There's no future for you if ya can't love me back—if you aren't mine."

Karramis wanted to run. She wanted to summon her magic and allow it to erupt from her, giving her a chance to live. She was not ready to die yet.

"I fought for so long," Lucas continued, resigned. "And I'm done now. I'm tired. I give up. I'm lettin' ya go. I've wasted too much time, and it was all for nothin'."

"So, have you had sufficient time to consider my offer, Mr. Fraye?" Merrick asked amiably, almost eagerly.

"I have," Lucas delivered, devoid of emotion.

"And?"

"I rescind our previous deal."

"Excellent." He held out a hand to Karramis, pure pleasure in his features. "Come here, sweetheart."

Karramis did not want to comply, but the insistence behind the command was terrifying. Now she understood how Rhiannon felt—the presence of this man was already intense, but when he was determined and dominant, it was so penetrating it was as if he was trying to control them from the depths of their very souls.

She moved, fear and curiosity driving her forward.

His fingers were so soft and surprisingly warm as he trailed them down one forearm and along her wrist. Lifting her arm, he pressed delicate kisses on her skin along her pulse points.

"Just one taste," he said, a seductive plea.

Karramis did not fight him. If all he wanted from her was some of her blood, then so be it. She knew when to pick her battles, and this was nowhere near worth the fight.

And if she wanted to, she had no doubt she would lose.

Fangs pierced her skin along her wrist, the pain equally sharp and blunt as the teeth dug in deeper. She winced and sucked in a breath.

Eyes closed tight, she held back a whimper as tears formed.

It hurt.

It hurt so bad.

The agony accompanying the pointed teeth burrowing deeper was like tiny lances impaling the layers of flesh, the fiery shards of pain like glass slicing through her skin. Her hand and arm went numb as he pulled blood from her vein, but the penetrating sting remained.

A moan rang out, the euphoria growing as Merrick's tongue licked under his enclosed mouth. She tasted exactly as he had expected—like sin and pleasure and lust, like danger and sanctuary, like life and death, like something ancient and powerful.

Solid black eyes lifted as Merrick withdrew his fangs slightly, his lips still against her blood-coated skin. "What are you?" he asked in an almost hypnotic cadence, awe and wonder dripping in his tone.

Mouth lowered, he sunk his fangs in again.

This time the pain was barely registering, his teeth slicing through the same puncture marks with absolute precision. Only a slight sting traveled through her nerves as more blood was sucked from her body.

Merrick moaned, long and guttural, the feel of it rumbling along her arm. He sucked harder, pulling deeper with each swallow.

A wave of dizziness washed over her, her muscles going weak and her limbs becoming pliant.

He needed to stop, or he was going to kill her.

"Stop," she pleaded weakly, yanking her arm away, the jerking motion forcing his fangs to slice along her wrist and cut her. She hissed in pain and backed away. Clutching her palm over her wrist, she covered the two puncture marks and gashes pooling blood.

"Very well," Merrick said as he wiped her blood from his mouth, his features and teeth returning to normal, the picture of casual charm returning. Holding her gaze, he retreated, staring at her like she was a mystery he wanted to solve. A moment later, he strolled over to the door, stopping in the doorframe and facing her. "You are far more delicious than your daughter." He sighed. "I am rather disappointed I'm not the one who gets to indulge in the finality of your extraordinarily luxurious essence." His pale blue eyes swung over to the vampire watching with pure smugness on his face. "Revel in her, Leif. She's a rare one." He went to turn but halted. "Leave the body fer me."

And with that, he disappeared down the stairs.

Leif flashed an elated grin, the gesture evil and cold as it angled toward Lucas. "Does this mean I can finally kill her?"

Images of her family flashed in her mind.

Fight back.

Do not surrender.

She refused to die. This could not be her destiny.

But as the thoughts of dying sank deeper, she wondered, maybe this was part of the plan all along. Maybe the prophecy had been right, maybe this was her fate. She always knew she was meant to die for her kids. But even now, as death lingered close by, she felt like this was not supposed to be the legacy she was meant to leave behind.

"Do whateva' ya want with her," Lucas voiced flatly, pulling her away from her thoughts. "Defile her, beat her, kill her—I don't care anymore."

Leif cooed, "Aww, look what you did, you finally broke him. Good job, witch." He stalked toward her, his body language a clear warning he was eager to take hold of her. "Now then, any last words before I have some fun with you?"

"Don't touch me," she snapped, backing away from him.

Summoning the last bit of strength she had left, she made one final decision. If they were going to kill her, and she could not summon her magic to help her, then she would do exactly what she told James she would do.

Fight back.

She twisted just as his hand reached for her, moving around him. Kicking out her leg, she rammed her booted foot into the back of his knee, his height being a problem to manage any offensive tactics.

But everything was cut short as Leif unleashed on her.

A slew of punches crashed into her—her back, her stomach, her face. She barely had a chance to register a new blow before another one struck her, the vampire's agility and precision carefully timed and administered with just enough force to disorient her but not completely incapacitate her.

Well, if she was about to die, at least it was from being beaten to death. Because there were worse ways to die.

"Stop!" Lucas bellowed.

Relief escaped in a sigh as the tightness in her chest eased, and she crashed onto all fours on the stone floor.

She knew it. She knew he would never allow Leif to kill her.

Helping her to her feet, with her wincing through the pain, Lucas said, "You asked me in France why I hated ya, do ya rememba' that?"

"Yes," she managed to say with a nod, the slight movement causing an ache to shoot through her.

"And what did I say?" There was a deep void behind his gaze, an emptiness.

Her voice was so soft and strained when she said, "That you didn't hate me—that you never hated me."

Leif strolled up behind him just as Lucas twisted his head back toward the vampire and lifted a hand, their movements seeming planned. The blade of a black-handled dagger slid into Lucas's palm, Leif being cautious of the sharp edges as he handed it to Lucas. Flipping it in the air, Lucas took hold of the handle.

"Well, love . . ." He leaned closer, angling the tip of the dagger against her abdomen. "I do now."

Panic and fear and desperation flooded her entire body.

He would not do what he was about to do. He could never kill her. Right?

"You wouldn't dare," Karramis whispered, the declaration weak and imploring.

In that moment, he had no soul, no conscience, no trace of any humanity. He was devoid of all human emotion. Only the undiluted rage of a caged beast simmered in his cold eyes. "Ya wanted a villain . . ." The blade plunged through her stomach, the slice deep and clean. No hesitation. No regret. "So, here's your fuckin' villain."

A sharp, searing pain blasted through her center, shooting outward and ripping through her nerves. Oxygen expelled from her lips in a gasp, the piercing intrusion burning along her stomach. An electric shock shot down her spine, instantly shutting down her senses in a rush of agony. Her muscles stiffened, the contraction coiling around the invasion still sticking out of her, the tightening causing even more pain to course through her and flood her veins. Her limbs weakened, causing her legs to crumble beneath her. Flesh smacked against the floor as she cried out, the pained moan coming with a trail of tears.

Kneeling and pushing the blade deeper, Lucas leaned in and whispered into her ear, "Look what you made me do." He kissed her cheek and stood, leaving the blade embedded in her. Strolling through the door, leaving her alone with Leif, he called back, not even giving her another glance, "Goodbye, Karramis."

He was gone.

Lucas had stabbed her and left her there to die.

Closing her eyes, she gave in to the darkness wanting to consume her.

But Karramis was lurched upward like she was weightless as Leif held her up by her arms. Her own body was no longer in her control as she bent over slightly and leaned into the vampire's chest. The pain seared deeper into her as the blade shifted. Her eyes widened as more blood seeped from her. Heavy, uneven wheezes escaped her parted lips. She shoved him, wanting nothing more than to escape his presence, but the action was a feeble attempt to fight him off. Her knees buckled, her entire body wanting to collapse, but Leif held her tight, the hands gripping her upper arms barely registering against the pain. She grasped his shirt along his sides and dug her nails into the taut skin, a pathetic effort at again trying to fight back.

One side of her body sagged as Leif released her.

She screamed, the sound surprisingly loud and alarming, as the vampire twisted the blade, her telekinetic powers exploding outward on their own accord. But even her magic was too weak, the vampire only stumbling at the impact.

"Stop fighting. It's over," Leif taunted with a wicked chuckle as he yanked the blade from her body, the metal clanking against the floor.

Karramis's entire body slumped, and Leif allowed her to fall. She collapsed to her knees and toppled onto her side. She could not breathe, the pain making even the most basic bodily function difficult. Eyes closing, she could feel her magic fading as the warmth from her blood soaked into her clothes.

Leif squatted down beside her and gripped the hand holding her stomach and forced her to lift it. She moaned but kept her eyes closed as he slid two fingers very slowly into her open wound. Screaming again at the intrusion, she forced her eyes open and tried to wiggle away, but the movement was stifled, his fingers still inside her causing more pain to surge through her every movement.

She panted as his fingers pulled out. Their eyes locked as he lifted his hand and placed the digits into his mouth, a soft moan flowing from him as he sucked.

"Mmm," he moaned deeper, slipping his fingers out with a popping sound. "You taste so fucking good."

Lifting her to her knees, he grinned down at her, an inappropriate comment lingering on the tip of his tongue. But he refrained as he lowered to his knees and cupped her face with both hands, the struggle to hold her up interfering with the need to keep eye contact with her. Running a finger over her lips, he reveled in her one final time before he uttered, his eyes going black, veins deepening, and fangs descending, "Brace yourself, witch. This is going to fucking hurt."

Giving in to the defeat, she did not even scream.

Pain.

All there was left was pain. So, she allowed it to take over her, consume her. Allowed it to sink deeper into the depths of her mind, washing away everything else and leaving nothing but the end of an unfair fate.

This was it. Her life. It was over. A life of an unknown fate, of loss and heartbreak and no chance of a happily ever after.

And with that, she released it, her magic. Giving it permission to leave her to her destiny, desperation giving her strength.

As the blood flowed from her body, she could see it, her magic.

The mist swirled around her, embracing her one final time with its familiar welcome. And as her body landed on the other side of the goodbye, she opened her eyes, wanting to see the world around her just one more time.

It was cold. So cold.

And wet.

And white.

All of it was so bright and covered in white . . . before it all faded away.

Chapter 20

Life Given

The cold released its hold on Karramis as she gently pressed her lips against Will's chilled cheek, every ounce of her craving just one more moment of happiness.

"I'm not cold anymore." Her voice was strained and barely above a whisper as the wind whipped wildly around them.

Jerking back at her words, Will peered down at the glossy brown eyes staring up at him. "No." She was dying. He had been too late. "No, this isn't happening. Not again." He had already lost her too many times before—having to tell her and his newborn children goodbye and a death he had not known was false until nearly a year ago. The idea of never seeing her yet again weighed heavy on his heart. "Not now."

Her eyes fluttered, the battle to keep them open waning. "I love you . . ." Unable to fight it, she gave in, the world around her going dark. "All of you."

Every part of her became simultaneously weightless and heavy as the darkness devoured her, the shadows claiming her and slowly filling her with silence and emptiness.

Her name echoed in the distance as a raw hollowness seeped deeper into her body and wrapped around her heart, her mind, her very existence.

There was nothing around her. No floor, no ceiling or walls, no sounds, no air, no shimmer of light. Nothing. Even her own body felt foreign and distant, as if her mind was no longer connected and all parts of her were floating in this dark oblivion. As the shadowy vast of nothingness pulled her further and further into it, a sudden yank jostled her forward, hard and swift.

A presence. An energy her entire essence called to, held on to. It was an anchor, refusing to allow her to wander into the abyss. But she could not hold on to it.

Come back. Don't leave me.

Will.

He had been here. He had come back for her.

She clung to him, his presence trapped behind a wall of solid blackness, as trepidation and desperate anticipation coiled in her chest. Her heartbeat fluttered, straining to stay alive, the soft thumps like a finger tapping gently against her skin. A warm breeze filled with a familiar scent coasted around her, but the phantom wind collected all that was left of Will as more of the coldness faded from her ethereal form, stealing the last of him away from her.

No. Not yet.

But he was fading in and out, getting farther away as more of the darkness blanketed her, her body giving in and fully surrendering to her injuries.

She searched, reaching out for anything, craving something real and solid to take hold of her again.

I'm not ready.

But there was nothing but emptiness.

Will was gone. And she was alone. All that remained was a complete void.

Fear consumed her, just like the blackness all around her.

It was dark. So dark.

It was only her.

Alone.

Lost.

She could not feel, or smell or hear. She could not see.

Only darkness.

Darkness and . . .

Wait.

Heat. There was a blazing heat slowly wrapping around her. A heat growing more intense by the second.

Trying to draw in a breath, she struggled as the air around her grew hotter, the heat masked behind the shadows.

Another presence lingered. This one both recognizable yet so strange and foreign somehow. But this was definitely not Will. No, this was something else. Something formidable. A force like no other.

Light flashed up ahead, the spontaneous illumination like an explosion. It raged as it grew closer, the heat shooting toward her at an unstoppable speed.

It was going to hit her. There was no escaping it. She could not move. Her form remained frozen, floating in midair as if tethered to something. Something strong and powerful. Something light and dark. Something real and alive.

A rush of energy blasted through her, igniting something deep inside her core and rising to the surface with the intensity of the light racing toward her.

No, not light—flames. Fire. It was an explosion of flames, bright glowing shades of red and orange zooming straight for her.

The energy inside her and the flames called to one another, like two lost souls finally finding their other half. It burned from the inside out, the internal force wanting nothing more than to be free and join the element rushing toward them. But the pain did not hurt. No, it was almost pleasurable. A mix of right and wrong. It was welcoming and warming yet hostile. It was protective yet dangerous. It was fierce and gentle and completely all-consuming. It was magically euphoric and life-altering.

The flames raged closer, and the energy inside her built, opening its arms to greet the inferno.

Pulling in a deep inhale, she tightly closed her eyes, anticipating the burning impact.

This was it.

The glow behind her eyelids grew brighter, the heat nearly unbearable as the blaze intensified just as a white flash sparked. She popped open her eyes and screamed, but her voice was inaudible, completely lost within the nothingness she was trapped inside as the flames crashed into her.

But nothing happened.

There was no searing pain. No burning flesh or singeing hair. In fact, it did not hurt at all. No, it was more like a comfort. An invisible energy swooping in and forcing her heart to beat again.

A lifeline.

The fire disappeared into her, the flames pulling into her chest, her stomach, and trailing along her arms before dipping beneath the skin. She was glowing as the flames began to pulse below the surface, the fire heating every inch of her insides, forging itself within her veins, blood, bones, and her soul. Wrapped in a veil of fire, the flames caressed her nerves, the element forging into something more, something powerful. Something ancient and unstoppable.

A phoenix.

Encouraging her to take her first real breath, the energy and element combined inside her, completely driving away the darkness.

She was alive.

The air around was clean, crisp, and fresh—smelling of cold rain, pine trees, and a wonderful familiar aroma of wild nettles, of suede and cedar, and the subtle undertones of lavender and jasmine.

Eyes open, she tried to observe her surroundings, but everything was out of focus. A touch she had grown accustomed to slid over her face and caressed the top of her ear, sliding her hair behind it, just as her body went limp. A cold wetness pressed into her legs as her body was lowered, the chill seeping through a soft barrier along her upper thighs.

She blinked and stared up into familiar, beautiful blue eyes.

"Hello, darling." His voice was like a caress against her nerves, calming her.

He was here. Will. Her missing piece, lost but found again.

She was home.

~

"I'm going to slaughter them. All of them. Starting with the son of a bitch who stabbed me."

There was so much conviction and rage in Karramis's declaration, but Will wanted nothing more than to savor this moment.

Karramis was here.

Awake and talking.

He could feel the warmth radiating from her, proof the blood in her veins flowed freely. He could see the pulse against the smooth, clean skin along her neck. Her heart was beating. Condensation blew from her mouth as she drew in shallow exhales, evidence there was air in her lungs. She was breathing.

She was alive. Karramis was alive.

Will gently pulled her body closer to his, wanting to confirm she was really in his arms, and it was not a dream. "For a moment there, I thought I lost you." His words were taut, the burn in his throat matching the burn in his eyes.

A calm settled over her as she monitored the disbelief and shock flooding his relieved expression. Swallowing down the realization again that she had, in fact, died, she reached up a hand and cupped his face, Will leaning into her touch. "You did."

He nodded imperceptibly, not wanting to fully believe her words.

The next word from her mouth was a desperate plea, a question she needed answered more than anything, accompanying a widened gaze. "Kids?" But it was so soft and strained, choked behind the fear coursing through her. Had Merrick kept his promise to keep them safe for now?

"They're all right, my love," Will answered quickly, seeing the worry in her expression and feeling the rigidness of her body against him. Glancing over at the twins, who were only a few feet away, Will added with a soft smile. "They're here."

Karramis sagged in relief as her eyes shifted to her children, her heavy breathing holding back her tears.

"Hi, Mom," Rhiannon offered with a slight wave, her own tears winning the fight and escaping down her cheeks.

"Hi, sweetie." Karramis gave her a gentle smile. "Are you okay?"

Rhiannon nodded. "Yes."

As Karramis glanced over at James, her son remained still, his face emotionless and his bloodshot gaze unblinking. But before she could question if he, too, was all right, Aidan stepped closer.

"It's a miracle." There was awe in his tone.

"No," Will said calmly, shaking his head and peering down at his wife with pure astonishment and adoration, "it's magic." He chuckled. "And tenacity, I'm sure."

Aidan snickered. "You always were a stubborn one, lass."

"Shut up," Karramis said, trying to appear serious but failing as the response came out with a playful lilt.

"You really are a miracle, though," Will added, refusing to break eye contact. "You know that? I always knew you were. But I also stand by my original statement from before about you." Grinning, he added playfully, "You are definitely a bloody fool as well."

"Yeah, well," Karramis stated simply, "this miracle is glad to be alive. And as for the bloody fool part, I'd have to agree with you. Because . . . if it came down to me and you again, just know that I will always save you."

"I thought we agreed to save each other."

Karramis let out a soft huff, humor filling her features and tone. "Yeah, we did. So, tag, it's your turn."

Laughter filled the desolate area just outside the infirmary, everyone joining in except James, who remained almost in shock by his mother being alive before him.

Noticing the light flurries, Karramis muttered as the chill began to make her lower extremities numb. "I'd like to point out that I'm still on the ground and completely naked. And it's freaking freezing out here."

Will offered her a devilishly handsome grin as he released her and lifted to his feet, reaching down to help her up. "Let's get you inside and warmed up, darling."

Karramis grabbed his hand and held tight to the blanket wrapped around her, but as Will lifted her up, the muscles in her legs gave out and she collapsed.

Will caught her just as Rhiannon called out softly, concern etched along her brows, "Mom."

"I'm okay," Karramis promised as Will lifted her into his arms. "I'm just a little weak."

"And tired, most likely," Will added.

"Jeez, Kare," Aidan said, wrapping an arm around Rhiannon and James, the three of them trailing behind Karramis and Will, "ye're the livin' equivalent to the sayin' 'What doesn't kill you only makes you stronger,' aren't you?"

"But it did kill her," James corrected bluntly, stepping out of Aidan's comforting embrace.

Opening the door of the infirmary, Will strolled inside, Karramis closing her eyes and welcoming the heat of the room wrapping around her. The cold was starting to wear her down, along with the dying and coming back to life.

"Well then, I guess it's a good thing she's now immortal," Aidan said, attempting to drive the tension surrounding James away with a comical retort.

"About damn time," Karramis declared weakly as Will lowered her down onto one of the couches near the large fireplace in the parlor room. "Because this shit is getting ridiculous."

"But she's not immortal," Rhiannon admitted matter-of-factly, not a sliver of uncertainty in her statement as the details of phoenixes flowed to the surface of her mind.

"What do you mean?" James asked with a bite in his tone.

Rhiannon narrowed her eyes and observed her brother, sensing the range of emotions coming from him. She reached for him, mind to mind, but only silence bounced back.

Exhaling, allowing him to process things on his own for now, she continued, "There's not much about phoenixes in the documents and archives, but what is in them states that they are only folklore. A pure, genuine myth. No real phoenix has ever lived—at least, not during a time when the alphabet and record-keeping existed. But in the myths and actual stories I've read, it was always a fire bird, never a person. And in one set of documents, phoenixes were never immortal."

"They weren't?" Will asked, careful not to expose Karramis as he removed the wet blanket draped around her and covered her with a dry one. "But they are known as the eternal flame."

"No," Rhiannon continued, averting her gaze from her parents, along with James and Aidan, all of them giving

Karramis some privacy as she got situated on the couch. "A phoenix's magic isn't immortality, but rather resurrection. Immortal literally means never dying, yet phoenixes die. Mom died." She swallowed down the emotions, saying it out loud making it all too real. "But she was reborn. She's not truly immortal. She's just resistant to staying dead."

Karramis scoffed, fighting the tiredness creeping in. "Add resurrection to this ridiculous list of tropes my life seems to be throwing in my path, and I'm a damn walking, talking fairytale gone wrong."

"Does it say how a phoenix is created?" Aidan asked, wrapping his head around this revelation.

Rhiannon rubbed her forehead and thought about his question, racking her brain for the information. "It's said that phoenix magic could be created when powerful fire magic came together when life and death are joined as one. That it could happen when an over-abundance of fire magic was in one place when death arrives. But every story I came across stated a true phoenix can only be born upon its death when both phoenix magic and fire magic flow within the same vessel. That's probably why they are called the eternal flame—a fire can be created from the smallest ember. Her phoenix magic was the ember, and her fire magic was the fuel feeding it." She swallowed. "And her death ignited the flame."

"So, my mother dying is what made me a phoenix?" Karramis asked, more alert, already knowing the truth. Her daughter's words not only creating some questions but answering some as well.

Karramis was a Fire Witch, and so was her mother—in fact, they were part of the bloodline of the very first Fire Witches. And when her mother was pregnant with her, her father had given her the blood of a Fire Dragon to protect her. So, with the blood of three fire magics, and the fact her mother was killed instantly while Karramis was in her womb, most likely transferring any remaining blood to her unborn child as her tiny heart fought to stay alive, and the blood of the dragon also likely trying to heal the child, as well as the natural magic connected to the fire raging around her mother's dead body, the magic of a phoenix was created.

And given to Karramis.

This is the reason she did not die that night at the manor. She had phoenix magic inside her, but it was trapped. Her spell could not remove it. Because one could not remove magic that was not there. Dormant magic was untouchable. Unbinding. You could not remove something that was not truly present. It had been a safeguard magic had put into place way before humankind had been given any powers—to protect itself and the vessel from any malicious intent. And knowing she was not powerful enough nor skilled enough to divide her abilities, Karramis had to remove all of her magic, even the one keeping her alive. But with the phoenix magic still inside her, inactive but present, she could not fully die because the fire magic inside her was gone. The lingering phoenix magic, though dormant, kept her in a magical stasis, both alive and dead. Trapped between two worlds until she could die with fire magic wholly inside her.

"I think so," Rhiannon admitted softly.

A wave of guilt washed over Karramis. Her mother died, but she survived. She had cheated death now four times—once as an unborn baby, then again when Lucas nearly killed her trying to take out Will with an arrow, again when she was willing to remove her powers if it meant keeping her children safe from the clutches of Lucas when he found them, and now. She had died only a short time ago. Actually died this time. But now, she was alive.

Noticing the paleness blanching her face, Will lifted her into his arms, comforted that the fire had warmed her body by a substantial amount. "I think she needs to get some rest." Stopping in front of James, he whispered, the last few moments being focused on his son and the distance in his gaze. "Let me get her settled, and we'll talk. All right?"

James nodded, reluctant to argue, despite his unwillingness to join in any conversation fully at the moment.

Footsteps moved down the hall through the interior door from the parlor, the sounds fading as another door opened and closed.

"Hey," Rhiannon said gently as she placed a hand on her brother's forearm. "Are you okay?"

James wanted to lie and tell her he was fine, a lie she had once uttered multiple times to him just a few months ago. But he knew she would not let him off that easily. He had pushed and pushed her to open up, never allowing her the chance to feel as though she was truly alone. But now he wanted to shield her from everything he was feeling. Protect her from his own demons coming to life in his head. They were dark and vicious, telling him he was the reason his mother was killed.

She had died. His mother was dead—there was nothing left inside her, only a shell of a body remaining. He had seen her lifeless figure and touched her cold, pale skin, the kiss of death leaving its permanent mark on her.

Just moments ago, he watched as his father cradled his mother, desperate for her to come back to him.

His mother was dead.

And he had been the one to kill her.

"No," was all James said, not even glancing her way, as he strolled out of the infirmary into the blustering evening and closing the door behind him.

Will lowered Karramis's naked body into the steamy, warm water of the claw-foot tub, the large bathroom more of a luxury suite rather than part of an infirmary. With black-and-white speckled marble countertops and white cabinets with gold fixtures, white tiled floors, and dark gray accented walls, this room was beautiful and serene. Even the solid black tub, with its sleek sides and extravagant gold-plated faucet added an elegant charm to the tranquil atmosphere.

But it was the hands in her hair, gently scrubbing and massaging, that made everything about this moment peaceful.

Allowing herself to disappear into his touch, she closed her eyes and sank into the water. She was so exhausted. Everything inside her screamed for her to just sleep.

As fatigue settled into her core, she closed off her mind and gave her body fully over to Will and his attentiveness, welcoming him rinsing her hair and gently running a cloth along her skin—all remnants gone from her newly-born body birthed among the flames of her phoenix magic. She barely even recognized the strong arms lifting her from the bath and holding her up as Will dried her off, his touch so gentle and caring, before carrying her naked over to the bed. She sank into the mattress, the softness of the bedding and warmth of the heavy blanket causing her to fall even deeper into a sleepy trance.

Kissing her forehead before crawling under the covers next to her, he held her tight against his body, breathing in her scent. "How do you feel, my love?"

Inhaling deeply to remind herself he was actually there, she whispered into his chest as she drifted off to sleep. "Safe."

Chapter 21

Here and Gone

The dusting of snow falling from the sky was not due to James, who stood outside, taking in the aftermath of the explosion of power that had detonated from him and Rhiannon a short time ago.

The twins' powers were here. They had finally arrived.

Broken glass lay strewn about, the various windows being the victims of the earthquake which had been unleashed. Luckily, it had only been some of the larger ones on the top floor, rather than the smaller casements lining the walls of the bedrooms on the main floor where his mother and aunt now rested. The areas where fire burned among the snow now appeared muddy, exposing the dead grass to the dusky sky. Flower petals rested throughout the open field surrounding the backside of the infirmary, James having no recollection where they had come from. A large disjointed line lay across the charred land a few yards away, the fiery fissure that had been created now gone. He did not remember doing that either. Or maybe it had been Rhiannon. Either way, the distance from it and where he stood near the steps was entirely too close for comfort.

The infirmary could have been destroyed and everyone inside could have died or been seriously injured. Not confident who had created the crack in the earth which left the land scorched, James wondered who could have been responsible for the possible deaths of three more people, him or his sister? Aidan had said Nina, Alfina, and his aunt were all right afterward and only a few things had been broken, but what if it had been worse? Everything about that moment was so distant, like a dream he was slowly forgetting.

He was not even sure how he and his sister had managed such a destructive outburst of magic, but seeing his mother dead was the catalyst of so much emotional turmoil he could not contain everything inside him, and the magic wanted out. It wanted to fight and maim. To kill. It had wanted revenge. *He* had wanted revenge.

They had killed her. This time, they had been the reason for her actually dying on him. His mother had made a deal with the devil, and she had paid the final price for it.

But it was a price he was supposed to pay. Not her. He was who the prophecy foretold would stop Merrick, not her. He should have been the one to fight. Not her. So, why was fate constantly throwing her into harm's way? Why was she the one destiny kept trying to toss to the monsters who wanted all of them dead?

It was because of him. It was his fault. It was not fate or destiny. It was him. He was the one who had nearly gotten Rhiannon killed months ago, and it was he who was to blame for his mother's death. She had been trying to protect him, to give him more time to prepare and fight and summon all his magic.

Well, it worked. His mother had sacrificed herself, and in doing so, he was now fully capable of stopping Merrick from stealing any more magic.

And he would.

James was going to kill Merrick and anyone else who got in his way. He just had to figure out how.

~

The parlor was warm when James stepped inside and made his way over to the couch across from where Rhiannon sat on the sofa with her arms wrapped around her bent knees.

He did not have to ask to know what she was thinking about—the same thing he had been.

"How are we going to stop him?" James asked, sinking into the plush cushions, fatigue starting to take root.

Rhiannon turned her head, her watery blue eyes reflecting the flames in the fireplace. She had been crying. James had known she had been, having felt her finally give in to everything as her thoughts began to race. The same thoughts and emotions running through him as well. Rage and grief and shock were near the forefront of the emotional rollercoaster they were on, but relief was definitely the winning emotion. Relief their mother was alive. Relief their aunt would be okay. Relief that Harkin was alive, injured but still alive. Relief they had survived another run-in with Merrick. And relief they not only had full access to their powers, but because of their mother, they had six months to figure out how to use them. And six months to formulate a plan to stop Merrick.

Shrugging, Rhiannon said quietly, "I don't know."

"Yet." There was so much certainty in his voice. "You—no, we—*we* don't know yet. But we will. We will figure this out. I'm not letting them get away with this."

The voice of Terramina filled both their minds, providing them with an update. Everything was all clear outside, no signs of anyone trying to get through the wards around the village or Stoweward. And Phosmeratae had just completed another sweep along the northernmost tip of the island. Nothing seemed out of place or a cause for any concern. Ignara had remained with Harkin, protecting him while his wings healed enough for him to return to the cave, his magical flames causing the worst of his injuries. The wooden beam lodged into Harkin's leg had been removed, Ignara yanking it out with her mouth, but a few splinters of wood had remained, making it impossible for the dragon to heal.

"We need to help him," Rhiannon said, not wanting the Fire Dragon to suffer any longer than he had to. Harkin had fought for them, protected them. And now, he needed them.

Will strolled into the room. "I'll go."

Rhiannon took in his sluggish stride and messy hair. Sleep was wanting to claim him. He had been through a lot the last few hours, and he needed just as much rest as her mother. "I thought you were sleeping? You need to sleep, Dad."

"I know, I will, but I wanted to check on you both first."

"We're fine." Rhiannon glanced over at James and back at her father, realizing her choice of words. "Okay, maybe not fine, but it's a lot to process."

"Yeah," James agreed, his voice low, "we just need some time."

Will nodded, not wanting to prod but still hesitant to just let it go. They were just kids. Sixteen-year-olds who not only just saw their mother dead *and* come back to life, but they also unleashed an extraordinary amount of magic all at once.

Curiosity winning his internal debate, Will asked, "What happened back there?" His eyes shifted between the two of them. "How did you do all of that at once?"

"I don't know," the twins admitted together, both shrugging.

Not even acknowledging their perfectly synced answer, James continued, "It was like I was no longer in my body, like something—"

"—else was controlling me," Rhiannon chimed in with him.

James allowed her to continue on her own.

"Yes, me too." Rhiannon stretched out her legs on the couch. "I mean, I was there, but I wasn't. Something else completely took over me."

"That was your magic," Will said, furrowing his brow and showing them the defined crease between his eyes as his mind pulled in all the facts he could remember about magic. "The full force of it surfacing. But it was too much at once, so you lost control of it."

"Is that bad?" Rhiannon asked, concerned.

"It can be, if you don't train properly. See, as you know, magic is alive—it's an actual living thing—and because of this, it can fight to take control sometimes. It can reveal itself at the best possible time or even the worst, but it does it when it wants to take control. Magic wants to live, and when it feels threatened, it becomes extremely powerful."

"But magic can't die," Rhiannon reminded him. "So, how can it feel threatened?"

"Magic is far more powerful when it has a vessel to contain it, so it fights to keep the one holding it alive as well. Magic is only an essence, like a ghost. But along with the elements or a living, breathing thing being joined with it, it's an unstoppable force. But we have to remember, we can't let magic take total control over us. It can't fully take over or we could lose ourselves to it, or something far worse could happen."

"But how do we control all of it? I mean, I can't even remember half of what happened, but I do remember feeling like nothing could touch me, like I was an invincible force. I wasn't afraid or scared—I wasn't anything. I wasn't even me really. I was just . . . there. How do you control something that powerful?"

Will paused for a moment, remembering more of the things he had learned over the years and from Karramis. "Remember, magic is all about mind over matter, so we have to control it—fight it when it wants to take over. We have to be powerful enough to reel it in and take the reins again. But you also have to realize magic isn't unlimited, at least not the way you think. It's like a battery—you have to recharge it, or else the power eventually runs out. Just because you felt invincible, doesn't mean you are, or that you will always feel that way when you draw strength from your magic."

Silence fell as the twins processed everything their father said. After some time, it was James who spoke.

"What I don't understand though, is how is it that the magic has always been inside of us and yet it hasn't?"

"Yeah," Rhiannon went on. "How can we possess something that isn't really there?"

Will rubbed his chin, careful of the injuries along his lips. "Think of it like this—think of dormant magic like oxygen, like the air in your lungs. It's in you, it's there, but you can't really feel it or see it. You can't hold it. But once magic fully surfaces, it's now like the blood flowing through your veins. It's tangible. It's definite. You can feel it, taste it, smell it, see it. Magic is your blood now—you can feel it, manipulate it, create it, contain it."

Nobody in the room knew the dangers and struggles of powerful magic more than Will. He may not have had personal experiences with this kind of formidable abilities since his Drolnogard magic came naturally to him—only having to master distance and pushing the thoughts through—but he had been around to experience the powers his wife possessed and the strength her magic had when mastered. It was her magic and her undeniable ability to control it that had saved him, after all, and it was her magic which had saved her numerous times before. If it was not for the strong and fierce magic inside her, Karramis would not be alive just down the hall from him.

Looking between the twins, Will asked, reluctant due to the dangers but aware they had just as much strength as their mother now, and they would never find the same inner might and determination as her, if he did not give them the space to do it, "Would you like to go help Harkin?" The word had been delivered to Terramina to relay to Will just a few moments ago that the Fire Dragons had made it safely to the cave—the infirmary being inside the wards and Emrys Cave being a tad too far from the village, as well as a literal solid mass of stone, making it impossible for Will's magic to penetrate. "I can ask Nina for some suture supplies. Come to think of it, you may need some actual tools to remove the wood pieces, depending on the size of them, which I may be able to find around here somewhere. Once you remove the shards, he should heal without any permanent damage other than a scar or two."

"You're letting us go?" Rhiannon asked, surprised. "By ourselves?"

Will gave her a gentle smile and nodded. "Yes, you are just as safe in the cave with them as you are here." He headed toward the door leading into the hall. "Plus, I think the dragons have proven they are quite protective of you both." Stepping over the threshold, Will called, "Be right back."

James breathed a soft chuckle. "Yeah." The memories of the ogre, Gastell, getting eaten by Harkin flashed in his mind, the sight sending ease through him. He was grateful he was on the side where dragons fought with them and not against them. Dragons were definitely dangerous, but also, so freaking cool. "I guess the whole 'dragons don't eat people' thing is now in question."

Rhiannon laughed under her breath at the thrill running through her brother. "To be fair, though, I wouldn't count that thing as people. And he kind of deserved it."

"They all did." His tone was serious now. "Maybe we can just get Harkin to eat Merrick." James chuckled again. This time it was forced. "That would solve all our problems."

James knew the prospect of that idea was highly unlikely, Merrick proving he was strong enough to fight against the dragons already. But, even now, James wondered if there really was a way to stop him. Merrick's stolen magic was far more powerful than any other person's on the island.

Or was it?

"We'll stop him," Rhiannon said into his mind before saying out loud, "We just have to figure out how."

The room went quiet as the two of them considered their next step.

"James?" Rhiannon said softly, a look of reverence and appreciation in her expression.

James glanced back over his shoulder, pulling his pensive gaze from the fireplace over to her. "Yeah."

"Thank you."

He twisted his body around. "For what?"

"If you hadn't been there, holding my hand, I don't think I would've survived all of this."

A warm, gentle half smile curled one corner of his mouth. "Yes, you would have. Because I wasn't the one holding your hand, you were the one holding mine."

After a few minutes, Will returned with a backpack full of supplies. With a hug from their father and the condition that they have the dragons keep him posted, the twins left on Oakley and Raeth with Terramina staying behind to guard the infirmary and provide any updates.

~

The twins had returned to the infirmary a few hours later completely exhausted, the last few hours finally catching up with them as the adrenaline subsided. Each taking a room down the hall from their parents, James and Rhiannon had decided to sleep, asking both their father and Aidan to wake them if anything came up.

And with his wife and children under one roof, safe and guarded, Will finally decided to give in to the exhaustion washing over him as well and opted to retreat to his room and sleep next to Karramis, reveling in the idea he could hold her. But not before a quick shower and replacing some of his bandages.

His body was sore, the temperature change from the hot, steamy water to the warm yet slightly cool air of the bedroom erasing some of the relief the shower provided along his bruised muscles and injured ribs. Pain still throbbed across his face, but it was his midsection that ached more than anything.

With a towel wrapped around his waist, Will quietly strolled over to the wardrobe at the foot of the bed, glancing over at his sleeping wife before pulling a pair of gray sweatpants from the shelf inside the massive closet housing items for both him and Karramis. Alfina had raided the storage room in the basement and pulled some clothes she thought might fit them. Luckily for them, clothing was plentiful on the island—new and old items having been left behind by various residents over the recent years, as well as new articles collected from the non-magical world when traveling from the two realms had been more popular. Despite some of the clothing being outdated by twenty years, give or take, they were still clean, warm, and extremely helpful right now. Especially since most of his and Karramis's clothes had probably been lost in the fire.

Once things settled down a bit, Will knew they would have to venture over to the cabin to see the damages and figure out where they were going to live. But for now, he was content just being here, in the infirmary, next to his wife. A thought he welcomed as he removed a plain white T-shirt from the wardrobe and draped it over the wooden footboard, wanting it within reach just in case it was needed in a hurry in the middle of the night. He clicked off the soft-glowing lamp on the nightstand and crawled into bed. Soaking up the heat of Karramis's body, he pulled her backside into him, the two of them fitting into each other just right, and closed his eyes. Within moments, sleep claimed him as the smell and feel of her blanketed him.

~

Will opened his eyes as his hand reached out and felt the cool sheets of the empty bed next to him. He had no idea what time it was, but it was still dark outside the window. Unable to see the face of his watch in the unlit room, he reached for the lamp, the light illuminating the room in a soft amber glow.

"Darling?" Will called quietly, glancing at his watch. It was a little after midnight. Panic filled his chest as he threw the covers back and jumped to his feet. "Karramis?" he whispered loudly, trying to fight the uneasiness taking root in his stomach.

The sound of water running caught his attention, his eyes shifting toward the closed door of the bathroom. He opened the door slowly to find the room cast in darkness, but the shower was on. Flipping the switch, Will let out a deep sigh of relief at the sight of Karramis.

But something was wrong.

Karramis was sitting on the floor in the white T-shirt he had placed over the footboard, leaning against the black-tiled wall with her legs pulled into her chest and her face pressed into her palms with her elbows tucked in between her stomach and thighs. The stream of the shower pelted against the top of her slightly inclined head and completely drenched her. Steam billowed behind the glass door, but Will could see her shoulders were shaking. She was crying.

Will pulled open the glass door and stepped inside, instantly hissing at the searing heat of the water burning his skin. He angled the showerhead away from them, his sweatpants partially wet as he knelt down in front of her and took hold of her face. Her eyes were open as he forced them up to meet his, but her gaze was distant, lost.

With a soft, pleading voice, Will whispered, "Come back to me, darling." His wet hands slid into her hair, and he leaned his face closer, their noses almost touching. "Look at me." He waited, but she continued to stare right through him—she was somewhere else. "Darling." He pressed his lips against hers, just a gentle caress. "Look at me."

Karramis blinked, registering who was in front of her and where she was.

"I have you, darling. I'm here." Will sat down and pulled her into him, lifting her and placing her onto his lap. The shirt she wore was drenched, the feeling of the hot and wet material against his bruised midsection almost soothing.

She swallowed and closed her eyes, giving her head a quick and subtle shake before lifting it and focusing on him. "I'm fine."

"Don't," Will argued gently, his tone firm but kind. She was lying, whether for his sake or her own, he did not know. But either way, he would not allow her to fall back into the darkness again. "Don't lie to me." Caressing her wet strands away from her face, he wiped away the tears joining with the water along her cheeks. "You don't have to be strong right now. I have you."

Karramis curled her arms against her chest and leaned into him, nuzzling her forehead into the crook of his neck, letting the tears fall.

With one hand wrapped around her waist and holding her against him, Will rubbed her back with the other, reminding her he was there and soothing her. She was not alone. He would be there for her for as long as she needed him. And when she was ready, he would help her get back up. But until then, he would hold her while she cried in his arms.

A short time later, her crying slowed, and she pulled back and stared into his eyes. Pain filled her own expression, her dark brown gaze, now containing honey-gold speckles, rested among bloodshot eyes.

"I died," she said through the tightness in her throat. "I was dead." She released a heavy exhale followed by a shuttering inhale. Confusion and disbelief plagued her face as her voice dropped. "I was dead."

Will glided a hand up to her face and cupped her cheek, the soft and sympathetic tone matching his entire demeanor. "Do you feel this?" he asked, running his thumb carefully along her cheek, wanting her to focus on his skin against hers. "Feel me?"

Karramis closed her eyes and leaned into the touch as she nodded.

His hand moved slowly down her neck and over her collarbone before stopping at her chest, his palm splayed over her left breast. "Do you feel this?" He began to move his index finger in rhythmic taps, perfectly in sync with her heartbeat.

She nodded again, her eyes never leaving his.

"You are real." His finger continued to tap against her chest, his low and tender voice like a lullaby soothing her. There was so much adoration in his expression, so much compassion, affection, and devotion. "You are alive . . . You are whole and perfect and mine." Placing a hand at the nape of her neck, he pulled her in, kissing her passionately. His forehead leaned against hers. "And I am yours. I'm here, my love. We are both here and alive."

"It's gone," she whispered, her voice raw, the tears again forming in her eyes.

"What is?" Will asked with narrowed eyes.

"My magic."

Will's lips parted, inhaling a slight gasp at her words, the understanding hitting him instantly.

Karramis had died with fire magic in her blood, thus summoning her phoenix powers to the surface to bring her back to life with the gift of resurrection. She had been reborn a phoenix, but in doing so, she had actually died. Meaning, when she was dead, her other magic had been released back into the island. Karramis no longer had her other powers. She was no longer a Guardian or a Fire Witch. All that magic, gone. And her portal? She would never be able to open another doorway again.

She was empty—her magic completely ripped away from her. Magic she had finally mastered. Magic she had finally grown to respect. Magic she loved. Magic that had saved her time and time again. Gone. It was all gone.

Sliding his arms around her again, Will held her as she began crying, the pain and loss of everything she was going through something he could never understand. So, instead of offering her words, he cradled her in his lap as the water continued to fall and the steam filled the shower. He might not be able to shield her from everything she was dealing with, but he knew this—he would not let her go until she was ready, being the lifeline she needed, the one thing refusing to let her drown.

~

Karramis bolted awake and hurried to her feet, racing to the wardrobe. The sky outside the window was colored a dusky blue with soft yellows and pinks just along the tree line.

"What's the matter?" Will asked, startled and disoriented by her frantic actions.

Throwing on an oversized sweater and black leggings, the lack of undergarments not seeming to bother her, Karramis searched the room for shoes.

"Keep an eye on the kids," she demanded, her tone calm and absolute. "I'll be back."

Will gave her a bewildered shake of his head as it jerked back, his feet flying from the bed and moving swiftly toward her. "Where the bloody hell do you think you're going?"

There was a fire behind her determined, unwavering gaze turning to face Will, one filled with genuine thrill and raw vengeance, deep brown eyes wanting nothing more than ruthless revenge. "To the castle."

Karramis was no longer the person she once was. She was no longer a witch nor a Guardian. No longer a protector of the realm. That person was gone. Dead. A new person had been born. A person with the rage of a fighter and the heart of ice to do it. One who would do anything to protect her children and family. One who wanted justice and revenge. She would stop at nothing to get it. And as she took in the bruises and bandages along Will's face, really taking in the damages and realization she almost lost him, she vowed to herself she was going to get it. One way or another.

"Like hell you are," Will protested, halting her advancement toward the door with his hands on her upper arms.

Every moment leading to now flashed before her as all her pain, fear, and heartbreak shifted into endless rage and pure confidence. They had killed her, so now it was time to pay them back in full force. An eye for an eye. "I'm going to murder those fucking bastards."

"With what, your bare hands?" Will asked curiously but with a teasing tone, somewhat frightened and concerned by the woman before him but also slightly entertained. She was on fire, the wrath and undeniable strength exuding from her both extremely attractive and awe-inspiring.

Karramis wanted vengeance. They had stolen a life from her, and she wanted them to suffer for it. "Listen, with everything I'm feeling right now, I think I can handle myself. And I want them to pay. I want to feel the life drain from their bodies. I want to see the emptiness in their eyes as their soul dies. And I will not fail this time. And I sure as hell will not think twice about it."

"Again, how?" Will grinned and ran his hands along the sides of her face, pushing her messy hair back. "Darling, I think you've gone mad."

"No," she said, calm but tight, "I'm fucking pissed. They killed me, Will. *Killed* me. And I want them to suffer."

Will kissed her, sensing the tension fading almost instantly at the action. He had to help her think rationally right now. They could not go in there unprepared and frantic. That would only work against them. "And they will. But you can't go in there ill-equipped to defend yourself. You don't have magic to protect you anymore, my love." The gentle reminder was harsh but necessary. "Yes, you can fight, but being a phoenix doesn't make you invincible. They can still hurt you. They can still kill you again and again. And you will feel that pain every single time—that emptiness and darkness. And eventually it will only drive you completely mad. You will lose more of who you are each time you taste death, especially by their hands. Please, darling. . ." He kissed her forehead. "Think about it before you do anything reckless."

He ran a finger along the scar on her left temple, slowly gliding it down her cheek. He gently coasted the pad of his thumb over the area where her bruises no longer were. "Remember, the wounds you bear, the ones inside and out, are not the marks of defeat, but rather the marks of strength. Wear them proudly, for they show how you survived something that was meant to kill you. You have been broken. You've been beaten and battered. You've bled and cried. You've fought and failed. And yet here you are."

His hand lowered, tracing the area along her neck which once contained two puncture marks. But they were gone. He did not stop there, his never-ending sensual caress moving down to the invisible marks no longer on her wrist before his fingers lifted the hem of her sweater and found the smooth skin where the new stab wound had been, but it, too, was now gone.

"You are resilient," he uttered softly, his touch soothing her anger and transforming it into something else, something corporeal and hypnotic. "You are a force to be reckoned with. But you are not invincible. And you are definitely not rash with your decisions."

Karramis closed her eyes at his gentle inspection, his feather-light touch finding another knife-inflicted injury, this one raised and still present on her skin.

Will was not certain why the most recent injuries on her body had disappeared—he could only assume it was somehow due to her phoenix magic—but he was glad the others remained, the beauty of her wounds proof of her resilience and strength. His wife was a fighter, a trait he found utterly attractive.

Karramis settled her flirty gaze on him. "Are you trying to distract me from my revenge?"

Will flashed her a knowing grin. "Is it working?"

"No." Defiance gleamed in her eyes, her flirtatious expression fading into playful resignation. "Fine," she drawled, "I'll wait."

Will halted his perusal and cocked his head. "Really?"

"You sound surprised."

"To be honest, I am. I seriously thought I'd have to do a bit more convincing."

"Why, though?" she asked with a teasing shrug. "You're right. I can't go in there like a raging lunatic and without a clear-cut plan." She pressed her body into his and stared up at him through sensual eyes. "Plus, I'm a bit distracted now."

Will stared at her, surprise and longing lingering in his eyes.

"What?" Karramis asked with a delicate grin, baffled but intrigued by the way he was watching her.

"Say it again," he pleaded, his voice low and husky.

Karramis understood exactly what he wanted. "You. Were. Right." Her tone was seductive and dreamy.

"Mmm," Will hummed, deep in his throat. "I love hearing those words on your lips."

Karramis arched a suggestive brow.

Will looped an arm around her waist and yanked her into him. He kissed her, hard and claiming as he moved them both toward the bed.

Any strategizing could wait until later.

The Keep

Karramis and Will sat atop Callie along the exterior wall near the front gate of Casteya Castle as the sun began to rise. Rhiannon was close by on Raeth, hidden within the forest just a few yards away from her parents. James waited with Oakley, the two of them barely noticeable as the dragon stood on the roof of one of the smaller towers on the western side of the castle, their figures nearly camouflaged within the predawn light, the dragon's dark hues and James's black attire adding to their veiled presence.

Terramina and Ignara remained within range of the others, their guards up and ready to strike if needed, while Harkin and Phosmeratae scouted the area of the forbidden side closer to the forest, cliffs, and caves, monitoring for any movement. With the typically asocial Air Dragon's stark white appearance and large body, he would be obvious to anyone paying attention to the skies on this side of the island—and potentially even cause an uproar at him being so close to the castle—so he had remained closer to the ground, his presence making even the vampires uncomfortable at times. And with the word of what Harkin had done to Gastell, the Fire Dragon had remained farther away, his flight path seeming more casual as he observed from higher altitudes.

Harkin's injuries were almost completely healed, but his wings were taking longer to recover due to his own flames being the one to singe through the membranous tissue. So, this was just a casual flight for the healing Fire Dragon, nothing to see here. It was something most of the dragons did on a regular basis, never landing but always visible when taking to the skies on the east side of Kiluemar.

It had been a little over a week since the attack at the cabin, the inferno having taken out more than half of the structure. But the twins and their parents had not yet returned to see the actual damages for themselves yet, everyone agreeing to remain within the confines of the wards until everyone had recovered more and a solid plan was set in place before moving forward. Safety was everyone's major concern, but living within the protective walls around the village was a safeguard they appreciated. No rumors had been given on anything happening with Merrick and the others, and word of what happened at the cabin and to Kavana and Karramis had remained tight-lipped among the guard, deciding the less knowledge anyone else had, the better. And Lucas and the others finding out Karramis was, in fact, alive was something she wanted the privilege of doing herself. The element of surprise yet again.

Viktor had increased his nightly patrols between Stoweward and the village, while Quinian and Tenarick had provided more weapons to those who had decided to remain on the island after another warning was given that things were about to become increasingly dangerous. Many of the non-magical ones left, but most of the magically inclined humans and creatures stayed, especially those who were unable to go unnoticed. Most of the werewolves had nowhere else to go, and the dangers they were to society in the non-magical realm outweighed the dangers they faced staying here. None of the werewolves wanted to hurt anyone in the non-magical world, so all those who had activated the curse chose to stay, and many of their non-magical families decided to stay as well. But as long as those who remained kept within the protective wards around both the village and Stoweward, they would have an advantage and be safe.

But Will had been correct in assuming the wards had weakened upon Zarrius's death, every Guardian and member of the guard being the anchor to hold the barrier in place. But with Karramis also dying and Kavana hurt and Pavian gone, the protection around the areas had severely weakened, thus prompting James and Rhiannon to offer up their blood to strengthen them, along with the blood of each dragon. Now, the wards were stronger than ever, and the only thing keeping those who stayed behind completely safe.

But only when inside them.

Everyone waited patiently as dawn crept closer, their window to strike only consisting of mere minutes if discovered before everything fell into place.

Karramis rubbed her arms, thankful for the heat from Will radiating along her back. The snow had melted, but the chill was still in the air, the new year bringing cold temperatures but fewer storms. Callie shuffled, the winged horse sensing the tension building as they waited for the signal.

But this was not an attack, the moment Karramis had craved shortly after coming back to life. No, this was not her finally seeking her revenge. This was something bigger than vengeance. Something life or death.

This was a rescue.

Kavana had woken four days after the ordeal at the cabin, her injuries and the medication making her incoherent and overly exhausted, forcing her in and out of consciousness.

Upon inspection, Nina and Alfina had discovered the extent of her injuries had nearly killed her. They had hoped her Guardian magic would help heal her from some of the minor damages or speed up the regeneration of her blood, but unlike Pavian, all her healing abilities had completely diminished.

Pavian had learned from the way his hand had healed when they reopened the portals that his healing powers had remained—nowhere near as strong, but present nonetheless. However, Kavana's cut on her hand never healed, leaving behind a scar on her palm. No one was sure why Pavian's ability to heal was still active inside of him, but Alfina presumed it was because his abilities were older, thus stronger than hers, but there was no real way to test that theory. So, Alfina and Nina had to heal her the old-fashioned way, with medical treatment.

When Kavana woke a few days afterward, she was frantic and insistent on getting back to the area where they had held her captive. A place they called the Keep.

The Keep was a feeding ground for the vampires. A dungeon created to house magical and non-magical humans as living, breathing blood bags. It was a prison to those people. A death trap. The last place many of them would ever see.

And to Karramis's shock, one of those people had been Avery—one of her childhood best friends. A friend she had thought was in Isreal all this time with her family, introducing them to her new husband. But the truth was, according to Kavana, who had been in a cell next to her, Avery and Caleb had returned over the summer, just a month before Merrick returned.

Avery and Caleb had been prisoners and tortured for months. And there was no telling how long the others had been there. Kavana had said there had been at least a dozen more cells around her, but she was unsure if all of them were occupied, most of the feedings having been administered downstairs and during the night when the lights were out inside the Keep.

Kavana needed to save them, but her injuries had been too severe, her body still not strong enough for a rescue mission.

But Karramis had agreed with her sister, they had to save Avery. They had to rescue all of them. This was not up for debate. So, they were going to storm the Keep and get every single one of them out of there.

Although, the idea of storming the castle seemed rather barbaric and somewhat idiotic, so another plan was devised.

Relaying as much as she could, Kavana had informed them the Keep was not heavily guarded. In fact, it was pretty much empty except between dusk and dawn when all the vampires would come to feed. Kavana had noted at least eight vampires, not including Leif or Merrick. The cells had been thick iron bars and most of them had no windows, so the chance of breaking out was nearly impossible. And from what Kavana could tell, Caleb and another individual, one she could never fully identify, had been the only two with any dangerous powers, something the vampires took into consideration the night after she was taken—the night of the full moon.

Caleb Kittleman was a werewolf, along with his two younger brothers. The three of them had arrived in Kiluemar shortly before Will had. After realizing he carried his father's curse, he fled with his brothers and mother to the island after his father was killed during one of his shifts.

Kiluemar had solely been a realm for magical creatures, but for reasons like Caleb, and many more before him, non-magical humans were given permission to live here over a century ago. And with this, many of the modern amenities were provided due to the ones without magic wanting to be beneficial to the island—therefore becoming plumbers, electricians, teachers, nurses, engineers, and so on. And Caleb's mother had been a botanist before coming here, so her skills with plants and herbs came in handy. But unfortunately, Karramis had eventually learned, his mother had been one of the ones who had gone missing during the fifteen years she had been away.

But Will had become friends with Caleb over the years, the two of them being new residents during the same time. So, Will refused to allow his friend to fall victim to the monsters of this world like Caleb's mother had. They were going to get them out of there. All of them.

James waited, the heat of Oakley keeping him warm as the cold air kissed his exposed skin along his face and hands. Everything about this mission sent a thrill through him, this invigorating sensation of danger and anticipation buzzing through him. But there was also something else humming just below the surface. It was a raw sense of power and strength yet a slight hesitancy. He did not want to mess this up, but everything inside him told him he could do it. It felt visceral and all-consuming. He was determined to complete this task without any mistakes. No one was going to die this time. No one. He was going to ensure every single person made it back to the infirmary today. One way or another.

"It's almost time," he said to the Earth Dragon as he zipped the coat up to his neck, the thick material warm and soft.

Oakley gave a single nod, confirming he was ready.

"James," Rhiannon called, her inner voice traveling up to her brother as she waited inside Shadow Forest. *"Are you okay?"*

Rhiannon had been worried about her brother. There was something off about him, something she had noticed more and more over the last few days. He had shut himself off to her, but not like she had before. No, this was not in terms of their connection, but rather in a deeper way. Like a part of him changed when he saw their mother dead. It was like he was lost almost, but he, himself, was determined to find his own way. There was a fight inside him that scared her. An emotion that was far more powerful than fear. It had been hard for her too, the nightmares making it difficult to sleep again, but with James it was different. He was not suffering in the same way she was. She was still so afraid of everything, all the unknowns and dangers. And with losing her grandfather and nearly losing her aunt, and seeing her mother dead, Rhiannon was terrified and so anxious about what was coming.

But with James, he craved it. He wanted to fight, to learn, to just run down the path of destiny and face all of it head on. He embraced his powers, his strengths. More than before. It was a hunger almost. He had become a predator wanting to hunt its prey, this prophecy being the thing he craved more than anything. There was no fear but rather a fearlessness making him impervious to everything they both had suffered through lately. It was as if everything that had happened was fuel to the fire building inside him. He had a drive to attack, a determination to strike the enemy before they had a chance to hit first. And that, too, terrified her. James had always been spontaneous and reckless with the things he did, but there was definitely something brewing inside him, and Rhiannon was not sure what it was. Those thoughts she was not privy to. But she was concerned whatever it was would get him killed.

"I'm good," James said, anticipation thrumming through him.

He was the one who had insisted his parents allow him to help them, going so far as telling them he was the one with all the magic now and they were both powerless against all the dangers they could face. James would not be left behind again. And he would not let them send him away. Not this time. This was his fight. Period. And when Karramis had recognized the stubbornness and defiance in his gaze, she had decided whatever she would have said did not matter. He was going to come one way or another.

And so, here they were, waiting for the signal. The signal that would set the plan in motion. The plan Karramis had come up with, along with her husband, their children, the dragons, and Aidan. It would be a dangerous plan, but only if they were caught, and if executed right, it would work.

A golden eagle waited on the roof of the Keep, Aidan's shape-shifting form watching below with the expert precision of a bird of prey on a mission.

A set of three quiet footsteps moved away from the Keep just as the slow progression of the wall of sunlight breached the exterior of the first castle, coasting across the brown, overgrown lawn of the inner ward. As the footfalls disappeared behind a door along the side of the interior wall of the older structure,

Aidan waited, observing the area one final time, the silence and stillness filling his heightened senses.

His bird called out, the high-pitched whistling sound traveling across the early morning sky.

The signal.

Raeth outstretched his wings as Rhiannon leaned forward and clutched her legs together and held tight. Wind swirled as the dragon shot into the air and headed toward the castle. Oakley jumped and coasted downward, James grinning as the zooming descent sent a wave of excitement shooting through his abdomen. Oakley landed among the shadows still lining the backside of the Keep near the wall of stairs, the front of them around the corner just as his call-to-action reached Terramina, Ignara, Harkin, and Phosmeratae, backup already heading their way but the Air and Fire Dragons ascending into the clouds overhead, awaiting further instructions.

Will clicked his tongue and gently nudged Callie, the winged horse taking to the sky as Karramis leaned back into her husband's arm and held tight to the wrists holding the mane. Callie and Terramina closed in on each other, the two creatures landing on the other side of the walls near the main door of the second castle—the same castle housing Merrick's and the others' bedrooms.

Aidan landed next to Will and Karramis, shifting back into his human form. Will jumped from Callie and unfastened the cross bow from around the winged horse's neck, handing the weapon and quiver with a handful of wooden-shafted bolts to

Aidan. Unsheathing the sword Raina had given him, Pavian's sword, Will readied himself just as Karramis's feet landed hard against the frozen-solid ground. She raced over to the Keep as Aidan and Will monitored the door of the castle, hoping it would remain closed but ready to fight.

Phosmeratae circled overhead, his large shadowy form casting the castle grounds in darkness as he and the two Fire Dragons disappeared into the clouds.

Raeth landed next to Oakley, and the twins quickly ran to the front of the Keep, the dragons following behind them slightly, remaining close and vigilant. James bolted toward the stairs of the Keep and raced upward, throwing open the door as Rhiannon followed behind him. The heavy metal door crashed against the back wall, the sound reverberating through the stone room like a deafening alarm.

"James," Rhiannon chastised in a loud whisper.

He frowned. "Sorry."

They both waited, their eyes and ears on alert. When only silence settled back in the building, they jumped into action.

Kavana had told them the keys to the cells were on a single rusty iron ring, which they kept by the front door on a hook, allowing anyone to open the cell doors to feed. But they could not find it. The hook was there, screwed into the stony interior, but no keys.

The sunlight started to creep in through the few barred windows lining the open entryway, the entire hallway to the right absent of natural light. Stone walls consisting of various-sized boulders lined the sides leading into the corridor as the twins made their way farther into the Keep, hoping the keys were somewhere nearby.

Making their way into the medieval-style dungeon, the area surprisingly clean despite the subtle odor of blood, human waste, and body odor slamming into them as they moved past the first wall. Two sets of cells lay before them, one on either side of the hallway. Iron bars created the main wall while the same mismatched stone barriers at the front of the hall provided the rest of the prison chamber. The area was small, no larger than eight feet in all directions, but a pile of blankets rested in the back corner of each cell and two wooden buckets sat inside, one near the makeshift sleeping space and the other near the heavy iron door.

"They're empty," Rhiannon whispered.

"We need to check the others," James said, gesturing with his chin to move deeper into the Keep.

Rhiannon focused on her side, rushing down and eyeing each cell.

A moan drew his attention as James reached the next cell. A petite woman, no older than him, with matted black hair and bronze skin, leaned against the back wall as she sat on the blankets. Blood coated her clothes, and her cheeks lacked any color. She appeared severely malnourished.

James gripped the bars and shook the door, the slight hope it was unlocked fading when it held tight. "Listen, I'm going to get you out of here." Desperate to help her, he tugged on the door again. "Dammit! Where are they?" He twisted around, eyeing the other cells.

Rhiannon halted two cells down from him. "I think I found her." Her voice was quiet but sure. Her mother had described what Avery looked like, the adult woman before her matching the description with her wavy blonde hair and fair skin. "Avery?"

Please don't be dead.

James heard his sister's internal plea, the same words he thought as he stared at the young girl.

"Hey," James whispered, and the girl's eyes fluttered open, fully aware of his presence.

"Avery?" Rhiannon called again. "Can you hear me?"

This was taking too long. They were going to get caught.

Rhiannon tapped on the iron bars, the sound hollow under her fingertips.

The woman sat on the stone ground with a layer of blankets, appearing almost clean, draped over her body up to her neck. Was she even breathing anymore? The Keep was freezing, and there was no telling how injured the woman was, everything appearing as if she was simply sleeping beneath the blankets, so Rhiannon let out a relieved exhale when the frail and motionless woman moved.

"Back wall," a soft, delicate voice croaked to James.

Glancing up, his focus moving from the old-fashioned lock back to the young girl, he questioned, unsure if he actually heard her. "What?"

"Back wall," she said again, her hazel eyes meeting his.

Hands gripped James and twisted him around, the powers inside him reacting on instinct as the air whipped around him and crashed into the figure.

Aidan landed on the floor with a heavy thud, a grunt exploding from him.

"Shit!" James hurried to help him up. "I'm sorry."

"It's all right, lad." Aidan rose to his feet, his body radiating with adrenaline. "We need to hurry. What's takin' so long?"

"We can't find the keys," Rhiannon said.

James peered at the girl, then down the hall toward the back wall. Without hesitating, he raced by his sister, seeing two more figures shift inside the cells. He searched as he halted in another area, this one filled with chairs and a small table in the center of the room and what looked like a bookshelf of various canned goods lining one wall. Two more barred windows rested higher on the wall on either side of the rectangular room.

His brown eyes settled on a hook matching the one up front just inside an arched threshold leading to a set of stone stairs spiraling downward into the darkness.

There they were on the hook. The keys.

"Got 'em!" James whisper-yelled.

Rhiannon waved him forward. "Hurry."

James rushed back into the corridor, unlocking the first cell of the two closest prisoners. Aidan rushed forward, jumping into action and lifting the person, another woman with mocha skin and long-white hair, from the cell on the left. He carried her outside just as James raced to the other cell, pushing open the door. Moving swiftly, he stopped at the cell in front of Rhiannon, the key sliding in and unlocking without any resistance.

James did not wait another second as he came up to the cell with the young girl, the door flinging open as soon as the lock clicked. Dropping the keys on the floor, he lifted her into his arms, the action effortless under her fragile body.

Her eyes met his as he angled himself sideways, avoiding her head from hitting the doorframe. "Downstairs." The word was forced as pain creased her brow.

His shoes pounded against the stairs, his movements swift as he rounded the corner, meeting Aidan and the two Earth Dragons on the backside of the Keep.

It was still quiet outside.

James lowered the girl to the ground, leaning her carefully against the wall next to the woman Aidan had removed from the building.

"Open your eyes," James said softly, pushing the girl's hair out of her face as her head lulled to the side.

Heavy eyelids fluttered, the sallow appearance on her face a deep contrast to her perfectly tanned skin. Dark circles filled the hollows under her eyes. Her long, wavy raven-colored hair was matted, but still appeared healthy, the shiny locks nearly reaching the middle of her back. Various puncture marks lined both sides of her neck near the artery, all but one appearing old and healed.

James blinked as he stared at her. She must have been here for months.

Blood coated her oversized white shirt, and her bare legs had traces of more blood along her thighs, the dark stains appearing as disjointed smears. James noticed another set of fang marks on one of her wrists, this one seeming recent, most likely the cause of the blood along her upper legs, the location of the smears near where her arm would rest on her side.

Rich hazel eyes, more green than brown, collided with his as he lifted his perusal back up to her face. Sadness mixed with hope flickered in her gaze.

"You're safe," James muttered. "I'm getting you out of here."

"Downstairs," was all she said, the same word she uttered earlier finally registering to James.

He ran back around the building and up the stairs just as Aidan carried a blonde woman outside, Rhiannon trailing behind him.

Avery.

"Is she going to be okay?" James asked, concern and panic racing through him at her bloodied appearance.

She had far more puncture marks on her neck and wrists than the girl, but she also had them on her forearms and inner thighs, her oversized shirt barely covering her lower half. Old and new, the wounds had appeared to have been administered in careful succession, the vampires making sure she healed before drawing more blood from her.

"She's alive," Aidan said, his voice sounding unconvinced by his statement as he continued down the steps without stopping.

Avery was, in fact, alive, but barely. Her heart beat, but it was slow. Too slow.

Aidan whistled, and Karramis and Will faced him.

Karramis bolted as her eyes widened at the familiar sandy-blonde tresses attached to the lifeless body in Aidan's hands.

Will followed behind her, no longer focused on whoever might storm out of the castle.

Karramis reached Aidan, but before she could ask, he reassured her, seeing the fear in her eyes, "She's alive."

Relief tore through her chest, a light sob falling from her lips.

"She needs help." Aidan handed Avery over to Will, his emerald eyes relaying an urgency not present in his firm, steady tone. "Now."

Will nodded, calling Callie, his whistle echoing throughout the courtyard. His arms cradled her under her upper back and beneath her bended knees, angling her into his chest as her head leaned into his shoulder.

Cold, frail fingers twitched against his chest, the touch so soft but intentional.

Will glanced down and looked into familiar, piercing blue eyes. "It's all right." The words were a whisper on his lip, the state of her ashen skin, sunken, bony face, and frail figure making his tone tight with disbelief. He swallowed down the lump in his throat. "We have you. We're going to get you out of here."

"Cal-eb." She could barely speak.

Will turned his eyes upward and aimed them toward Aidan, a silent conversation transpiring between them.

Aidan shook his head and pursed his lips, his eyes sad and his expression filled with defeat.

Caleb was not inside.

And the only other person, a young man in perhaps his early twenties, was dead. The body was not even in full rigor mortis yet, but with the cold temperature and the possibility of having all his blood drained, there was no way of telling how long ago he died or if they had been just a few hours sooner, if he would have survived.

"We'll find him," Will said, hopeful his words would not be a lie as he hurried over to Callie and lifted her up, Karramis already ready to go and taking her best friend into her arms. "Get her out of here."

"Help," James called, his voice traveling farther than he wanted as he stumbled through the door of the Keep with a man at his side, James nearly carrying the weak and limping guy.

"Go," Will said to Karramis as he gently tapped against Callie's side. "We'll get the others."

Karramis did not argue but only nodded, the state of Avery worse than she could imagine. Her best friend was barely hanging on, death knocking at her door.

Callie lifted into the sky, Karramis not even concerned by the prospects of being airborne by herself as the winged horse headed toward the infirmary.

Aidan traded places with James and helped the man down the stairs, lowering him to the ground next to the other two.

Within moments, James and Will had removed two others from the Keep, one of them being Caleb, who had been downstairs locked up with another werewolf and a woman, the three of them being the most recent meals for the vampires.

Ignara and Harkin swooped down and landed beside the three Earth Dragons as James climbed up onto Oakley. Will lifted the young girl with black hair, and James took hold of her and cradled her in his arms as the dragon took flight. Oakley hovered overhead as Rhiannon aided Caleb and the other werewolf up onto Ignara's back. Thankfully the two werewolves were strong enough to ride solely on the Fire Dragon, but the fear was evident as they remained as still as possible on top of the massive creature. The werewolf curse may be a curse, but in this moment, it was a blessing, the two men healing quickly.

Harkin kept his eyes and ears alert, the danger still present until they all took to the skies.

Will helped the woman from downstairs onto Ignara, Caleb and the other man nestling her in between them. She was weak but awake.

Rhiannon mounted Raeth as Will pushed the other semi-conscious woman, the one with rich brown skin and stark white hair, into his daughter's lap before jumping on behind her, making sure the woman and Rhiannon were secure on top of the dragon. He held tight as all of them sprang upward, Terramina following behind them.

After doing one more quick sweep of the Keep, Aidan exited the door and shifted, heading straight for the infirmary, the sight of the dragons against the early morning sky allowing him to relax.

They had done it.

But unfortunately, not all of the ones there had survived. Four bodies had been found in their cells downstairs, as well as the young man upstairs.

The mission may have saved some, but not all of them.

And once Merrick and the others discovered what they had done, taking away their food supply, many more would fall victim to their hunger, their wrath. And there was no telling how many more would die before this was all over.

Chapter 23

The Aftermath

It had been weeks since the twins' magic had arrived, the full extent of the power inside them forging itself into the very essence of their souls. They could feel it, an innate potential. An energy spreading through their veins and along their bones and swelling deep inside their core and taking over every organ, every drop of blood, every nerve. It was building and maturing into a force, an intense and potent strength. They could sense how powerful they could be.

The only problem was, neither one of them knew how to access and control the full power that had been unleashed from them when they saw their mother dead. And both never wanted to witness it again. They never wanted to gain that kind of power if it meant losing someone. If they had to see their mother—or anyone—die, James and Rhiannon did not want to be able to control the powerful magic inside of them.

But the twins dealt with the uncertainty of what would happen next and the future of this prophecy differently. Both did not want to lose anyone, especially if it was to protect them.

James had taken what had happened to Karramis just as hard as Rhiannon, but something shifted inside him. Instead of fearing the potential losses they might face, he had made a promise to himself to fight, deciding he would train and practice as often as he could to prepare himself for the battle soon to arrive. A battle he vowed would be *his* fight as the prophecy foretold, without any outside forces helping, minus his sister, of course. But Rhiannon had reverted back to being afraid all the time, her fear taking control of her once again. But James could not allow that to happen. Not this time. Too much was at stake. A battle was coming, whether she wanted to admit it or not, and the only way they were going to survive it was to outsmart and overpower the one who wanted them dead. And James was confident, with the right plan, cunning and thorough, and the right amount of training to counter Merrick's stolen abilities and natural strength and agility, they could, in fact, succeed in taking him down.

It was only a matter of convincing Rhiannon to step away from the research she believed would be the ultimate way to defeat Merrick and train her abilities. James knew she was powerful, more powerful than him even. Possibly. She had exhibited such strength before, such control. It was only that she had wandered too far into her head, yet again, allowing her mind to whisper lies to her. A voice she often listened to. But James believed she could do so much more, if only she would stop giving in to the demons inside her head. The doubt that she was not good enough, the fear and worry of failing, and the anxiousness that no matter how hard she tried, she would always be the weak link.

However, James knew the truth waging war inside his sister—a truth he, too, thought about often. That despite how much they wanted to save everyone, some of the ones they loved might not make it out of this alive.

~

A few days after the rescue of Avery, Caleb, and the others, James, Rhiannon, and their parents moved out of the infirmary. Space was limited, and the supplies were getting scarce, and with Karramis fully healed due to her phoenix magic, they felt staying would only cause more stress for Alfina and Nina, running the whole place by themselves, with the occasional assistance from Tenarick and Tiffasa.

Tiffasa Hernandez, along with Avery, had been best friends with Karramis for a long time. Tiffasa and Karramis had been friends the longest, having met each other when Karramis was only eight, just a few months before she had met Lucas. And Avery came into the group when Karramis was sixteen, the two of them instantly connecting and forming a friendship. The three of them had been inseparable for years, along with Lucas. But it was Karramis and Lucas who had been the closest over the years, the two of them joined at the hip until Lucas started disappearing for months at a time once he turned eighteen. And once Lucas had professed his love for Karramis, a little too late according to Tiffasa and Avery, Lucas vanished completely from the group.

But over the years, the three remaining friends flourished as women, confidants, and magical individuals, remaining by each other's sides through the worst and best moments of their lives. And that did not stop, even when Karramis was presumed dead. Both Tiffasa and Avery continued to check in on Will for years, until he went missing. Even now, the friends were by each other's sides.

Tiffasa had opted to stay inside the realm after learning Avery had been captured, tortured, and rescued, making sure she was there for her best friend—as well as Karramis, who had literally died. But as a precaution, she had decided to finally send her three sons into the non-magical world to stay at one of the safe houses with a few other residents she had grown close with over the years.

Even Alfina thought it would be safer for the two humans that had been captured and rescued to continue their recovery in the non-magical realm. So, with the aid of some of the residents, they left, along with many more after learning of Zarrius's murder, deciding to stay at the many safe houses scattered around the world in hopes that, one day, they might be able to return to Kiluemar.

But with Tiffasa living at the infirmary, along with the rooms being needed for Avery, Caleb, and two others who were rescued, it was best for the twins and their parents to leave.

Kavana had also been discharged upon her request, stating her being home with Aidan would be the best medicine for the final stages of her recovery. But everyone knew it was just her way of getting out of there and to step right back into her role as a member of the guard, focusing on that instead of what had happened. When she finally learned about her father's death, she took it hard, crying for days and blaming herself for his life being taken. She had been the bait, and they had succeeded in catching the one they wanted.

Caleb had recovered relatively fast, his werewolf blood regenerating at an alarmingly swift rate and healing his injuries. Not a single mark marred his skin. However, Avery was not so lucky. She had multiple puncture wounds scattered along her body, and there was just enough blood left inside her to keep her alive. Caleb had mentioned they rotated their feedings with all those in the Keep, the months being torturous with minimal food, horrible sleeping conditions, and the foul way they had to relieve themselves when nature called, but it was still not as bad as it could have been. The state of the Keep was uncomfortable but clean. Yes, vampires did feed on them, but they made an effort to keep them all alive. There was no overindulging, and for the most part, the vampires seemed grateful. They did not need to hunt, and their food source was unlimited to a certain degree. Now, there were moments some of them could barely control their bloodlust, but every vampire who came to the Keep had another individual with them, almost like a safeguard to keep the others in line. It was only Merrick and Leif who had come alone—the ones the other vampires were most likely terrified of and the reason for them all abiding by whatever rules were set in place.

But something changed. A few days before they were rescued, Leif and Merrick had come in and taken two individuals out, and both did not return. And over the course of what seemed like only a few hours afterward, the vampires came in and just fed on them randomly as if given permission. However, when too many more had died, Merrick had informed all the vampires there that if any more were to fall victim this close together, all the vampires would suffer the consequences of taking their food source from them. He had stated all would be punished and the sins of one would be the sins of all. But even though Merrick appeared angry about too many of the captives being dead, Caleb noted how the monster removed every single body with a strange delight in his expression.

And since returning to Kiluemar over the summer, Caleb had witnessed over three dozen different individuals come in and suffer the fate of death at the hands of the vampires. Many of them were non-magical humans stolen from the other realm, taken to the Keep to be the food for hungry vampires, only to eventually succumb to their injuries after a few weeks of being tortured and enslaved. It was only magical individuals they had made more of an effort to keep alive longer, their blood being far more enticing, quenching, and overall more succulent.

The others had also learned that Caleb, along with the other werewolf, a twenty-nine-year-old guy named Jaxon, had been allowed out the morning of the full moon, being told to leave the grounds and head into the forests. Both werewolves would travel in opposite directions and go as far as they could, hoping to avoid the attack that would likely ensue if they encountered each other. Luckily, for the most part, most werewolves avoided one another once shifted, aiming to hunt down the blood of anything other than their kind, but werewolves were still very territorial, not to mention extremely dangerous. So, the two werewolves would likely kill each other if they crossed one another's path. But every morning over the months, Caleb returned of his own free will, due to the threats against his wife. He would not leave her there. Although he was always kept on a different level than Avery, just being able to see her when he passed by each month or when they brought her downstairs into the chamber they designated as the feeding room was enough to keep him hopeful they would get out of there alive. That one day someone would save them.

Jaxon also chose to return both times he was let out, but without any discernable reason to Caleb, no real ties to the Keep. However, it was eventually learned after being rescued that Jaxon did have a reason. The motive being if he did not return, one of the captives would die—the life of a young girl solely in his hands. A girl he had not known but somehow felt responsible for after being told she would die if he escaped. And so, he returned. And luckily, she too had been rescued.

Ava St. Martin was a seventeen-year-old girl who had ended up in Kiluemar after being in the wrong place at the wrong time. Although a witch, Ava had never known about the magical island off the coast of Norway. She did not even know there were other people out there like her. She thought her earthly abilities were simply unique to her. Her mother never had powers, and she never knew her father or his side of the family. But after her mother died unexpectedly, she wanted to investigate her strange death—something she later learned was due to a vampire, her mother also being in the wrong place at the wrong time. The coincidence was not lost on her. But it was not until she was captured and taken to the Keep that she learned all about this place and her abilities being not as rare as she had thought, the information given to her by Avery, the two of them growing close over the last few weeks.

Taken mid-November, Ava had questioned if she was truly a product of a person in the wrong place at the wrong time, or if she and her mother had been targets all along. Avery had informed Ava of a group of people called magic hunters, a faction of mostly non-magical humans who aided in searching for magical individuals. Something Ava also learned was that it was not just for consumption of their magical blood, but also for potentially being the source for a ritual to steal magic. But it also turned out, magic hunters feared magic as well, so when given permission, they would simply kill the individual or creature out of spite. Hence why many lived on the island, resided at the magical school, or remained hidden and suppressed their magic. But Ava was not part of a magical family and had never learned how to control it or why she even had it, so after her powers surfaced, she and her mother would often flee, never keeping roots in one place for too long.

But when Ava had been captured and found herself here after she accidently caused a small tremor one afternoon a few days before her mother died, she knew she was in trouble and maybe she had been the reason for her mother dying. Maybe they had been following her all along.

~

Merrick and the others had not taken their actions lightly. The rescue had taken their entire food source, so they had retaliated in the only way they could since everyone refused to leave the protective barriers around the village and Stoweward once the others left, making the large group's trek to the portal the last chance anyone was willing to take. It was an unofficial rule and promise made by all the remaining residents inside the wards. Only a few guard members left, keeping the two locations informed with any news, as well as monitoring for any disturbances. However, not all the creatures resided within the safeguards set in place.

Many of the animals around the island had been mutilated and dismembered, their body parts strewn about along the outskirts of both locations and piled outside the gates. Deer, wolves, elk, rabbits, even the wild horses, both winged and normal, did not escape the wrath of the vampires. Crimson soaked the grounds all around, the animals' blood tainting the air. Vampires could not drink animal blood, so this was a warning, a threat. It was all intentional. A massacre to prove a point.

It was only a matter of time before more creatures were discovered and killed. The merpeople within the waters along the island, the dwarves left among the caves, the giants behind the falls, and even the dryads in the forest were in danger.

And this was causing James to get stir-crazy. The idea of staying another night in Caerwyn Village, while Raina and Liam remained alone and unprotected in Stoweward, made his skin crawl. He had made a promise to his uncle to stay with them, protect them, and he had failed miserably. Granted, James had been advised that they were safe and monitored regularly, by Viktor and Tenarick, as well as getting updates from Zeus, his Messenger, but it still did not ease the anxiousness of not seeing them for himself.

The full moon was only a couple days away, and James hoped Pavian would finally return. But as time ticked by, James's nerves started to get the best of him. He was worried. He knew there was no way Merrick or any of the vampires could get into Stoweward, and even Lucas was no real threat, but that did not ease the trepidation that Raina and Liam were potentially in danger, that they could be a target. They would be much safer here in the village with him and his family.

And he was going to make it happen. He just needed to contact her first.

James lay in a borrowed bed, a bed nestled in a small room within one of the various homes abandoned in Caerwyn Village. One of the stone-and-wood-slated houses near his Aunt K's and Aidan's house and not far from where Randolyn, his step-grandmother, lived—alone now that his grandfather was dead. He stared up at the ceiling, or what he knew as the ceiling, but the darkness around him did not allow him to peer beyond the shadows of the rising moon casting a soft, silvery glow along the wooden floorboards. The entire house was silent. Even the crackling sounds from the fireplace down the hall outside the open bedroom door had gone quiet. But he knew his mother was still out there, her footsteps never having retreated back to her room after she awoke and crept out past his door a few hours prior.

His mother had struggled to stay asleep almost every single night since coming here, some of her dreams startling her awake with an echoing gasp, while other nights left her whimpering in her sleep until his father gently woke her up and soothed her back to sleep, the soft whispers of his voice lulling James into a slumber as well. It was hard to comprehend what his mother was going through, the idea of dying and remembering every moment of it once coming back to life had to be something anyone would struggle with. She had felt the kiss of death. That was not something many could say they experienced, and James was sure it was not something she took lightly. She had died and yet survived, while her father had not.

Groaning at his inability to concentrate, he threw back the blankets and sauntered out into the room at the end of the hallway. The area was warm, the gray-stoned fireplace still radiating heat despite the lack of flames. A single candle sat lit on the small table next to the wingback chair near the window, his mother painted in the softest hues of orange and silvery white, the flickering flames and moonlight creating an image of ethereal beauty—a fiery angel.

"Mom?" he said softly, trying not to startle her as she held a mug in her hand and stared out the window with her legs bent into her chest.

Karramis turned her head toward him, the movement so slow and relaxed it was as if she was far away somewhere, but the sound of his voice pulled her back. She swallowed and shook her head, seeming to remember where she was, and sat up straighter. There was distance in her gaze when her brown eyes locked on his, the two sets no longer fully mirroring one another as the golden specks in hers glimmered under the reflecting flames.

"Did I wake you?" she asked, her voice gentle and low.

"No," James answered. He hesitated before asking, worried and already knowing the answer, "Mom, are you all right?"

Pursing her lips, she nodded. "Yeah."

He recognized the lie, unsure if it was her way of protecting him or of convincing herself. The same lie Rhiannon told herself over and over again all those months. But unlike his sister, James did not know how to help his mother. Maybe he was not supposed to. But he wanted to, he wanted to help her the same way he had helped Rhiannon. But he knew this was not something he could fix. James understood, deep down, this was something only her and his father could handle—his parents having a love like no other, a bond like he had with his sister, but different. And James had every bit of faith they would find a way to do it. They would overcome this. Either with time or something else. But they would, one way or another.

"Why are you awake, then?" Karramis asked, pulling him from his thoughts.

"I never went to sleep."

Concern flashed in her expression as her interest piqued and she dropped her legs and faced him fully. "Is everything okay?"

"Yeah."

Karramis narrowed her eyes, also sensing the lie, but she refused to ignore it.

It was harder for him to lie, both his mother and Rhiannon always reading him like a book.

"Okay, no." James sat down in the chair across from her, the soft, velvety material of the antique chair silky against his bare arms. "No, everything is not okay." Desperation filled his tone. "I've been trying to astral project myself to Raina, but I haven't been able to do it. I have to check on her and Liam—I have to see for myself that they are okay. But I can't seem to do it. And I don't know why. I was getting so good before with Raina helping me, but now . . ." Head shaking in defeat, he let out an exasperated sigh. "Now, I can't seem to do it. I can create the astral body, but it won't go far enough to reach her."

Karramis placed her mug on the table in between the two chairs. "I know why." Nothing but certainty lay in the casual declaration.

James straightened, his rapt attention focused on her every word. "Why?"

"Magic cannot penetrate the wards from the outside. Remember? That's why Lucas was never able to read your dad's mind after we left, and he returned to the village. And that's why we haven't left again. That rescue was dangerous for a number of reasons, but one of them was that no one on that side knows I'm alive yet. And there's no telling what Merrick might do once he learns of my new abilities. He may not have wanted my other magic like we all thought, but now, with me being a phoenix, he might find me a powerful commodity in whatever plans he has."

"So, we're never leaving again?" James asked, the unease of not being able to get to Raina and Liam sounding tight with worry. He stood and paced, running his fingers through his messy dark hair. "Mom, I can't just sit around waiting for something to happen. I need to get to them. They need to be here, with us."

Karramis stepped in front of him and gently gripped his upper arms. "I know." She waited for him to understand and see the sincerity in her eyes, and when he met her gaze, she said again, "I know."

Karramis had seen what the worry and anxiousness of not knowing firsthand if her sister-in-law and nephew were truly safe had done to her son over the last couple of weeks. But it had intensified since the bodies outside the borders started showing up. And even though Tenarick and Viktor, along with Quinian and a few others, monitored and guarded the two locations with as much caution as possible, it was still nerve-racking to not know what lay ahead. And with the full moon approaching, the werewolves in Stoweward would have to venture out into the highlands, but even they had grown hesitant to leave the protective borders. Shifted, they had a chance against the vampires and any other malevolent creatures, but as humans, they were still nowhere near as strong as the blood-thirsty monsters. And the werewolf blood could heal certain injuries, just not fatal ones.

And with Merrick and the others on a revengeful path to prove their power inside the realm, the werewolves were surely not off limits. Karramis and the others had to do something before anyone else got hurt, or worse.

Karramis was tired of living in this void of unknowing and fear. It was becoming too overwhelming, too suffocating. And she could tell it was affecting her son as well.

And so, the time had come to no longer allow the forces outside the wards of the village to dictate her life and the lives of her children.

With absolute conviction in her tone and an unwavering confidence in her expression, Karramis declared, "It's time."

"For what?" James asked, confused by the shift in her demeanor, the energy around her now almost electric.

Karramis had been formulating this plan for the last few days, something she refused to allow anyone to tell her she could not follow through with. A taunt and a challenge. A warning and yet a promise. A plan of equal measures of evasive maneuvering and strategic preparedness. It was risky and absolutely dangerous, but Karramis was certain it would raise caution and maybe even fear in the other side. And despite his original reluctance, even Will knew this was something she had to do. Something that would help her overcome the demons in her head. The darkness wanting to consume her.

The time had come to face Lucas. To show herself to him and the others, and she was going to do it on her terms and in their domain. No, she did not have her other powers to protect her anymore, but it did not matter. She was not powerless. She was a force to be reckoned with, and she again had the element of surprise on her side.

As well as a little something else.

Chapter 24

Unfinished Business

"Are you serious?" Rhiannon questioned her mother pointedly, her expression tight with skepticism. "That's the plan? You're just going to waltz right in there like you own the place and knock on his door like, 'Hello, is anyone there?' "

James stifled his laughter at his sister's smartass antic.

"James," Will chastised, trying to fight the amusement on his face.

"This is serious," Rhiannon argued, not at all entertained as she crossed her arms. In fact, she was terrified, the idea of storming the castle with the intent of causing a scene making her nerves ache with dread. This was not going to end well for anyone. "Mom, this is stupid. They already—" She cut herself off, not wanting to voice the words, not just to herself but to her mother. Rhiannon had seen firsthand the struggles her mother faced due to the aftermath of dying. She exhaled, centering herself. "I'm just worried," she voiced, her tone much calmer.

Blue eyes lowered to the ground for a moment before landing on her mother. "And scared." The declaration was timid and delivered in a low tone.

When James had learned of the plan his mother devised, he was adamant about coming along. Unlike Karramis, he had powers. He could protect her. And with his father also going, refusing to allow her to face them alone, stating he would never leave her side again—something even Karramis could not force on him this time—James was beyond insistent. But to his surprise, neither one of his parents argued, just like when he declared he would be part of the rescue at the Keep. Though his mother had not seen the powers unleashed that day, his father had witnessed it, and it was enough. Will had been an advocate for his children, knowing the powers inside them were far more advanced than anyone before them, and the only way to fully master them was to practice. And there was no better way to practice then in real-life situations. It was Karramis who had been hesitant to allow them to come along at first, but when Will told her about what happened when their magic fully surfaced, she relented. Because it was true, her children would never be able to stop Merrick and face whatever destiny had in store for them if she kept them from embracing their full potential.

The only problem was Rhiannon. She was still not convinced magic had chosen the right person to save it. Even with her new abilities, more powerful and stronger than anyone she had read about in all the archives and documents, she still questioned where she fit in within this story.

But Karramis understood, for she too was unsure of the path she was now on. A path with so many twists and turns, she was worried she had lost her way. That no matter how hard she tried, she would never figure out which way she was supposed to go, and if the new life she had been given was all a mistake.

Karramis stepped toward her daughter and took her hands into hers, holding her gaze, her eyes soft but filled with unshed tears, the sadness and fear distant but still present. "I'm scared too."

Surprise flittered into Rhiannon's expression. "You are?"

Karramis closed her eyes, the motion so quick it was barely noticeable as she exhaled and nodded softly. "Yes."

"We all are," Will said, coming up behind his wife and placing a hand on her lower back.

And it was the truth. Even her parents were scared because no one knew what the future held for them. No one knew who would survive in the end. But one did not truly live when life was filled with fear. The what-ifs would never stop something from happening. No matter how hard someone tried or how well they planned, sometimes the inevitable would happen. The safest thing anyone could do was prepare for the worst and hope for the best.

"How do you fight it, then?" Rhiannon asked, her eyes shifting between her parents. "How do I fight being so afraid all the time? I'm not like you all. Even with all this magic, I'm not brave. I'm not strong enough."

Karramis gripped her daughter's face, her touch warm and comforting. "You don't need magic to be strong or even brave. All you need is the inner strength to know you can do anything you want without it." She cleared her throat, her emotions rising to the surface. "Let me ask you something. What do you think triggers your abilities outside of being able to control them?"

"Emotions and physical pain."

Dropping her hands, she stepped back, her attention on both her children. "What kind of emotions do you think trigger your own magic?"

"Fear, of course," Rhiannon said truthfully.

"That's part of it. Maybe. But what else? What made you want to stay and fight every time before?"

Rhiannon shrugged. "I don't know."

Karramis's eyes landed on her son. "What about you, James?"

"Anger?"

"Again, maybe. But no, not really. Yes, your powers have shown up when you were afraid or angry or even when you were trying to prove a point, but that's not what truly triggers them deep down. In every event that has happened so far where your powers have shown themselves the strongest, what were you feeling?"

Rhiannon thought for a moment before answering, "Fear, but not just for myself, for those around me. And sadness—the loss."

"Anger that I couldn't stop it," James added. "Fear that I might not be able to save them. Guilt because I was the reason for what happened."

Karramis gave them both a slight smile. "Exactly. And what emotion do you think controlled all those other emotions?"

The twins shrugged.

"It was love."

"Love?" they both said.

"Yes, love." Karramis embraced the hand gliding along her back and resting on her hip, Will's touch relaxing her. "Love is the strongest ability one can possess. It's the purest and rarest form of magic. It's the only thing that cannot be controlled or altered by an outside entity. The ability to love someone is the easiest thing to do, and yet it's also the hardest. Love is authentic, primal, and instinctive. And it's the one thing fate cannot dictate the final outcome of."

James's brow creased. "How come?"

"Because," Will answered, his gaze set on Karramis and his tone laced with admiration, "love is more powerful than even destiny."

Rhiannon could not process the information, her mind overwhelmed with everything. She loved her parents, and she loved her brother, but how could love be the trigger of her magic? Love was not something Merrick seemed to possess, so how was he so powerful and in control of the magic he had, yet she still could not master her abilities enough to stop him and save her family? If it was that easy, why was she still struggling?

And why had she not been able to stop Merrick from doing everything he had done at the cabin? Why had her mother still died?

"You don't have to go," James said to his sister before aiming his next words at his parents. "Maybe it's best if she doesn't."

James was trying to protect her, but he was also giving her an out. He wanted to be part of this plan, but she did not have to be. James did not want his parents going into the lion's den again without proper backup. His mother was powerless, aside from her resurrection abilities, and his father's magic would not be any use inside the castle walls. He was the only one who could protect them from the dangers they would likely encounter.

Karramis saw the relief in her daughter's eyes. And mirroring her daughter's emotions, she let out a slight exhale. Karramis was not sure how things would go, but having to worry about Will and James was enough to send her anxiety spiraling. Maybe having Rhiannon stay behind was for the best. But she knew Rhiannon would have to face the fears controlling her if she and James were going to fight Merrick and come out of this alive. Rhiannon had to find the strength to fight her emotions and welcome the darkness in her head before it was too late. She had to embrace her flaws and make them into something powerful, something fierce.

And she could. Karramis knew that kind of strength was inside her daughter. Because like her mother, Rhiannon was stronger than she believed and far more resilient than she thought. She was a fighter, and no amount of darkness would hold her down.

As James and Will headed for the front door, Karramis lowered her voice and gave her daughter a gentle smile. "Only among the darkness will you see the embers burn the brightest. So, welcome it. Use it. Let the darkness consume you. Make it your strength, not your weakness."

~

The plan was simple, albeit dangerous, but simple nonetheless—get in, say what needed to be said, and get out. To create enough of a distraction to keep any focus on them instead of what was happening on the other side of the island.

To show them all Karramis was alive—that despite their efforts, she survived. It was something she needed to see firsthand—the look in their eyes when they saw she was not so easy to stop. She needed them to see that they failed.

But Karramis had also taken James's concern to heart, knowing Raina and Liam would indeed be safer in the village with all of them. It would also be something Pavian would want. And with him returning soon, and everything she would have to fill him in on, Karramis wanted to make sure his wife, son, and unborn child were safe, and they had a home ready for him upon his arrival. So, various plans were taking place besides the one Karramis needed to do for herself.

First, Raina and Liam would be moved from Stoweward to the village, with the help of Aidan and Kavana, along with Galahad. Despite Aidan's disapproval, stating she was not fit to fly, let alone to put herself in any possible danger, Kavana was the head of this task. She was determined to get this done without any mistakes. She owed it to her brother to get his family to a place where they could be protected and much closer to all of them. Not to mention, the infirmary was here, and though Raina was still months away from delivering, she needed regular medical care. So, Kavana and Aidan would fly in once the sun was up and transport Raina and Liam to the home that was previously owned by Raina and Pavian before they moved back to Stoweward.

Next was the issue regarding the possible threat to the werewolves. So again, once the sun was up, Tenarick, Viktor, and Quinian would lead the werewolves needing to reach the highlands before tomorrow night's full moon out of Stoweward and to Lunar Cave. Will had requested both Harkin and Ignara guard the convoy of people and remain at post to protect the cave, as well as monitor the werewolves once shifted. Tenarick would also inform the dryads of the added dangers that could occur, making sure they were on high alert. And if any vampires were seen anywhere near Lucien Valley, the dragons were given permission to take them out. Even the Water Dragons would monitor the waters below the cliffs, just in case the vampires decided to swim to the highlands. The only real issue would be if Merrick flew in, being a major threat to not only the dragons with his new abilities, a proven tactic he knew very well, but also the werewolves. But Karramis was hopeful he would not deem the werewolves worth the effort after she followed through with her plan. She was optimistic once Merrick knew of her resurrection, he would focus on her, rather than the werewolves for the time being.

But it was not just the werewolves she was worried about. It was also the portals.

Karramis was also hopeful this ploy to focus the attention on her and what she might be and the powers she contained, the portals would be safe enough for Pavian to return. It was farfetched, but it was something else she was holding onto while moving forward with this plan. The last thing she wanted was for Pavian to come through, only to be killed like her father. Karramis was positive Merrick would send people out to monitor all the ones left, and with Merrick having some control over them, there was no telling where they all would end up.

But even with everything else they were planning, it was finally revealing herself to Lucas, and showing all of them they had made a huge mistake in killing her which thrummed through Karramis. The adrenaline. The power. The need to take back something they stole from her. She wanted control back over her life. It was selfish in a way, maybe even foolish to put herself in that kind of position again, but she had to do it. She needed to be in control again—to no longer fear being discovered on someone else's terms. Being vulnerable and defenseless and helpless to those who plagued her dreams was going to stop now. She was no longer going to exist in a living nightmare, afraid of who might be in the dark just waiting to strike, anymore. She did not just want to survive. She wanted to live. Karramis had been given a second chance, and she was not going to waste it. Tomorrow was never promised, so she was going to fight for today.

Karramis had not originally planned for her husband and son to attend this reunion, but both rejected the entire idea if she refused to allow them to accompany her, Will going as far as threatening to tie her up if she so much as thought about going without him. He would never let her out of his sight again. This was just as equally his fight as it was hers, and she was not going to face them alone, if he had anything to say about it. He was her husband. He was supposed to protect her, and he was hell-bent on making sure he proved he would do anything to keep her safe. It was them, together—always and today, now and forever, until the end.

Karramis understood his need to come along, the idea of losing her again not something he wanted to think about right now. The wounds were too fresh, too deep. He had lost her three times now, but only once had he held her dead body in his arms. And Will could not face that kind of heartbreak again. Not this soon. In fact, he had not left her side for more than a few minutes after finding her in the shower after coming back to life. She needed him. He grounded her, being the anchor to this new life, always reminding her she was alive and real. That this was not a dream, and they had been given another chance. A chance she did not take lightly, considering tomorrow was never promised. For anyone.

But as the three of them landed—she and Will on Terramina, and James on Oakley—she was grateful she was not alone, the trepidation warming her lower abdomen and burning in her chest.

Raeth, Harkin, and Ignara remained overhead, the sun peeking out from the overcast clouds sending their shadows circling along the ground inside the castle walls as Oakley and Terramina remained just a few feet outside the second castle's main entrance.

It was a bold move, to walk through the front door, but it was a statement Karramis needed to make. She was not afraid. She was not weak. And she would not cower. Her magic may be gone, but something else flowed through her body and filled her soul, a power like no other, a strength she had discovered unlike anything she had ever felt before.

And it was time to let it out.

She was still pissed, and she finally wanted to unleash it.

It was as though there was something different inside her, her own thoughts and actions being controlled by something deeper. Something feral and inhuman. But even though this new sensation was foreign, this need for revenge, for vengeance—for her father, her sister, for Will and their children, Avery, for all the people on the island and MUSE, for herself—there was also a sense of validation, of purpose. She was not a killer, and she did not want to harm anyone. But she would. She no longer operated on a code of ethics that had been branded into her from birth, all morality and honor to protect having died with her. No, now she was going to give them a taste of their own medicine when the time came for it. And when she did, Karramis was going to make it hurt.

Taking a deep breath, Karramis closed her eyes and steadied her racing heart. A warm hand slid into hers, and she opened her eyes, taking in the beautiful features of her husband—the subtle scruff along the strong and sharp-edged jawline, the dimple nestled into his chin, the slight curve along the ridge of his nose, the near-flawless symmetry of his features, the gentle lines appearing on his cheek with the soft grin lifting on one side of his mouth, his soft, kissable lips, and his eyes, his captivatingly beautiful, deep-blue eyes. This man was absolutely perfect in every way, but it was his love, kindness, passion, understanding, and loyalty that elevated him in her eyes, the admiration he had for her being something she never thought she needed but knew she never wanted to live without. The trust and respect he gave her day after day. Will was her everything.

"Are you sure you want to do this?" Will asked reverently as he interlocked their fingers and pulled gently, angling their bodies to face one another.

"Absolutely." There was no hesitation as she opened the door and strolled into Casteya Castle.

Everything was how she remembered it, her memory seeming more like a dream than reality until now. But as she moved down the hall, taking in all the familiar architecture, art, and décor, Karramis was growing more confident with each step.

Will and James trailed behind her, both equipped with weapons. Will still had Pavian's short sword, and it was now sheathed at his waist with his hand gripping the hilt. The need to have the full weight of the sword in his hands made Will uneasy, but Karramis had wanted this to go smoothly, noting the death of any of Merrick's men would not end well for them, either before they even reached the front of the castle or with another round of slayings. And so, Will kept the weapon readied at his side and his attention on their surroundings.

James opted for his well-acquainted ranged weapon—his custom-made bow and newly crafted arrows, arrows meant to kill vampires. But it was his magic he held tight to, keeping it just below the surface, while his bow and the quiver full of arrows remained slung over his back.

They kept their footsteps quiet as they moved down one hall, turning and reaching the narrower corridor leading to the various bedrooms. One of those being Lucas's. Karramis tapped her finger against her mouth, remembering one of these rooms housed a vampire, and likely a few others. Although it was barely after dawn, she could not be certain the vampires were asleep yet. But with the grounds being deserted and the castle seemingly quiet throughout, she was hopeful.

Reaching the door of Lucas's bedroom, she halted and faced Will and James. "I'm going in alone," she said without any room for argument.

But apparently, Will did not care about her tone. "Like hell you are."

"I have to agree," James added, crossing his arms.

Karramis lifted her finger and hushed them again, her voice dropping to a whisper. "No. Let me do this myself." She glared at them both. "This right here is my fight." Her eyes stopped on Will. "I got this, okay?"

Will did not trust Lucas whatsoever, but he trusted his wife. And she needed this. This was something that had been eating away at her for weeks, and now it was her time to show Lucas just who he helped create.

"We'll be out here, if you need us."

"Are you serious?" James asked his father.

"Trust me, she can handle herself."

James released an annoyed exhale but did not argue.

As Karramis slowly eased open the door and stepped inside, Will and James leaned against the framing, this time their weapons drawn and their senses taking in everything around them.

The door clicked shut, and Karramis stood in a practically dark room. With the curtains closed and the fireplace only containing the glow from soft embers, she searched for a way to turn on the light she had seen before but her eyes snagged on a nearly extinguished candle flickering next to the couch on the opposite side of the room. She took a step toward it, but halted as her foot pressed into a floorboard, sending a creaking echo through the room. Movement shifted behind the faint orange glimmer, the subtle radiance casting the shadowy figure in light and revealing a familiar face as it turned her way.

Lucas.

She remained still as she squinted through the darkness. He did not move again. He appeared to be sleeping. Closing her eyes, she eased her foot off the floor, grimacing as it squeaked again. She observed the room once more, deciding what she wanted to do. And without a second thought, she shrugged and strolled over to the window, ignoring any creaks emanating under her carefree stride.

It was now or never.

"Fuck it," she whispered to herself as she tugged on the tassel and the room illuminated, the soft blueish hue of the morning lighting up the room just enough for her to see.

Her feet pounded against the floor as she made her way over to the fireplace and tossed a few of the logs next to it into the hearth, not at all caring about the amount of noise she was making. Then, grabbing the entire container of matches, she threw them into the embers, the hundreds of igniters bursting into flames as the hiss-like sizzle sound filled the room and fire roared to life along the logs.

A blanket flew up from the couch as Lucas bolted to his feet, narrowing his eyes as he scanned his dimly lit room.

Time to have some fun.

"Hello, Lucas." Her voice was melodic and delicate, almost angelic.

His gaze cut to her, and his eyes went wide. The air around them becoming taut, the silence thickening as he scanned her from head to foot. He blinked, seeming to test his eyesight as he made his way closer. Cautious. Careful. Confused.

Karramis kept her gaze locked on him as she stood perfectly still. Lucas reached out a hand to touch her, but she took a single step back, making herself just out of reach. He gasped and his advance faltered. He took a few steps to the side and braced a hand on the wall, his blue eyes wide again.

"Karramis? You . . . you're alive." The statement was filled with both shock and relief.

"I am," she replied with a venomous glare as she remained unnaturally poised.

He swallowed and fought the urge to step closer. He wanted to touch her. Feel her. Just to make sure she was real. "They told me ya died." The statement was slow, the disbelief she stood before him clear even in his words.

"Did they?"

A ripple of confusion flashed in his eyes, the small twitch of his head coinciding with the narrowing of his brows. "And . . . when I went to find you—search for your magic, it . . . it was gone."

Lucas had always been able to sense her and her magic. It was a permanent imprint embedded into the very essence of his being. Every time he had encountered a magical individual, he could call forth his powers and brand that person's abilities and essence into his psyche. They became a beacon, and he was now the tracker. And when they were younger, Lucas had done it with Karramis. Her magic and very existence had been linked to him and his abilities, something she never took into consideration when she had fled with the twins, having forgotten over the years that was how he used his Telematra powers to track people.

He did not need to form an imprint on someone to track them, but it was stronger if he had. And even with the spell around the manor and refusing to use her magic, Lucas still could have sensed her because her magic was still alive, the imprint of her blood and magic still linked to him. However, the spell was preventing him from actually finding her. That was why he never believed she was truly dead before. But this time she really had died, and her magic had died with her.

Karramis let out a breathy yet humorous exhale. "That's because I was dead."

"How?" The word was faint and breathless.

She squared her shoulders as her brown eyes remained fixed on him. "It would seem I wasn't just born from the ashes with fire magic coursing through my veins." Her tone was steady and relaxed, almost hypnotic as she inched closer, slow and calculating. "No, I *was* the fire. I was the flames, the embers, and the smoke. And my death ignited a spark hidden deep inside me, bringing to life a new, raging wildfire." She paused as she stopped inches from him. Lowering her voice, she leaned into him, making sure he could see the certainty in her golden-amber-speckled brown eyes. "And you, Lucas, are in the path of my destruction."

"Your eyes," Lucas managed, terror joining the bewilderment plaguing him. "What—what happened to you?"

The golden flecks grew as a rich honey-colored ring lined her eyes and her pupils narrowed. A menacing and taunting smirk graced her lips. "Like I said, I died. I was killed. And you helped make it happen."

He shook his head, the dispute forming with ease. "I neva' really wanted ya dead."

"Bullshit," she declared with a sharp bite in her tone. "But it doesn't matter anymore. All that matters is that you know that I'm coming for you. And when I do, you'll have nowhere to hide."

Every other emotion faded from him as the threat of her words slammed into him, transforming him into a man ready for the challenge, the boldness she exhibited like a spark of adrenaline, a rush of excitement.

A low chuckle rumbled through him, his lips curling into a devious grin. "You could neva' win against me, love. Haven't we proven this already?"

There he was—the other side of him, the one she never truly recognized before. But not anymore. *This* was the real him. The true evil, living as a man but clearly a monster.

"Try me," she countered, provoking him, taunting him.

"If you died, that means ya don't have your magic. And we both know ya could neva' overpower me on your own." His eyes flicked down to her bare hands. "Ya don't even have a weapon." He tsked her. "That's a ratha' stupid move on your part."

She cocked her head, her eyes becoming dark and threatening. "That's because I don't need one . . . I *am* the fucking weapon."

Lucas did not flinch. He did not even react. Her declaration nothing more than a failed attempt at intimidating him. "What are you gonna do, love? Hmm. Kill me?" He paused and glared at her. "No, you could neva' kill me. Ya just don't have it in ya. That's not the girl I know and love."

Karramis's expression was like a predator sizing up another threat—composed, cunning, and patient. "Yeah, but according to you, that girl is in the past. And that version of me is dead. She's *dead*, Lucas. And you're the one who helped kill her."

"Then why wait?" he challenged. "Why not just do it now?"

The golden-amber flecks sparked, and the honeyed ring disappeared as red and orange rimmed her eyes and glowed. Lucas jerked back in disbelief, the smugness radiating from him washing away behind the paleness seeping into his features.

"Because," she finally said, drawing out the word with a snarl rumbling in her throat, "I want you to live in fear of me for once." Her voice eased, the calm and casual tone far more terrifying. "I want you to stay up at night wondering if I will show up while you sleep. I want you looking over your shoulder, wondering when I'm going to strike. I want you to fear the dark—fear what lies beyond the shadows outside your window."

He scoffed as the arrogant glint returned to his eyes. "I will neva' fear ya because we both know you'll always fear me. Remember, love, I'm the villain in your story."

"Yes, once upon a time you were, but not anymore. Things changed. Because I'm now the villain in *yours*. I'm the enemy now, Lucas. And as real as the oxygen is in my lungs, so are these words—I promise you this, as the life drains from your body, my face will be the last thing you see as you take your final breath. And fear *will* be the last thing you feel next to pain."

And with that, Karramis pivoted and headed away from him.

As she reached for the handle of the door, Lucas grabbed her arm and twisted her around. "Don't you dare walk—"

Karramis rotated her arm around and slipped from his grip just as she stepped into him and slammed his back against the wall and smacked her open palm against his heaving chest, holding him in place with only her hand. The strength she released was not something he had ever witnessed from her or from anyone who was not an immortal or cursed being.

Excitement filled his features, mixing with arousal and pride as he took in the power she had just displayed and the heated rage flowing from her entire body. "My, I thought you were strong before, but this . . . I think I might enjoy this version of ya, love. Could be fun." Winking, he grinned and lifted his arm and reached for her wrist.

A fist slammed into the side of his face, the impact sudden and sending his head sideways. Blood erupted from the gash across his cheek, the powerful blow slicing open his skin.

Dazed, Lucas wiped the blood from his face as he met her unyielding and almost inhuman gaze, her newfound savagery and dominance stimulating. He lunged forward and gripped her upper arms, twisting and slamming her hard against the wall, the sound of the impact resonating through the room.

The bedroom door flew open and crashed against the wall just as Will came into view.

"Get your hands off my wife!" The demand was stern, commanding, and oozed pure dominance. It was equal parts possessive and protective.

Lucas's gaze shot to Will, and he rolled his eyes. "Fuckin' hell. Always such a fuckin' nuisance."

"Will, it's okay," Karramis said calmly, trying to stifle the rage growing below the surface. "We're done here. I got this."

"Oh," Will said as he moved closer, his stride determined, "I have no doubt, darling." His fist flew through the air and slammed hard against the side of Lucas's face. "But I have a score to settle."

Wide-eyed and mouth agape, Karramis watched as Lucas's body jerked back and tumbled to the floor.

Reaching for his wife, Will gripped her hand and tugged Karramis into him, his gaze examining her for any injuries. "I bet he didn't see that coming," he joked with a grin. Once he realized she was unharmed, he gave her a quick kiss on the forehead and pulled her toward the door. "Let's get out of here."

Karramis gently pulled Will to a stop as they reached the threshold. "Oh." She turned and faced Lucas, who sat on the floor, rubbing his jaw and chin. "Touch me again," she continued, her stance firm and her glare fierce, "and I will not hesitate to stab you in the fucking throat." She strolled over to him and crouched before him. "Don't test me, Lucas. Remember, I'm the villain now, and this villain won't be so easy to kill. I can't say the same about you." She gently tapped her palm twice against the uninjured cheek, his lip now split from Will's blow as blood pooled along the new injury on his face. "See you around." Feet pivoting, she strode toward the door and placed her hand on the handle. "Oh, and one more thing," she called as she turned her head to face him. "You tell them I survived. And when they ask you who or what I am now, you tell them I'm the one you couldn't break. You tell them the Karramis you knew is dead. And when you see Merrick, you tell him I held up my end of the deal. The debt has been paid in full. Now, it's his turn."

Will exited the room first, Karramis following behind and slamming the door as she stalked past James, the anger inside her burning along the surface of her skin.

To everyone's surprise, the door remained shut.

"Damn, Mom," James said, having heard every word and witnessing the final moments in the room, "that was badass." His eyes flicked to his father as the continued forward. "I bet that felt good, huh?"

Will laughed under his breath as the three of them moved down the hall, all weapons now put away. "You have no idea."

It was instinct to protect her, to punch the man who continuously threatened and harmed his wife. The man who had his hands on her yet again. But it was also something more. Something animalistic and territorial. Will had wanted to show his dominance. Karramis had given herself to him a long time ago. She was his and he was hers, and he just needed to remind Lucas of that.

Making their way down the corridor, they halted as footsteps echoed nearby, the sounds coming from around the corner.

"Let's go the other way," Will announced, backing up, redrawing his sword.

There had to be another exit somewhere, the rest of the hallway also curving into another hallway along the other end.

But Karramis had other plans.

"What are you doing?" Will called in a whisper as his wife continued forward.

She paused and turned back, her eyes blazing with a determined fierceness. "Taking back control."

"By getting yourself killed? That isn't taking control, darling, that's losing it."

"Just trust me."

"It's not about trusting you. It's about questioning your sanity."

She winked at him as amused defiance tilted up the corner of her mouth before she continued down the hall.

Will could not help the twitch of his mouth, the bravery and tenacity of his wife just as troubling and reverent as always. "Your mum is utterly mad."

James reached for his bow and nocked an arrow as the two of them did not hesitate and trailed behind her.

As they turned the corner, the three of them halted, coming face-to-face with four individuals—ones Karramis recognized right away.

Leif. Tressa along with her minotaur companion, Theseus. And Niko.

Leif's eyes went so wide, Karramis could see all the blue. He was visibly dumbfounded and shocked by who stood before him, but it quickly shifted into something like intrigue or exhilaration. And Tressa appeared equally confused but also just as mesmerized by Karramis. The other two were emotionless and almost bored at whatever was happening around them.

Leif gave her a critical once-over before he sighed in faux irritation. "Well, fuck me. I guess you're even too damn stubborn to stay dead."

Karramis just gave him a dismissive shrug. "I guess you couldn't finish the job." She arched a suggestive, snide brow. "Shame."

And with that, she pushed past him with a smug grin on her face, completely ignoring any threat any of them might pose. All she needed was for her presence to be known—she would show all of them she was not someone they could control anymore. Fear was not something that was going to consume her again.

Annoyance filtered in the vampire's expression at her flippant nature and the nerve she had to walk away from him, completely disregarding him and acting as if he was not the man who had ended her life.

"Careful, witch," Leif noted pointedly as he snatched her arm, forcing her to stop.

Karramis twisted around. Will and James reached for their weapons, but she threw up an arm, signally them to fall back.

She did not need them to escalate the situation.

"Don't forget," Leif continued, his voice low and gravelly as he stared Karramis down, ignoring her husband and son. "If you mess with fire, you're going to get burned."

"That's right," she agreed, pure delight and amusement in her steady voice, "you will." Her eyes sparked and the fiery gaze deepened, the red and orange growing and bursting into flames, the dancing fire among the golden-amber hue now taking over her entire irises. The air grew thick as it crackled, simmering to life with power as her skin heated, igniting the embers of rage and power deep inside her veins. "So be careful, Leif. Or you just might burn."

"What the hell?" Leif released her with a slight recoil as he shook his head and blinked, trying to process what he was witnessing. "What are you?" he drawled, something like fear flashing in his expression.

"Impossible," Tressa whispered in a breathy exhale.

"I'm something that was forged in the fires of hell," she offered stoically, a regal fierceness to her. "The place you sent me." She flashed him a gentle but cunning smirk. "And I loved the way it fucking felt."

Karramis sauntered away, James and Will following, the two of them fighting the grins wanting to spread across their lips.

Frozen in place, Leif and the others watched Karramis and her family stroll out of the castle like they owned the place, not even bothering to close the door behind them.

"Bloody hell," Will announced, completely amazed and impressed as they stepped outside. "All right, I take it back. That was definitely taking control."

Chapter 25

Return

It had been a few hours since the full moon reached the highest point in the night sky, and word had finally reached James that his uncle had actually returned. But after discovering his home empty in Stoweward, Pavian had taken the portal closest to the town in search of Raina and Liam, only to find a golden eagle circling overhead. Thanks to Aidan, Pavian had been informed his family was safe, and he had opted to see them first.

Multiple people had taken to the skies throughout the night, trying to monitor as much as they could with the werewolves out, the possible dangers lurking, and the portals opening, thus making sure they were aware of any new arrivals. Without the full strength of the Guardian magic, Kavana and the rest of the guard had been worried about the portals and any potential threats or unknown entries of magical or non-magical beings. So, from the highlands to the Ember Cliffs, from the desert along the north shores down to the Lookout, and even on the forbidden side, a surveillance party was underway. The skies were filled with winged horses, dragons, a golden eagle, and a gargoyle, all protecting the island from above.

But as the sun began to crest along the horizon, James was convinced the island and residents were safe for another day.

Ignara landed just outside the northern gate leading into Caerwyn Village with James mounted on her back just as Harkin came into view from the south. Coasting downward, the dragon banked, giving James a peek at his sister, who had perfected flying with such elegance and grace. Her fear of heights had been minimal when atop the flying creatures, her trust in the dragons the only reason she allowed her feet off the ground.

Large, clawed feet pressed into the sage-and-tan-colored grass, the winter air still crisp and washing away all the bright colors of the once plush landscape. Even Fayemeara battled against the temperatures to keep the garden flourishing, something the others were surprised had been left untouched thus far. But even the Garden Nymph had been reluctant to leave the village to tend to her plants and herbs, the hours she would spend there having been limited to minutes. And moving the large plot within the borders was not an option. It would take weeks to regrow the amount of food sprouting just outside the gates. Fayemeara may be powerful enough to grow and maintain a steady flow of food for the people, but even the Garden Enchantress—as she is known around here—had her limits. The acres of land consisted of rows of corn, a variety of beans, various squashes, herbs, tomatoes, root and cruciferous vegetables, wheat and other grains, berries, melons, and so many different types of foods—this was the livelihood of the island. And what was canned and jarred in the communal root cellars in both Stoweward and Caerwyn Village would not be enough to feed the remaining residents for more than a few weeks, so the garden needed to remain intact and protected. And so, the boundary line was extended, the wards now stretched out past the main border of the village and included the garden, stopping just a few feet in front of the portal still remaining nearby and inside the forest to the west.

Rhiannon flung her leg over the Fire Dragon and slid down as Harkin lowered his body closer to the ground, giving her less of a fall in her descent.

"Have you seen him yet?" she asked as her booted feet hit the ground and she readjusted the loose-flowing, knee-high skirt of her dress.

Dressed in a thick jacket and jeans, James dismounted, just as smooth and agile in his movements, as he landed and strolled over to his sister. "No, not yet. I figured he deserved some time with them before I went to see him."

"Yeah," Rhiannon agreed solemnly as she straightened the slightly twisted hem of her black leggings under her skirt, lining it back up with the inside of her leg. Eyes lifting, she folded her arms over the thick material covering her chest. "And they tell him everything that happened."

Raina and James had both agreed that she should not be the one to tell Pavian about his father. It was something only his siblings should do. It was still a hard realization for his three younger sisters to come to terms with, and they all knew Pavian would take it just as hard, if not harder—having been by his father's side since Pavian was a young boy. This was something he would need, something all four of them would need, a sibling bond being the only thing powerful enough to help mend the heartbreak and utter devastation of losing a parent.

Sadness seeped into her gaze as she continued, "I don't think Mom has fully accepted it yet, and Aunt K and Aunt Meadow aren't really talking about it either. It's almost like it didn't really happen, even though I know it did. But, I think, once Uncle Pavian knows, it will be all too real for all of them."

James nodded, not quite sure how to respond. But every part of him ached for his mother and aunts, the pain and agony they were all struggling with, and the suffering his Yaya was having to endure, the life without her husband. However, for James, it was his uncle he had been worried about, the guilt and suffering Pavian would likely have to live with the rest of his life— knowing he had not been here to try to save his father. Plus, everything that had happened to his sisters. Kavana had been kidnapped, tortured, and nearly died. But Karramis had actually died. Now, she was a phoenix—a mythical creature come to life right before everyone's very eyes.

It was a lot to process even for James, but he knew Pavian would somehow blame himself. A feeling James knew all too well.

"Is everything okay?" Rhiannon asked, concern dripping from her tone. "You seem different. Quiet."

It was true, James had gone quiet, both outwardly and inwardly, the need to silence his inner voice the only way to stop the guilt and anger eating away at him. But he was dealing with them himself. He did not want to discuss this with her. Nor did he need help trying to manage his mental state. He was strong-willed, resilient, and brave. Figuring out obstacles and hardships was branded into him. Being part of a powerful bloodline of witches and an even more formidable line of steadfast and tenacious men, who fought and never gave up, he wanted to prove his worth. Prove he was given these powers for a reason. Prove that no matter what, he would not give in. He was determined to fight this alone, proving to himself he was strong enough to control not only his magic but himself, his mind, body, and soul.

Rhiannon exhaled, not out of anger or annoyance but out of defeat. "Okay, well, I think this needs to be returned to its owner." She pulled something from the pocket of her jacket. Reaching out, she took his hand into hers and set the mystery item into his palm, closing his fingers around it. "When you're ready, you know where to find me." Similar words he, too, had spoken to her when she was in her lowest moment, lost in the darkness.

James watched as she offered him a gentle smile and hugged him. And without another word, she headed over to Harkin.

Opening his hand, he stared down at the small leather pouch, his eyes going misty. He shook it and felt the weight of the small stones inside as they clanked together. The same stones he had been carrying in his pocket the day she saved his life when they were younger. All kept inside the same pouch she had handmade him for their birthday. The one item he had always held on to— the one thing always reminding him he had her by his side. The same item he had always made sure he took with him wherever he went. Even the night at the manor, the night their entire world changed, he had removed it from under his pillow and slipped it into the pocket of his pajama pants. And when he and his uncle had abandoned their life on that island to return to Kiluemar, it was the one thing he made sure he had with him.

A piece of her. His sister. The calm to his chaos. His other half.

But before he could thank her, for everything, she was gone, both her and Harkin disappearing into the darkened sky.

Later.

He would tell her later.

~

They were ready. It was time for all of them to return and finally see what was left of their home for themselves.

Anxiety surged in Karramis's body, a mix of fear-induced butterflies fluttering wildly among the gloomy sadness building in her stomach and the raging anger of a swarm of killer bees in pursuit of whomever dared enter their territory roiling in her chest. Trepidation, fury, devastation, heartbreak, it all took root inside her core, burrowing deeper and deeper as they neared the cabin.

Will noticed the way her body pressed into him with each deep breath she took and how her hands balled into tightly clenched fists around Callie's mane.

"Are you sure?" Will whispered into her ear from behind as he held her close to his chest.

He had asked her that very question just before they mounted the winged horse, her husband's own worry of what they would face overshadowed by the concern he had for his wife.

This was their home. The place he and Karramis had lived and built a life together. The place where their children were born. It had been their sanctuary. The place they had both felt the most at home in—a place of countless laughs, warmth and comfort, of cozy evenings and lazy mornings, of passion and desire, of tears of joy and tears of sorrow, of promises, truths, and secrets. This was more than a place. It was the heart of their lives and the soul of all their memories. It had been the first place Will ever truly felt at peace since becoming an adult and leaving his childhood home. And it had been a safe haven for Karramis, a symbol of independence and strength.

Karramis leaned her head back and angled it just enough to rest her cheek against his, offering him a soft nod as she closed her eyes.

She was ready. She had to see it for herself.

The partially charred remains came into view, and Karramis took in a shuddering breath.

Her feet touched the ground as her eyes stayed glued to the cabin.

The only thing identifiable about the single-story cabin was the rear portion of the building, the walls of the hallway leading to the two bedrooms and adequately sized and beautifully modern bathroom were still standing, as was the back half of the structure. But the front was nothing but a pile of rubble and scorched remnants of the home that once stood here.

"I'm so sorry, Mom," James said solemnly as he came up behind her and wrapped an arm around her shoulders.

Tears welled in her eyes as the pain in her chest tightened and traveled up her throat. "It's okay." She swallowed and cleared her throat. "It's only stuff. And more importantly, none of us were inside."

Will came up beside her and placed his hand into hers, their fingers interlocking as they both squeezed. Their eyes locked as Will lifted their hands and placed a gentle kiss on her knuckles before ushering them both forward.

They had decided to not only see the cabin for themselves but also, if the structure seemed safe enough, they would rummage through the remains to see if anything was salvageable. Any memories they could find, they wanted to have them.

James had offered to come along, while Rhiannon stayed with Kavana, the two of them joining them later with Pavian.

Matters needed to be discussed. Matters the whole family needed to be part of.

Karramis, Kavana, and Meadow had finally told their brother about what had happened to their father, as well as how Kavana had played a part in all of it. During the conversation, Kavana had also informed them how she had fought like hell to escape, going so far as actually landing a few good punches to Leif, something he did not appreciate. And apparently, the volatile vampire had risen to the challenge, taking matters into his own hands to handle the downright disrespect—as he so boldly claimed—and not only beat the hell out of her but also brought her close to death, leaving her with barely an inch of life just to be alive long enough to finish out their plan to kill their father.

Pavian had been silent through it all, his emotions and mind visibly battling it out in front of his sisters. There had been sadness and anger, so much anger, but there was something else, something Karramis could not quite place, but it almost seemed like guilt.

Karramis had also informed her siblings what had happened to her—the whole dying and coming back to life thing in full detail. And how she no longer had any of her other magic. But now, there was something else raging inside of her, something strong and ancient and fierce. The new magic in her was dominant and active, having shown her some of her powers within a few days of receiving them.

Strength, something akin to that of vampires—well, maybe not to that extreme, but definitely a werewolf maybe.

Werewolves had an unnatural strength in their shifted forms, but even as humans, their muscular vigor outweighed that of a common man by a large percentage. And fire, she still had fire inside her, but it was different, it was unique. And when she had realized she could call forth that spark through her eyes, something Will had actually discovered one evening, she had never been more relieved. She still had magic. It may not be the powers she missed now more than anything, but she still had magic. And it fulfilled some of the ache inside her, some of the loss. But even with being reborn, given a second chance, she never felt more alive, more vivacious, and yet she still felt empty. Her other magic had been taken from her, stolen right when she had fully embraced it.

The wood creaked beneath her feet as Karramis made her way through the black-and-ash-covered ruins. She made her way over the small niche jutting out slightly from the rest of the front wall, the area that had once been the kitchen along the front of the cabin. The old-fashioned wood-burning stove and stone-slatted countertops were the only thing recognizable among the rubble. This had been the place Harkin had crashed into the night of the attack. So much was damaged in the collision, and the rest had been lost to the fire. The living room just on the other side had also been completely destroyed. Even the furniture was barely noticeable. The back wall of the living room was missing, giving her a clear view of her bedroom, the room she had shared with Will. The sacred space filled with love, lust, desire, happiness, and so many other memories. The place she birthed her children. A room filled with hopeful dreams and horrible nightmares.

Karramis jerked her head sideways, the sound of James slipping pulling her attention.

"I'm okay," he called as he stepped over a charred beam leading past where she was looking and toward the open door at the end of the hall. The bedroom he had shared many nights with Rhiannon.

Her eyes scanned the remnants of her home, taking in all that was left. The shower still stood, and most of the walls were still intact. Only the wall connecting her room to the bathroom was damaged. Karramis was surprised by how much of the cabin actually remained standing.

Harkin was a large creature, a very large creature, and when he crashed into the cabin, it appeared as though he had done a lot more damage. But luckily, the cabin—although only consisting of two bedrooms and a single bathroom—was fairly large. Plus, the covered porch provided even more space, the addition being attached to the cabin soon after Karramis and Will were married.

Stepping over a pile of what looked like what was left of one of the chairs, Karramis moved toward the area of her bedroom. Will had made his way here first and had begun rummaging through the pile of what was once their overly large wardrobe. He tossed aside fragments of wood and pieces of singed material, all that was left of their clothes.

The decorative metal bedframe still stood, but it was no longer the brushed bronze color it had been the last time she saw it. Now it was solid black. Springs lay on the floor under the metal bars, all that was left of their mattress. Something she had to wait months for after moving in—the bed originally here having been only a large wooden box frame with rolled-up padding and dozens of blankets.

Her entire body ached, all her emotions rendering her numb and yet making her overwhelmingly tense. Her mind was in another place, in a far-off land desperately trying to hold on to every single memory, while the darkness slowly began to wrap itself around her again, oozing from her bones and creeping into her veins. She wanted to cry. She wanted to scream. She wanted to throw herself on the floor and just fold in on herself.

Nothing. She wanted to feel nothing.

But she felt everything. It was too much. This was all too much.

It hurt, everything hurt. Her head, her heart, her soul. Even her lungs hurt. They burned, the pain building and building and taking over her chest. She wanted it to stop. Her skin tingled, the sensation like a live wire inching closer, the hairs along her body rising to greet the electrifying energy. The air was dense and too thin, hot yet so, so cold. Her chest heaved as she fought the invisible hands covering her mouth and nose. Chills slithered up her spine and sweat beaded her hairline.

Make it stop. Someone, please make it stop.

Her body was no longer hers as her eyes closed, the lightheadedness taking over. Black and gray blended with the blue and white and green. It was too bright, the kaleidoscope of colors blinding.

Her blood rushed in her ears, her heartbeat pounding and pounding like a war drum. Pain, the pain in her chest tore through her like a monster wanting out.

Breathe. She needed to breathe. She wanted to breathe.

But did she?

It was like desperately wanting to take in that deep inhale but hoping it would never come. It was like wanting to feel yet wishing to never feel again. It was like drowning, the fear and despair and anguish of knowing it was coming, that any moment it would be your last, but still wanting to sink. To see just what would happen if you stopped fighting and gave in. To descend down, down . . . and down. Deeper and deeper into the darkness. It was wanting to live but not. It was the forbidden fruit.

Just a little taste.

But she had. She had sampled the bitter taste of death. No, not sampled, she had eaten the whole thing.

No!

Breathe.

Warm, comforting hands gripped her face, the touch gentle and soothing. "Open your eyes."

She had not realized she had even closed them.

"Darling, open your eyes."

His voice was like a beacon in the night, bringing her home.

Safe. She was safe.

Her eyes opened as her chest continued rising and falling unsteadily. In and out. In and out. The struggling inhales and shuddering exhales were shallow. Too shallow.

"Breathe," Will soothed, his voice calm and encouraging. "Look at me." When she finally focused on him, her brown, golden-speckled gaze concentrating on the most beautiful deep blue eyes with a delicate brown in one corner, the lifeline she held on to, he continued, "I'm here." His fingers slid into her hair as he gripped the base of her head, running his thumbs along her lower cheeks and jawline. "You are safe. You are real. And you are not alone." He kissed her forehead before they locked gazes again. "I have you, darling. Feel me. See me. And breathe with me." Taking a few deep breaths, Will gave her a gentle nod, urging her to follow his steady inhales and exhales.

Air filled her lungs as she matched his actions, perfectly in sync with him.

In—for three.

Out—for three.

In and out. Slow and steady.

Calm settled into her, never faltering from his gaze and mirroring each inhale and exhale.

The breeze around them kissed against her bare skin, the chilled caress pulling her deeper into her body. Each pounding beat slowed before vanishing from her ears, the sounds of the trees swaying and soft clattering filtering in. A wave of contentment eased through her veins and soothed her nerves.

Karramis blinked and drew in a long, deep inhale, her eyes closing as she blew it out and released it, giving it to the breeze to take far, far away.

Will gave her a tender smile, the gesture making him so ridiculously handsome. "That's my girl." He kissed her forehead again, everything about him making her love him even more, if that was even possible.

He lowered his hands and tucked one into the front pocket of his dark blue hoodie and pulled out a necklace, holding it up by the chain and dangling it in front of her. "Found it."

Will had been looking for something, searching through the wardrobe with determination on his face.

At the base of the silver chain hung a beautiful charm, the eight-pointed silver star with Celtic knots in the middle of each point covered in soot and slightly blackened, but still whole and undamaged. Even the hexagon-shaped deep-red garnet in the center, and the tiny black obsidians, tiger's eyes, and bloodstones were all in place.

It was the necklace Will had given her soon after he found out she was pregnant, the one to protect her. And the one that had housed her magic just long enough for Will and her siblings to close the portal. When he met his children again for the first time since they were babies. The necklace he had Quinian make for him—the weaponsmith surprisingly not at all reluctant to make jewelry. Dwarves were known for their craftsmanship, their skills ranging from metalwork to carpentry to even engineering, but Quinian did not seem the type to create such a delicate and intricate piece of art. But he had. And it was the same necklace Will knew Karramis loved just as much as the round ruby ring with two heart-shaped black sapphires atop it—her mother's ring.

"I think this belongs to you," Will added with a smile.

Karramis's mouth pulled upward, the matching gesture genuine but not revealing any teeth. Her eyes were soft, grateful, but filled with emotions. "It survived."

Will placed the necklace in her palm and folded her fingers over it before cupping her face and giving her a firm but gentle kiss, her lips welcoming. "And so did you."

"Hey," James called as he made his way over to them, not at all bothered by his parents' intimate embrace—in fact, he had grown to value these moments and appreciate and admire the love they had for each other. A love story not written in stone or sand, but in the stars. "I have a question. One that has been bugging me for a while now."

Will faced his son, but not before giving Karramis one more kiss, a gentle peck, and just one more glance, the silent 'I love you' clear in his eyes. "And what might that be?"

James stepped over a pile of wood, the rounded logs of the wall charred in some spots but still recognizable. "How did Phosmeratae put out the fire?"

James did not know all the abilities the dragons possessed outside of them having healing powers, as well as healing blood. But he was fully aware they did, in fact, have magical abilities. However, having no powers to control or manipulate water himself in unison with his air magic, he was genuinely curious as to how the dragon had been able to do what he did.

Will observed the two books tucked under James's arm, books that were surely novels of some kind based on the size and thickness of them. Rhiannon's books. James had found some of his sister's books she had left here.

It had been a while since Rhiannon had been to the cabin, opting to stay inside the wards of the village with her aunt and Aidan. Something both Will and Karramis understood and respected. Life at the cabin was not for the faint of heart on any given day. Add the new threats and the nightmarish memories of all the other bad things that had happened here over the last few months, and Will was not even quite sure why he and his wife had remained here for as long as they did.

But now, they did not have a choice. Their home was gone.

"That's actually a really good question," Karramis said. She had not been aware the Air Dragon could control water in the manner in which Phosmeratae did, having maneuvered numerous clouds containing a large amount of water over the cabin to extinguish the flames soon after they had entered the portals and headed to the castle.

"Magic," Will joked with a sarcastic drawl.

Karramis rolled her eyes. "No shit, Sherlock."

"Such language, darling. My, my, so cheeky."

Rolling her eyes again, Karramis huffed out something between a snort and a chuckle.

Will grinned and kissed the side of her head before addressing James. "Phosmeratae only moved the clouds, clouds he created, but the Water Dragons are the ones who placed the water into the clouds and released it."

"What?" James and Karramis echoed, equally baffled.

"When the fire broke out, Ignara called to Phosmeratae for help. The fire needed to be put out, but with it being Harkin's magic that had created the flames, Ignara could not call forth her abilities to control it. Fire Dragons can only manipulate a naturally occurring fire, or one not magically produced, unless it was generated by their own powers. So, Ignara called Phosmeratae, and the two of them summoned their telepathic abilities to reach out to the Water Dragons. The dragons then used their powers to raise the water from the sea into the clouds Phosmeratae had created. And once the clouds were moved to the right location, they were told to release it, pulling the water out so it could fall onto the fire."

"The dragons can communicate from that far away?" Karramis asked, trying to gauge the distance from the northern side of the island—both Dragon Cove and Arista Bay being where the Water Dragons usually lived when not swimming around the island—and the cabin, or wherever Phosmeratae had been that night.

"Dragons can speak telepathically from hundreds, if not thousands, of miles away. It all depends on telepathic strength and their bond. They once were able to communicate with Drolnogards in the same manner—from very, very long distances, but that particular ability weakened over time as more and more of the Drolnogard bloodline faded and more dragons died. I've only been able to go as far as the distance between the cabin and a few hundred yards inside Emrys Cave to commune with the dragons—something I'm quite sure was done intentionally with the placement of this place. You and your sister's Drolnogard abilities are far more advanced and stronger."

"Why, though?" James questioned, intrigued yet grateful his telepathic abilities had finally strengthened over the recent weeks.

Will shrugged as he held Karramis's hand and began moving them through the rubble. "I'm not quite sure, if I'm being honest. I could only guess it may have something to do with there simply being more Drolnogards. Or maybe it's just unique to you both. An added enhancement given to you by magic itself."

James eyed Terramina, who had been the one to fly him in. She had been by all of their sides over the last few weeks, never leaving the village and always within range of all three of the Drolnogards, just in case. She even went as far as sleeping outside the house where the entire Cassil family slept, guarding them every single night. Even Raeth and Oakley remained nearby. None of them had even been back to the cave, staying either inside the village or just above, monitoring the area. Harkin, Ignara, and Phosmeratae had chosen to return to their homes every day to rest, but remained the constant aerial watchdogs of the sky during the night.

James had grown close to the dragons, seeing them as not only companions, protectors, but also his family. They were loyal and honest, protective and caring. He trusted them, valued and respected them. Loved them.

Terramina bowed her head slightly as she took in the admiration and gratitude in his eyes, the adoration. James did not need to speak mind to mind for the dragon to know what he was feeling, she could sense it.

"Heart to heart, mind to mind, you are mine to protect, mine to guide, mine to defend, and mine to love. Until my final breath, my life is that of yours and your bloodline. Wholly and without regret."

The dragon's words were so sincere and honest, so heartwarming, it made James swallow the emotion rising in his throat. But before he could respond, another voice filtered into his head.

He angled his head toward his parents. "It's time to go." The command was simple, no fear, no worry, no sense of urgency, just a gentle finality in his tone.

"Where to?" Will asked, helping Karramis over the last pile of debris as they left the wreckage and made their way over to Callie and Terramina.

Rhiannon had contacted James, their telepathic powers having strengthened as they continued to practice more, learning to control the entering of the other's mind without invading each other's privacy, as well as shielding themselves from invasive eavesdropping and making their long-distance communication travel farther and more efficiently.

"Uncle Pavian and Aunt K want us all to meet in the Grand Hall in half an hour."

"All right," Will said, his voice filled with somberness as he angled his head to face Karramis, the two of them twisting back and taking in what was left of their home. "Are you sure?"

Karramis paused for a moment, closing her eyes and taking in one long inhale, the smell of jasmine, sea salt, and the collective trees surrounding them filling her nose. Opening her eyes, she nodded at her husband as she exhaled, nothing but acceptance in her gaze.

"Yeah. I'm sure."

And with her words, Will and Karramis mounted Callie as James hovered in the sky a few yards above them. Tapping the side of the winged horse, Will gripped Callie's mane, making sure to squeeze his arms and legs to hold tight to Karramis as they all jumped into the sky and joined James and Terramina. Glancing down at the cabin, all of them watched as Harkin flew over the trees to the east, banking upward slightly before coasting down. Hot, orange flames spewed from his open maw lined with sharp teeth, trailing across the ground and charring the land just before the straight, fiery projectile slammed into the cabin. Fire erupted, the inferno blazing as the flames danced higher and the smoke billowed, completely engulfing the cabin.

Karramis watched as the rest of her home was destroyed, the thoughts of tomorrow filling her mind.

Someday. Someday they would return here and rebuild.
Rebuild their home.

One day.

Maybe.

Chapter 26

Death and Destiny

The light outside the stained-glass windows dimmed as dusk approached. Flames roared in the oversized marble fireplace located on the back wall of the Grand Hall. Heat filled the long, open room, the warmth a welcome contrast to the chill outside the rounded wooden door. Chatter echoed off the interior stone walls, the conversation taking place filling everyone in, all those who sat at the long wooden table or paced the room, on the activities Pavian had endured in the non-magical realm.

The entire guard—which consisted of Kavana, Viktor, Tenarick, Alfina, Quinian, and now Meadow, Aidan, and the twins, both having the only active Guardian magic left—along with Karramis, Will, and Randolyn had discovered the full extent of the devastation at MUSE.

In addition to the fire that had occurred, destroying more than half the large estate, a massacre had taken place. The muses were no more, the last remaining ones completely wiped out. A magical creature who had been around many millennia had been erased from existence. They were all gone. Extinct. Along with many of the instructors, who had been both magical and non-magical. Witches and regular humans just disposed of as if they were nothing more than a quick meal. Blood had filled many of the bedrooms, the attack happening in the dead of night, but smears and splatters lined the hallways, the floors and walls coated in crimson as many of the others tried to escape.

There had been over a hundred students residing inside the estate, some who had no magic but had only been part of a magical bloodline, and ranging from nineteen to as young as eight, and most had been found among the wreckage. But some had not. That had been Pavian's top priority after cleaning up the mess, more so with the local authorities rather than in literal terms. He had to find those remaining children.

Pavian had handed off the responsibilities of the actual estate, including the destruction of the building and arranging for removing the bodies for burial, to one of the local caretakers who had been off-site during the attack. Pavian had pondered what should happen to the school, deciding to level the remaining structure, the choice not an easy one considering the estate had a history to it. But after having any salvageable documents removed, he figured it was for the best—the massacre not being something the school needed to be remembered for. So, they would rebuild it, somewhere along the other side of the lake on the property, deciding the magical community still needed a school. But they would wait a few years, giving everyone time to heal and recover from the tragedy. And to wait and see where things were by then.

Because Pavian was certain if his niece and nephew were not able to stop whatever was coming, there might not be enough of them left to rebuild or even instruct the new generation. That is, if magic even existed in the end.

All of the children who had not perished had eventually been found by Pavian in a nearby town, taking refuge at a church. Two of the older students had helped aid in an escape through the underground tunnels, a precautionary addition added during the fifties, along with bunkers and root cellars for food storage. In total, thirteen children had survived. Only thirteen. And from those thirteen, none of them had witnessed the carnage. Thankfully. But Pavian knew exactly what had happened, the evidence that had been found clear.

It had been vampires.

Vampires had broken through the wards and attacked, without any reluctance or remorse. They had drained every single person inside, killing them as though they were nothing. Even the children.

Children. The thoughts and images Pavian still could not come to terms with. They were supposed to be safe. MUSE was designed with some of the strongest spells to shield it from any tracking abilities, and yet they had failed. Even the protective barriers to keep any malevolent creatures out had failed.

No, they had not failed, they had been overpowered.

Merrick had found them.

He had broken through all the wards and entered the grounds, murdering all the muses and thus severing the magic around the school and giving full access to the rest of the vampires.

Pavian was not quite certain why they had attacked. At first. But something had eventually been discovered on the grounds weeks after the massacre. A ritual site—a ritual leaving two dead. Two teenage boys. Brothers, in fact. Brothers linked to the original Fire Witch bloodline, the Llewellyn witches. Karramis's bloodline. But their ancestry had not been directly linked to Pavian's younger sister, the boys' lineage distant and removed through many generations from Karramis. Even their magic seemed faint, nowhere near as powerful as the fire magic that had coursed through Karramis's blood. But they still had the magic, something Merrick apparently wanted and needed for himself. A magic that left the two boys victims of the prophecy slowly coming to pass.

Others had also potentially been killed at the ritual site, but no other bodies had been discovered. Only blood. So much blood had stained the pebble stones along the shores near the lake where the suspected ritual had taken place. The dark crimson lined the inside of the makeshift circle consisting of larger stones, leaf-covered branches and dead flowers, and burned logs.

Pavian had spent most of the rest of his time over there transporting the children he had found to their homes and back to their families. But when he had planned to come home himself, he faced a problem—another portal had disappeared, leaving only three doorways left into the realm. So, he had missed his chance to return, needing to travel to another and wait out the rest of the month until they opened again. He had decided to make the trip early, just in case that one, too, had disappeared. But luckily, it had not. And, to add to Pavian's newfound luck, it had been within a close distance from a safehouse.

However, the luck ended there. The portals were disappearing, both inside and outside the realm. Soon, there would be none left, leaving everyone either trapped inside or stuck outside. The only way in or out once the doorways faded completely would be to bring down the entire barrier, thus risking exposure of all magic, including the creatures unable to hide, in the non-magical realm. And the portals left on Kiluemar were also malfunctioning. Although, Pavian had learned Merrick was the cause of some of that. But still, there were no longer any portals linked to him or his sisters. In fact, James and Rhiannon were the only ones who had their Guardian magic, and they were not quite efficient in controlling those particular abilities. And even then, the magic of the Guardian bloodline was fading, just like the portals.

The realm was in danger.

"The balance has shifted," Pavian said, the authoritative tone matching his posture as he stood at one end of the long table, his stance wide and arms folded over his broad chest. "It's off—no longer whole or equally measured. And if it continues to be off kilter for too long, the magic will continue to deteriorate, and once that happens, the realm will cease to exist. Magic will be fully exposed to the outside world again. Everything will start to unravel into chaos, and we won't be able to fight it, let alone survive. With the advances in technology and all the weaponry, it will be genocide to our kind yet again."

Rhiannon analyzed his words and asked, "The balance of what exactly? The realm or magic itself?"

"Both most likely, but I was referring to the realm. The magic here is fractured and weak. There are cracks, it seems, in the structure of it. This island was created with pure, unfettered balance. The balance of male and female, life and death, created and cursed, dark and light magic. There was an equal balance within the four elements. It was a gift given for a gift taken. The blood of the fallen and the blood of the living. It was a ritual of complete balance. But now . . ." Pavian exhaled. "Now there's not enough magic within the island to keep it alive."

James leaned back in the chair next to his sister and mirrored his uncle by crossing his arms, his demeanor serious and contemplative. "So, the island is dying, then?"

Pavian gave a single nod. "Yes."

"How do we fix it?" Rhiannon asked, her thoughts churning, desperately hoping he had an answer.

"By releasing the stolen magic back into the island."

Rhiannon narrowed her eyes as the others watched with rapt attention. "You mean, by killing Merrick?" She wanted it to come out as a statement, a statement she knew was true, but the uncertainty came through in her voice, making it a question.

"Yes," Pavian answered with another curt nod.

"And how do we do that?" James asked, almost excited and ready for whatever was next.

Pavian glanced over at Karramis and Will, who sat across from the twins, knowing the weight of all this was solely on their children's shoulders, yet he had no way to help them, his niece's and nephew's lives and the survival of this island and all magic left up to fate. "I have no idea," he finally answered with a defeated shrug.

James let out a frustrated sigh and lowered his arms to his lap. "Well, that's helpful," he delivered with a sarcastic lilt.

James and Rhiannon had been trying to figure out a plan for weeks now, the two of them actually working together in the library with Ryan, all of them searching the documents, archives, and stories for any solution. Any fragment of a possible key left in the past to help them. Different strategies were discussed, but nothing concrete—just unrealistic ideas and ridiculous schemes being spewed.

Eventually James gave up, stating sitting around was not going to solve their problems. But Rhiannon had chosen to continue to focus all her mental strength on something she knew she was good at, research. She was certain something in all her reading and investigating would be the answer they were searching for. But her brother thought otherwise. James preferred a more physical standpoint on preparing for their impending future.

"We need to train harder," he informed his sister, the steadfast statement containing slight irritation. "We are never going to win this without the full power of our magic." He eyed the others before rotating in his chair and facing her wholly. "We were given these powers for a reason, so we need to practice them. We aren't going to beat him by hiding out in the library. We have to train."

Rhiannon knew this. It was something he had mentioned many times before. But even without the reminder, she knew—she knew magic was a big part of how they might survive this. How they might actually save everything—and everyone. But it still scared her. Not her powers, not even the future, but rather the ones she would have to face again. Merrick and Haydrin still haunted her dreams, her nightmares a constant reminder they were still out there, and that her inability to master her magic might be the reason someone might die. The idea of that was the worst kind of failure. And she did not want to fail.

But in learning everything about what Pavian had gone through, they had also learned the truth about Haydrin, something Pavian was reluctant to discuss due to his father's death still being fresh in his mind. But he had, and it was adding to the fear Rhiannon had for the werewolf. That, and the fact that she learned werewolves did crave the blood of the victims they tasted. Meaning Haydrin would continue to hunt her until he killed her. However, it was not just the realization he wanted to end something he started with her, but rather, it was the true reason why the werewolf had been the one to kill Zarrius. It had been revenge. Justice. A life for a life. The irony of it somewhat poetic.

But it was not Zarrius who Haydrin originally wanted, it had been Pavian. But when the time came, it would seem the werewolf was happy to take the parent of the one who had killed his mother instead.

Haydrin's mother had been in labor the night of a full moon, but once the baby was born, Haydrin's mother had begun to shift. Pavian was called into the infirmary to handle the situation, trying to administer a sedative to the woman, hoping it would allow him to transport her to a safer location before she shifted completely. But the dosage was too much for the woman, who had not shifted completely and had just suffered blood loss due to the delivery, and Haydrin's mother had gone into shock and died. It had been an accident. Pavian did not know the sedative was harmful to their human forms, but Haydrin did not care. Pavian had killed his mother, and when Haydrin activated his curse years later, he planned to slaughter Pavian for what he had done. But when Haydrin had attempted to attack inside Caerwyn Village, Pavian again had to administer the tranquilizer, but it had not worked on the new werewolf—Haydrin's new abilities had been too strong and potent. So, another was given to him, and again, the sedative was too much, and it caused some damage to Haydrin's human form. He could no longer heal from minor injuries, even in his werewolf form, and it had caused some damage to his eyesight.

Zarrius had been part of the whole ordeal that had robbed Haydrin of his mother, leaving the teenage Pavian in charge of such a dire situation, and it left another teenage boy to take on the full responsibilities of his newborn brother. Even though Zarrius was insistent on aiding Haydrin and his brother over the years, even offering to house them in his home and provide them with a family, it was not enough. Haydrin wanted nothing to do with the Guardian or his children. As he grew up, Haydrin's hatred developed into what it had become, vowing to kill Pavian and going so far as working with Merrick to make it happen. But when the time came to finish their deal, Haydrin opted for Zarrius instead. A parent for a parent.

And now, after learning all of this, Rhiannon was scared that with one task done, Haydrin would come for her next.

With all eyes on her, she remained quiet, unsure what to say, but also hesitant to voice her concerns. Shielding her mind, she blocked out her brother, silencing any chance of him hearing her inner thoughts. Although, she could tell by the softening of his features, he felt it. He could sense the emotions waging war inside her.

But James had so much faith in his sister. He believed she could do it, if she just stopped giving in to the thoughts in her head. He believed she was far more powerful than she thought. She just needed a small push. His sister had proven her strength before—at the beach when Ryan and Haydrin attacked, the control she had, the concentration and might of her magic. She had shielded them from an entire tidal wave. But that had not been the first time she had shown her potential.

Sliding his hand over the pocket of his jeans, he felt the reminder of the first time her magic surfaced. A magic neither one of them even knew she possessed. Yet she had controlled it with such manipulation and power, it was awe-inspiring. A miracle. It was downright magical in all sense of the word. She just needed to find that again—find the unwavering drive to fight.

"Are we done here?" Rhiannon asked, pushing back her chair, the sound of it scraping against the floor. She would not give in to the emotions. She would not cry again. She was done crying.

"Not quite," Pavian answered, sensing the tension but ignoring it. There were still things to discuss.

Rhiannon ignored him and stood. "I wish to be dismissed. I . . . I just need a moment."

When Pavian went to object, Aidan interrupted smoothly, "Just give her a minute." There was no dominance or anger in his voice, just understanding.

Rhiannon did not react, but her eyes silently thanked him as she made her way outside.

Karramis watched her daughter, identifying and relating to everything Rhiannon was going through right now. Fear was debilitating. It was suffocating and all-consuming. And for some, it ruled their lives. It was not something one could simply get over. It took time and strength, strength only the person facing the fear could master. Rhiannon had to find the strength for herself. Even with the love and support Karramis had—Will being the anchor keeping her from drifting away and the hand to prevent her from sinking—it was something she, too, had to figure out on her own. Karramis understood now, being afraid does not make you broken or flawed. It simply makes you human.

"Let me talk to her," James said to his uncle, his gaze shifting over to his parents.

Karramis and Will nodded, agreeing, but it was Karramis who spoke. "We'll finish up here and meet you both outside."

There was not much more to talk about, but whatever was left could be relayed to the twins later. However, Karramis was certain the final thing her brother needed to discuss was not related to her children but rather their father.

James opened the door of the Grand Hall, the cold air smacking him in the face as he stepped outside of the heated room. Darkness had fallen over the village, the stars dotting the night sky. His shoes slapped against the stone stairs before landing on the solid dirt pathway, and he searched the area.

Rhiannon was nowhere in sight.

But he knew where she had gone.

~

Rhiannon entered the library and made her way past the towering shelves filled with books. The rows and rows of classic novels, historical documents, tomes, spell books, realm archives and records, and tales of folklore called to her, the pages and pages smelling like home.

The small alcove on the main floor, across from one of the fireplaces, with the old wooden desk, was her favorite place to do her research. While the oversized chair tucked into the nook in the large room upstairs was where she loved to sit and just read. And sometimes even nap. Sleeping at the library had been a common occurrence with her over the last few months, even more so lately.

Making her way up the stairs, Rhiannon cringed when the wooden steps creaked, the sound so loud in the open space.

"Blaze?"

Ryan's smooth voice filled the area, the echo of it distant. He was on the second floor, but the other rooms on this level could not be accessed from these stairs. These led to the open alcove on the top of the landing, the space most likely used as a workplace or possibly a private sitting room when it had been a brothel when the building was first built.

"Ryan?" she called, heading back down the stairs. Rhiannon did not know what time it was, although it had not been too late. But she was still curious as to why he was here. She thought he had returned to Stoweward before the full moon a few nights ago. "What are you doing here?"

She strolled by the shelves along the back wall and made her way over to the second stairwell, this one slightly wider and in much better shape. Glancing up, she spotted Ryan leaning over the railing, the casualness of his demeanor seeming almost mischievous.

"I could say the same thing about you," he teased with a grin in his smooth English accent. He must have seen something in her expression because the corner of his mouth drooped, and he pushed off the railing and headed toward the stairs. "What's wrong? What happened?"

"Nothing," she answered unconvincingly.

The door of the library opened, and James's voice traveled in. "Rhiannon?"

"I'm here," she said, not at all surprised by his arrival.

James followed the sound of Ryan coming down the steps, the three of them now standing on the base of the stairs.

"What happened?" Ryan asked again, moving his gaze between the two of them. He took them both in, sensing the apprehension in Rhiannon and the determination in James.

Ryan had grown even closer to Rhiannon since he had attacked her and James at the beach. An attack he still could not figure out how or why it had happened. He had never lost control over himself like that before. But he had also developed an even stronger friendship with James. Ryan had visited them after learning Karramis had died and come back to life, making sure he could provide as much support as possible. But Ryan had noticed something happening to James the more he got to know him better. Unlike Rhiannon, James was not ruled by his emotions. He controlled himself in a way that was almost inspirational. There was a drive inside him, a determination unlike anyone Ryan had ever come across. He had a confidence to him, a composed assurance that was almost unnerving. And

Ryan could see it in his eyes now, James was on the verge of doing something, something Ryan could not seem to place.

"Nothing," Rhiannon said again. "I mean, nothing really. It's just . . ." She exhaled. "You would think I would have all this figured out by now. You know?"

"All what?" Ryan asked. "Your magic?"

"That and the prophecy. The symbol. Something. How am I—*we* . . . How are we supposed to do all this when we have no clue what to do?"

The door of the library opened again.

"Rhiannon?" Karramis's soft voice filtered into the room. "James, are you two in here?"

"Over here," James stated just as Rhiannon said, "Yeah."

Karramis came into view with Will trailing behind her, both giving their children a gentle smile.

"Hey," Rhiannon added, her expression apologetic, "I didn't mean to just storm out like that."

"Don't worry about it, sweetie," Karramis offered sincerely.

"I'm sorry anyway, though." Rhiannon curled her hands into fists, taking some of the material of her skirt into her grip. Inhaling deeply, she released it and continued, "I just can't figure out how we are going to fix all of this when I can't even master all my magic. I haven't been able to do . . . *whatever* it was I did before when you—" She cut herself off, eyeing her mother regretfully and with sadness in her gaze.

"Died," Karramis finished for her. "You can say it, Rhiannon. It's okay. It's not going to break me. Not anymore.

Yes, I died. But I am not dead. And one day, I'll die again . . . And one day I might never come back. But I am here now."

Rhiannon admired her mother's strength and resilience, her tenacity and willpower to overcome everything she had been through. Rhiannon wanted to be her mother when she grew up. She wanted to be able to face every obstacle with the grace of a lady but the fight of a warrior.

"How do I do it, Mom?" Rhiannon asked, admiration and awe coating the question. "How do I fight against this idea of not being good enough? That magic didn't choose right in picking me. How do I fight this constant fear of whatever waits for me in the dark? I know the power is there—the ability to counter it, and even produce it, but how do I stop allowing my emotions to cause me to hesitate and question myself? I want to control it. How do I do that?"

Karramis focused on her daughter, speaking only to her despite the others being nearby. This was something she, too, had to discover for herself, and now, it was time for her daughter to find the ability to do this for herself. "You're still running from it. But you can't do that anymore. Because we all know it's there—we've seen it. It's been right in front of us. So, stop running away. Stop hiding. Those things don't work for us."

Rhiannon kept her gaze locked on her mother, even as her voice wavered slightly. "What does work, then?"

"Running toward it. Facing it, fighting it—challenging every part of it and using it to your advantage. Manipulate it into fearing you instead. Stop struggling and just give in to it. And once you do, it can no longer hold you hostage. And only then will you be the one in complete control."

Eyes dropping, Rhiannon took in the hands of her parents, interlocked as if they refused to let go of each other even for a second. "How do I do that? You make it seem so easy, like flipping a switch in your mind."

"Oh, trust me, it is not that easy. I spent most of my life afraid of my powers, resentful of being different from everyone else. I spent so many of those years running from my magic, trying to hide from it. Then I hid again, literally. Afraid magic would get me and you both"—Karramis glanced over at James—"killed." Her brown gaze returned to Rhiannon as she gave her a soft smile. "Magic and I have never seen eye to eye on things. Eventually my fears relating to my powers, the rumors of an unknown future, and those who wanted some claim on me or wanted something from me they couldn't have, started to take control of my life. I wasted so much of my life worried about the what-ifs and the possible dangers of what tomorrow might bring that I lost out on so many todays—the here and now. No one is promised tomorrow, no one, and it took me a long time to realize that I just needed to live in the moment. To not focus so much on a future I may or may not be given." Tucking a strand of hair behind her daughter's ear, she added wholeheartedly, "You are like me in so many ways, but this is one thing I don't want you to inherit from me. Don't be afraid of tomorrow, Rhiannon, because you'll miss out on today. Embrace right now. Fight for it."

Wiping an escaped tear forming on her lower lashes, Rhiannon asked, fighting back the lump rising in her throat, "What if I'm not strong enough?"

"You are." So much certainty and sincerity were in the declaration. "It took me a long time to find my inner strength to stand up and fight back. But first, I had to surrender to it. I had to allow everything I was feeling to consume me, to accept things I didn't want to accept and embrace the path I was on. But I did. I gave in, so I could be reborn into a person who refused to give up. And now, it's your turn. You can do this. You are strong enough to fight. But you have to give in to all of those fears and let them consume every part of you. Let it flow into your very soul, fusing deep inside of you, so you can draw strength from it. Only then can you use it to fight back."

Rhiannon pulled in a shuddering breath. "Do you really think I can do it?"

"It doesn't matter what I think, it only matters what you believe." The statement was directed at both Rhiannon and James. "But everyone has an innate desire to survive. It's the fight-or-flight response triggering us to react one way or another. Right now, you want to flee. You want to avoid the situation instead of facing it—something I'm all too familiar with. But unfortunately, we can't hide from this. What we are running from will never stop chasing us. It will always be there, coming for us. It's a shadow, following us in the light, and the ghost in the darkness. You can't outrun it. So, stop. Stop running from it, and instead face it."

"But what about the prophecy—our destiny?"

"Destiny isn't a predetermined notion. It's all about choices."

Rhiannon's blue eyes landed on her father. "Yeah, that's what Dad said."

Karramis smiled over at her husband and squeezed his hand. "And he's right. Destiny isn't a one-way path. It's not that simple. If it was, then there wouldn't be right or wrong, good and evil. Destiny is all about perspective. It's about which vantage point you see it from. But our journey, our path, is up to us to decide. Nothing can control our final fate. Only you have the power to do that with the choices you make. Destiny might be a path you are placed on, but that path can lead you in different directions. There are twists and turns, left and right, and even obstacles. It's not always linear. And the way you decide to go will dictate where you end up. Destiny isn't the final destination, it's simply the journey to get there. You control which way you go." Karramis paused for a heartbeat. "Remember, strength isn't about being strong physically, it's about being strong mentally. Strength is more about fighting through the limitations of the body and being able to control the mind into believing you are capable of doing so much more than what is in front of you. Strength is overcoming doubt, fear, grief, and anger, and all those negative emotions, and showing yourself you refuse to give up. Power over the mind is one of the hardest things to manipulate, but once you win that battle, nothing will be able to hold you down anymore.”

James hooked an arm around his sister’s shoulders. “You can do this. You’re powerful and strong.” Encouragement radiated in his voice, his eyes, but it faltered, quickly turning to a teasing manner. “You are the other half of me and all.” He nudged her playfully.

Rhiannon could not help but smile. “Shut up.” Remembering where she was as she glanced around the library, she asked her parents, “What are you both doing here?”

“Looking for you, of course,” her father answered. “We wanted to make sure you were all right.” He tossed a quick peek over at Karramis. “And to let you both”—he took in their children—“know something important.”

Excitement raced through James as Rhiannon’s heart sank into her stomach, the tone of their father’s voice not giving any hint as to whether this was something good or something bad.

“Nothing is wrong,” Will added, making sure to ease any concern after realizing his statement could be taken as something dire.

“Okay,” James said curiously, “what is it, then?”

Karramis’s chest rose as she took in a deep inhale, a look of sadness in her eyes. “It’s time to say goodbye.”

~

James sat on the shore of Half Moon Harbor, the sand cool under the material of his jeans and black hoodie. It had been nicer over the last week, the chill of winter washed away slightly by the heat of the sun beating down overhead without a cloud in the sky. The sound of the cerulean waves lapping over the ivory sand filled the bay, the calm and beauty of the beach making it impossible not to relax, to just live in the moment. Salt and an atmospheric cleanliness flittered through the air along with the crisp aroma of flora and fauna drifting down from the cliffs.

This place was one of James's favorite locations on the island, something about the seclusion and view of the southwestern sky at sunset so peaceful and beautiful. Even with the memories of the attack on him and his sister all those months ago, both of their blood soaked into the sand by now, it was still such a serene place. With the trees swaying along the cliffs behind him, the sensation of the sand beneath him, and the soft echoing of the wind caressing through the mouth of the caves, James felt connected to his magic here. There was something so powerful about this side of the island for him, the caves and grotto somehow making his powers seem alive inside of him. One day, he would have to travel into those openings into the island and explore the wonders underground.

The sun trailed farther down along the horizon as numerous shadows came into view along the shoreline, the shapes differing in size. Silhouettes, with their long tails and outstretched wings, circled around, coming closer and closer, their shapes growing.

James had known they were nearly here, the other dragons joining Oakley, who had been scouting the area since the Earth Dragon and James had arrived nearly an hour ago. What was supposed to take place tonight would not happen until sundown, but James wanted some time to himself, to think. To clear his head.

It had been five days since learning about everything his Uncle Pavian witnessed at MUSE, and five days of mulling over all the thoughts and ideas fluttering around in his head. Granted, strategy was more Rhiannon's forte, but there had been something gnawing at him, an idea—well, ideas rather. Although the execution of one in particular was still not quite certain, yet the other was on the forefront of his mind and clear as day. At least, he hoped it was.

As all the dragons circled overhead, Terramina, Raeth, and Ignara landed, allowing the people atop them to dismount. Pavian jumped from Terramina, his descent from the Earth Dragon flawless, and reached up for Liam before placing the little boy down and grabbing hold of Raina and helping her as well as she cradled her very pregnant stomach. Kavana, too, removed herself from Raeth as though she had been a dragon rider all her life. Marks still littered her body, the wounds on her neck healed but permanently scarring her skin. Aidan swooped down beside her and shifted a few feet from the ground, his shoes landing in the sand, his transformation effortless and perfectly timed. Ignara lowered her body down as Rhiannon and

Ryan dismounted, the look on Ryan's face telling James the poor guy was still not used to being on the back of the dragons.

As all of them headed over to James, who had remained sitting on the shore, Callie and Galahad appeared just over the cliffs. The two winged horses landed with such grace, and they trotted to a stop. James's Aunt Meadow and family—her husband, Tristin, and two young daughters, Ivy and Iris—sat atop Galahad, the solid black creature one of the most majestic things James had ever seen. With his silky black coat, massively large frame, and formidable demeanor, Galahad was absolutely breathtaking. He was all elegance and power. Wings lowering, Callie sank down, allowing Randolyn and her sister, Aayrah, a shorter distance to slide off the winged horse.

And like clockwork, James's parents arrived, Karramis and Will coming into sight as they rode in on Harkin. Squinting, James noticed another passenger with them, the braided gray hair and bright floral pattern on the flowy dress making James recognize the person right away. Fayemeara.

Viktor, too, arrived within minutes of the others, the massive gargoyle landing and taking up a wide stance and eyeing his surroundings as if guarding the area.

They were all here. His family. His friends. All of them were here. The only ones missing were—

Figures emerged from the portal along the beach.

James could barely make them out due to the distance, but as they came closer, he rose to his feet and dusted off his backside.

Nina, Tenarick, Alfina, Quinian, Avery, Caleb, and Tiffasa all made their way closer. Even a few others had come, some James recognized from seeing them in the village or Stoweward, but did not know them by name.

Everyone was here.

Here to say their final goodbyes to Zarrius Ward, a beloved father, a dear friend, a loving husband, a caring grandfather, and an amazing Guardian—a protector of his family, his friends, his guard, magic, and everything inside this realm.

The silence floated across the vast area as everyone began hugging and greeting each other with sorrowful grins and teary eyes.

Making their way toward the water, everyone lined up as the last of the rays reached into the sky, the soft yellow glow painted alongside the vibrant hues of magenta and orange before fading upward into the rich shades of dark purples and blues. Stars appeared high overhead against the midnight blue of the approaching night.

Pavian kissed Raina's forehead and strolled over to the front of the group, turning to face them. Sadness plagued his features, his dark brown eyes fighting the urge to water, but he stood tall, forever the collected leader.

James drifted his attention from his uncle to the others, taking in every single one of them. Their faces, their eyes, everything about them, burning them into his memory.

For them. He had to do this, for them. The prophecy, this magic, this gift, it was all for them. To save them. To give them a life, a life he was unable to give to his grandfather. A life that his mother would also no longer have, if she had not been given a gift too.

He took in his young cousins—Liam, Ivy, and Iris, the three of them still so young yet just as equally in danger. They had their whole life in front of them. And even now, the risk of being outside the wards as the light of day was erased by night with each passing second was high. But everyone here knew the dangers, yet they still showed up. No weapons, no fears, no doubt or regret. Everyone wanted to be here, despite the possibility of whatever might come.

Pavian exhaled, readying himself. "We all deal with loss differently, so I'm not going to stand here and tell you all how to feel or how to cope. But my father was a good man—a firm man, a strict man. A man with so much seriousness yet an amazing sense of humor, you never really knew which side of him would show up sometimes. But he was an amazing leader, a great family man, and one of the best human beings out there. There will never be anyone quite like him for me, and for many of you."

Quiet sobs broke out around them, everyone trying their hardest to keep themselves together.

"But—" Pavian continued, his voice wavering, the need to also keep it together making him clear his throat. "But you all know this already. So, in lieu of reminding everyone of what we lost, I'm going to tell you something similar that he told me a long time ago when I first joined the guard." His eyes met James and Rhiannon, knowing his next words would help them with whatever the future held for them. "We live in a world where it's all about survival, and I don't just mean here. I mean out there too. Every day everyone is faced with the possibility of death. Even immortals. Life is about existing within the chaos of the unknown, and we live among the harshest of that chaos. Here, it's harder. It's dangerous—unpredictable. Here, some days, it's kill or be killed. Every action has a reaction. A consequence. But some consequences have their rewards. Sometimes doing the right thing isn't always good, and doing the wrong thing isn't always bad. It's all about balance. And sometimes, a good mistake is necessary. Because it keeps us alive, both literally and metaphorically. Mistakes help us. They allow us to grow and thrive. Right or wrong, good or bad, it's all part of the same coin, just different sides. But it's up to us to decide which side we want to stand on when it matters most."

Pavian lowered his head, the emotions building. Swallowing them down, he glanced up to continue, but his eyes went wide, and his mouth dropped open, shock lining his expression.

Silence.

Everyone faced where his eyes remained locked, the cliffs behind them.

James turned and mirrored his uncle's reaction.

Astonishment. Disbelief. Admiration. All of it slammed into him.

Lining the cliffs stood nearly a hundred people.

Flickering illuminated their silhouettes, the glow coming from candles in what James could only assume were glass containers, considering the breeze blowing was not extinguishing the flames. It had to be all those who had remained in Stoweward, all the families of the werewolves with nowhere else to go, and the few others who had chosen to stay in the village.

Shadows moved across the moonless sky, the celestial wonder having not breached the horizon yet. The dragons circled high overhead, their focus glued to the entire area surrounding them. The Earth and Fire Dragons were the eyes and ears and monitored this side of the island while Phosmeratae remained vigilant on the forbidden side, going so far as to prevent anyone from entering the portal just outside the castle. Every precaution was taken for tonight.

Splashing sounded just as a familiar twinge filled James's chest. Heads turned toward the beach just as long necks breached through the surface of the water inside the harbor.

Water Dragons.

"Look," Liam called excitedly as his little finger pointed toward the cliffs near the West Shores.

Brown eyes went wider as James gawked in absolute wonderment and shock at the numerous figures standing at the edge of the bluffs. Tall—massively tall, that is the only way he could describe the shadowy forms watching them from above. Giants. James was looking at the giants for the first time. Creatures who rarely left the caves under the waterfall inside the

Valley of the Giants. James hated that he could not make out more of their features in the dark, but he knew, without a doubt, they were magnificently magical.

Bright colors caught James's attention in the corner of his eye, and he glanced over at them. It was in that moment he understood why they had chosen this location as the place to say their goodbyes.

"The Dancing Waters," Ryan whispered to himself, the awe in his voice matching everyone's expressions.

Pink, blue, purple, white, and yellow lit up the waters of the bay, the vibrant colors swirling together. The glow sparkled underneath the lapping waves, the illumination lighting up the entire harbor as the Water Dragons dipped below the surface, a soft blue emanating from them. A kaleidoscope of colors swayed among the water as the glimmering lights created a rainbow of bright rays shooting into the night sky.

"How are they doing it without the full moon?" Ryan asked no one in particular.

It was Tenarick who answered, serene and steady. "The Water Nymphs never needed the full moon to create the Dancing Waters. All they needed was the natural power inside the element itself."

"Water Nymphs?" Rhiannon asked, confused as she eyed the flicking of a smaller tail, bright pink and glowing, breaching the surface. "I thought the merfolk were the ones who did the Dancing Waters, along with the dragons."

Tenarick angled his head, considering her words. "Merfolk." It was not really a question, but rather an observation. One he found quite entertaining by the look of his pleased expression. "They are one in the same," he continued. "Long before they were given the name mermaids—or rather, merfolk—they were referred to as Water Nymphs, and in some cultures, Water Sprites. But they are all the same."

"I didn't know that," Rhiannon said, even more confused by the lack of this information not being in the archives and various documents.

"Many do not. This was long before the realm existed—quite a few generations in fact. Many cultures have given them different names over the millennia, but it was *mermaid* which seemed to catch on the most, the written word making it even more popular."

James knew elves were not immortal but rather they aged very, very slowly. And it was his sister who had informed him of this fact, something she had considered based on the next words out of her mouth.

"How old are you exactly?"

Tenarick simply smiled as he continued to watch the Dancing Waters. "Old."

The area went quiet again as everyone returned their attention to the bay, the lights among the water the only illumination in front of them.

A few minutes later, James noticed Pavian tossing a single nod over to Will. The curiosity faded within seconds as the presence of Harkin zoomed overhead. Spinning in a downward spiral, the dragon soared through the sky, heading over toward Ember Cliffs. An orange glow filled the dark, rainbow-lit sky just before fire erupted from the dragon's open mouth. Flames shot through the air and crashed into the top of the cliffs, igniting a large pile of wood just at the edge of the bluffs. A bonfire.

James remembered how they always burned the bodies on the island now when one died, so this must be the ceremonial sendoff. A symbolic gesture with the flames giving everyone the closure they needed.

Everyone sat on the shore and watched in silence, holding or leaning against one another as the flames danced across the cliffs and the colors of the bay continued to glow bright.

Over the next few hours, more and more present disappeared, their goodbyes concluded as the fire finally started to dwindle and the Dancing Waters stopped completely. The only ones left as James watched the last of the flames flicker out were his parents and Rhiannon, and to James's surprise, Viktor. The gargoyle had remained positioned a few yards behind his family, never taking his eyes off scanning the entire beach. Even the dragons stayed nearby, never leaving them despite the late hour.

It was not until the dragons landed and James and his family stood that Viktor strolled over.

James would never get over the massive size of this man, this creature. The fact that a walking, talking seven-foot-tall stone figure stood before him, not only real and alive, but a fully functioning being, who breathed, blinked, understood, listened, and was incredibly kind, docile, and wise. And scary, definitely scary. And intimidating.

Viktor's heavy stride moved closer, the power and grace of his advancement somehow comforting despite his hefty proportions and monstrous appearance.

"Hello, Viktor," Karramis said kindly. "It's good to see you."

"As you, my dear," the gargoyle offered in an accented, low and gruff tone, with a slight bow of his head. His solid black eyes narrowed, and his expression softened. "I wanted to offer my condolences about your father. Zarrius was a great man." When Karramis nodded in agreement, the sorrowful gaze never faltering from him, he continued, "But I also wanted to offer my deepest sympathies regarding the loss of your magic and the life you were robbed of." There was so much sincerity in his words, so much regret and remorse in his expression. "And I apologize for not only my part in your father's capture—I should have never left him unprotected—but also my inability to protect you from what transpired. I not only failed your father, I also failed you." There was something there behind those words, more than just regret. It was almost as if it pained him, that the mistakes he believed he made were breaking his heart. "I should have been aware. So, I am deeply sorry for the lack of knowledge regarding your own death. I promise I will do better to protect you and your family."

Karramis stepped away from Will's touch and placed her hand on Viktor's forearm, the coarse gray skin rough against hers. "Viktor, you have nothing to apologize for—"

"Please, do not downgrade my mistakes. As much as I appreciate the words you were about to speak, I do not feel they are that of truth. So please, my dear, just accept my apology."

Karramis nodded, conceding his plea. "Very well." A smile graced her lips. "Apology accepted."

"Thank you."

Karramis backed away, giving him a nod conveying a silent *you're welcome.*

"Now then," Viktor said, his dark gaze shifting over between the twins. "Which one of you believes yourself to be the weaker of the two?"

Rhiannon's brows shot up. "Uhm . . ." She cleared her throat and awkwardly raised her hand. "Me." Her hand dropped. "How—why . . . How'd you know about that?"

"Zarrius," he answered somberly. "Your grandfather had informed me one of his grandchildren believed magic was wrong in choosing them. Do you truly believe that?"

Rhiannon hesitated a moment. "Sometimes. Yes."

"Because you believe your magic to be weaker or that you are the weak one?"

"Both?" she drawled, conveying both truth and uncertainty in her answer.

"First of all, magic is never wrong. Magic can be used incorrectly, but it, itself, is never wrong. I beg you to remember that in the future. And second, everyone has a weakness. Everyone. And it is far better for your weaknesses to surface now rather than later."

"How come?"

Viktor glanced over at Karramis before he spoke. "Because every failure, every mistake only makes you stronger. For all weaknesses can be strengthened. You, my child, are the sword, and life is the forge. If you want to be stronger, you must endure the pain of living. But remember this, even the weakest blade can land a killing blow if given the right opportunity." His large muscular wings extended outward. "You will never know if you can truly fly if you are not willing to, at first, jump." He bowed, giving all four of them one final nod before flapping his wings and flying away.

And it was with those final words James decided what he needed to do next. It was no longer an idea but rather a solid plan. And it was not about hope anymore, it was about faith.

And certainty.

James was going to help Rhiannon learn how to fly. Metaphorically speaking, of course.

Chapter 27

Wave of Power

"Have you not realized yet?" Ryan teased as he reached out a hand, the urge to smirk threatening to break through. "Never turn your back on your opponent."

Rhiannon glared up at him, her eyes like daggers slicing into him. Almost like the dagger now lying a few feet away from her.

Ryan had been training her since a week after everything happened at the cabin. Like James, he had been insistent Rhiannon learn how to protect herself. But unlike James, Ryan wanted her to train in self-defense, taking her mental sharpness and combining it with some knowledge of the dagger she now carried—a gift he had given her. After Ryan had seen the state of Kavana while visiting them in the infirmary, he could not allow Rhiannon to go any longer without some defensive and even offensive tactics. Magic was great, it was resourceful and powerful, but it was not always reliable, especially when in dire situations. And with Rhiannon still trying to combat the ability to turn her emotions into something she could control and manipulate, hand-to-hand fighting and weapon maneuvers were the next best thing to keep her safe and alive.

Rhiannon huffed, her scowl never wavering as she reached up and slid her palm into his offered hand. "But I didn't turn my back."

They had been practicing for a little over an hour inside the grotto under Ember Cliffs. This place had been one of Rhiannon's favorite locations to train, the seclusion providing cover from curious eyes, but even more so, it offered security. There was only one way in and out of the cavern. Well, the only one above ground, that is.

The twins had learned the caves under Kiluemar were connected, but very few knew how to access the passages attaching the forbidden side with the rest of the island. That news was something James and Rhiannon both felt relieved about considering it was rumored there were still many unknown creatures living deep under Maevis Mountains. But the truth of those rumors had not been proven in recent years. So, Rhiannon always picked the grotto for any training. And since her mother had made her resurrection known to all those outside the protective wards, and things having settled down in the last few weeks following her grandfather's memorial—even the slaying of the animals that had been left to rot outside the village and Stoweward had stopped—and no signs of any activity on this side of the island, things went back to normal. Or as normal as they could be considering the countdown to the twins' next birthday literally ticked by closer and closer every single day.

Aside from researching, trying to figure out how to stop Merrick, Rhiannon had been training. Lately it had been with self-defense, but she still practiced her magic. James had been hounding her to train, train, train, and when she was done, train some more. And, in all honesty, she was getting much better with all her magic. Still not perfect but better. Her fire magic was getting easier to control and manipulate. She had even been able to create fire from her hands a few times. But it was extremely difficult to do so. It was far easier to summon it to the wick of a candle or call it forth to a fireplace filled with logs. She could even pull it from the earth, like she had when her mother died. Sometimes. But creating it within herself was much harder. Something her mother told her was the most difficult thing to master, if given the ability to do it.

Her water magic was the easiest to control now, even creating it. But unlike her fire magic, she had never been able to pull it from her own body but rather her surroundings—the ground, the sky. Water was everywhere, in everything. But it was also what most of the body was made of, so she knew it was possible. But fire, fire was not part of a person's genetic makeup or even a normal component of the human body, so pulling fire from herself was seemingly impossible, and yet she had done it before.

But her defensive training? Well, it had definitely gotten better, and her evasive techniques, quick reflexes, agile movements, and even her physical strength had greatly improved. However, her ability to stay on her feet seemed to be her biggest issue.

"All right, then," Ryan offered with a low chuckle as he pulled her to her feet. "Correction. Never *look away* from your opponent."

Rhiannon gave him a snarky grimace as she rolled her eyes and dusted her skirt. "Oh, shut up."

Ryan gave his head a humorous shake as the corner of his mouth ticked up. In addition to her smartass personality and snarky teasing, he still found it amusing how she wore dresses and skirts, even when training. But as he took in the knee-length black dress, the black embroidered swirling designs on the bodice with its higher neckline, the quarter sleeves, and the intricate etching of silver-threaded designs along her waist, giving the dress the appearance of it being two separate pieces, he had to respect the idea that she refused to allow anything to take away from her feminine side. Even fighting.

Although, he did appreciate how she always wore leggings or tights under her skirt, making all floor training a lot less awkward. Yet she still argued about wearing proper footwear, stating if she ever needed to fight in a real-life situation, she would be stuck wearing whatever shoes she had on, which were usually boots or sandals. Or barefoot. But Rhiannon hated sneakers and despised anything between her toes, so she was going to wear what was realistic, not practical.

Rhiannon pulled the tie from her hair, releasing her long caramel tresses from the high ponytail and ran her fingers through the sweaty strands, giving them a gentle fluffing. "It's getting late. We should probably start heading back."

"Right," Ryan said. "Of course." Strolling over toward a pile of dark gray material on the area where the sand and stone met, he picked up his hoodie and headed back over to her, gesturing for her to go first. "After you."

"Such a gentleman," she teased with a mocking curtsy before making her way in the direction of the large fissure in the cavern wall.

"Nah, it's just if something is out there, it will get you first."

Rhiannon halted and turned, her boots digging into the sand. She stood there, silent, her mouth agape with playful surprise.

Ryan laughed. "I'm joking." He placed his hoodie over his head and pulled it down, tugging on the hem and adjusting the collar. "But let's be honest here, you are the more powerful one out of the two of us. I'm not ashamed to say this, but if it came down to it, I might just have to be the one saved by you rather than the other way around."

"Who says I'd save you, huh? I might just decide to run away and let you fend for yourself."

Ryan narrowed his eyes, considering with a roguish gleam in his brown eyes. "Nah," he concluded as he placed an arm around her shoulders and escorted her toward the opening, "you'd totally save me."

"You're sure?"

"I'd bet my life on it, Blaze."

Rhiannon eyed him and grinned at his ironic choice of words as they exited the grotto.

Ryan's lips curved upward, his gaze locked on hers, the blue of her eyes bright against the late afternoon sun along the horizon beyond the harbor. "Don't even say anything, smartass."

Rhiannon grinned and dropped her gaze, watching her feet move through the sand, biting back the facetious retort she was about to say as they continued forward in silence.

Her stride slowed as they neared the portal. Trepidation coiled in her stomach, the sensation instantaneous but somehow distant. Concentrating, she attempted to pinpoint the cause of it, the origin of this sudden onset of something not quite right.

"Rhiannon? Are you all right?" Ryan asked as he matched her steps and lowered his arm, trying to get a better angle of her face.

Rhiannon could not place what was happening. She scanned the area, taking in the cliffs, the shores, the entire bay, even the opening of the caverns across the way. Nothing. She even listened internally. Maybe one of the dragons was reaching out to her. Still nothing. And James, he had been known to block her from their connection recently. Not out of anything malicious but rather to protect her from his own thoughts. His constant need to berate himself for the things that had happened. But as she reached out to him, searching for that link, that bond, there was a distorted disconnect. A veil of some kind. Yet she could feel it in her gut—something was going on with her brother.

But as soon as it appeared, it faded, leaving her feeling as though she had imagined it. However, there was something else now causing her to worry. Something pulling her attention toward the water.

A distant energy called to her, singing a lullaby, soothing her deep inside her soul. It was a gentle caress. A warm hug wrapping around her. It was the sound of the waves, the feel of the rain, the taste of the most succulent fruit—sweet and tempting and forbidden. Everything inside her relaxed, a lulling whisper like a tonic flowing through her bloodstream and washing away all her inhibitions.

"Rhiannon?"

She could hear Ryan's voice, the concern and persistence in his tone, but she could not pull herself away from the ballad of sin and danger humming all around her. It called to her, beckoning her to go to it. To dance among the waters. To kiss the salty air. To wash away all her fears. To trust the depths of darkness, to give in to it and just take the plunge.

And so, she did.

Rhiannon drifted . . .

Deeper and deeper.

Just a bit farther.

Closer and closer.

Almost there.

Lower and lower.

I'm coming.

Down, down, down—

"Rhiannon!"

Fingers dug into her shoulders as hands shook her, the force behind it pulling her back from whatever trance she had fallen into.

Blinking up at Ryan, Rhiannon squeezed her eyes tight to erase the rest of the haze. "I'm okay."

"What the bloody hell just happened?" An equal mix of unease and interest was in his question.

She opened her eyes, the salty air burning them as they went wide, and she peered down.

Water sloshed under her feet, her boots sinking deeper into the sand as the waves pulled away.

She was standing in the harbor.

Why was she standing in the harbor?

"What happened?" she asked, moving away from the shoreline and trying to ease the panic pounding in her chest.

"That's what I want to know."

"I . . . I'm not sure. Maybe—maybe I'm just tired. I think I just need to get home and get some sleep."

Ryan was not convinced. "Are you sure?"

"Yeah," she lied. The truth was, she had no clue what had just happened. And lack of sleep was not the cause of whatever that was.

"All right." He returned his arm around her shoulders, this time to make sure she did not head back toward the water and steered her toward the portal. "Let's get you home."

Ryan regretted not flying in on one of the dragons this time, but Rhiannon had figured they had been doing so much lately to keep everyone safe, the last thing she wanted to do was have to make them do more. So, they had been coming here to train lately through the portals. The doorways closest to the village and Full Moon Harbor were still in place, so traveling down here was fast and easy.

Stepping out of the portal, they strode a few feet and made their way under the wards and continued under the archway of the north side of the village.

Rhiannon halted.

Ryan stumbled slightly as he kept moving despite her sudden stop. He noticed her thoughts going inward, instantly recognizing the signs of her talking telepathically. Her eyes went distant as her head tilted a little to the left, lifting her right ear ever so slightly upward as she slid her hair out of the way. Even though all the voices were in her mind, Rhiannon always angled her head and tucked her hair behind her ear as if giving her better access to her telepathic hearing. Her lips parted faintly, and her breathing slowed, her chest rising and falling with a steady pace.

But as soon as her eyes widened and her breathing picked up, Ryan knew something had happened. "What's wrong?"

A squawk sounded overhead, and Ryan's gaze shot upward. An owl soared high above the village. Athena—Rhiannon's Messenger.

"Who?" Ryan asked, the panic he was feeling filtering into his tone. Someone was in danger.

Confusion gleamed in her blue gaze, but it was her entire demeanor which made Ryan on edge—she was afraid. "James."

~

Thick, gray mist rose up from the surface and coasted across the deep blue waters, inching closer and closer. Waves ebbed and flowed, the gentle lapping harmonizing with the rhythmic melody of the sea. They were out there, calling him. The song was hypnotic and angelic, the beauty of the smooth humming seeping deeper and deeper, soothing the fear and hushing the hesitation creeping into his mind.

Come, the water seemed to sing.

His bare feet sank into the dark, pebbled sand along Dead Man's Bay as the sun made its way closer to the peak over Maevis Mountains. Everything around was calm, serene. Only the sound of the waves filled his ears.

But his mind . . . His mind was filled with the most beautiful, enchanting tune.

Come to us.

Waves crashed into him, the water soaking into his jeans.

Cold. It was so cold, the iciness of the sea slicing into him.

But he still did not stop.

More and more of his body dipped beneath the waves.

Come.

Treading water, he dove, the chill washing over him completely. His eyes opened. The salt burned, but he did not care. He just wanted to swim.

Deeper and deeper.

"James?" Rhiannon's voice shouted behind the beatific melody in his mind. *"James!"*

He could not stop. He was almost there. Almost to the paradise awaiting him.

Down and down.

"James!"

The voice was louder in his mind, more insistent as her presence grew closer.

She was coming. His sister was almost here.

Rhiannon had gotten his message.

Perfect.

James pulled himself back inward, and his astral body disappeared from the ocean below.

Standing up, he wrung out the water in his shirt as he took in the mist still crawling closer from Siren Sea out toward the peninsula where he waited between the Forbidden Bluffs and Mystic Woods.

Below had been where he had appeared in his astral projection the first time he traveled magically to Kiluemar. This being where he had felt the most fear, apart from seeing Phosmeratae—but the Air Dragon had no longer scared him. So, this was where he had to do it. He knew the real fear he had for the sirens, even now, was going to be the breaking point for Rhiannon. She would sense everything he was feeling and come.

And she did.

Now, it was time for his sister to see just how powerful she was.

Thanks to Raina's continued help, James had created an alternate version of himself, an astral image, and projected himself where he knew the sirens would likely sense him and call him to them. And he was correct.

Once the sirens began to enchant him, or rather his astral body, he allowed his astral mind to believe the hypnotic summons of the sirens. He then magnified it and sent it down the mental bond and straight into Rhiannon's mind. She needed to believe he was truly in danger. Granted, it was not entirely false, considering the rest of his plan would definitely put him, and her, in a seriously foolish and downright risky situation. But James had all the faith in the world it would be worth it.

He had spent hours researching the sirens, something that was particularly hard to do when Rhiannon was always at the library. But after some help from his Yaya, he learned a few things about the sea creatures.

Aside from once being Water Witches, the sisters could only use their song on the opposite sex. Females were completely immune to their call, something James could only assume had to do with them having killed their husbands, but that was only a guess. He also learned how the sirens could only use their magic to lull men into the water when the man—or multiple men even—was within feet of the ocean. Now, the sisters could sense their prey from about a mile away, but their song could only be heard from the shores. However, if a man was *in* the water, the song was much stronger and could potentially travel even farther. But the sirens' call had a glitch, or rather a protective loophole for any man who heard it. Once they entered the water and became fully submersed, the trance would fade deeper they got, allowing any man to be fully aware of their surroundings again. But by then, it would usually be too late.

And to test some of those facts, James had wanted to create an astral version of himself when sending the warning to Rhiannon. James needed to be completely coherent to control everything he wanted his sister to feel. And he also believed the mental power he needed to create his astral body, maintain it, and send everything to Rhiannon would interfere with the magic of the sirens. He also needed to make sure the sirens did not get to him before Rhiannon had arrived, so he could not physically be near the shore. Thus, creating an astral body was the safest way of doing all of that. He truly did fear the sirens, the creatures still plaguing his dreams sometimes, but he also understood their magic was all mental. So, all he had to do was maintain a stronger mindset to counter their abilities. And with astral projecting, he was able to sever the full connectedness of his alternate self and actual mind. Two bodies, two separate minds.

And now, the real magic was about to start.

James had timed it all perfectly because just as the mist filled the entire bay, Raeth came into view, coasting down from the southeastern side of Maevis Mountains.

This was it—it was time to test his theory.

Rhiannon needed to call forth the entirety of her magic again, she needed to be able to access every part of her powers—the control, the manipulation, the creation. And this was going to do it, this was going to show her she was not the weakest link. No one else was going to die because of them, and James was going to make sure of it. Even if it meant nearly getting them killed to prove it.

Rhiannon swung her leg over Raeth's back and jumped from the dragon, the smoothness of her landing worth admiring. Taking in the smug look on her brother's face and how he was not actually in danger, she glared at him, the rage in her expression littered with confusion.

"James, what the hell are you doing?" she demanded, her eyes snagging on his boots and socks piled at his feet before focusing on him.

James gave her a dismissive shrug. "Oh, nothing, just proving a point."

"By getting yourself killed?"

He grinned before taking a few steps closer to the edge of the cliff. "Maybe."

Rhiannon's back straightened. "What're you doing?" When James did not answer, his grin getting wider, she asked again, her tone both pleading and persistent. "James? What are you—"

James twisted and jumped.

"No!" Rhiannon bolted for the edge and peered down, just as her brother crashed into the water below, his entire body disappearing under the undulating waves. "James!"

He did not surface.

Fear curled in her gut. Not just because her brother could possibly be hurt, but the plunge was a few hundred feet. She had to go in after him. But it was too high, she could not do it, her fear of heights having never completely diminished despite being a skilled rider now. The dragons had always protected her, communicated with her, providing her with every upward motion, every descent, every twist and turn, reminding her they would never allow her to fall. But now, she had to, she had to purposely jump off the cliff and fall.

But without giving another thought to the fear wanting to take over, she jumped.

Adrenaline surged as the air whipped around her. For a moment, exhilaration took over, wiping away all her fear, all her apprehension.

She was flying.

Nope! Not flying—falling. Definitely falling.

The reminder hit her seconds before her body smacked into the waves, the collision with the water sending pain shooting through her.

Cold wrapped around her, masking the ache as her skin soaked up the freezing temperatures of the water, the chill leaking into her muscles.

Eyes opening, Rhiannon kicked and reached upward, desperate for air as a figure moved beneath the water. A rush of fear shot through her, the possibility of what was nearby making her kick harder. Her head broke through the surface, and she pulled in a deep breath. Salt water dripped into her eyes, everything around her blurry, the blending of the clear blue water and gray mist seeming to distort behind her gaze. She blinked and rubbed at her eyes, opening just as another figure broke through the water in front of her.

It was James.

And he was smiling as he treaded water.

"Seriously!" Rhiannon barked, her annoyance and rage burning in her gaze as she ignored the thick gray fog moving in around them. "What the hell, James? What are you think—"

A fin broke through the surface behind her brother, the sight of it making her eyes go wide and her mouth snap shut. It was a few yards away, but the pointed, dark gray fin grew larger as it trailed through the water, slicing the surface like a hot knife through butter as it banked to the right. Another fin appeared through the mist hovering over the water. Then another.

Rhiannon slowed her movements, her feet barely kicking as her arms swirled in larger, gentle arcs. "James . . ." she said with a soft warning as her heart pounded in her chest. "What's going on?"

The fins spread out and began circling them.

"You're going to save us," James announced with absolute certainty.

"What?" she snapped, a little louder than she meant as her brows knitted, the bewilderment spiking to the same level as the fear coursing through her. Lowering her voice, she added sharply, "And how exactly am I supposed to do that?"

"By controlling—"

A fin sliced through the water between them, the twins jerking back as the body of the animal glided under the waves.

Rhiannon's hand brushed along it, the contact causing her to push herself back through the water. A section of the skin was rough, yet part of it was smooth, almost slimy.

"By controlling the water and pushing it away from us."

James's words took a moment to register.

"What?" she screeched, the question again coming out much louder than she anticipated. He could not be serious.

The water moved behind her, the animal swimming a little too close to her just as its fin came into view to her right before dipping under the water. Movement swept beneath her feet, and Rhiannon fought every urge to look down.

"Push the water away from us," James went on, the confidence in his tone faltering.

Rhiannon took him in—his wide eyes frantically scanning the surface of the water and the circle of fog around them, the heaving of his chest, and the panic in his pinched expression. She did not need a connection with her brother to know exactly what he was feeling. He was scared. Genuinely scared. And nervous. She could feel it. It was manifesting and growing.

Through clenched teeth—from fighting the clattering due to the cold water, as well as from the irritation at his lunacy—she demanded, "You want me to move the whole damn ocean?"

James hissed in pain as he lifted his arm from the water.

He was bleeding.

Bright red rivulets trailed down his skin from four deep gashes on his forearm, these joining the long-since-healed scars given to him by the very creatures circling them like prey.

A slight flicker of hope sparked in his eyes, the confidence and conviction returning. And something like humor joined the mix. Nothing like laughing in the face of danger. "No, I want you to split it."

Rhiannon watched as he lowered his hand and red tainted the water. "Seriously, James?" she snapped in protest. "I'm not a damn prophet!"

Another sharp inhale came from James from his clenched teeth just as more blood flowed to the surface. Pain lanced through his leg as the burn of the salt water added to the agony of torn-open skin.

James fought through the pain. "No, but you're stronger than you think." He knew she could do this. "You just have to believe it." A smile appeared on his lips, the appearance of it genuine despite their current situation and the pain he was in. "Like I do."

Rhiannon shook her head at the insanity of her brother. This was crazy. She could not possibly part the entire ocean.

"You might want to hurry before—"

"James!" Rhiannon yelled as her brother was yanked down, all of him being swallowed by the waves.

Something wrapped around her ankle and yanked, her entire body plunging under the surface. Her throat burned as her gasp was silenced by a large gulp of water. Down, down her body was pulled. Opening her eyes, she glanced up and watched as the surface got farther and farther away, the last of the sunlight breaching the thick fog lighting up the sight above her. A figure zoomed across where she was glancing, the long, dark silhouette swaying its tail side to side as it swam overhead.

She glanced down as whatever was holding her squeezed hard, tugging her deeper and deeper. Through the burn of salt water, she saw it through the clear water.

A siren.

Rhiannon had to fight the urge to gasp again, or maybe it was a scream. Either way, she needed to suppress it, knowing only more water would enter her mouth.

This creature was terrifying.

The siren, with its long, spindly, clawed fingers and webbing between the five digits, was ghastly even through the murky haze of the deepening water. Scales covered the upper half of the body, the color of the fishlike skin pale gray and mottled with a greenish-brown hue. It had the appearance of a woman with long black hair flowing behind it as it swam, the strands moving in a wavelike motion as it ended just before the fin located at the base of the creature's back. However, it was anything but human. Rhiannon could see the scales trailing up the neck and stretching along the shoulders and arms and continuing upward across the creature's face.

Rhiannon needed to breathe, the ache in her lungs starting to burn. Urging the water down with a powerful thrust of her arms, she kicked hard, the action meaning to fight against the tight grip pulling her deeper, but one of her booted feet made contact with the arm of the creature.

Both Rhiannon and the siren halted, floating almost motionless in the water.

Two monstrous eyes turned toward her as the siren held them both in place. Rhiannon's eyes went wide at the even scarier features gazing upward. Solid, lizard-like eyes focused on her, the blood-red surrounding a slitted, white pupil, a contrast to the grayish film blinking over it, the strange eyelid translucent.

Rhiannon gaped at the creature, terrified to even move. Jagged, sharp teeth protruded from the uneven maw of the lipless siren as the mouth slowly opened, the jaw unhinging. Rows of teeth filled the oversized jaw as the mouth widened, the skin along the corners of the nonexistent lips webbing as it stretched. There was no nose on the creature's scaly face, just two long and narrow slits slicing vertically in the center. A pointed tail moved behind it, the side-to-side motion and shape of the fin confirming the stories she read about and the memories her brother recalled from his astral projection—the bottom half of a siren was similar to a shark. A very large shark.

And like a shark, with its mouth gaping and ready to snap shut, it was, without a doubt, a true predator. And this thing was about to take a huge bite out of her.

A pulse erupted from Rhiannon's hand, the shock wave reminding her she was running out of oxygen. The tremor through the water flowed outward, and the rippling motion flowed into the siren.

Her magic wanted her to fight. To survive.

The creature canted its head, its open mouth going slack.

Rhiannon shoved out her magic again, this time with control and precision. The water pulsed around her. Energy swirled in her core, the magic in the water combining with her own.

The siren's eyes narrowed, making the creature appear even more ominous, and she quickly released Rhiannon just before it dove deeper into the water.

Rhiannon kicked and moved her arms through the water like her life depended on it—which it did. Head breaking through the surface, she gasped and instantly started searching the area, no longer caring about the threats as desperation and helplessness flooded her.

"James?" she called frantically. He had to be okay. She had only been down a few seconds less than he had. "James!"

A gasp exploded behind her, and she turned, spotting James a few yards away. A thankful exhale burst from her. They had let him go. The siren that had pulled him down had released him too.

She swam toward him but pulled back just as a shark fin cut through her path to him. Another fin appeared, the two of them now circling her. Something bumped against her feet right before the third siren emerged and joined the other two.

Around and around, they encircled her. Closer and closer.

"Any time now!" James yelled, swimming over to her, not caring what the sirens would do to him or even slightly fazed by having nearly been drowned.

"You know," Rhiannon shouted back with a teasing yet serious tone, the ridiculousness of their situation almost unbelievable as her head flipped around, trying to keep her sights on all three of the sirens, "you're the idiot who got us into this mess." She flinched as one of the sirens got too close. "And now you want me to fix it?"

"Yes!" James sent back, matching her mocking attitude. "Now, hurry the hell up."

"Don't rush me!"

"Rhiannon, if you don't do something, they are going to kill us."

"You don't think I know that!"

The fins disappeared, all three of the sirens diving deeper.

Rhiannon did not like this. "Where'd they go?" Her eyes scanned the area, the gray mist still hovering around them, leaving them all in the center of a foggy dome. "James, do you see them?" No answer. "James?" She faced where he had been.

The water was painted red.

And James was gone.

"James!"

Without thinking, Rhiannon took a deep breath and dove, swimming down toward the trail of blood swirling up from the depths. The water around her somehow grew lighter, less dense and almost airy, as she pushed through it with ease. Down and down she went until her brother came into view, his lifeless body being pulled deeper by two of the sirens. Her body thrummed as she called her magic forward.

She needed oxygen, she needed to breathe, but she continued to kick, driving herself closer to James.

What she really needed was to save her brother.

And she was going to.

Something shifted inside her. No, it was something more, something deeper. It was a full transformation. A change. The fear she had soaked into her—her bones, her blood, her entire body, switching to an unwavering courage she had never experienced or felt before. Helplessness turned to hope, defeat morphed into determination, every weakness became a strength. And all of it, every emotion, became one thing. Anger. It flowed wildly and without reservation through her veins. Anger for always being afraid, for always allowing the world around her to make her cower. For always wanting to run and hide. But not anymore. She would not yield. She would not surrender again. She would finally fight back. Fight for herself, for her brother. For once, she would be brave.

A figure appeared in her peripheral, and she gazed sideways, just as a large, gaping mouth rushed toward her. She pulled back, narrowly missing the sharp teeth snapping shut. The siren spun around and dashed toward her once more as it again unhinged its jaw.

Fury and unfettered resolve exploded in Rhiannon's chest, sending a wave of molten-hot adrenaline through every nerve, releasing an undeniable fearlessness and fortitude from her core as waves of power washed over her.

Rhiannon lifted her hands and opened her palms to the creature, drawing back her arms. She could feel it, the magic—both hers and the natural energy inside the water—it was not only real and pure, it was visceral. It was ancient but new. The giver of life, yet the bringer of death. It was nurturing yet destructive. It was powerful.

Remembering the way she blocked the tidal wave the night of the attack at the beach, Rhiannon offset that ability. Instead of shielding herself from the water, she called to it, allowing it to forge as one with her and giving it permission to rise to the surface.

A rippling wave shot out of her palms and crashed into the siren, sending the creature rocketing backward through the water. As the siren circled around, Rhiannon did it again. This time, the water pulled away from her, dipping her closer to the seafloor. Her eyes darted to the other two sirens, who had halted their descent but still held tight to her brother.

James was not moving, and blood continued to seep from the various open wounds on his body. Fear and anger and panic raced through her nerves, the emotions again mixing together.

Her breath caught as she fought the urge to breathe, making her throat ache and chest burn. A scream built, the muscles constricting her airflow, the pressure tightening and expanding. The pain grew, hotter and hotter, scorching as the force inside her intensified, desperate to release.

And then, she unleashed it.

Rhiannon screamed, the sound muffled beneath the water. But it grew clearer. And louder. Louder and louder as an explosive force discharged from her entire body, the shock wave traveling outward through the water. Rhiannon started to sink—no, not sink, but drift. Down and down. She was drifting farther as her screaming suddenly halted and she pushed out her arms, the magic from her body now coming from her hands.

Her feet touched down against silty sand as she shoved the water away from her, splitting the ocean in two. She pushed and pushed, her attention on her brother just beyond the wall of water roaring in front of her. She could see them, the sirens and James on the other side. Focusing on the only siren still holding on to her brother, Rhiannon summoned even more of her water magic and shoved harder, creating another break along the ocean floor.

James and the siren flopped against the bottom of the ocean, blood coating the sand next to her brother and . . .

A woman.

Long, silky black hair partially covered a nude woman with smooth, golden skin moving next to James, who had rolled from his side to his back, sputtering and spitting. The woman hurried to her feet, and Rhiannon raced over to her brother and dropped to her knees, her mind still on the water she was holding in place.

"James, get up."

She pulled him to his feet and urged him away from the woman just as two darkened figures moved through the water not far from where they all stood.

The sirens stopped at the wall of water that was shooting up into the mist-covered, dusky sky. They both dipped lower toward the sandy ground, their bodies mere inches from the bottom of the ocean floor. Four sets of webbed, clawed hands burst through the water, the creepy and monstrous appearance instantly disappearing and morphing into human limbs. Like the black-haired woman, their skin was beautifully tanned, the golden hue smooth and flawless. More and more of their bodies came into view as their human feet stepped into the sand. The three women looked very much alike, except for one thing. Unlike the first woman, these other two had different colored hair, something Rhiannon had not noticed before. The one on the right of the black-haired woman had strands the color of the richest caramel, while the other had platinum-blonde tresses. All three had perfectly straight hair reaching down to their lower backs. And they were absolutely gorgeous, a major difference to their cursed counterparts.

Taking in deep breaths as he leaned against his upper legs, James started to come around, taking in his surroundings. Eyes down, he opened them, staring at his bare feet and . . . sand.

Why was he standing in sand? Dead Man's Bay was a mix of light gray sand and dark pebbled stones. This—this sand was ivory and seemed untouched, the wavelike formations along its surface littered with various rocks and seashells.

His eyes lifted as he rose to his full height, his gaze snapping and trailing up, up, up along the wall of water in front of him. A thrilling awe filled his chest, along with admiration, pure satisfaction, and even a slight twinge of jealousy.

He was standing at the bottom of the ocean.

She had done it.

And he had been right. His sister was extremely powerful.

Brown eyes drifting downward, he took in the three women standing before him. The three very beautiful, *very* naked women.

James averted his gaze, his head jerking toward his sister. "Nice job on the parting of the sea, Sis," he stated with a teasing tone but with nothing short of amazement in his expression. "But uhm . . ." He placed his hand on the side of his face, shielding his next words from the women, and the fact that he wanted to look over at them again. "Why are they naked?"

Chapter 28

A Threat Removed

The three sirens stared at the twins, their deep red irises analyzing them as if James and Rhiannon were a puzzle they were trying to solve.

"And who might you be?" the black-haired woman intoned, her melodious voice silky and pleasant.

"You first," James countered smoothly, keeping his eyes directed upward.

"My name is Marryn," the black-haired siren said. "And these are my sisters." She presented a hand toward the woman with rich, caramel hair, her movements so graceful. "Mariska." Her body twisted toward the other woman, the brilliant blonde of her hair making her red eyes seem even brighter. "And this is Malena."

"James," Rhiannon whispered, even though the sirens could not hear her inside her brother's mind, *"I don't know how much longer I can hold this."*

"What do we do?" James asked. "If the water comes back in, they'll come after us again."

"You didn't bother to think about that before devising this ridiculous plan?"

"Well—no. I only got as far as this point."

Rhiannon went to deliver a wry comment, but her mind was pulled back into her body, the full extent of her surroundings coming back wholly as the three women stood in front of her and her brother.

"Shit!" James breathed as he jerked his head back, registering their presence too.

Neither one of them had even noticed the women moving, the ethereal way they moved seeming to flow like a delicate breeze.

James's eyes dipped, his gaze trailing down Malena's lean, toned figure, the sight of her entire body sending a wave of heat through him.

This woman was absolutely gorgeous. The most stunning woman he had ever seen. Her lips were so plump and luscious, the idea of feeling them, tasting them, made his mouth water. He wanted to caress the high arches of her cheekbones, touch the smoothness of her beautiful, perfect skin. And her hair, the long, silky blonde hair, wet and draped over her shoulders—he wanted to run his hands through it, feel it slide through his fingers. He wanted to be the beads of water trailing along her collarbone, down and down, sliding over the curve of her perky breasts, the size of them perfect for his hands. Down and down the water glided, against the smooth skin of her stomach, past her belly button . . .

Down and down—

"Stop!" Rhiannon demanded, pulling her brother back to the present.

James shook the soothing echoes of the siren's call from his lust-addled mind. Well, it would seem he did not think a few things through all the way.

"Apologies," Malena said, not sounding at all sorry for her actions.

"Listen," Rhiannon started as she grabbed her brother's wrist and began moving backward, still keeping a watchful eye on the sirens as they backed away, "I think it's time for us to go."

"Go," Marryn crooned, her and her sister's eyes becoming hungry. "But we have yet to learn who you are." The three of them advanced closer, one single step. "And we would very much like to do so."

"No, that's okay," Rhiannon objected plainly, her head moving insistently side to side with the statement. "Our parents told us to never talk to strangers."

James snickered at his sister, the seriousness of her demeanor not at all matching the humorous retort.

"Shut up," she snarked, now trying to mask her own amusement. "This isn't the time."

The wall around them shuddered, causing the water to slosh, sending some of the element to rain down in large droplets.

"Let's go," James said, all the humor gone as he snatched Rhiannon's wrist and twisted them both around.

But they stopped, the sudden arrival of the sirens on the other side of them forcing their feet to burrow into the sand at the abrupt halt.

The three women advanced, their movements again smooth and ethereal. Even with their feet pressing into the sand, they almost appeared wraithlike.

Pain started to burn into Rhiannon as her head throbbed and her muscles began to ache. She could not hold on to the magic for much longer. She was not even sure how she had held on to it for so long. In fact, when it shuddered before, she was certain it was about to come down.

But James was right, if she let go and the wall came down, they would be, again, at the mercy of these women—these very hungry-looking, evil women.

Rhiannon called to Raeth, praying he had remained close. And when he had, she blew out a breath. Hopefully, he could come down and get them. The part along the ocean floor was large enough for the dragon, in fact, to Rhiannon's surprise, she had made the opening a lot larger than she had originally thought.

But as her plea to rescue them reached the dragon, she had learned her plan would not work. Raeth could not see beyond the mist. It was too thick and dense. And as Rhiannon glanced up, she could tell, even through the concealing fog, the shadows of night were closing in on them.

And they were still on the forbidden side of the island.

"We have to get out of here." Rhiannon eyed her brother as another silent plea reached out, praying it would hit its mark. "Now."

"What do we do?" James asked with a slight panic in his tone as he side-eyed her, too nervous to look away from the sirens. He could feel them pulling against him again, their call attempting to send him into another trance.

Rhiannon crouched down for a second, the action going unnoticed by her brother as she took his hand. "Swim."

The soothing melody instantly faded and was replaced by Rhiannon's powers surging deep inside him. The strange sensation similar to when they had touched before when one of them had summoned their magic. It was then he could feel it, another presence deep beneath the waves, a familiar yet unique energy. This, too, was calling him, but he welcomed this one.

"What?" James said with a derisive snort, mirroring his sister's retreat toward the wall behind them as he finally took in her comment. She did not seriously expect them to outswim the sirens. Did she?

"Swim," she said again, their eyes locked. "Fast."

"Rhiannon."

Her name came out in a drawn-out protested warning, but she ignored it. The magic inside her vibrated, the pain and power merging into one. The control was there, the magnitude of her strength still thrumming, but it was faltering. And as another pulse of the magic holding the water shuddered against the wall, she knew, in that moment, the ones she called had been here all along—the presence of her and James in the water having already summoned them to the twins.

And with that, she said to her brother, absolutely certain of what was about to transpire, "And hold your breath."

The wall began to surge downward, the sound of it roaring and splashing in a thunderous rumble.

Twisting, the twins dove through the water, swimming as fast as they could as all sides of the wall crashed down, creating an echoing boom and sending a rippling undercurrent surging outward in all directions. The underwater tidal wave slammed into them, and they allowed it to carry them. But their escape was futile, as all three of the sirens in their monstrous forms, swam up beside them.

Rhiannon threw up her palm and pushed against the water in front of her and James, the magic behind the force causing the twins to slow. With her other hand, Rhiannon shoved the magic downward and propelled her and her brother upward.

Breaking through the surface, the twins gasped and pulled in deep, hurried breaths just as a fin sliced through the water not far from them. Then the other two.

Movement surged beneath them, the powerful shifting of the water below causing the twins to bounce along the waves, their frames buoyant and seemingly weightless.

They were here—the Water Dragons.

Both the twins had felt them.

Rhiannon had known all the dragons could sense them, but as her power erupted when she unleashed it, she had unknowingly called to them. But it was not until she actually felt their presence and then reached out to them mind to mind that she had realized they had already arrived. But her and her brother's attention had been so focused on the sirens, neither one of them knew they were there at first.

The three fins continued toward them, the zigzagging movement through the water coming closer.

A massive, powder-blue head broke through the surface right in front of the twins, the neck attached to it trailing up and up. A large open mouth shot downward, the sirens banking and narrowly missing the powerful snap of the jaw filled with razor-sharp teeth.

James and Rhiannon watched in shocked astonishment as two other figures rose from the water, and the three fins dipped down and disappeared under the waves, the mist above them vanishing as well.

Treading water, Rhiannon spoke internally to the Water Dragon closest to them, her voice also filling James's mind. *"Thank you."*

The dragon turned its head back, eyeing the twins before swirling its whole body around to face them.

Its neck was so incredibly long, reaching feet in the air. The color of it was the softest shade of blue, almost the same color as the clear blue water it swam in. Its skin appeared sleek and smooth, similar to a dolphin. Not a single scale in sight. Possibly along its body, but not on its neck and face. The rounded snout of the creature protruded out slightly and housed two long slits on either side of the bridge of its nose. Black irises sat among white eyes and rested in narrowed, inset sockets. Frills the color of light gray and even lighter blue sat on either side of its head, along the entire length of its cheeks, and a pewter horn jutted out along the top of its slightly tapered head.

The creature appeared very familiar, like the various marine reptiles of the past. But as two large things rose from the water on either side of the dragon, it was clear this creature was definitely not like those other animals—this was, without a doubt, a dragon. A very unique dragon, but a dragon nonetheless. Because it had wings. Large, leathery wings the same color as its head and neck.

Rhiannon had learned the Water Dragons' wings were not used for flying but rather to help them with swimming.

Bowing its head as its wings moved, pushing the water around to keep itself afloat, the dragon said, *"You are welcome. It is a pleasure to finally meet you both."* The voice was gentle and dreamy, similar to Terramina with its motherly charm. *"My name is Thalayssa."*

The sky overhead grew darker as the rich colors of the sunset began to fade into darkness.

"It's nice to finally meet you as well. I'm Rhiannon, and this is James."

The two other dragons moved closer, the twins both unable to tell any of them apart.

One of them said, the one on the right of Thalayssa, *"My name is Nerissa."*

"And I am Aenoc," the other dragon stated.

The only difference between the other two was Nerissa had the voice of a female, while Aenoc appeared to sound more masculine.

"And those," Thalayssa went on, gesturing behind the twins, both James and Rhiannon following the dragon's line of sight and spotting three other figures not too far away, *"are Ellwyn, Neptune, and Delphina."*

Six, there were six of them.

Rhiannon had felt the Water Dragons a few times now, but she had not known there were so many. Taking them in again, specifically their color, she wondered something.

When Rhiannon astral projected, she had ended up on this side of the island, not far from where she was now floating. And as she jumped into the water, she had started to drown. She could never figure out why she had not been able to swim, something she always just assumed was due to her not being as powerful when it came to controlling her astral body. Or possibly it was some other reason. But something had saved her. It had pushed her to the surface, and when she broke through the water, it had forced her back into her regular body.

"Did you sense me a while back and save me?" she said to Thalayssa.

"No," the dragon answered.

"I did."

Rhiannon eyed the dragon to Thalayssa's left with gratitude, the dragon who had called himself Aenoc. *"Thank you."*

Another question popped into her head, the inquiry not aimed at any particular dragon. *"Were you the ones who kept the wall from crashing down on us?"*

"No," Thalayssa answered again. *"That power came solely from you. The only thing we aided in was making sure we removed the threat."*

Rhiannon could not believe it. She had done all of that on her own. Even with the pain and the small blip in the magic, she had still managed to control it, to maintain that wall. She had allowed herself to fully become one with the water, and it had actually worked. She guessed she needed to make sure she thanked her Aunt Meadow for that bit of magical advice.

"Rhiannon," James said, trying to get her attention, "I think we should go."

Attempting to gauge the emotion she heard in his tone, she studied him, noticing the trepidation immediately. The sirens were gone, so why was he so nervous? And she knew it was getting late, but she doubted anyone would mess with them with the dragons here. Maybe it was that they were still in the water?

"What's the matter?"

His hand lifted, the droplets dripping as his finger pointed up toward the Forsaken Bluffs.

She had not even realized they had made their way this far into Siren Sea.

Light brown brows shot upward as blue eyes zeroed in on the black wolflike creature with glowing red eyes staring down at them through the shadows along the cliff.

"Why is he here?" Rhiannon questioned, her voice slightly unsteady as she kept her gaze on Raamko, one of the creatures who still haunted her dreams.

"I don't know," James answered, "but I really don't want to stick around and find out."

Rhiannon nodded in agreement.

"We can take you some place safe," Nerissa offered.

"Really?" The excitement was clear in James's voice.

With a single confirming nod, James and Rhiannon climbed on the top of Nerissa's back, both situating themselves between the wings where the neck and body met. Water splashed around them as the dragon moved through the water, the up and down motion and lack of anything to grip onto making it difficult for the twins to hold on. But as Raeth came into view as Nerissa and the twins moved past the same peninsula they started this all on, the dragon slowed. The Water Dragon allowed the twins to step up on her back, so they could mount atop Raeth. But before flying away, the twins thanked all the dragons again and vowed to come visit them soon.

Raeth landed on the peninsula, allowing James to grab his socks and shoes before the three of them coasted upward over the peak of Maevis Mountains, the night almost completely taking over the sky.

Rhiannon pulled something from the pocket of her drenched skirt. *"Here,"* she said to her brother through their bond, pushing her voice into his mind, the wind whipping around them just too loud for her to talk over right now.

He reached out a hand. *"What is it?"*

"Something to add to your collection."

James could hear the smile on her face. Opening his hand, he peered down at a seashell, a small conch with various shades of brown and tan painted on it.

"I mean, I saved you again from drowning, so it only seemed fitting."

James grinned as his fingers closed around the shell and he held it firmly in his grip.

She was ready. They were both ready.

All they had to do now was figure out how to use their magic to stop him.

Chapter 29

Failed Plans and Dangerous Ideas

Rhiannon bolted upright, tossing the book sprawled open on her chest onto the floor as her bare feet slammed against the wooden boards, and she shoved up from the oversized chair nestled in the darkened alcove. Racing down the stairs, she paused abruptly before her swift movements hurried back up the few steps she had descended. She slid her feet across the cool boards near the makeshift bed she had just been sleeping in.

Back and forth.

Back and forth.

"Where are—" Her foot hit the sandals strewn about haphazardly on the floor. "Aha!"

Gliding them on, she continued her fast-paced descent down the stairs, the perfectly pleasant night washing over her as she raced out of the library and ran down the dirt path toward her aunt's house. Despite no longer living with her aunt and Aidan for nearly five months now—having decided to live with her parents and James after they all left the infirmary—she still considered their house one of her homes. It was her home away from home, other than the library, of course.

Allowing the moon and a few of the lampposts to light her way, she ran through the dirt-covered streets, the adrenaline and elation driving her feet to move.

She had figured it out. She knew how they were going to stop Merrick. The idea having come to her in a dream of all places. But hey, at least it had been a dream and not another nightmare that had pulled her in a rush from her sleep.

Her only complaint was this should have been something she had figured out on her own, the literal answer having lived with her for months before she moved back home with her family, and not in a dream about being chased by a cartoon version of Merrick, dressed as a pink dog wearing a purple, glittery tutu, through a forest made of gingerbread on a white tricycle only to have him shape-shift into a live version of Aidan, who was hovering over a field of dancing sunflowers while his little white fairy wings flapped behind him, releasing pixie dust as he moved. That would teach her to drink three cups of hot chocolate and eat almost a dozen homemade cookies before falling asleep.

But it had been one single thing from the dream which her subconscious had focused on and pulled her from her sleep— Aidan shifting into Merrick.

If Aidan could get close enough to Merrick, maybe he could use his shape-shifting abilities to take some of Merrick's essence *and* stolen magic, and use it against him, to subdue him. Then

Rhiannon and James could come in with all their powers to fully counter all his magic and kill him.

The prophecy foretold of the twins stopping him, but it never said they could not ask for help. Maybe the reason James and Rhiannon needed all their powers was because it was not necessarily to use against Merrick, but rather to protect them from all the others who might show up to defend him. Maybe the twins' magic was more for defensive tactics rather than offensive.

It would work!

She just knew it would work.

It had to work.

Right?

~

It would not work.

After Rhiannon had barged into Kavana and Aidan's home in the middle of the night, and nearly scaring her aunt half to death, she had delivered her idea to a very sleepy, albeit very alert and slightly annoyed Aidan, only to learn her plan was not only useless, but also impossible.

And now, she sat with Aidan, learning exactly why her idea would not work.

Rhiannon composed herself, taking a moment to not only register what Aidan had just said but also the fact that her plan had just been foiled with one simple fact. One she should have learned by now.

"So, wait," she said as she and Aidan discussed this on the couch in the living room. "Okay. So, shapeshifters won't take in the magic of the person when the essence is taken?"

"No," Aidan stated as he casually leaned back against the plush cushions.

After she had told Aidan and Kavana her plan, her aunt had immediately shot it down by telling Rhiannon the idea of the prophecy predicting her and her brother and magic creating them only for them to simply be the ones to kill Merrick while Aidan did most of the work seemed rather ridiculous. Not only that, but she had informed her niece shapeshifters could not use their magic that way, without giving her any clarification. But after Kavana had retreated back to bed within moments of bursting Rhiannon's bubble—her aunt stating that if anyone woke her again without a cup of coffee ready for her, she would suffocate them with her pillow—she had ruminated over her aunt's words.

And Kavana had been right. There was no way she and James had been given these extraordinary abilities simply to be the side characters of this prophecy.

"Shifters can't absorb magic—we don't have that kind of power," Aidan continued. "I believe it was another protective measure put into place by magic as a means of defense. Most shapeshifters refuse to do this anyway, especially to another human. Animals are different, in a way. But with humans, it's not only painful, from what the legends state, but it's also quite unethical."

Rhiannon could already comprehend why, but she still wanted to hear it from him. "How so?"

"Well, when a shifter steals the essence from a livin' bein'—yes, it allows them to shift into said bein', but it also leaves a permanent impression within the shifter's mind. A brand of sorts. It's almost as if they steal the very soul from the person. But the first time a shift takes place with the essence of said bein', it forges to them. It becomes a part of them forever. That other bein' takes up residence inside their mind. The shapeshifter retains every memory, every emotion. They can remember that bein's pain, sadness, anger, happiness, desires—everythin'. And when it's a human essence that has been stolen and imprinted into the shifter, it can drive that person who took it absolutely mad. However, when it's stolen by a malevolent bein', it can make more of their humanity shine through."

Rhiannon considered, realizing Aidan not only had some serious knowledge about shapeshifters stored in his head, things even she had not known despite reading all she could about the magical ability, but there was something else about the depth of his knowledge that made her wonder. "You talk as if you know all of this from personal experience."

"I do," Aidan said simply, breaking eye contact for only a second as his gaze dipped before lifting it again. "Merrick killed my mother for her magic."

Rhiannon drew in a stunned breath. She had known Aidan's father had died, but she had never learned what had happened to his mother. She assumed his mother had also died, but she never imagined maybe she had been one of Merrick's victims. "I'm so sorry."

He offered her an appreciative nod. "Thank you, but it was a long time ago." The room went quiet for a few heartbeats, his eyes going sad and contemplative as if he was lost in a memory. But when he continued, his voice remained just as steady, never revealing his emotions. "But when Merrick killed her, she had been the first person to have their shiftin' abilities stolen. The first and only. At least, that we know of. Because shape-shiftin' magic can't be stolen. So many of us think Merrick doin' that caused the magic to backfire on him. We think the first time he tried tappin' into her powers, my mother's essence forged to him."

"So . . . Merrick has your mother's essence inside of him?"

"Yes."

The idea of having her own mother's essence—her memories, her emotions, her soul—trapped inside someone like Merrick, or anyone for that matter, was not something she ever wanted to have to think about. It was an unimaginable fate, a life trapped inside someone else, never fully able to live, yet never able to die. It was an eternal prison sentence. And the idea of not only being able to morph into someone else, that concept alone unnerving, but also living forever with another person stuck inside you, inside your head, Rhiannon could only imagine that had to be torturous for some. The literal definition of a split personality.

"Okay, wait a minute—hold up," Rhiannon said, the realization finally hitting her like a smack to the face. "So, Merrick is a shapeshifter?"

Aidan nodded soberly. "He is. Now."

No! Then that means—

"So . . ." She hesitated. "He can turn into your mom?"

"If he wanted to, yes." Aidan could see the shock and horror plastered on her face, so he added, "But I've never seen him in her form and neither has Nina."

"Oh," she breathed, the tension in her body easing. "That's good."

"And I honestly don't believe he ever would."

"How come?"

"Because every time a shapeshifter transforms into the essence they stole, they take on more of that person. Merrick already had a weakness with me and my sister simply because he possessed our mother inside him, and too much of her already seems to be in control. So, I don't think he would jeopardize losing any more of his control."

"That's why he has a soft spot for you then, huh? A part of your mom is inside of him. He actually cares for you."

"In a way, yes," Aidan acknowledged with a dejected nod.

"Why would he want that, though? Why would he want to feel some sliver of humanity?"

"I don't believe he does. A lot of the shape-shiftin' knowledge is unknown to most outside the magical bloodline, so many believe, includin' myself, he didn't know it would happen. And it's for reasons like this that most of the records and facts about my kind are kept secret. Too much information can be deadly. Or in Merrick's case, detrimental to his plans."

"Yeah." Rhiannon was not sure what else to say, so she said again, "I'm sorry, Aidan. I'm sorry your mom was taken from you."

"It's all right, piuthar beag." Leaning over, he grabbed her arm and tugged her across the couch, pulling him into his chest and wrapping her in a side hug. "Just promise me this . . ."

Rhiannon withdrew from the embrace, taking in the kind smile he was offering her.

"When you do finally kill him," Aidan continued, "make it fuckin' hurt."

Smiling back, she nodded.

~

James and Rhiannon had spent the last few weeks mulling over every book, archive, document, even going as far as reading fantasy and paranormal novels to see if they could figure out how they were going to stop the prophecy from happening. Well, it was already happening, but rather preventing the rest of it from coming true. The twins did not want to die, but their time was running out. Their birthday was only days away, which meant by next month, they might be dead.

Even Ryan had offered to help, spending countless hours with the twins devising plans, only to have them ruined by some other fact they had learned.

But eventually, the focus had shifted to one thing—the ritual. And it had been James who had decided it was the ritual they needed to really direct their full attention to. Because he firmly believed with Merrick having stolen the magic that was supposed to go into the island to keep Kiluemar alive and the barriers working properly, then the ritual had to be the key to unlock how the prophecy wanted them to stop him. If they could somehow use the same elements needed in the ritual, or maybe even render him powerless by removing all the stolen magic, then maybe they would be able to take him down once and for all.

And James had come up with a plan. All he had to do now was convince his sister to go along with it.

"Come on, Sis—the closer we are to danger, the farther we are from harm."

Mouth agape, she asked with her tone equally sharp and confused, "What does that even mean? Danger and harm literally mean the same damn thing. That is a contradicting statement."

Not at all shocked she did not get the reference, he explained, "We need to get the upper hand in all of this. We need to be one step ahead of him. So, it means we face the dangers head on, so we can see what exactly is in front of us—so we can prepare."

Rhiannon pondered a moment, her brow creased with both skepticism and understanding. "Because he won't be expecting it?"

"Exactly."

"So . . . we bring the fight to him, then?"

"Yeah," James said, a little too thrilled by the idea. "That's exactly what we're going to do. But first, we have to set some ground rules." He pulled back his shoulders, a sense of seriousness filtering into his tone and demeanor. "The first rule of this plan is we *don't* talk about this plan."

Rhiannon was seriously wondering if her brother was losing his mind. "What?"

Letting out an exaggerated scoff, he rolled his eyes. "Just keep everything we talk about to yourself. Just you and me—no one else. And anything specific, keep it internal only. This is only going to work if no one knows what we're doing."

A crease again appeared between her eyes, but it accompanied an arched brow. "What about Mom and Dad?"

"Especially not them," James announced adamantly. "I'm not having them fight our battles anymore. We already lost Mom, and I won't jeopardize her life again, or Dad's."

That was something Rhiannon could agree with her brother on. Their parents would not be put in the same situation that had happened months ago. But she knew, once they did finally find out, they were going to be very upset. "They're going to kill us."

James let out an amused, low chuckle. "Not if Merrick does it first."

"That's comforting." Rhiannon released a long, drawn-out exhale. "Well, let's get started."

Chapter 30

The Shadow of Darkness

"We've been over this a thousand times already," James said as they traipsed through Shadow Forest. "Just have a little faith."

"This is never going to work," Rhiannon admitted, the statement flustered but firm, her logical side quickly mapping out all the possible outcomes, good and bad.

The moon was slowly making its way toward the peak in the night sky, the early summer temperatures cool and crisp in the late evening hours. Not at all smothering just yet, something no one was looking forward to again. But James was positive if they could pull this off, not only would Merrick finally be gone and the threat eliminated, but the realm would hopefully return to normal.

They just had to survive first.

James's dark brow lifted in unison with the corner of his mouth, the look of delight beaming in his eyes, a rush of adrenaline controlling his certainty. "Not with that attitude."

A derisive snort sounded, a hint of amusement behind the action. "Why do I always have to be the voice of reason?"

"Because one of us has to be the rational one."

"Right." She had to agree with him there. "Well, fine, then let me just say this. This is a *stupid* idea."

This was definitely a stupid idea, not to mention absolutely dangerous and extremely risky. They were taking a chance here, one Merrick might not be willing to take because it would not only leave him unable to counter the decisions, the twins finally being one step ahead of him, but it would also go against his word to their mother.

Karramis's deal with Merrick had been he could not go after the twins until the full moon after their next birthday.

But their birthday was just a few days away, and now, they were about to walk right into the castle and offer themselves up to him. A whole month early.

"Probably," he agreed with a frivolous shrug.

Her blue eyes burrowed into him, nothing but exaggerated annoyance radiating in her scowl.

"What?" he asked innocently with another lift of his shoulders. "I said probably."

As they exited the forest, they stopped at the path leading to the front of the castle, the structure a silvery-blue mass as the moon shone down on the citadel.

"If we don't survive this," she stated with an added cadence of a faux threat in her teasing tone as she stood next to her brother and stared at Casteya Castle, "I'm going to kill you."

James took her hand into his. "That'll be a neat trick."

Squeezing, she teased, "Shut up."

~

They both knew this was not going to be easy, but as they stood just outside the door of the second castle, Rhiannon could not help but question the lunacy of their current situation.

Large flames clung to the ground in a circle around them, the fire charring the grass as three vampires, all of which neither James nor Rhiannon recognized, ogled them with their hungry eyes like they were a delicacy they could not wait to taste. Thankfully, the fire Rhiannon had summoned had kept them at bay, and the twins remained inside the large fiery circle, and the vampires lingered on the other side of the wall just waiting to strike as soon as Rhiannon's magic faltered.

But it would not.

After Rhiannon had *become one with the water*, she had used that same tactic on her fire magic. And, lucky for her, it actually worked. After focusing on only her fire magic over the last few weeks, knowing this would most likely be their best defense against Leif and the other vampires, she had finally mastered calling forth her magic fully and had learned how to summon it to her hands.

The door of the castle flew open, and two figures emerged.

"Well, well, well," Leif crooned, "what have we here?"

The twins had demanded to see Merrick as soon as the vampires tried to attack, but as they both stood there, staring through the flames, all sense of hopefulness and certainty drained from their bodies.

Merrick observed the twins for a beat before eyeing the wall of flames, studying them with an intense curiosity. "Dismissed," he finally said, his command not directed at anyone in particular, but the three random vampires strolled away without a second thought. Eyes on Rhiannon, he continued, "Drop it, or I will."

Rhiannon did not argue. She needed to present a sense of civility, along with allowing Merrick to believe he not only had the upper hand, but he also held all the control.

The fire evaporated as Rhiannon lifted a hand and swiped it through the air as if swatting away a bug. Smoke billowed along the grass as James and Rhiannon stepped over the charred line and strolled over to Merrick and Leif.

"We have a proposition for you," James announced, displaying an authoritative side to him.

Merrick lifted a curious brow. "And that would be?"

Rhiannon lifted her chin, trying to match her brother's composed and collected demeanor, even though her heart was pounding in her chest like it wanted out. "We will offer ourselves up now, if you promise to leave the rest of our family and all the residents and living beings on this island alone. No more threats or injuries or harm of any kind. No more kidnapping or torture. No more blood spilled, or it being taken by force. No more death. Period." Her gaze faced Leif. "And this extends to all of you. To any living being who needs blood or flesh to survive or for some form of pleasure or entertainment."

Leif admired her boldness. "What's the catch?"

"No catch," Rhiannon continued, addressing both of them but her focus on Merrick. "If you agree to this, leaving out any tricks, manipulation, play on words, or any other disingenuous tactics, or decide to counter our agreement due to any negligent or misconstrued notions, then we will move forward and allow you to perform the ritual on us. But if you don't accept now and move forward with the ritual next month, we will fight, all of us, possibly making this drag out even longer."

"Why would you offer such a noble yet deadly proposition?" Merrick asked, his interest piqued.

"I wasn't finished," Rhiannon added boldly, surprising even herself.

"Well now," Merrick replied roguishly, tossing her a deceptively saccharine grin, "it would appear the little kitten has finally grown some claws like her mother."

Rhiannon took that as a compliment and an indicator she could continue. "We will both meet you at the ritual site and offer ourselves up as a sacrifice. But . . ." She drew out the word, emphasizing this was the important part. "No more killing inside the realm. At all. And no more rituals. Allow the magic inside those here to return to the island." When Leif went to interrupt, she cut him off. "Allow all the previous residents to come home and stop all the hunting, stalking, and slaying of *all* the living beings within the entire realm—land, sea, and air. Any killings will only be done inside the non-magical realm. And all previous deals regarding any injuries, dismemberments, torture, death, or harm of any kind to any member of our family or living being on the island is null and void. *And* . . . no more massacres or slayings of the masses—out there, beyond these borders." Rhiannon exhaled. "Okay, I'm finished now."

Rhiannon had thought long and hard about what she wanted to say, making sure to include the right verbiage as to not provide Merrick with any loopholes.

Merrick waited, not saying anything for what felt like forever. But then, he finally said coolly, "That's quite a list of demands there, sweetheart."

"Yes, but—"

"*I* was not finished."

Rhiannon pressed her lips together and offered an apologetic nod.

"But I feel it is a fair one, considerin' you would be offerin' up both your lives and providin' me with the powers I crave."

James and Rhiannon had learned through rumors Merrick mostly wanted all the stolen magic not simply for the power and greed behind it but because he wanted them for his curse. They heard Merrick believed with all that magic inside him, he could control his transformation of the monster he became, making it less torturous. And now, they were testing those rumors.

"There is a small kink in your well-thought-out plan, though," Merrick continued. "I do not control every single vampire or creature inside this realm or in the other. How do ya reckon I manage such matters?"

Rhiannon had actually considered this as well. "You do have sway over most of the more aggressive beings on Kiluemar and those on the forbidden side, so you will send out orders to all of those, thus taking full responsibility for their actions. And if such actions do occur, you are required to handle them with whatever punishment you seem fit. But ultimately, if you so choose to allow them to live, they are to be banished from the realm. One strike and they are out. And any future residents who find themselves under your command or living on this side of the island also become your responsibility. And as for those on the outside, any that work for you, associate with you, or are linked to you in any way are also to follow the agreed-upon deal or face death by your hands. You will have even more power once you take our magic. There will be no one to stop you from doing what will be necessary for you to keep your word."

Now, Rhiannon was taking a page from her mother's book and using his ego against him. His need for not only power but also control. Merrick was not a born leader, one of values and honesty, a true ruler, but rather a man born with a dictator's heart. A man who thrived on standing tall while the world around him cowered on their knees at his feet.

"Please, please, please," Rhiannon chanted in her head, her voice reaching her brother.

James was optimistic based on the expression on Merrick's face—he was considering their deal. *"He's gonna take it."*

"You would just die—like that?" Leif asked, not at all convinced this deal was without a catch. "Without a fight?"

"Yes," the twins responded without hesitation.

Rhiannon added, "The prophecy said we're supposed to stop him from destroying the realm and unleashing chaos. It never stated we would be alive in the end. So, this is us doing what the prophecy foretold."

Leif arched a brow. "You truly believe you were only born to hold all this magic just to hand it over freely."

"Sell it," James said. *"Come on, Sis, you got this."*

Part of their plan was to allow Rhiannon to do most of the talking because not only was she more diplomatic when it came to discussing serious matters, and had a much better way with words, but James was convinced if she was the one to do it, Merrick would latch onto the fact he believed Rhiannon was the weaker link and would yield without too much consideration. Plus—and this part James kept to himself—he wanted his sister to face her fears. He wanted, again, to prove she was far more powerful than she believed.

"Yes," Rhiannon said convincingly, so refined and level-headed. "He is just too powerful for us to fight—he has proven that many times now. And no, we don't want to die, but we also don't want anyone else to die for us. And even if we do fight, there's no guarantee we will save the realm. So, this is the only way to make sure, in the end, all are safe, and the realm will survive."

By now, even James was convinced by her performance. *"Damn, girl. See, this is why I said you needed to be the one to talk. I would've fucked this up by now."*

Rhiannon kept her face neutral, but the urge to smile rose to the surface.

Merrick waited again to speak, his expression impassive. But his eyes—which seared into Rhiannon as if they were trying to see any trace of dishonesty or malicious intent—revealed he was considering their offer.

"Your acquiescence is admirable," Merrick finally announced, his stance wide but still, and his features so even and unmoving it was hard to read him.

"What the hell does that mean?" James asked, his inner voice sounding confused but his features still stern and observant.

"He respects what we are doing," Rhiannon answered him quickly before she asked out loud, "So, do we have a deal?"

"Oh," James continued through their bond despite her external question. *"Well, why not just say that?"*

"He did," she shot back before telepathically shushing him.

Considering one final time, Merrick observed the twins. But after a moment, he declared smoothly, "Deal."

Rhiannon reached out her hand, and as Merrick took it and they shook, she repeated, "Deal."

"But first." Merrick did not release her hand, the grip on it leaving no give for her to pull back. "Leif?"

"Yes," the vampire answered.

"Go fetch Tressa."

"As you wish," Leif offered, deliberately polite as he bowed.

After what felt like forever, Merrick finally released Rhiannon's hand and she stepped back, leaving her, James, and Merrick waiting silently in the dark with only the moon watching over them.

"What is going on?" Tressa asked calmly, stepping outside wearing a purple robe and a black silk-and-lace nightgown underneath.

Despite appearing to have just woken up, Tressa was still well put together. Her black hair was smooth and not at all messy from sleep, and even her face was flawless, her features enhanced by only her raw, natural beauty.

Merrick had filled Tressa in on everything, the woman not even reacting to all he was telling her, her face remaining completely impassive and her body language appearing unbothered.

The twins had learned by the conversation between Merrick and Tressa, the woman was the witch he would use during the ritual, and he had wanted to make sure she was ready to perform the task at hand.

"I'll need their blood," Tressa said, eyeing the twins. When Merrick's gaze turned toward her, a look of confusion gracing his face, she added, "Their magic is too powerful, so I will need their blood to place into the ritual site to enhance the magic already there."

Merrick seemed convinced by her answer, so he gestured for her to continue. "Proceed."

Tressa smoothly stepped forward and glanced back at Leif. "Dagger, please."

The twins took in how relaxed she was, so at ease around these two, despite how dangerous they were.

"Hand," Tressa said to James, holding up her palm as she took the dagger from Leif.

James was reluctant at first, unsure how much the woman was about to hurt him and unnerved by this slight misstep in their plan. He had not thought to consider them needing their blood.

Tressa noticed the hesitancy, the slight fear in his eyes. "I don't need much." Her voice was soft and dripped with sympathy, almost as if she felt sorry for what was happening.

James nodded in understanding and laid his hand into her palm, wincing as the blade sliced open his skin along the tissue just below his thumb.

"Fuck, that hurts," James hissed under his breath.

Tressa gently slid the edge of the blade again along his skin, using the angle to scoop up and coat one side of the dagger.

"Your turn," Tressa said to Rhiannon, closing the distance between them.

Rhiannon did not like this. She did not like this at all. Blood was sacred in the magical community. But she did not argue. Instead, she lifted her arm and held her breath, hoping the act would diminish some of the pain.

It did not.

A heavy hissing sound echoed as blood pooled along Rhiannon's hand. Doing the same thing she had with James's blood, Tressa collected Rhiannon's on the other side of the blade, the crimson staining both sides now.

Turning, Tressa said to Leif, "You'll get this back later." And then she addressed Merrick, "Am I finished here?"

"Aye. You are dismissed."

Tressa gave him a single nod and strolled back into the castle, tossing back one more sympathetic gaze.

"See you both tomorrow night," Merrick said to the twins as he followed behind her, Leif doing the same.

Discussion over, deal in place.

It was not until James and Rhiannon stepped out of the portal still located by the cabin, closest to where they left Raeth and Oakley and told them to remain, that they both finally took in one full breath.

~

The twins had chosen ahead of time to walk to the ritual site from Guardian Lake, but the portal located near there had disappeared or moved recently, something they found out after they had stepped out only to find themselves on one of the beaches. So, to their dismay, they had to call for help getting to the site before time ran out.

Rhiannon had called Raeth to escort them back to the village, only to get Callie and have her take them to the spot between the lake and forest, opting to walk to the site instead of having the winged horse fly them directly in. Both James and Rhiannon had agreed not to give any sign to Raeth regarding their plans. Like James had mentioned before, this was only going to work if no one else knew about it. And if Raeth even suspected the twins were about to do something dangerous, he would intervene either by protecting them or summoning the others, and possibly their parents. So, they left him in the village and took Callie. But they also did not want to leave her in any danger, so they dismissed her once they had dismounted.

"Dammit!" James bellowed as they made their way through the trees.

"What?" Rhiannon asked with a startled jump as her hand flew to her chest. "What's wrong?"

His fingers snapped. "I forgot to ask Merrick if he really wanted our magic still because we have Guardian powers." His tone was filled with humor, his attempt at lightening the mood.

Panting, Rhiannon lowered her hand and scoffed out an annoyed exhale. "You're an asshole, you know that?"

James chuckled to himself, amused by her jab and completely entertained by his own antics. After a moment, he asked, the lightness still present in his voice, "So, do you think he might decide not to try and kill us if I mention that?"

"No," Rhiannon said plainly as she ducked under the branch of a lush tree. "When Merrick dealt with Adalaide, he did not have all the magic he has now, so I highly doubt he even cares anymore."

"Well, it doesn't hurt to ask."

Rhiannon could tell he was only trying to stop her from getting too far in her head and second-guessing everything they were about to do.

James had told his sister the answer to everything was in the ritual, so both of them focused on devising a plan to recreate the original one but with a slight change. Merrick. With having all four elements inside him and the curses, Merrick would be all the things needed for the sacrifice. And with a slight change to the spell, they would not need him to be a willing component. And with both of them also having all four elemental factors, they would be the witches needed to perform the spell. Plus, the twins would represent the balance of male and female. The only thing they needed was a way to subdue him, something they were relying on their magic to provide. And with how much they had been practicing, they believed they could counter his abilities just long enough to do it. If they were successful, Merrick would die, and all the magic inside him would release back into the island and hopefully restore it completely.

Still trying to keep his sister distracted, James offered her a random thought, something he reflected on recently after witnessing his parents' affection for one another soon after he had awoken from another nightmare in which his mother had not come back to life, and she was still dead. "It's hard to think of Mom not being here, but I know it will happen. One day. And when it does, I think it will be harder for us than Dad."

Rhiannon eyed him suspiciously, wondering where that thought came from, but she played along, wanting to know why he believed that. Their father loved their mother deeply, more than she thought any person could love another. Their love was something to be admired and desired, a love written in fairytales. One she hoped to find, too, one day. "How so?"

Without missing a beat, he said matter-of-factly, grateful she decided to take the bait, "I don't think Mom will ever be dead completely for him."

"Why do you think that?"

"Because death cannot stop true love. All it can do is delay it for a while."

Rhiannon stopped in her tracks, completely bewildered by his poetic and absolutely romantic statement. "Wow, that was beautiful, James."

"Thanks," he replied proudly. "It just came to me."

They continued forward, the two of them now walking in silence for a few minutes.

"It's from a movie, isn't it?" Rhiannon finally guessed, knowing her brother had to have some help with his sudden burst of hopeless romanticism.

"No," James countered, completely offended. "Of course not. What, I can't come up with something so beautifully romantic on my own?"

Rhiannon eyed him skeptically, her brow arched as high as she could lift it.

"Okay, fine," he admitted, driving his eyes upward with an exaggerated roll as he let out a gargled scoff. "Yes, it's from a movie. But still, it's a great line. Not all of us can—"

James halted, his movements following his abrupt cutoff as Rhiannon remained frozen just a few steps behind him.

"What are you doing?" he asked, curious why she had stopped.

When she did not answer, he followed her line of sight.

Just through the clearing, in the center of the open field, lay the ritual site. And lining the outside of the circle were lit candles.

Taking each other's hand, they continued forward in silence, even their minds remaining quiet.

This was it.

They were about to literally step into a deathtrap.

The moon shone down on the large stone circle, the boulders on the outside almost sunken into the ground, and a tall, barren oak tree as they neared the site. But as they moved closer and stepped over the first set of stones, they slowed to a stop.

Rhiannon squinted to get a better look at a figure lying on the ground inside the second circle, which was also lined with lit candles. "What is that?"

"I don't know," James said as he made his way over to it, taking his sister with him.

The figure was unmoving and hard to make out. Only shadows surrounded it. But as they cautiously sauntered closer, they realized instantly what it was.

A body.

Someone was lying on their side, facing away from them.

Dread twisted in Rhiannon's gut, the horror of who it might be making her want to vomit.

"No," Rhiannon pleaded quietly. "No, no, no—"

"We don't even know who it is," James pointed out, trying to calm her down.

Not wanting to touch the person or get too close, just in case it was some trick, James let go of his sister's hand and moved around the body, keeping his eyes zeroed in on the figure, trying to spot any signs of movement.

A gasp sounded as James took in the face of the person before him.

"What? Who is it?" Rhiannon nearly begged in a panic.

Eyes glued to the figure, he announced with an airy exhale, "Merrick."

"What?" Rhiannon snapped, loud and extremely confused as she hurried to his side, certain her brother was mistaken.

"It's . . ." He pointed down at the body as soon as his sister came up beside him. "It's Merrick."

Another gasp erupted, this one from Rhiannon.

He was right.

It was Merrick. On the ground. Dead.

Shock, confusion, and trepidation shot through Rhiannon like an explosion of unruly, out-of-control fireworks, zooming and exploding through her whole body.

Dead.

Merrick was *dead*.

"What are you doing?" Rhiannon whisper-shouted as James moved closer to the body, certain her voice might somehow revive Merrick.

Whispering back, seeming to feel the same way, he answered, "Making sure we don't make a classic horror movie mistake."

Silence. Absolute silence.

Head angled back, James stopped as he noticed the perplexed expression on his sister's face. "Oh, come on! Always verify the kill. Just in case."

Continuing forward, James reached out a foot and gently nudged Merrick, the motion making the body instantly slouch backward and rest flatly on the ground. Peering down at Merrick's face, James took in his appearance. Merrick had always been slightly pale, but now he was grayish and twinged with blue. His pale blue eyes were glazed over and opened to the sky. He definitely looked dead.

But was he?

James nudged him again with his foot.

And again.

And again.

"I think he's dead, James," Rhiannon noted pointedly, her voice still quiet but not as much as before.

James moved away and made his way back a few feet toward his sister. Folding his arms over his chest and letting out a small muffled *huh* sound, he said teasingly, completely proud of himself. "Well, that was easy."

Rhiannon was immediately on guard, not only by the fact that was definitely too easy—way too easy, not to mention unexplainable—but also that someone had been the one to kill him. And it had definitely not been them.

James continued, a faux pout pulling at his lower lip. "And a little anticlimactic, if you ask me. I was expecting fireworks or something." He gestured with his hands, mimicking explosions. "Maybe even a round of applause." He shrugged. "Oh well. Maybe they'll throw a party in our honor. Ooh, maybe there will be cake. Or ice cream. Or maybe cake and ice cream. I mean, there should be. We just saved—"

Merrick pulled in a deep, long, and loud inhale, his chest rising as his back arched and his skin flushed back to his normal paleness.

James jumped back, taking Rhiannon with him. "See! I told you! The villain always comes back from the dead."

"Fuck you!" Merrick wheezed loudly, his voice raspy and raw and sounding dry like he had not spoken in years.

James flinched at the outburst, slightly amused and offended by the comment. "Well, that was rude. What did *we* do? He was already dead—but not dead—when we got here."

"I don't think he's talking to us," Rhiannon considered quietly, her instincts having been right.

Growling filled the area, the sound low and guttural and eerie.

The twins twisted around, trying to find the source as Merrick pulled in even more breaths, deep and almost pained as he remained prone on the ground as if frozen in place.

"There!" James called, pointing toward the trees to the south.

Rhiannon's eyes went wide, and all her fight-or-flight instincts faded as she froze in place, completely unable to react other than stare.

A shadowy silhouette strolled away from the trees, low to the ground and moving like an animal. And among the dark figure, two eyes glowed red.

Raamko.

The black, four-legged creature prowled forward, stalking closer, his red eyes burning bright and fixed on the twins. It moved with such grace and power, the muscles along its shoulders swaying with fluid movements.

The beast was just as Rhiannon had remembered, being up close and personal offering more of the terrifying features that she had witnessed when she had astral projected. The other two times she had seen him had not done the creature justice when it came to reminding her just how large and deadly he was.

A snarl rumbled from his slightly open mouth, offering the twins a glimpse of his razor-sharp teeth.

But as the monstrous wolf crept closer, his mouth closed and eyes dimmed just as the rest of his features started to morph, the moonlight providing just enough illumination but creating an even more ominous ambiance to the situation.

One of the front paws lowered as fingers sprouted from the claws, a hand being the one to press into the ground. Then the other. Bare feet emerged along the back paws, now attached to legs and hips. Skin appeared beneath the black fur, the coat disappearing completely. The snout pulled in, and the entire front of the face revealed human features. And before long, a person stood before the twins.

Shock erupted through Rhiannon, masking some of the fear. "You," Rhiannon said as she exhaled the breath she had been holding.

Raamko was not just a beast, he was a human—a shapeshifter.

However, that was not the only surprising part, but rather the creature was not even a *he*. It was a woman.

And she was completely naked.

"Hello there." The feminine voice was delicate and pleasant. "Let me officially introduce myself. My name is Tressaya Raamko, but you may call me Tressa."

The twins watched in silent shock as Tressa strolled casually over to the edge of the stone circle and grabbed for a pile of clothes. She slipped a black dress over her head and down her perfectly-shaped, curvy body. The material clung to her torso and accentuated her chest, the lower half of the garment flaring slightly at her hips and flowing down to her bare feet. Lifting another article of clothing, Tressa wrapped a corset over her midsection, positioning the black-laced covering perfectly over her breasts and zipping it up. Finally, she reached for a dark purple cloak and wrapped it around herself, the copious fabric covering her from the neck down completely.

Tressa kept her gaze on the twins the whole time with something akin to satisfaction on her face. She strolled over to Merrick, the stoic movement swift and determined yet quiet, regal, and dignified, the fluidity of the woman's poised demeanor apparent even within the dim glow of the moonlight. Silky tresses—the streaks of silvery-blue from the sky above shimmering off the dark color—rested over a set of dark purple-clad shoulders, the ends stopping a few inches from the smooth and rich golden skin just above her ample chest.

"If you'll excuse me a moment," Tressa said, her tone becoming deep and cold as her gaze dipped to Merrick on the ground, pain etched on his face, "I have matters to attend to."

Taking the fact that Tressa had seemingly just dismissed them by her final words to them, James and Rhiannon took that as permission to leave. Slowly, they began to back away, equally confused and horrified, but keeping their eyes on the woman.

Tressa knelt down beside Merrick and glared at him, giving him a sweet yet callous grin before she delivered in a soft, diabolical voice, "Checkmate."

A deep, guttural scream rang out, covering the whole area like a booming explosion. The twins paused their retreat just before they reached the outer edge of the stone circle and stood in disbelief as the sound faded—the cry of pain only a short-lived echo—their eyes fixed on the bloody heart in Tressa's hand.

"What the hell is happening?" James asked under his breath, taking his sister's hand into his, needing to remind himself this was not a dream.

The first line of the third verse of the prophecy filtered into Rhiannon's mind, the words etched in her psyche after months of trying to decipher their meaning.

"You said it was too easy," Rhiannon whispered, the declaration flat and emotionless, her thoughts still processing what she was trying to comprehend. "And it was."

The shadow of darkness will soon emerge.

Will soon.

It will *soon* emerge.

Meaning . . . it had not yet been discovered.

The third verse was delivered after the twins had already been born, and by then Merrick had already been the one everyone believed to be the one the prophecy foretold. But they were wrong.

They were all wrong.

"What does that mean?" James asked quietly, his mind connecting with hers as the words of the prophecy and her final thought registered, refusing to glance away from Tressa.

Rhiannon swallowed, the task difficult as fear made all her muscles tense. "Merrick was not the one whom the prophecy warned us about. It was her."

James did not need time to process. He had no doubt his sister's instincts were correct.

"We need to go," James declared through their bond as he gripped his sister's hand and urged her to follow.

They bolted, walking in a fast pace, choosing not to run and draw too much attention to themselves. But as the two of them reached the stones, they both slammed into an invisible wall.

"What?" James breathed as he eyed the empty space in front of him.

"My apologies," Tressa said behind them, the cadence of her tone calm and sweet. "But you two aren't leaving."

James and Rhiannon twisted back toward her.

She grinned, pure delight and malice in her gaze. "We're not finished here."

To be continued and concluded in:

Path of Destiny
Magic of the Realm ~ Book Five

Character Art

James and Rhiannon Cassil

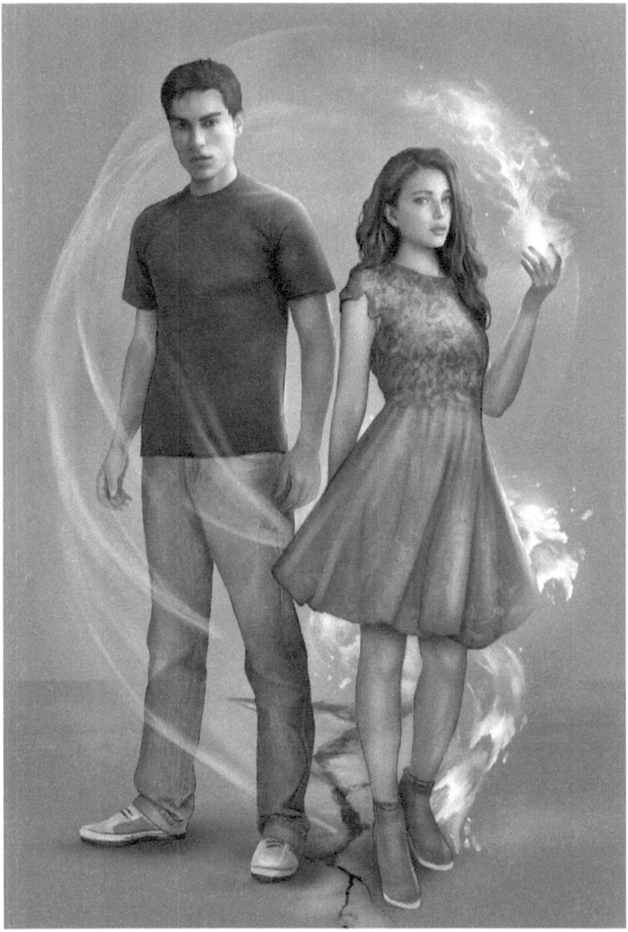

Leif Nyland

Haydrin Tevlak

Pronunciation Guide

New Characters

Aenoc: A-NOCK

Delphina: DELL-FEE-NUH

Ellwyn: ELLE-WIN

Nerissa: NUH-RISS-UH

Thalayssa: TH-UH-LAY-SUH

Tressaya: TRESS-A-YUH

Refer to other books for more pronunciations

Translation Guide

Mo ghràdh – My love
Piuthar beag – Little sister

Content Warning

This book contains the following:

Death, including family member

Physical abuse - mild and severe

Violence

Murder

Mature language

Mature situations

Suggestive language

Mention of sex, lust, and pleasures

(Not descriptive/Vague terms)

Mental health struggles,

including PTSD, depression, anxiety,

and trauma from loss of family member

Blood and gore

Details of nudity

Use of sedatives/Being drugged

(Not for sexual purposes)

Death of pregnant woman (Mention only)

Death of an unborn child (Mention only)

Acknowledgements

First and foremost, writing this book took a lot of long nights, many stress-induced tears, and a whole lot of determination, and without my children being a constant source of strength every single day, I might not have finished it, and I definitely wouldn't have survived this long. To Isabelle and Ian, I love you so much.

To my beautiful daughter, thank you for being my number one fan and for being the one who shows me the kind of strength I strive to have in myself. This entire series would not be out in the world if it weren't for you.

To my mom, Anna, and best friend, Stephanie Kittleson. You two have been my voice of reason these last few years and the ones constantly helping me off the ledge when things got a little too much to handle. I love you both so much, and there are not enough words to describe how much you mean to me.

To my friends, Jenn G. and Carmen T., thank you for your continued love and support through the years.

And a special thanks to Jenn and Isabelle again for being a beta readers for this book. Your advice and suggestions really helped.

A big thank you to Nadine T., Ashley B., Samii C., Jess K., Kaely S., Brittany K., Elle D., Amber S., Felicia G., and Mary R. for being a huge part of this past year and for making my days a little better. I'm so glad you and I found our ways into each other's lives. I am so proud to call you all my friends.

Also, a huge shout out to Enchanted Ink Publishing, Dennis Doty, Stephanie Saw, and Beth Gilbert for the work you have done for this book and series. I seriously couldn't have done it without your hard work and talents.

To Jacclyn James (also known as Jacci Prior) and Keval Shah, my narrators, you two are such amazing people and ridiculously talented. I can't wait to see what you bring to the audiobook world. Hopefully, we can work on the rest of the series soon.

Last, but definitely not least, to my readers, thank you so much for giving this series and me a chance. I can't tell you enough how much your support drives me to be a better author. I truly hope you loved this book and you are excited to read the next one. Without readers like you, authors would have no one to cherish their work.

www.ingramcontent.com/pod-product-compliance
Lightning Source LLC
Chambersburg PA
CBHW022009300726
48970CB00003B/804